DAEMON WORLD

GOLGOTH RAN OUT past the treeline and held his axe high. 'All who can hear me!' he yelled. 'All who call yourselves men! Torvendis has sent us an omen! It has sent us destruction! All who wish to see the city fall, charge!'

He ran out alone towards the daemon and its infant army, suddenly light on his feet and feeling as strong and deadly as a hundred men. Maybe there were some warriors following him, maybe he was completely alone. He didn't care.

Because, as Ss'll Sh'Kar tore at the battlements and his daemon followers gained form at his feet, Lady Charybdia's wall was falling.

More Warhammer 40,000 from the Black Library

• WARHAMMER 40,000 TITLES •

SOUL DRINKER by Ben Counter
ANGELS OF DARKNESS by Gav Thorpe
EXECUTION HOUR by Gordon Rennie
SHADOW POINT by Gordon Rennie
STORM OF IRON by Graham McNeill
FARSEER by William King
PAWNS OF CHAOS by Brian Craig

• GAUNT'S GHOSTS •

FIRST & ONLY by Dan Abnett
GHOSTMAKER by Dan Abnett
NECROPOLIS by Dan Abnett
HONOUR GUARD by Dan Abnett
THE GUNS OF TANITH by Dan Abnett
STRAIGHT SILVER by Dan Abnett

• THE EISENHORN TRILOGY •

XENOS by Dan Abnett
MALLEUS by Dan Abnett
HERETICUS by Dan Abnett

• LAST CHANCERS •

13TH LEGION by Gav Thorpe
KILL TEAM by Gav Thorpe

• SPACE WOLF •

SPACE WOLF by William King
RAGNAR'S CLAW by William King
GREY HUNTER by William King

• ULTRAMARINES •

NIGHTBRINGER by Graham McNeill
WARRIORS OF ULTRAMAR by Graham McNeill

A WARHAMMER 40,000 NOVEL

DAEMON WORLD

Ben Counter

To Helen

A BLACK LIBRARY PUBLICATION

First published in Great Britain in 2003
by BL Publishing,
Games Workshop Ltd.,
Willow Road, Nottingham,
NG7 2WS, UK.

10 9 8 7 6 5 4 3 2 1

Cover illustration by Adrian Smith.

A CIP record for this book
is available from the British Library

ISBN 1 84416 001 7

Set in ITC Giovanni

Printed and bound in Great Britain by
Cox & Wyman Ltd, Cardiff Rd, Reading, Berkshire RG1 8EX, UK

See the Black Library on the Internet at
www.blacklibrary.com

Find out more about Games Workshop
and the world of Warhammer 40.000 at
www.games-workshop.com

IT IS THE 41st millennium. For more than a hundred centuries the Emperor has sat immobile on the Golden Throne of Earth. He is the master of mankind by the will of the gods, and master of a million worlds by the might of his inexhaustible armies. He is a rotting carcass writhing invisibly with power from the Dark Age of Technology. He is the Carrion Lord of the Imperium for whom a thousand souls are sacrificed every day, so that he may never truly die.

YET EVEN IN his deathless state, the Emperor continues his eternal vigilance. Mighty battlefleets cross the daemon-infested miasma of the warp, the only route between distant stars, their way lit by the Astronomican, the psychic manifestation of the Emperor's will. Vast armies give battle in his name on uncounted worlds. Greatest amongst his soldiers are the Adeptus Astartes, the Space Marines, bio-engineered super-warriors. Their comrades in arms are legion: the Imperial Guard and countless planetary defence forces, the ever-vigilant Inquisition and the tech-priests of the Adeptus Mechanicus to name only a few. But for all their multitudes, they are barely enough to hold off the ever-present threat from aliens, heretics, mutants – and worse.

TO BE A man in such times is to be one amongst untold billions. It is to live in the cruellest and most bloody regime imaginable. These are the tales of those times. Forget the power of technology and science, for so much has been forgotten, never to be re-learned. Forget the promise of progress and understanding, for in the grim dark future there is only war. There is no peace amongst the stars, only an eternity of carnage and slaughter, and the laughter of thirsting gods.

CHAPTER ONE

SOME SAY THAT Arguleon Veq came to the world of Torvendis when the Maelstrom was still young – a long time ago, for that jewelled wound in reality is old indeed. Others maintain that his deeds on the planet were within a breath of living memory, and that he fabricated the weight of history to turn his life into a legend. Most, however, agree that it was during the time of the Blind Crusade, when the mindless herds of humankind were united in the Imperium of the Corpse-God, that Veq began his conquest. Perhaps one hundred and fifty centuries passed between that time and the current age, and yet the legacy of Arguleon Veq still covers Torvendis like a thousand scars.

There are many stories of Arguleon Veq, some of the time before he arrived in the Maelstrom, and some (told by liars) from the time afterwards. But most concern the battle with the Last, the power that held Torvendis in the face of blessed Chaos. For centuries the fight raged, with Arguleon Veq pitting his cunning and devotion to Chaos against the sheer strength and arrogance of the Last, and there were more stories forged in the heat of that contest than could ever be told. But the story that really matters tells of how, with the Last finally defeated and slain, Arguleon Veq claimed Torvendis in the name of the Chaos gods, and turned that world of symbolic and actual power into a place alive with the celebration of Chaos.

Where once the planet had been barren and drained by the malignancy of the Last, now it was flooded with life that pooled in the scars left by the battle. Barren wastes were covered by teeming oceans. Mountains of shattered rock rose. New moons were drawn into orbit by the magnetism of Torvendis's newly-released power. The Dark Gods looked on the place with envy and with every new master the landscape changed once again. New layers were added to the strata of history that built up around the planet like skins waiting to be shed.

This, then, is Torvendis – a world made of legends, delivered to the dread gods of Chaos by a champion of myth and fought over by violence, stealth and deception for more than ten thousand years since. Everywhere are wounds of history that bleed stories, and the sky still rains blood from time to time as if in memory of all those who died, or worse, to win mastery of Torvendis. Every rock and snowflake and drop of blood is a story waiting to happen, and every breath of every living thing is a legend that will one day be unlocked.

COLD. BLOODY COLD. Golgoth had scaled these peaks once before, to prove that he was man enough to endure the freezing storms and isolation, and the hallucinations that sometimes rode on the winds that came before a blizzard. It was the initiation that every true warrior of the Emerald Sword tribe had to undergo – and though he would never admit it to anyone, Golgoth had barely survived. Now, even with the massive lupine skin wrapped around him over the layers of padded leather, it felt as if death was trying to drag his bones away. Though he was not much more than twenty winters old he was a big man with ropes of muscle wrapping his arms, and yet the wind cut right through to his soul. Despite his youth, with his wild, uncut hair and beardless face turning to a dark dust of stubble, Golgoth knew he looked like a leader – and he could not let the men who followed him see that the mountains were wearing him down.

The sky was clear above him, scattered with the sharp cold stars and the smears of nebulae that some said were the bloodstains of the gods. The Canis Mountains, hard and unforgiving, stretched all around him in towering blades of stone. The chasms between them were so dark they looked bottomless. Golgoth had lived his whole life in these peaks, but he had never ventured this far into the interior of the mountain range, and even he was impressed by the sheer majesty of the hostile peaks.

The Slaughtersong, a bright silver star named after the legendary steed of Arguleon Veq, was high in the sky – a good omen for swift travel and stealth. For a moment Golgoth forgot the throat-rawing cold and saw himself as chieftain, taking the pride of place when the Emerald Sword tribe gathered to contest their strength, and in the heart of the shieldwall when the tribe gathered for war.

The Emerald Sword had not marched to war as one for many years. The tribe was now broken up and scattered all across the Canis Mountains. Many lived in isolated settlements that had more to do with the neighbouring tribes than with the rest of the Sword. The tribe's accursed chieftan, Grik, ruled a whole city of the Sword, and took tribute from the rest.

The elders claimed the tribe had existed for as long as the mountains and the seas, but if the Emerald Sword continued to hide in the mountains while Lady Charybdia ruled to the west, soon the tribe would stagnate and die. It would take someone with true strength to drag the Emerald Sword from the oblivion that threatened it. It would take someone like Golgoth.

He glanced behind him. He had started out ten days ago with fifty men of the tribe, travelling on foot from his home settlement in the foothills to the east. Now thirty-five warriors remained to follow him up the mountain's peak, lupine fur billowing around them, axes and swords slung under shields on their backs.

Fifteen men dead. That was good going for this weather. The Emerald Sword bred them tough, thought Golgoth proudly. They could be so much more. They could be great again.

Hath stumbled up the blade-like rock to Golgoth's side. 'Kirran's snapped an ankle,' he said. 'Do we leave him?' Hath was older than Golgoth, about as old as a warrior could expect to get at nearly forty winters – his face, picked out by the starlight, was lined and dark with age, his hair and beard sparse and grey. His voice was gravelly and he was short of breath.

Golgoth looked out across the landscape of shattered rock, like knives stabbing at the sky. Hostile as it was, the way ahead that picked its way from peak to peak was the safest across the mountains and Golgoth's men would have to make good time if they were to stay on the trail of their quarry. 'We can camp in an hour,' he said, pointing to the shelter of an overhang some way down the opposite slope. 'If he can't walk that far, he doesn't deserve to make it.'

Hath nodded, and waved the rest of the Emerald Sword warriors forward. Lonn, the youngest, had to be helped up the steeper inclines. If the lad hadn't been one of the Touched, Golgoth wouldn't have taken him, or would have outpaced him and left him for exposure to claim to show the rest of the men how he treated weakness. But Lonn's opaque eyes, white with whorls of red like blood in milk, could pierce darkness and murk. He was too useful to leave behind.

The boy was hauled up beside Golgoth, fully a head shorter than the warrior. Golgoth cuffed him round the head.

'What do you see?' snarled Golgoth.

Lonn kneeled on the cold stone, peering down at the broken rocks below. The light of the Slaughtersong was cold and sharp, picking out blade-like edges but leaving the cracks and ravines deep black. There was a thin, shrill whistling as the wind blew through the narrow fissures.

Hath put his grizzled face close to Lonn's ear. 'If we've lost them, boy,' he growled, 'we'll be one short with full stomachs come the morning.'

Lonn said nothing, scanning the hostile landscape. 'They passed this way,' he said at length. 'They've lost two more men.'

'And the wagons?'

'They're still hauling all three. Grik's sorcerers must be speaking with the rocks.'

Golgoth was impressed, though he wouldn't voice it. Grik was no kind of a leader for a tribe which lived on war, but he could be clever. A single caravan, guided by spells that melted a clear path through the rock, travelled once every third winter and brought all the gifts and tributes straight to the chieftain's tent. In the times before Grik each tribe had sent their tributes separately and many were lost, often deliberately. Now, Grik's sorcerers could ensure that the tribute caravan made its long circuit of the tribe's settlements in safety and bring back everything that was his due.

It was all show. What good were spears of dragon's bone or daemon-wrought skeletons of gold if they filled the coffers of a chieftain who was letting his tribe die?

'Wait,' said Lonn. 'There's someone close by... A stranger...'

'Where?' said Hath, crouching down low, trying to see through the darkness.

Suddenly a tiny point of light flared below them on the far slope, and as Golgoth's eyes focused he saw it was the light of a flame being applied to a campfire. The fire flickered at the feet of a hooded, robed man, hunched against the cold. Though he was barely visible and the warriors were in deep shadow, the man seemed to see them, stare for a moment, and wave in greeting.

'Have you heard of a hermit walking these mountains?' Golgoth asked.

'Here? No. Nothing survives without sorcery here, save us,' replied Hath.

'Is he one of the men from the caravan?'

'He looks old,' said Lonn, seeing details of the stranger's face that no one else could pick out. 'Would Grik send old men to guard his tribute?'

'Unlikely,' said Golgoth, turning to the men gathered behind him. 'Varkith, Tarn, with me. The rest of you, head for the overhang and make camp.'

The Emerald Sword warriors picked their way towards the overhang, and Golgoth struck out for where the hermit was sitting and warming his hands, oblivious to the fact that a night on the Canis Mountains was one more way to die.

GOLGOTH HAD KILLED old men before. Old women too, and children, and horses and warhounds and just about everything it might cross a man's mind to kill. He had crept into Kordar's war host when he was still too young to earn his first kill, and had fought alongside his older tribesmen as fiercely as any thrice-blooded warrior. Eight years later Golgoth had killed Kordar, a contest both men had seen coming ever since the day when the beardless boy had ignored the rules to take his first lives, and taken control of the Bladestone settlement.

In the raids and skirmishes that followed, Golgoth lost count of how many he killed in dreary, petty bloodlettings. The days of Kordar were gone. Lady Charybdia had subdued everything west of the Canis Mountains. There was nothing left the tribes could fight against, and no leaders who would challenge one another. The times of battle were to become another legend, like the million other legends that hung in the air of Torvendis like the morning mist.

When Grik was dead and Golgoth led the Emerald Sword, the times of battles would return.

Yes, he had killed enough old men. He was fully prepared to kill one more.

This particular old man didn't look so old up close. His skin was lined but his eyes were bright, as if it was weather and not age that had preyed upon him. His hair was dark and his hands still strong. Golgoth could tell a warrior when he saw one – the hermit's nose and cheekbone had been broken long ago, his knuckles were lumpen and scarred. He stayed sitting by his small fire as Golgoth approached.

'Who are you, stranger?' barked Golgoth as he strode up to the hermit, Varkith and Tarn at his side.

The hermit looked up, smiling faintly. 'A traveller making his way across the Canis Mountains, much like yourselves.'

'No one travels alone here, old man.'

The hermit poked the fire at his feet, though it gave off little heat. 'I am not alone. Torvendis is with me. I can read its ways so well it speaks to me like a friend.'

Golgoth stepped closer. 'Are you armed?'

'What you see,' replied the hermit, spreading his arms, 'is what you get.'

The hermit did not waver, though Golgoth and his companions were an imposing trio of men. Varkith was nine heads tall, his fists as big as a normal man's head. Tarn, on the other hand, had once worked for the chieftain Grik before being cast out and joining Golgoth – he had strangled Grik's enemies in their beds and killed with no more thought than most men gave to drawing breath.

'A caravan passed this way,' said Golgoth, still unsure what to make of the hermit. 'Three wagons and twelve men, led by a sorcerer. What do you know of it?'

'Eleven men,' replied the hermit. 'And harpies.'

Tarn glanced at Golgoth, and Golgoth knew they were both thinking the same thing. Harpies were feral, daemonic, bat-winged creatures that flocked to the bleakest peaks of the mountains; it took a powerful man indeed to tame them. And the most cunning harpies were only seen if they wanted to be, so even Lonn could miss them if he didn't know what to look for. Had Grik fathomed that Golgoth would stalk the caravan and bring a true-sighted Touched with him?

'You were close enough to see all this, and they let you live? I find that difficult to believe, old man.'

The hermit stood up. He was taller than Golgoth had expected, as tall as he was. 'Age has its benefits, stripling. I know things that your people thought were forgotten. Perhaps there is something you could learn before you kill yourself and your tribesmen taking on an enemy you can't handle.'

A barely perceptible gesture from Golgoth kept Varkith from tearing the hermit's head from his shoulders. It was

some time since anyone had spoken to Golgoth like that,
and longer still since they had done so and remained
unscathed. But Golgoth knew he could kill this man at any
time, whether with his own hands or through the two warriors beside him. But anyone surviving to reach old age in
the Canis Mountains was rare enough, and one who could
spy on one of Grik's tribute caravans with impunity was simply impossible.

Golgoth was curious. So the old man lived, for the time
being.

The flicker of a flame caught Golgoth's eye. Some distance
away his warriors were making camp and setting a fire of
their own – Golgoth would have to join them soon if he
was to get any rest at all before dawn. It was another five
days' journey before they got to the Snake's Throat, a deep
pass that marked the only path around the daemon-
infested lower foothills on the other side of the Canis
Mountains. They needed to stay tight and focused – an old
vagrant shouldn't be allowed to take their minds off the
mission.

'This man,' the hermit was saying as he looked first at Tarn
and then at Varkith, 'is a killer and nothing more. And this
one is an animal with a human face, which I see you have
trained well. But you… you could learn.'

The hermit held up a hand. There was light dancing
around his fingertips, pale and blue-white. As Golgoth
watched the fire flowed up and turned in on itself like a
knot, forming a sigil like a snake tied into a figure of eight
and swallowing its own tail. Golgoth watched, mesmerised,
as the flame flaked away in tiny silver sparks, each one dancing in its own intricate pattern, leaving trails of light in the
air that weaved into a glowing tapestry.

'You have thirty-five men, Golgoth. Grik has half a tribe at
his side, sorcerers and daemons. If you face him as you are,
you will die. But there are things I could teach you, and if
you learn, you might just survive.'

The tapestry of light coalesced into an image – a barbarian with axe in hand, surely Golgoth, striding through the
knee-deep remains of his enemies, beneath the cured skins

of the chieftain's tent. Then, suddenly, the image dissolved into the night, and left only the hermit's face, suddenly serious.

Not a hermit. A sorcerer? A Touched? Or something else?

'My name is Kron,' said the old man. 'When the dawn comes, we can begin.'

It was a risk, Golgoth knew that. But then again, it had been a risk to sneak into battle when his beard had yet to grow, and to challenge Kordar – but he had blooded himself a hundred times over since then and still wore Kordar's jawbone on his belt. There was something about Kron that Golgoth couldn't shake out of his head – his every word was afire with conviction, and it seemed that Golgoth had waited a lifetime to meet someone who could speak to him without fear. In any case, he told himself, he needed someone who knew these mountains, and he had lost enough men so that he could make space around the fire for one more.

Golgoth led Tarn, Varkith and the old man towards the warriors' camp, imagining himself wading through the corpses of Grik's lackeys, feeling a new determination to make the hermit's illusion become real.

It never occurred to him to ask how the old man had known his name.

To THE WEST of the Canis Mountains, beyond the rolling foothills and past the toothed banks of the Blackwater Delta, the heart of a continent was bounded by a wall of bone-white stone that grew in great plates and ribs from the broken earth. Soldiers swarmed along it like insects picking over a skeleton, pikes and spears bristling. Within the wall a city grew denser and denser like a spider's web, first with isolated colonnades and plazas melting from the ground, then with massive chunks of fortress walls that lurched upwards as if trying to haul their stones into Torvendis's jaundiced sky.

Paved streets were ribbons of stone diving in and out of the grey-brown earth, running further into the city which grew closer and taller as if there was something at its heart that nourished it. Mushroom-like blooms of polished rock were ringed with windows in which barely-human knots of limbs writhed. Shanty towns clung to larger buildings like frightened pets, blossoming and dying as their inhabitants were dragged this way and that, draining into incense-filled catacombs or flooding out in great purges to turn the ground dark with their shadows. Pleasure-cults, in pack-animal mobs, roamed as the buildings grew taller and broader, sought out new sensations in streets that narrowed and crushed as the buildings expanded and contracted like huge stone organs.

Further towards the centre the ground fell away into massive strip mines torn beneath the city, spindles of rock remaining to which buildings were chained to keep them flying away. For this was a place saturated with power, flowing up through the wounded earth below and seeping from the orgiastic sense-rites that thronged the walkways and platforms above. Precarious top-heavy factory hulks, like inverted pyramids, shook as they belched the smoke of rendered bodies. Streams of elixir distilled from hordes of sacrifices ran down their sides and rained onto screaming cultists. Silk-clad legionaries, their armour bright metallic like beetles' carapaces, kept key intersections clear of the pleasure-seeking crowds and policed their infinitely complex ceremonies with shock-prods, halberds and guns.

Observation towers leaned insanely, shaking as if with laughter, and trained spindly arrays of clockwork sensors on the heavens, seeking new experiences in the patterns of Torvendis's many moons. Temples to Slaanesh were suspended on ropes of human hair above bottomless pits, silken pavilions protected by huge sweeping blades of gold and silver, armatures and daemon-bound engines studded with diamonds.

Billowing clouds of incense turned the sky purple-black, where segmented sky-wyrms coiled and banners to the Pleasure God rippled up into the sky. In a wide ring around the city's very heart stood spiked barricades guarded by the Traitor Space Marines of the Violators Chapter, their armour sky blue with purple-grey ichor weeping from the joints. And beyond these barriers stood Charybdia Keep.

The city itself didn't have a name, and was usually referred to as the 'City', or the 'Capital', or not mentioned at all. For it was simply the hinterland of Charybdia Keep. The mines beneath the city supplied its materials, and the city was itself a mine for slave-courtesans and the substances that could only be rendered down from the living. The keep was the seat of power on Torvendis, a power that had achieved dominance such as few had ever achieved in the planet's long and tortuous history. The keep was the spiritual, military, political and physical lynchpin of the planet.

It was built of pale grey fossilised remains precisely quarried from the rocks of Torvendis and tesselated into massive straight-edged blocks. Polished ribs and gleaming teeth sparkled on its surface. Corners were braced with webs of skeletal fingers. Schools of ossified sea monsters were packed into the dense foundation blocks that formed pillars sunk deep into the earth. The keep was a kilometre high, and every stone in its construction had once been something living.

A chamber at the very peak of Charybdia Keep had once been the eye of some unimaginably huge creature, now a vitrified crystalline dome that sat on the battlements like a diamond in a crown. From here an observer would command a magnificent all-round view of the city, and watch as the buildings rippled slowly, shifting and changing like something alive. Which, in many ways, it was.

THERE WAS ONLY ever one such observer at the pinnacle of Charybdia Keep. Not because no one else was permitted there, but because there was only one person on Torvendis who could survive the insanity that was the keep long enough to reach the chamber. That observer was Lady Charybdia.

Lady Charybdia sat back in the deep upholstery that filled the lower half of the globe, feeling it close around her. She waved a hand and the transparent surface above her clouded, shimmering with many colours as she focused her sight through the crystal. For a moment she let her senses relax, dulling them to the warmth of the chamber and the feel of the silk against her skin, the whispers that caressed her face after travelling as screams far across the city.

It was as if she was sinking from some rarified, divine place into the drudgery of reality. The air was still. The thick velvet around her pulled back from her skin. The scent of all the emotions of the city died away. Everything was quiet. Lady Charybdia could throw her senses back into hyper-reality with a thought, but she always liked to dampen them now, for the few moments before she used the chamber, so she would not get flooded by a planet's worth of sensation.

She usually felt as if she were just a receptacle for sensations, pure and transparent. She was suddenly very aware of her body, the same vessel of flesh that had served her for so long, but one that was very changed from its original form. Her fingers were too long, jointed in many places like spiders' legs. Her face was like porcelain with wide gleaming eyes and high cheekbones, running up into a forehead split with a ridge of hardened skin that ran back along a grossly distended skull extending back for a full metre. The blades of her pelvis flared like petals of bone curving up from her waist, and her spine was greatly elongated with hundreds of vertebrae that writhed of their own accord. Her skin was decorated, not with anything so crude as tattoos, but with elegant spirals so faintly etched that they were only visible to someone who concentrated for many minutes on the play of light against Lady Charybdia's body. Very few people, however, would dare to stare at Torvendis's ruler in such a way. The thought pleased her.

The clouded crystal swam, and images emerged. Lady Charybdia willed them into distinct columns and rows, each one a different facet of the planet that she considered to belong to her. It existed for the pleasure of Slaanesh, the god to whom she offered all her praises – but the rocks and the seas and the flesh and blood of its inhabitants, those were hers to mould like clay into whatever form she saw fit. It was this act, and the place of her imagination in it, that formed her worship. For Torvendis to be dedicated to her god, she had to own and control it completely.

Focusing on each image in turn, she looked out upon Torvendis. A writhing slab of flesh throbbed in one of the city's many buildings, bathed in the light of their lust – Lady Charybdia felt a faint nostalgia for the days when she had been young and naïve, and had thrown herself with abandon into the orgiastic rites of Slaanesh. She had suffered the degradations and triumphs of those times and emerged as a true emissary of the Prince of Pleasure, given to the pure pleasures refined from the bodies and souls of her subjects. Though she herself was an aesthete, there were still untold millions of her underlings who worshipped Slaanesh in only as sophisticated a manner as their unenlightened minds could comprehend – hence the pulsing knot of tangled limbs.

One strand of her attention sought out the corruption-drenched lands to the south, where magic saturated the earth like blood on velvet. Those who survived there farmed the land and traded with one another for the basics of existence, but their bloodlines had been devolved and they were blank-faced, cattle-minded people. She could feel the cloying stupidity that lay behind their eyes – it smelled thick and spongy, it felt damp and sticky, and sounded like bubbling mud.

In the oceans that bounded Torvendis's largest continent schools of sea creatures lolled in the lightless depths, gnarled and mutated versions of those from which the keep's foundations were built. The constant fear of predation and lust for prey was a sweet, sharp tang in the salt water.

A straggle of barbarian warriors hiked across the tooth-like mountains. Charybdia cared little for such people – they led raids on the settlements that grew up around her outer walls, but they were like flies that could be swatted away by her legions if she ever got round to paying them any attention. The warriors were muscled and battered by a life amongst the elements – they had weapons slung over their backs and murder in their eyes. Charybdia had seen such men grow up, fight, and die a thousand times over. She moved on.

Deep below her, slave-gangs laboured in the shadows of the keep's foundations. The slaves were drawn from the city's unwanted childrenand the able-bodied captives that Charybdia's forces took in battle, and the vast majority of them lived and died in the mines. Though they would never know it, their labours provided most of the raw ingredients for Lady Charybdia's life of aesthetic excess, for beneath the earth lay endless slabs of the dead. Torvendis's history was so long and crammed with conflict that the battlefield dead lay thick in layers like geological strata – it was from these seams of violent death that the slaves hacked fossilised bone and blood-rusted weaponry. Every now and again they would uncover something that could produce a completely new experience – a specimen of a species previously unused in the keep's architecture, a nugget of surviving tissue potent with age, a talisman still drenched with magic that could have the memories of battle and bloodshed wrenched from it.

Hundred-strong gangs sweated in the infernal heat and darkness of a rock face from which jutted stone claws gnarled in death and spikes of still-sharp steel. The slaves' limbs were corded with muscles but their faces were drawn with fatigue. They were of all species – legions of indistinguishable humans, massive orks, monstrous ogryns, even a few shackled monsters from the alien fleets that traversed the cold space between the galaxies, goaded with shock-flails to tear at the rock with their claws. Most had been captured from those peoples of Torvendis who had at one point been in Lady Charybdia's way, with the others brought in by raiders throughout the Maelstrom and handed over in tribute. But none of them would live one tenth of their normal lifespan – the lucky ones dropped dead of exhaustion or were crushed by chunks of fallen bone. Those who did try to flee would be butchered by the guards who stalked them. The guards missed nothing – their outer layers of skin were pared off so every breath of air was a raw wind of knives against their raw nerves, every movement was like a radar blip of pain in their minds. They carried shock-flails for herding the slave crowds, and implanted vibroblades in their hands and feet to make short work of any potential escapee.

Lady Charybdia watched for a few moments as the slaves hacked away at the huge slope of rock, others sorting through the spoils that flowed down the rockface. They picked out finger bones, scraps of metal, the occasional jewelled armband or half-recognisable helmet. Many would call it a waste, thought Lady Charybdia – so many resources were poured into the mines that they probably formed her empire's primary expense. But she knew it was worth it. The constant refinement of sensation was her own form of Slaaneshi worship, and if the unwanted and defeated could not be put to work honouring her god, then what good were they at all?

And besides, the smell was wonderful. She reached out with her senses and the scent of despair filled her, thick and purple, hot inside her head. It was the first she had discovered, back when it seemed the galaxy itself was young, and she had never tired of it. They knew they would die, one way or another, and it was not just fear but an utter lack of hope. The smell of abandonment and tragedy. A million million broken spirits, bleeding out into the air and into the sense-centres of Lady Charybdia's soul.

She let the images shift and swim, looking for something amiss. Torvendis turned and its stories continued, every ending sparking a host of new tales. It was as it had always been.

Except... there was one thing. A tiny nugget of wrongness in the cauldron of Torvendis. Just past the Canis Mountains in the swamplands where nothing lived, a hard, sharp, cold thing glimmered. Charybdia looked closer, and the image in the crystal blurred into focus. This did not belong on Torvendis – it was from somewhere outside, maybe even from beyond the warp storm of the Maelstrom.

It was a spaceship. Shaped like a teardrop with a long tapering prow, the bulbous main body ribbed and studded with portholes. It was an old design, a shuttle or interceptor that had not flown in realspace since the Horus Heresy ten thousand years before.

There was a visitor on her planet, and Lady Charybdia made it her business to know of any visitors. And, usually, to order them destroyed.

She waved a hand and the images dissolved, leaving the glowing night sky of Torvendis shining down on her. The Slaughtersong was high, she saw, a curious omen of change and progress tempered with danger. Perhaps the visitor was more than a mere curiosity. In any case, they must possess some manner of sorcery or technology to arrive unannounced, and hence they were worth finding.

She would have to confer with her soothsayers. Lady Charybdia folded her arms around her, clasping her shoulders with her elongated fingers, and drifted down into the thick velvet. She sunk, and was disgorged several floors below. Around every corner of the keep's tortured architecture was a different style of decoration – the corridor in which she emerged was crusted with gnarled gothic mouldings, with a high vaulted ceiling and stained glass windows coloured with the blood of a thousand species. She had trod it many times – one way lay the grand staircase lined with statues in which were trapped the souls of innocents, which sang the unbearably sad song of their imprisonment. She headed the other way, towards the lair of her chief soothsayer, Vai'Gar.

This was a minor matter. While Lady Charybdia had many enemies on Torvendis, none had any real chance of threatening her. Once Vai'Gar had sought out the intruder and he had been dealt with, she would return to the depths of Charybdia Keep and enjoy the pure pleasures of her masterpiece.

IT WAS SIX DAYS before they caught up with the caravan. By that time they had lost two more men. One had succumbed to exhaustion, falling asleep one night and not waking up, while Kirran, inevitably, had tumbled down a precipice. Kirran had been out of sight of all but Tarn at the time, and Golgoth suspected Tarn had killed the lad to keep his murderer's hands bloody. Golgoth didn't mind, as long as the assassin didn't make a habit of it.

Golgoth crept on his belly along the rocks, the lupine skin folded beneath his chest to stop the ridges of sharp flint from cutting him. Night had ended and day was crawling up the sky, milky morning light seeping over the stones. The two moons were still above the horizon, the large milky disc of the Widow and the small, blue-green Vulture. He and his men had spent a hard night moving across rough ground and picking their way alongside precipitous drops, to ensure that they would have the best position come morning. Now, they waited above the one place his plan could have a hope of succeeding – the Snake's Throat.

The Snake's Throat was a pass that would lead travellers from the middle of the Canis Mountains clear through to the foothills. It was a huge channel burrowed through the rock, and old men said that it had been formed when Arguleon Veq hurled the world-snake, servant of the Last, down from the highest peak. The Throat was the impression the world-snake's body had made when it crashed down, broken, onto the rocks. Golgoth didn't know how many of Torvendis's many stories he should believe, but there were certainly the broken stubs of giant cyclopean ribs stabbing from the vitrified walls of the Throat.

Golgoth's heart rose to see his timing had been perfect. Down the curved channel of the Throat, the caravan lumbered. There were three wagons, each pulled by two hunched reptilian creatures, massive things twice the height of a man. The wagons were piled high with all manner of boxes and bundles, held down with ties of sinew and coverings of hide. Each one had a pair of drivers with barbed lashes, and they struck at the pack-beasts often, for the creatures were slow to feel pain.

Grik's guards rode on the sides of the wagons or walked alongside. They were warriors picked from Grik's own encampment – they had travelled across the mountains to all the barbarian settlements of the Emerald Sword, and were now making the equally dangerous return journey. They had to be men of the greatest stamina and determination. Golgoth recognised faces glimpsed on the battlefield – here was a man whose stag-horn bow could shoot through three men at once, and here was one whose two-handed war-axe had a blade hewn from a single slab of flint.

There must have been sixty men guarding the caravan, all warriors hardened by a lifetime of battle and the unforgiving passage across the mountains. But that was not the worst of it – on the top of the lead carriage sat a cross-legged man, naked from the waist up. The black skin of his hairless body and scalp were tattooed with vivid white designs, abstract swirls and patterns that would function to conduct the power around his body when he summoned it. A sorcerer – probably bought by Grik from one of the scattered desert lands to the south-west, trained and tutored even before he had been brought to the chieftain's tent. He would have been expensive, which meant that he must be good.

Kron had been correct. This was far too well-defended a quarry for thirty-three mountain warriors. Had they tried to take the tribute, as Golgoth had planned, they would all have been killed. Perhaps they would take a fair number of Grik's warriors with them, and maybe even force Grik to forbid the use of the Snake's Throat for his caravans again. They could cost him much effort and resources. But they would be dead, and Grik would be alive, and that was a concept intolerable to Golgoth.

But now, Golgoth had an advantage.

Kron's word was good, so far. He had, indeed, taught Golgoth much in the last few days as they clambered over the rocks or rested by the fire. Some of it was mere knowledge – Golgoth would not have recognised a sorcerer otherwise, and had certainly not known that a man could command fire like a tamer commands a beast. But there were other things – a word here, a gesture there, that could hook a strand of Torvendis's legends and from them draw enough power to do some commanding of his own.

Golgoth waved a hand and, though he could not hear them, he knew Hath and Tarn were sliding along to join him, with his warriors just behind them. They would have their blades and axes drawn just as Golgoth had, held out in front of him, with their shields unslung and tethered to their wrists with lengths of cured sinew.

'Ready?' whispered Hath at his ear.

'Not yet,' said Golgoth.

The caravan was passing right beneath them. The attack would be just like any other – the first wagon would be hit, then the last, then the one in the centre. Hath would take a handful of warriors to attack the last wagon, while Tarn would lead the assault in the middle, where the guards would be trapped and the slaughter would be at its hottest.

Golgoth would lead the initial charge on the first wagon. Not just because it was his right as leader to take the first blood, but because that was where the sorcerer was.

The centre wagon was passing under them. They could hear the lowing of the pack-beasts as they hauled the wagons over the ripples of stone.

'Yet?' asked Hath.

'Now,' said Golgoth, and leapt to his feet.

The glassy rocks of the Snake's Throat were slippery, but Golgoth kept his balance as he led ten men down the steep side towards the lead wagon. The guards were alert and had their weapons drawn as Golgoth reached them.

'For the Sword!' he yelled, and barged into the nearest enemy – a man with a single wide scar dividing his face in two, wielding twin handaxes in a shining figure-of-eight defence.

Golgoth led with his shield, letting his opponent rain blows against the cured hide. He kept his head down and swung low with his own double-headed axe, catching Grik's man on the knee and feeling the bones shatter. There was a cry of shock – Golgoth didn't need to look over the edge of his shield to know his enemy would be stumbling backwards as he tried to put his weight on his shattered leg. Golgoth pushed with his shield and stabbed down with the spiked butt of his axe, feeling the crunch of breaking ribs as he punched through the man's ribcage.

Voices rang out around him. The harsh crack of iron against stone told of a wild swing missing – the rush of air exhaled in shock told of another that hit. A glance backwards told Golgoth that Lonn, the Touched lad, had managed to blood himself, for he was rolling a spasming corpse off him and drawing his short sword from its belly.

His other warriors were barrelling down the slope to attack. Vrash was dead, taken through the eye by that stag's horn bow. The eight others were heading for the guards, battle in their faces.

Another arrow sliced the air and narrowly missed the massive Varkith. A man, Golgoth knew from experience, who would take that sort of thing personally. Knowing Varkith could look after himself, Golgoth ran forward over the moaning body of his opponent, heading for the lead wagon and the sorcerer.

Another of Grik's guards stood in his way, but Golgoth was feeling that rush of battle-lust that he had first tasted as a boy and never grown out of. He swung his shield like a club and backhanded the enemy across the face, dodged the wayward sword-cut the guard made as a return, and hacked deep into the enemy's shoulder with his axe. The guard was dead before he hit the ground, the axe blade biting through his collarbone and into his spine.

Golgoth felt a flush of heat and he knew that it was more than just the blood rushing to his head. He threw himself to the ground as a whip of fire lashed out at head-height. Golgoth didn't see who it hit but he heard the scream.

The sorcerer was standing, no, levitating a few hand's breadths above the top of the lead wagon, waving his hands in elaborate gestures. His fingers were aflame and spat fire that formed a long burning tongue, swirling like a sea-snake. The tongue lashed again and this time Golgoth saw one of his warriors fall, his torso sheared in two by the white-hot fire. The flame caught one of the reptilian beasts and it roared in pain, rearing its huge scaly body and rocking the wagon behind it.

Golgoth leapt up and scrambled up the hide-covered cargo on the wagon. He could smell the sorcerer, sweat mixed with spices, smoke and ash layered over the strange alchemies he had anointed himself with. The white tattoos on the sorcerer's black skin seemed to shift as Golgoth hauled himself on top of the wagon, as if they were alerting their owner to the danger.

It was time for Golgoth to put what he had learned into practice.

Sometimes, Kron had said, a warrior has a favoured weapon, or a design he must have on his shield, or a verse he must recite to himself on the eve of battle – something that gives him focus, something he can hold on to in the chaos of conflict. But the same principle could be used more deeply. A word here, a gesture there, an image in the mind's eye at the right time, would all help to link the warrior's mind and body and drive him to new heights.

Golgoth created the image as Kron had taught him. He imagined a bear, the long-toothed, grey-haired kind that had roamed around the Bladestone village of his youth. He imagined that the bear's fangs were in his mouth and the bear's claws were his axe. He spoke a few syllables that Kron had told to him, and leapt at the sorcerer.

Suddenly, he was everywhere at once. He saw Torvendis, a jaundiced orb surrounded by the boiling nebulae of the Maelstrom. He saw the Canis Mountains like a ridge of scar across the land. He saw how their peaks and valleys formed patterns in the stone, patterns that converged on a central point. He realised that he was at the centre, and that at that moment, the whole of Torvendis existed solely to witness his strength. Torvendis was full of stories, but in that second, the tale of Golgoth was the only one worth hearing.

The sorcerer was nothing. Golgoth threw his axe aside and grabbed the man by the throat, swatting aside the hands that tried to conjure a bolt of flame. He hurled the sorcerer away and marvelled at how light the man felt, watching him slam into the glassy stone of the Snake's Throat that shattered around him. Golgoth leapt off the wagon and bowled one of the guards to the ground as he landed. He reached down and ripped the man's arm off, then forgot about him as three more guards rushed to confront him.

Golgoth caught the blade of the first in one hand and shattered the second's jaw with the other. He wrenched the sword out of the first attacker's grip and rammed it hilt-first into the stomach of the second, in time to slam a head butt square into the face of the third.

Golgoth heard, impossibly, a gurgle from the sorcerer, a last message from the dying magician. Instinctively, Golgoth looked towards the skies.

Harpies. Three of them, half as tall again as Golgoth, with great leathery bat's wings that sent them diving towards him. With the hard light of the Vulture behind them Golgoth could see their muscular, brown-black bodies covered with bands of thick, shaggy hair, their pointed canine faces, the enlarged breastbones that pulsed with the beat of their wings and the yellow, filth-crusted claws that stabbed from their hands and feet.

Their tiny yellow eyes were fixed on Golgoth. He could see the sharp animal teeth behind their snarling lips and smell the carrion on their breath. He could hear the breath rasping in their throats. He could taste the blood that matted their fur.

He was supposed to dive to the ground, and hope those talons didn't sink into his back. He was supposed to lie flat and pray they took one of the other warriors instead.

But Golgoth was stronger and quicker now than any man had a right to be. He was supposed to die here, amongst the blood and the futility and the never-ending cold. But he had never been one to do as he was told.

He caught the first harpy, turning sideways and ducking between the splayed talons of its feet, reaching up and ramming his hand into its throat. He felt a shoulder pop but ignored the pain. With his free hand he grabbed the harpy's wrist and twisted, feeling the gristle of the elbow give way, pulling the monster close by the throat and holding it in the path of the two that followed it.

One harpy's claws speared into the back of its packmate. The other checked its descent with a massive beat of its wings, shrieking as it realised it faced a foe rather more impressive than the usual scraps that wandered the mountains.

Golgoth pulled the first harpy to the ground and stamped down on its throat. The second was disengaging its talons and rounding on him. Golgoth batted its swinging paw aside, barged with his shoulder, felt it jink to the side and used his momentum to step behind the monster. He grabbed a wing and yanked, snapping the hollow bone and tearing the membranous skin. He grasped the other wing and pulled in opposite directions, hearing the crackle of the creature's ribcage splitting open and grinning wildly at its gurgling howl.

It wasn't dead when he dropped it, but he knew it would be soon. The third harpy was keeping an almost respectful distance, hovering with huge wingbeats in the air above Golgoth, spitting in rage and frustration.

'Come on!' he screamed at the monster, knowing but not caring that it could only understand the dead sorcerer's tongue. 'What manner of prey am I? How do I taste?'

As if it knew when it was being taunted, the harpy dived, slashing with its taloned feet. Golgoth ducked and sprang up, shattering its shin with the edge of his hand. It squawked and dropped a metre, and Golgoth was on top of it. He leapt and brought his weight down on the harpy's back, crashing to the ground on top of it. Kneeling in the small of the creature's back he slammed his fist over and over into the bestial skull until it had given way and his arm was slick with blood to the elbow.

He picked up the dead creature to cast it aside, but suddenly the weight of corpse was heavy in his hands. Golgoth stumbled and the cold, raw air scoured his throat. His vigour drained out of him, and it was all he could do to keep from slumping to his knees. He dropped the corpse and looked around him, his head swimming with the heat of blood on his hands and the brittle lightness of breaking bones.

Five of Grik's men lay horribly mangled, the sorcerer amongst them. Three harpies, twisted creatures born of Chaos, were broken on the ground like fowl savaged by a fox. Had Golgoth done that? With his bare hands? He had always been strong, but this was the work of a daemon, not a man...

What had happened? What had Kron taught him?

Hath had done his job. His warriors had chased the
guards from the rear wagon into the centre of the caravan,
where they were surrounded by Tarn's men and those who
had survived the assault on the first wagon. This was where
the slaughter began, and where Tarn proved his worth. He
slit men's throats as his fellow warriors held them down.
When there was no need for a shield he fought with a dagger and axe, pinning men down with one and cleaving open
their heads with the other.

Normally, Golgoth would watch Tarn and admire the
cold-blooded artistry of the man. But Golgoth felt drained
all his energy channelled into a few moments of butchery.
Now the stench of harpy blood was making him dizzy. Pain
throbbed in his shoulder. And there was something else that
he had never felt before.

He was horrified. He was horrified at what he had done.

Grik's last half-dozen guards had been herded together,
back-to-back with their shields held up in desperation. As
Golgoth watched, Varkith wrenched a shield out of the nearest guard's hand and threw it aside, Tarn at his side hurling
a dagger into the man's eye. The other warriors joined in,
some battering at the enemies' shields while others struck
around their guard. Soon, they were all battered and broken
on the floor, and Tarn was finishing off the wounded with a
dagger through the throat.

Hath strode across the blood-slicked rock.

'Good killing, Golgoth!' he exclaimed, grinning. 'Grik's
lapdogs were no match for real men. And the harpy beasts!
Never have I seen such a thing! I feel there truly is hope for
the Emerald Sword, Golgoth!'

Golgoth forced himself to stop shaking and choked down
the urge to vomit. He had learned a long time ago that he
must never show weakness, not even to his closest comrade,
Hath. 'Yes, good killing. I must speak with Kron. Check the
wagons and see what we can do without.'

Hath nodded and turned to organise the surviving warriors, who were singing crude victory songs over the corpses
of their enemies. Golgoth clambered to his feet and headed
back up the smooth stones. The harpy blood was beginning

to dry and it pulled at his skin in thick clots. He would never get the stink out of his clothes – he would burn them all, once they found some suitable replacements in the wagons.

Where was Kron? The old man seemed to simply melt away when no one was watching him. It was one of many unnerving habits that Golgoth was only starting to notice now, when Kron's power was becoming apparent to him.

From the edge of the Snake's Throat, Golgoth could see clear across the Canis Mountains. He could just glimpse, in the far distance, the rolling foothills silver-blue in the light of twin moons. Somewhere between the fang-like mountains and those foothills was Grik's encampment, a nomadic tented city that moved with the currents of tribal politics, and at the centre of which was the chieftain's tent.

One day, Golgoth would walk into that tent and call out the weak-willed Grik to decide the fate of the Emerald Sword. And now Golgoth had the tribute caravan, that day was suddenly very close.

Golgoth gulped down the cold, clean air, trying to douse the nausea that still rose within him.

'The first time is the worst,' said a clear and knowing voice behind him. Golgoth turned and saw, as he knew he would, the cloaked form of Kron, silhouetted against the pale disc of the Widow. 'You are young, Golgoth. You think you have little to learn, but in truth you hardly know anything. The fear you have now is that you were something that you never realised, that you can commit acts you thought were impossible. You never knew you could be so savage, Golgoth, did you?'

'What have you done to me?' gasped Golgoth, struggling to keep from sinking to his knees.

'Nothing, Golgoth. You did it all. This is not mere sorcery, conjuring something out of nothing. I simply taught you how to reach into what lies within you already. There are few like you, Golgoth, and fewer still who ever discover what they are. You have depths of rage and hatred that will never be exhausted.

'You are angry now, and tired. But there will be a next time. How else can you hope to challenge Grik?'

Kron was right. If Golgoth could learn control as well as
strength, Grik would cower at his feet and the Emerald
Sword could march down the path Golgoth hacked through
the bodies of his enemies. But could there ever be control,
when Golgoth had torn five men and three monsters apart,
and lusted for more?

'You have potential, Golgoth. But at the moment, it is
nothing more. You have enough ambition to take a handful
of warriors across these mountains in pursuit of a lost cause,
and I can help you realise those ambitions. But you must
follow me, and learn what I teach you. You have seen what
you can do with my help. Are you too afraid to learn more?'

Below, in the bloodstained Snake's Throat, Golgoth's men
were stripping the dead and taking the iron medallions that
signified their allegiance to Grik. Hath, seasoned veteran
that he was, was checking the broken body of the sorcerer –
sorcerers were said to keep creatures sewn into their skin,
who would bite their way out and inform their employers
should the sorcerer die. Tarn and a number of the warriors
were laying the stripped corpses in neat rows, as an invita-
tion to the carrion harpies that would soon follow the scent
of blood. The wagons' coverings were off and the warriors
were rifling through the tribute to take the personal trophies
that were their due.

Anything small and valuable was quickly hidden in
pouches and folds of lupine skin – jewels that were the
frozen tears of maidens, necklaces of twisted golden snakes,
mined alive from the mineral-rich mountains to the north.
Several men took weapons or shields, or strapped pieces of
armour to their bodies, before pulling the coverings back.

Each warrior took care to make sure he had one particular
item of value – a small iron circle crossed by four bars, the
symbol carried by all Grik's warriors. They would identify
the men as the caravan's guardians, at least until Grik or one
of the elders came to meet it. By then, it would be too late.

Soon, Hath would soothe the lowing pack-beasts and the
warriors would move the stolen caravan towards Grik's
encampment. It struck Golgoth that he and his men had
succeeded in the most perilous part of their plan, at least

until they reached Grik. Perhaps he would pay a great cost for the strength Kron was offering, but if it was enough to ensure success as they had won here, there were few prices Golgoth would not pay.

The thought made him feel much better. The taste of bile in his mouth was gone. He tested his shoulder and felt the sort of pain that troubles for a few days, but heals. Kron walked past him, down towards the caravan and Golgoth joined him, already eager to learn more.

The twin moons faded in the brightening morning sky. Low on the horizon, small but bright, the Slaughtersong still shone down.

CHAPTER TWO

WHILE THERE ARE volumes of legends about Arguleon Veq, his greatest foe – the Last – is ever mysterious. Some say there were once many, and that all but one were swallowed when Chaos first bled through the Maelstrom into real-space, leaving the Last as the sole vengeful survivor of its race. Others say that it was, in itself, a creature of Chaos, a daemon who refused to accept the yoke of a god, a creature that in its madness desired the symbolic world of Torvendis for itself. Both scholars and liars claim many other things besides – that the Last was from another time, or a vast alien creature that became trapped in the Maelstrom like a fly in tree sap, or a sentient war engine from the insane times of the Dark Age of Technology.

But these tales are like oil on the surface of a lake. As if Torvendis was somehow embarrassed by stories of the Last, they shimmer on the surface of that planet's legends, sliding into obscurity when other tales remain stacked deep in the consciousness of the world.

But the Last fought long and hard against Arguleon Veq, that awesome champion of Chaos, and all agree that

sometimes the outcome of the duel was far from certain.
The Last must have been terrible indeed to truly challenge
Veq, perhaps skilled in sorcery, composed of energy, or
possessed of some other power that none can guess at. But
the most persistent impression is one of immense size.

The Canis Mountains are argument enough for many.
When the combat came to deceit and subterfuge, the Last lay
in wait for years, intent on ambushing Arguleon Veq. When
Veq let his guard down – a mistake, a lure? – the Last reared
up from beneath the ground and nearly devoured him. The
impressions left by the Last's huge maw remained in the
earth, as that range of sharp towering peaks called the Canis
Mountains.

THE MOUNTAINS WERE the first thing that Captain Amakyre of
the Word Bearers saw as the ocular arrays of the *Multus Sanguis* focused for the first time on the surface of Torvendis.
They were like a ridge of old scar tissue from a wound that
had healed and been re-opened a dozen times – ugly,
gnarled ripples of rock running the length of the continent
that dominated the face of the planet. Amakyre drew back
from the eyepieces of the array, his millennia-old power
armour whirring as he descended from the helmsman's pulpit to the bridge deck of the *Multus*. The *Multus Sanguis* was
as old as the Word Bearers Legion itself, and like the Legion
it had doggedly survived everything the galaxy had thrown
at it. Amakyre's mission was important and he had chosen
the *Multus* precisely because it was fast, tough, and had an
unusually active (if unstable) machine-spirit that could look
after itself if left alone. The ship was like a massive cluster of
cathedral spires, stained and encrusted with weapons
emplacements and gargoyles, that tore angrily through
space on the dull red glow of its engines. In addition to its
other qualities, it was the largest ship in the Word Bearers'
fleet that was capable of a planetary landing.

Inside, the interior of the *Multus Sanguis* was convoluted
to the extent that only a tiny fraction of it was habitable, the
rest open to hard vacuum or full of twisted metal. Only the
bridge, engineering decks and Word Bearers' quarters were

safe. This made the *Multus Sanguis* all but impossible to board, and it could run on the barest of skeleton crews as it did now.

Amakyre gestured at the pasty-skinned lackeys that cowered from his presence, and one of them flicked a switch that projected the image of Torvendis high above the amphitheatre of the bridge.

The black, age-stained ironwork of the bridge was edged with grey in the light of the holograph. Amakyre stared up at the pale, scarred world, trying to scry some meaning from its appearance: the tortured wound of the mountains, the sallow expanses of rotted swamplands, the multicoloured city of Lady Charybdia like a jewelled net cast across the centre of the continent. The shattered multitude of islands in the oceans to the west, the chewed-up peninsula to the south where slabs of rainforest crowded between bottomless chasms – where had the multitude of Chaos gods left their mark? Torvendis was a world of massive symbolic stature, existing as it did at the very heart of the Maelstrom where other worlds would decay and fragment, preserved by the way a hundred currents of the warp pulled in every direction upon the world and cancelled each other out. The eyes of every gloriously malign deity turned upon it, if only to see which one of them could claim dominance over it as the centuries flickered past.

Torvendis was tormented indeed, Amakyre saw. With sight honed by ten thousand years of contemplation, he could detect the wounds beneath the planet's surface and the currents of violence that had swept across it. All the more remarkable then that Lady Charybdia, misguided as she was to treat her god Slaanesh as prime amongst Chaos, had held on to power for as long as she had.

But Amakyre, captain of the Word Bearers Chapter, wasn't here for Lady Charybdia. He had made sure he knew enough about her to anticipate her reactions to the Word Bearers' arrival, but that was all he cared about as far as she was concerned. He was here for the one his Chapter called Karnulon.

Amakyre turned at the sound of the bridge blast doors opening. The circle of lackeys who crouched around the

edge of the circular bridge deck cowered at the noise, turning their eyes – those who still had them – to the riveted
floor.

Brother Prakordian stepped through the smoke that
boiled in from the noisome lower decks. Prakordian wore
power armour the colour of old blood, the same as
Amakyre's, and with the same snarling daemon emblem on
the shoulder pad. But where Amakyre's limbs were studded
with campaign badges and decorations from millennia of
war, the ceramite of Prakordian's armour was covered with
engraved ramblings. Prakordian was a deadspeaker, to
whom the words of the dead echoed in the half-trance that
Space Marines endured instead of sleep. When Prakordian
emerged from that non-sleep there would be another passage graven onto his armour, more words powerful enough
to survive death and reach Prakordian's corrupted mind.
Somewhere inside that pale, tight-skinned, hairless head
there were a million words circling, vying for the Chaos
Marine's attention, the last chance of the deceased to make
some mark on the universe. Prakordian's gift – and it was a
gift, for it made him useful to the Word Bearers and there-
fore to Chaos – meant that even those who gave up their
lives could still be interrogated.

'Praises!' called Prakordian, breathless with excitement as
soon as he glimpsed the mutilated disk of Torvendis. 'Such
a world! Such death!'

Some would have been amused by Prakordian, who
somehow still possessed wonder as well as the fanaticism
that tainted every Word Bearer, as if his devotion to Chaos
was more like the malice of a child than the cynical hatred
of an ancient warrior. But it took a lot to amuse Amakyre
now, when he had sought to bleed the galaxy dry of virtue
since the days of the Heresy.

'Take care you are not deafened, Brother Prakordian. There
have been more battles fought here than the rest of the Maelstrom together can claim. This is your first sight of the enemy,
brother, and it is an enemy indeed. This world is what Karnulon will be using as an ally. He will use its power against
us. Know your enemy, and do not let its beauty distract you.

If you can do your sacred duty here then the voices of the dead may be a little louder before we leave.'

And their duty was sacred indeed. Karnulon was one of their own, a Word Bearer of considerable reputation for viciousness in the face of war, and Amakyre had seen what could happen when one of their own lost his discipline. Though it was often scattered, fighting on a score of worlds at once according to the plans of its warlords or the Primarch Lorgar himself, the Word Bearers still retained their integrity as a fighting force. They still had discipline. They still had a chain of command. So many had lost it in the years since the Heresy – some Legions were just roving bands of butchers, others were insane predators who struck from the warp at random. The Word Bearers were a cohesive fighting force, capable of being wielded as a precise and devastating weapon by the enlightened Lorgar. Men like Karnulon had to be destroyed to protect the Legion. If rogues were left unchecked, the Legion would eventually become no better than the piratical Astral Claws or the madmen of the Thunder Barons.

Amakyre had known Karnulon. Karnulon had been there in the depths of the Heresy, and had weathered ten thousand years of war in the name of Chaos. Amakyre remembered those twin lightning claws that sent crescents of power arcing off his dark scarlet power armour, the hard-edged face that had never aged and was lined with experience rather than years. He remembered how Karnulon had been taken to the court of Lorgar himself, and had perhaps even spoken with that reclusive giant, before rumours of his education in sorcery and his rapid warp-mastery of magic.

Now Karnulon had disappeared and taken with him too many secrets of the true face of Chaos. Amakyre had been charged with finding him – and he had also been granted the power to judge his brother Chaos Marine, which allowed Amakyre to execute Karnulon once it was determined why the renegade had taken his leave of his Legion.

Amakyre was a captain of his Legion. A hundred Word Bearers had fought and died at his word, a hundred of the

warp's finest warriors. He had been relieved of that command to complete this mission, to find Karnulon and bring
back what remains he saw fit. Amakyre knew how important
he was, for he had overseen thousands of battles. The Legion
thought this task to be equally important, and Amakyre was
resolved not to fail. And fail he would not, for the six Word
Bearers he had with him were enough to accomplish anything.

'And we are sure he is here?' Prakordian was saying.

'No, we are not sure,' replied Amakyre sternly. 'We know
his ship came this way. We know this is the only place of
shelter for light years around. But we will not assume we
have found him until he stands before us.'

'But if we have found him, then why has he come here? So
many eyes look upon this world. It is no place for a fugitive
to hide.'

'That will be answered when we find him.' Amakyre waved
an impatient hand at the rag-clothed, scarred lackeys who
cowered at the edge of the amphitheatre. 'Navigation!' he
yelled, and a handful of them scuttled towards ancient black
iron consoles, where monitor screens blinked from inside
gaping daemon's mouths and tell-tale lights spelled out the
dark thoughts of the *Multus Sanguis*. Thin, dirty-nailed fingers scrabbled at keypads and a network of complex glowing
lines appeared around the image of Torvendis. Ghostly
equations and occult diagrams flashed here and there at random, symptoms of the ship's growing unpredictability – the
Multus was old and thoughts came to its machine-spirit
unbidden. In its senility, it was becoming more human.

The many trajectories the *Multus* could take were marked
out in glowing green. Sites large enough to land the ship
were orange patches projected onto the surface of the image.
There were places in the foothills of the mountain range, but
Amakyre knew the ship would be hard to miss from the
great walls surrounding Lady Charybdia's city. Much of the
swampland would swallow up the ship's huge weight and if
they landed on one of the islands the Word Bearers coven
would have to somehow find their way across hostile waters
before they could even begin their quest.

'There,' said Amakyre, pointing towards a place in the far north of the continent, where the mountains met the sea. The rocky terrain would be inhospitable, but flat and stable. Amakyre strode over to one of the lackeys and hauled it (Amakyre could no longer tell the males from the females, so riven with scars and malnutrition were they) to its feet. The Chaos Marine was about twice the height of the wretch.

'This is where we will land. Inform the machine-spirit.' He cuffed the lackey and sent it scurrying off down an access tunnel that would lead it to the housing of the *Multus's* machine-spirit, deep in the heart of the ship's prow. The machine-spirit would need feeding now, so while delivering the co-ordinates, the lackey would provide it with the warm blood it craved.

It was not surprising that Prakordian had been the second to emerge from the stasis-meditation the Word Bearers observed during travel through the warp. The youth (Amakyre could only think of Prakordian as a youth, though he was many centuries old) was filled with anticipation of secrets uncovered and blood spilt. The other Word Bearers of the coven would be waking now, and Amakyre would hold a sermon for them. He had to make sure they understood the importance of their task and the terrible consequences for the whole Legion if Karnulon reneged on his loyalties and went rogue, as no other Word Bearer had ever succeeded in doing before.

There would be weapons rites to observe for Vrox, who could not speak the litanies himself after the Obliterator virus had turned his mouth into a gunport. The landing would have to be supervised and the *Multus's* machine-spirit placated with more blood. There was so much to do even before they made planetfall, and Amakyre trusted all these tasks to no one but himself.

He strode off the bridge deck and into the roiling steam that billowed up from the lower decks, heavy with incense, sweat and decay. With every step he took he praised the pantheon of Chaos. With every task completed, he brought the galaxy closer to unification under darkness.

* * *

LADY CHARYBDIA LET herself drift down the shaft sunk deep into the immense foundation block, the sighs of spirits trapped in the walls cushioning her descent. Very few knew that it was even possible for something to travel this far down, for the foundation blocks of the keep seemed as solid as anything on the planet. But this one was networked with narrow channels and low-ceilinged galleries like flaws in a diamond, winding their way down through the massive stones and down to the same level as the most ancient of battle sites. The air was old and laden with the powdered bones of the war dead, the stones rough and traced with spiralling cross-sections of skeletons.

It pleased Lady Charybdia that she was the only one who both knew of these places, and was able to travel between them and the rest of Charybdia Keep. Most of the retainers she kept here had no idea that any world existed outside the cramped tunnels and blood-warm grottoes.

Lady Charybdia came to a junction where the shaft led to a long, torchlit passageway. She breathed a command and the lamenting spirits let go of her, letting her elegant, altered body in its white silks drift to the floor. The air here was warm and stifling, and she felt her lungs open up in response – a survival reflex, a relic of her earlier life when she fought and butchered like any Chaos champion.

The wall was studded with skulls, nailed to the stone with golden spikes. Normally such decoration was far too blatant for Lady Charybdia, but these skulls were special. They had been hacked out of the earth in the deepest mine her minions had ever sunk, so deep the heat killed off mortal men and precious daemons had to be summoned to complete the work. But it had been worth it, for these were not human skulls they had found.

They were eldar. At some time impossibly distant, eldar had walked upon Torvendis. They were a strange race, obsessed with eking out the secrets of the universe and then guarding them like a jealous child guards its toys – and yet the pursuit of knowledge had all but destroyed their civilisation, when their decadence had caught the attention of Slaanesh. Some claimed the eldar thus brought Slaanesh into existence, but such was heresy – Slaanesh was as old as lust, and lust was older than anything.

Lady Charybdia did not know why eldar might have visited Torvendis all those millennia ago. Perhaps they had become marooned on the world by accident, and the Maelstrom was certainly an easy enough place for a spacecraft to become lost. Then again, seeking out the secrets of Torvendis was just the sort of desperately inquisitive thing the eldar might do, so maybe they had been here deliberately. Whatever the case, Lady Charybdia was the only one on the planet to know the aliens had once been here, and that knowledge – like so many things – pleased her.

She admired the lines of the skulls as she passed. They looked human only at a distance, up close they were different in every dimension – wide-spaced, teardrop-shaped eyes, small jaws and teeth, elegant cheekbones, tapering craniums. It was easy for Lady Charybdia to imagine how Slaanesh might wish to take such an elegant species and turn their sophistication into a tool for his worship. They were beautiful, almost as she was beautiful, and the ultimate sensation of their dying must have given Slaanesh much pleasure when their planets were annihilated at his arrival.

The chamber ahead was large and circular, with rib-like supports holding up a domed ceiling of mottled red-black stone. It was one of the biggest cavities in the foundation, and standing on its threshold was like looking inside a great living organ, dark and hot, the hum of life felt through the soles of the feet.

In the centre of the room, where the floor sank into a circular depression, kneeled one of Lady Charybdia's legionaries. He was rather more than two metres tall, his skin so heavily tattooed it was impossible to tell what colour it originally had been. His torso was bare and around his armoured legs hung lengths of silk-like banners, embroidered with the symbols of the Pleasure God in hair shorn from the heads of those notables the legionary had defeated. One hand held a spear, the point a twin-pronged blade designed to pin down and disembowel. The other was

placed palm-down on the floor, feeling for movement, for
any sign that something below might be stirring.

Lady Charybdia approached the kneeling figure at the centre of the chamber. 'Arise, centurion,' she said. She knew his
rank because of the particular symbols he wore on his silks
and skin, but she did not know his name. To her, none of
them had names. They were just instruments she used to
maintain her position of worshipful pleasure.

The legionary stood, his eyes fixed on the ground. To look
on Lady Charybdia without due reason had become a crime
in the city without its ruler ever having to order it so.

'Has our guest woken of late?'

'He has not, my lady.'

'Then our hospitality must not be to his liking. Shall we
wake him, and see to his needs?'

'If my lady wishes.'

'Your lady does.'

The legionary stood aside, stepping up from the depression. He took a knife from his belt and, silently, cut a long,
deep cut in the side of his abdomen. Sheathing the knife, he
pulled a roll of parchment from the wound, slick with
blood, and unrolled it. Still averting his eyes, he held out the
parchment for Lady Charybdia to take.

On the parchment was written the code-rite, which was re-
divined and written down by Lady Charybdia's sorcerers
after every visit she made to her guest. The means by which
the guest could be woken had to be kept safe, and it had to
be different every time. If someone broke in and defeated
the legionary, his death would destroy the parchment as his
digestive acids broke through his prepared intestines and
dissolved it.

Lady Charybdia spoke the sacred syllables, her voice
barely above a whisper lest the power of those words bleed
into the foundation and pollute the purity of the keep. As
she finished, there was a grinding sound beneath her feet,
and Lady Charybdia and the legionary stepped back as the
stones shifted. The floor of the depression began to rise,
reaching the level of the chamber's floor and continuing to
form the top of a pillar of stone. The polished curve of the

pillar showed a cross-section of the stone, revealing smeared, stretched ribcages and distorted skulls ghosted into the rock.

A section of the pillar had been hollowed out, forming a man-sized alcove where a figure was chained to the wall. The chains were tongues, cured and sewn into loops linked together, that had once spoken the words that imprisoned the occupant.

The occupant was a daemon.

Lady Charybdia had often had cause to witness the form of daemons. The servants of Slaanesh, formed from a portion of his magnificence and given sentience, were enthusiastic if barbaric pursuers of pleasure and were unparalleled enforcers and soldiers. But this was not like those. The Prince of Pleasure had never looked upon this creature with lust or admiration. This creature was utterly inimical to Lady Charybdia and everything she believed in, for it hated all life and pleasure, and would rather swamp the galaxy with blood than contemplate one moment of decadence.

It was humanoid, after a fashion. It had too few fingers and its torso was lumpenly muscled, lopsided and hunched. Into its dark grey flesh had been hammered chunks of machinery, none of which seemed to serve a purpose, all still oscillating and pumping into the places where the stained metal met its bleeding skin.

Its face was grotesque, not like Lady Charybdia's own subtly hypnotic alterations but like a brutish animal. There were far too many eyes. The mouth was a fist of muscle covering thick yellow fangs. There was no nose, and horns sprouted from the daemon's forehead, temples and chin. On its massively muscled chest was a deep, charred brand, the crude skull-like symbol of the Blood God burned into the weeping skin.

Lady Charybdia would not let the name of the Blood God be spoken on her planet. Where Slaanesh valued life and the many entertainments that could be derived from it, the Blood God embraced only death. Its worshippers were blood-crazed thugs, and its daemons single-minded machines of destruction.

Once, in one of the many phases of Torvendis's history, the Blood God's daemon prince had held brief, insane dominion over the world. Ss'll Sh'Karr was the least blasphemous of its many names. Its word had commanded vast legions of daemons modelled after its own hideous image, legions that were eventually crushed by the next power to take a foothold on Torvendis. Lady Charybdia knew this because she had herself seen the rock face where the remains of that battle festered, and kept the malformed fossilised skull of Ss'll Sh'Karr deep within Charybdia Keep. The Blood God had had its time on Torvendis, and the captive daemon was the last vestige of its presence here.

Lady Charybdia very rarely came down to consult her captive. But there was something wrong with her world – she felt it in the sense-echoes of anticipation and approaching despair that tinted the clouds and the sky. Her scryers and scouts had found nothing of the visitor whose ship still lay in the swampland beyond the mountains. Lady Charybdia only knew that it had arrived in a pre-Heresy craft such as was used by raiders and renegades throughout the Maelstrom. She did not know who or what had visited Torvendis, or why. Such ignorance was entirely at odds with the way she wished to rule, and it displeased her. Displeasure had to be stamped out.

And there was more. It was as if the whole planet was seething, just too quiet for her to hear, thrumming with the weight of events to come.

The daemon looked at Lady Charybdia with most of its eyes. The others whirled madly as it snarled and slavered.

'Are you hungry?' she asked sweetly.

The daemon growled, dog-like.

'Good.' At her gesture, the legionary readied his spear. 'You will speak, spawn of ugliness. You know what I can do to you if you refuse.'

The daemon shuddered, trying to tear the spell-bound chains from the stone. It had struggled like this for aeons, ever since it had been unwittingly summoned from the rock face by the hapless slave-miners, and hunted down by the Chaos Marines of the Violators. Lady Charybdia had long since come to the conclusion that it was too stupid to give up, and had to be tormented into obedience like an animal.

'Bleed it,' she commanded, and the legionary plunged the blade of the spear deep into the daemon's abdomen.

It screamed, and Lady Charybdia winced to hear such discord in her domain. The thick red blood flowed out over the withdrawing blade and spattered down onto the stone floor, hissing as the boiling liquid touched the cold surface. The daemon shook as its beloved life-blood flowed out, and with it it's very soul. The prospect of exsanguination held a sort of cold horror for the Blood God's followers and servants, as if the blood loss somehow made them unworthy for the favour of their god, who despised victims above all else.

'I can make it stop,' said Lady Charybdia levelly, as the daemon watched its blood pooling uselessly on the floor. 'Or I can make it worse. Or I can make it slow. We will speak, Butcher God's slave. You will talk.'

'Speak what you will,' growled the daemon, its voice low and dark. 'I will tell you only lies.'

Lady Charybdia smiled. She had spoken often with daemons, and ones far wilier than this. 'Why is my world so disturbed?' she asked. 'Was there something planted here long ago that is coming to fruition?'

The daemon laughed. It was not a pleasant sound. 'Your world has a bitch-queen too scared to wage war. No wonder it shakes.'

'Who has arrived here? Why is he unannounced?'

'He has come to kill you.'

A straight answer. Something rare. Daemons lied, but it was dangerous to just assume the opposite of what they said was true. There was always some truth in what they said, it just had to be sifted from the lies.

'Why?'

'It would be quicker to say why not.'

Lady Charybdia tapped a foot and the legionary thrust the spearpoint back into the wound, twisting the blade and opening a long tear in the skin. The daemon groaned as a fresh gout of blood spurted onto the stones.

'I do not wish to be displeased, daemon.'

'I do not know the answers,' spat the daemon. 'I was young when this world was old. Your visitor spits on your god and mine, the Maelstrom did not give birth to this planet, and the things you see had begun to fester before Sh'Karr walked on these lands. I know no more. Rot your tongue, whore, you can demand no more of me.'

Lady Charybdia was bored with the interrogation. The daemon had come perilously close to admitting weakness – now its mind would seize up and it would retreat behind insults and threats.

She turned on a heel, with just a backwards glance towards the legionary. 'Leave it for an hour,' she commanded. 'Then send it back down.'

The legionary knelt in supplication. Lady Charybdia headed back along the corridor with its secret eldar skulls. She was displeased, for reasons she could not quite fathom. She would drown out her annoyance with the pure, scouring pleasures of the keep.

THE WEATHER HAD turned in the Canis Mountains. Instead of raw cold there was damp, clinging cold, a fine mist that hung everywhere and soaked through the leathers and lupine skins. Steam rose off the massive scaly pack-beasts as they hauled the wagons of the caravan through sheer-sided valleys westwards. Golgoth's warriors spat and swore, looking grimly at the grey-white overcast sky and grumbling about storms rolling in. The caravan was passing through the western edge of the Canis Mountains where the path ran through deep valleys winding their way towards the foothills.

Banks of mist clung to the mountains peaks and rolled down their slopes. Sometimes the fingers of mist reached into the valleys and the caravan creaked its way in near-blindness, other times it formed a slab like a ceiling just above them. It was as if the world had grown smaller, the endless wild darkness of the Maelstrom walled off by the mists.

'What can the mists give you?' Kron was asking.

Golgoth looked at the old man. Kron had refused to take a place on one of the wagons, along with the wounded, and walked alongside them as sure-footedly as any of the warriors.

'They can blind us and freeze us,' said Golgoth. 'They give us nothing.'

Kron smiled. 'Think, Golgoth. There is nothing on this world you cannot use. I have explained this to you already. You have a rare thing, an imagination, and you can use it to turn the sights and sounds and feelings you have experienced into something tangible. This is the essence of sorcery. This is the way Chaos interacts with this world, though very few can take advantage of it. What do you feel here?'

'The cold.'

'Cold what?'

'Everything. The stones, the air. Me.'

'You. Can you become that cold, Golgoth? Not just in body. In soul. Cold-blooded. Cold-hearted.'

Golgoth barked a short laugh. 'Do not talk to me of cruelty, old man. I have skinned men alive.'

'Not cruelty. Control.'

Golgoth, who had killed men and beasts with his bare hands and not been able to stop, suddenly paid attention. 'Control? I wish you had spoken to me of this earlier.'

'It is the hardest lesson to learn. I had to make sure you were ready.'

The mists ahead rolled off the last, fractured channel of the Snake's Throat. Beyond, the way would be crude and treacherous. Not bad enough to need a sorcerer, but still hostile. The mists drew back over the peaks like lips over teeth, and revealed a sight that Golgoth, though he had heard of it, had never seen with his own eyes before.

'Arrowhead Peak,' he breathed, his breath shortened by the suddenness with which the place had emerged from the mist.

The city of Arrowhead Peak had been carved out of the rock, a clutch of mountains hollowed and hacked until arches and galleries stabbed from every face. There were massive pillared halls and endless winding lanes running through the hearts of those mountains, plains under stone skies where whole armies could muster and gates that yawned back against the pale stone. Bridges connected the peaks like threads stretched over the dizzying chasms.

Arrowhead Peak was a sharp and deadly-looking place, with every tower topped with a tall spike from which banners once flew, and each pinnacle ringed by defences from which arrows could rain.

And rain they had, in the days when Arrowhead Peak was an inhabited place. Warriors from all across the mountains had vyed for a foothold there, where the chieftains of the tribes each held their court. Treaties were made and broken. Sometimes, blood flowed in the streets when war between tribes erupted, but this served only to strengthen other alliances. The city had been the lynchpin of the mountain peoples, a place where they could match one another's strengths and turn those strengths into real power. Back then, the tribes had marched as one when a large enough threat faced them all, with the stark white banner of Arrowhead Peak flying alongside those of the tribes. The Emerald Sword had held more than its share of power, and Arrowhead Peak had represented its best chance of taking over the dominion of the mountains.

As Golgoth watched, a flock of harpies alighted from one of the highest peaks, a grainy black cloud boiling from the windows of some ancient palace. There was nothing living now in Arrowhead Peak that did not live off carrion. Sometimes men of the tribes ventured up into the deserted city to bring back some memento of the days when the Canis Mountains were nearly welded into one of Torvendis's most powerful realms. Sometimes such men even returned, almost always mad, almost always alone.

Lady Charybdia had arrived a long time before Golgoth had been born . No one really knew the whole history of the degenerate princess's rise to power, but it was certain that Arrowhead Peak had been one of her first conquests.

She had war engines that could fly, and vomit whole legions of silk-clad, tattooed fanatics into the caverns of Arrowhead Peak. She had treaties with packs of daemons, and huge flying monsters were bound to her words. They even said there were Space Marines, Traitor Legion warriors a head taller than the mightiest Touched, with massive gore-stained armour and weapons that spat fire.

It had been slaughter. Lady Charybdia had an endless supply of legionaries and half-naked cultists, ferried in by skyships and lashed forward up the steep mountain slopes. The mountain warriors were penned in, with all their fighters committed and no source of help. Cultists died by the thousands and legionaries by the hundred, but there were always more. The Emerald Sword had held their great gathering hall for weeks, defending barricades of fallen pillars against waves of madmen who fought with their hands and teeth. But, like all the rest, they had fallen.

Then the legions had left, as if the capture of Arrowhead Peak was just a passing fancy for Lady Charybdia. She left the place an eyrie for ravenous harpies, and seeded it with dark tales that kept the tribes away. She had not assaulted Arrowhead Peak in the name of power – she had done it out of sheer spite, and then abandoned it when it gave her no more sport.

Perhaps, thought Golgoth sometimes, the mountain tribes had been weakening anyway, and one day would have fallen. But Lady Charybdia was someone to blame, and in this cold and unforgiving place, that was valuable indeed.

'When Grik is dead, I will take back Arrowhead Peak,' said Golgoth.

'Lady Charybdia cursed the place,' said Kron. 'It was she who branded the walls with daemons. They say a day in those halls will drive a man mad.'

'There must be a way,' said Golgoth, glancing at the old man and noting again how tall the old man was beneath his robes.

'So the stories tell us,' replied Kron. 'Concentrate for the moment on what you must do. Grik has killed more pretenders than we will ever know of. He will have more than one sorcerer and a handful of carrion beasts to defend him. Remember that control, Golgoth, because without it the strength you have will be worse than nothing. It will get you killed.'

'Grik is just a man.'

'No one on Torvendis is just a man. Listen, Golgoth. Learn. And never lose focus. The next lessons will be the hardest, because you will not want to learn them.'

The mists were peeling back from the slick, broken walls of the Snake's Throat. The beasts lowed and lumbered a little quicker as the view ahead opened up. Golgoth could see the place where the mountains rolled into the foothills, where the bladed peaks gave way to rolling foothills. In the distance, the jagged profile of the last peaks loomed pale like smoke and the foothills were ghosts just visible clinging to the horizon. From here there would be outposts and sentries, patrols of young tribesmen creeping through the shadows to blood themselves on wanderers. Grik's eyes would be everywhere, and it would take discipline to get through without being discovered.

Lonn sat on top of the front wagon, his Truesight scanning the rocks. Tarn was beside him, keeping his own watch with mortal, but experienced, eyes. The warriors, with Hath at the front, spread out as the ground roughened and the smooth trail was replaced by sharp, hacked channels and steps in the rock.

The hollow bones of Arrowhead Peak drifted past them as the caravan marched on, harpies flocking around huge windows like eye sockets, bleached battlements like teeth.

TORVENDIS WAS MANY things – not least, it was whatever its rulers made it. Lady Charybdia desired an immense altar to Slaanesh, a whole planet sanctified and corrupted to serve as holy ground for the Prince of Pleasure. Though she had done much, founding the city and using the resources of the planet itself to sate the pleasure-hunger and so praise her god, Lady Charybdia still had to extend a concrete influence over Torvendis as a whole. The mountains and the shattered islands that flanked her domain, and the lands to the south of desert and jungle and darkness, were beyond her direct control. The seething, swampy land beyond the mountains was further still from her rule.

Gradually, though, she was extending her power. The city itself crept outwards, growing from the ground or being hacked from the earth by peasants newly converted to the worship of Slaanesh. And elsewhere, temples of Slaanesh were built, to act as focal points for new followers. They also formed a kind of warning system for the city: when forces were massing against Lady Charybdia, they would hit the scattered temples first.

Yrvo knew this, and welcomed it. To die for the Prince! Not just to experience the ultimate thrill of violent death, but to do so at the will of the Lady, and help her eternal worship of Slaanesh! Yrvo almost wished some enemy horde would come pouring over the slick, rocky landscape towards his remote temple, just so he could feel their blades piercing his skin and help him reach the limits of his senses. To die here on the wet rocks and breathe his last of the salty coastal air – that would be an experience worth the life that preceded it.

But there was much to do in the meantime. Here, they were far away from most settlements and everything had to be done by the acolytes themselves. All around was slick, flattened dark grey stone, with the northern walls still many kilometres southwards and the harsh, barbarian-plagued seas to the west and north. Eastwards there was only the Canis Mountains, like a barrier at the edge of the habitable world. Yrvo's temple was as remote as they came, and he was proud – the word of Slaanesh had been brought to the furthest reaches of the planet.

The temple was delicate, and always needed maintenance. It was in a slight depression surrounded by a ridge of stone, like a scar, but the weather still took its toll on the structure. The body of the temple was a square of iron pillars which curved over to form a roof, like a cage a hundred metres on each side. Chains festooned with hooks hung down to shoulder height from the bars overhead, every link covered in tiny metal thorns and blades. Pennants and banners of every colour and design were everywhere, tied to the pillars and flying in the sharp wind that coursed right through the temple. When the wind was stronger the chains would make a sound like a choir singing, and spiked links would rain down to lie like caltrops on the rock floor.

The banners – silk and skin, woven hair and hide – would tear constantly, always needing the attention of Yrvo and his acolytes. And it was in this way that Yrvo would do the work of Slaanesh, for every time he crossed the floor of the temple the chains would gift him a thousand tiny cuts, the sweet agony feeding the pleasure-fire within him, the fallen links cutting into the soles of his feet.

In the centre of the temple was the altar, a metallic depression sunk into the ground in a curious star shape. Only when one looked long enough did it become apparent that it was designed to accommodate a spreadeagled human form. A chamber directly below was full of blades and drills, controlled by a system of levers operated by Yrvo's acolytes, that would stab or slice up through slots in the metal. The altar was rarely cleaned, for the rust-red stains were a testament to the holy work done there. How many unbelievers had Yrvo anointed with pain? How many had been introduced to the majesty of Slaanesh, manacled there as the words sacred to the Prince of Chaos were spoken?

'Magister Yrvo!' called one of the acolytes, scurrying into the body of the temple from outside. 'The Deacon sees strangers approach!'

Yrvo peered at the acolyte through the forest of chains – he was one of the young ones, judging by the relative lack of scars on his milky skin. He wore the yellow and white colours of a novice wrapped around his waist, leaving his upper torso bare to show the scars and tattoos of devotion. There were about a hundred and thirty acolytes here, living in the tents and huts clustered around the shelter of the nearby rocks. Yrvo rarely left the temple, and knew few of the acolytes by name.

'Who? How many?'

'It is hard to tell. Not many. They are coming quickly, but in hiding.'

They are always afraid, thought Yrvo. Those who had not had contact with the profane mysteries of Slaanesh were always frightened of what their senses could show them.

They had to be brought unwillingly to the fold of the Pleasure God. It was such a shame so many of these did not survive their anointing, but at least their lives were given to pleasure in the end, even if they did not appreciate it.

'Have the faithful arm themselves,' said Yrvo. 'Our guests will be bandits or scavengers. And gather some of the novices to prepare for the anointing, the altar shall see use before sundown.'

The acolyte bowed his head in acknowledgement. 'Praise Slaanesh, magister.'

'Praise Slaanesh,' said Yrvo.

Yrvo walked to the threshold of the temple, the skin of his face receiving many exquisitely fine cuts from the dangling chains. He never tired of that tiny, sharp pain when his skin parted, and the smell of the blood that ran down his face.

Beyond the fluttering banners he could see the ridges of rock that rippled up in the distance, across which the newcomers would be approaching. Acolytes were hurrying this way and that armed with autoguns and laspistols, valuable firearms given to the temple from the armouries of Lady Charybdia's legions. There were not enough to go round and many acolytes had swords or spiked flails. Yrvo was proud to see that just having such weapons in their hands was too much temptation for many, who drew thin red marks of devotion on their skin with swords and bayonets.

Yrvo saw the Deacon, who had been a fervent worshipper of Slaanesh for so long he no longer had any skin at all. His wet, red flesh glistened as he racked shells into a shotgun chased with gold and pearls. The Deacon had been at the temple for as long as Yrvo had, which was long indeed. In that time they had seen astounding pleasure-rites, the festivals of flesh that travelled the scattered temples like moving cities of sin, visitations from daemons on unholy nights and visions of new pleasures that lit up the sky. They had fought together often enough, too. The Deacon, as might be expected, felt no pain any more from conventional means, and to him combat was just another arena for experience.

Yrvo had still to arm himself when the first shots rang out. Not from his acolytes – from the newcomers, still out of sight. It was a ranging shot. The second shot took the head clean off one of the novices, a fountain of blood like a spray of jewels as he fell.

He saw a group of acolytes gathering beneath the lip of the rocky ridge where the novice had fallen, scattering random return fire. The Deacon was leading some of the tougher acolytes forward to flank the attackers. The attacking fire was suddenly heavier, and the acolytes by the ridge scattered, three or four falling in sprays of blood and rocky shards.

An acolyte running past thrust an autogun into Yrvo's hands. Yrvo felt the round slam into the chamber and sprinted towards the ridge. A sudden explosion blossomed, arcing past the ridge and blasting a handful of acolytes apart. Small arms fire chattered overhead, raking through the Deacon's men, punching raw red holes through torsos and sending limbs spinning from their bodies.

It was beautiful, thought Yrvo. There was a rare poetry in violence. But it would not do to lose too many followers, so Yrvo called out to the scattered acolytes falling back from the ridge as bright yellow-white lances of fire sheared through the air all around them.

'With me, sons of Slaanesh!' he yelled, holding his gun high. 'For the Lady! For the Prince! Feel the deaths of the enemy as your own!'

Yrvo ran up the slippery rock, one half of his mind urging him to move quickly and keep his head down, the other willing the bullets to rip through him so he could drown in his own blissful pain.

He reached the ridge, and saw the enemy for the first time.

Their attacker must have once worn armour, but the armour and flesh had become one. Skin grew in rags around the massive greaves, slick muscles for hydraulics, spines of bone jutting from rips in the dark scarlet metal. Each arm ended not in a hand but in a club-like slab of muscle covered in orifices from which weaponry jutted – on one arm were three cycling autocannon barrels spitting white tracers of fire, from the other stabbed the snout of a frag missile. The dead-skinned eyes and mouth opened and gun barrels poked out, chattering left and right.

The figure was three and a half metres tall with armoured shoulders just as broad, its armour plates packed with muscle, its shape shifting as new weapons were extruded from its flesh. Yrvo had seen Space Marines before, distant figures guarding the battlements of Charybdia Keep – but this was something different, ugly and brutal when Lady Charybdia's Violators were elegant in their strength.

Yrvo ducked behind the lip of the ridge as the missile streaked towards him, and half-rejoiced as shards of rock were driven deep into the skin of his back as it detonated. He fired back blindly, dazzled by shards and smoke, the kick of the weapon in his hands and the roar of its report flooding his senses alongside the pain.

The smoke cleared and Yrvo saw the acolytes were dashing up to join him, screaming as they fired wildly, blood fresh on their skins. Their bodies jerked and came apart under the autocannon fire, beautiful patterns of blood and ruptured organs cascading. There was nothing so aesthetically perfect as death – the reduction of living flesh to dead matter combined with the rush of escaping life that created the final, ultimate thrill.

Yrvo had to tear his eyes away from the spectacle. He had the Pleasure God's work to do. Another spray of bullets and his autogun's clip was empty. He took a lasgun from the mangled body of an acolyte that had tumbled beside him and fired blind again over the ridge. The metal was hot in his hands from sustained lasbursts, the thrumm of the power pack and the throb of the blasts spitting from the barrel pulsing through his palms.

He took his finger off the trigger and darted his head above the ridge.

The monstrosity was closer now, so close Yrvo could smell the deep, metallic reek of oil and taste the smoke that coughed from its many gun barrels. Its face was nothing more than another gun mount – too late, Yrvo realised it had seen him with eyes that blinked from sockets sunk into its armour.

The autocannon was levelled directly at his head, unerring as a compass.

The shells passed right through Yrvo's upper body. He could feel his organs shredded and his jaw shattering, taste the shrapnel and bone driven high into his brain. Cold rushed through him as his spine came apart, whiteness bloomed in front of his eyes as they spattered from their sockets. His tongue was in tatters and new tastes of pain and ruin flooded his mind.

Yrvo, now just a tattered column of torn flesh tottering from his waist, keeled over onto the rock. His last conscious thought was that death was not the cacophony of sensation that had been promised him – it was cold, and empty, and carried with it pain that he had believed he could never feel again.

Perhaps the revelation would lie in what followed. Yes, that was it. Just a little while longer, and he would feel that ultimate thrill.

Yrvo turned colder, and then thought nothing more.

IT WAS, AMAKYRE thought, dismal sport. Vrox, massive body sprouting a new gun every second, had the defenders penned in below the ridge. They were typical of Slaanesh's devotees, rushing into gunfire and scattering as they were cut down by Vrox's explosive shells and frag missiles. The cultists' eagerness for the sensations of battle warred with their instincts for preservation, and so it was simple for Vrox to keep them pinned back with sustained fire. Skarlan and Makelo the Tactical Marines, their boltguns sending controlled bursts spattering over the rock, were sprinting up to support Vrox.

The *Multus Sanguis* had landed five kilometres away, nestled on a salt-slicked plain between the mountains and the ocean. It was not safe for the coven to stay with the age-streaked old warship – Lady Charybdia or any one of Torvendis's peoples might discover the ship through sorcery or divination, and take exception to its presence. The coven needed somewhere else to plan their next move, and the Slaaneshi temple was the closest place where they might snatch a few hours' respite.

Amakyre could have joined his warriors assaulting the temple. But he knew how fine a warrior he was. This was the first chance he had to see the coven acting unsupported under live fire, and wanted to observe them.

Energy blasts impacted around the Marines. Skarlan ignored them even as they flashed off his power armour, while Makelo ducked to the side and strafed as he moved.

Far to the side, Feorkan was sniping at a flanking force led by a nightmare of a man whose skin was tied in flowing pennants around his waist. This group was more cohesive, using the broken rock as cover as they advanced to drive back Amakyre's Marines.

They could not know they were facing Word Bearers. They would know soon enough. To a lesser man, it would seem tragic, for not one of them would survive. But Amakyre was above such sentiment.

Two or three of the acolytes fell even as they fired, Feorkan's heavily customised bolter sending single shells punching through their bodies. Feorkan ducked and rolled as he moved to the side, and Amakyre saw he was trying to herd the skinless man's mob towards a knot of rocks.

He guessed Feorkan's plan before it began. Phaedos leapt from the shelter of the rocks and barrelled into the mob, chainsword throwing out fans of blood as it slashed, plasma pistol discharging a white-hot bloom of liquid fire into the centre of the acolytes. Prakordian was crouched in the rocks, covering the Assault Marine's attack, sending bursts of bolter fire into the attackers who tried to surround Phaedos.

Phaedos duelled with the skinless man, who was quick and determined as only a man with no sense of pain could be. It wasn't enough just to wound – Phaedos's blade lanced deep into the raw flesh time and time again, severing nerves and shredding muscle, until the man could fight no more. A second blast of the recharged plasma pistol reduced the nightmare to a melting, burning mess.

The mob were scrambling over one another to flee. Prakordian sprayed bolter shells into them as Feorkan picked them off one by one, every bolt sending a head snapping back as the life flowed out of their bodies.

Amakyre strode forwards and the sounds of slaughter cut through the wind, the stuttering roar of Vrox's autocannon mingling with the gurgling cries of the dying. The ground between the ridge and the temple was strewn with bodies, maybe fifty or sixty, with about twenty stragglers now cowering behind the pillars of the chain-festooned temple. The banners that billowed around them were shredded with charred bullet holes.

Amakyre despised these wretches. The weakness of character that prevented them from worshipping the full pantheon of Chaos was unforgivable. The Pleasure God was just one facet of the magnificence of the warp – to worship Slaanesh to the exclusion of all others was too feeble-willed even to register as heresy.

Death was too good for them. And they would get worse than death – to die here in the Maelstrom without having the favour of the Chaotic pantheon was to give your soul up to the warp. The enlightened of the Word Bearers would see the glory of Primarch Lorgar taking his place alongside the gods. These pathetic acolytes would see only madness and oblivion. Gods below, how Amakyre hated them.

He sprinted towards the temple, lasblasts and shells buzzing around his ears, heaving the heavy-bladed power axe from its holster on his backpack. The power field crackled to life without him having to activate it – after so long the weapon knew when its master was angry, knew when it would be ordered to draw blood.

The defenders were cowering. The iron of the temple was good cover for a scattered mob, absorbing head-height shots into the forest of dangling chains. Vrox, Skarlan and Makelo were grinding them back with twin autocannon and bolters, but it could take hours to winkle the acolytes out with gunfire alone.

These vermin dared waste the time of Word Bearers with their survival. In doing so, they impeded the work of true Chaos. This was what Amakyre told himself as he ran across the corpse-strewn rock, but it was drowned out by the hatred.

The first enemy was right in front of him, finger jammed down on his lasgun trigger. Lasblasts spattered off Amakyre's breastplate like rain, nicking his bare face, scoring the ancient gold and scarlet. He brought the axe down and it passed straight through the acolyte, so he had to check the swing to avoid burying it in the rock. The cloven body slumped to the ground before the blood had even begun to flow.

The shadows of the banners rippled over Amakyre as he tore into the body of the temple. He swung the axe in a massive arc, shearing chains and sending melted links spraying in a white-hot hail. He heard screams, and was glad, for every scream was a song sung in praise of his gods.

They were firing back at him, but he had been shot at and hit a million times. One shot penetrated between his forearm and elbow guards, the flare of pain an insult. Amakyre drew his bolt pistol and blasted at random, firing a salvo at the closest scrabbling shapes, seeing red blooms where he hit and bursts of barbed shrapnel where he missed.

One or two acolytes fled past him, into the covering fire of Skarlan and Makelo. One took refuge in a human-shaped depression of bloodstained brass that marked the centre of the temple – Amakyre sprinted towards him and swiped off the top of his head.

Others fled. Others failed. Amakyre hacked down the closest and shot down the rest.

By the time Amakyre had wiped the blood from the blade of his axe and returned outside, Feorkan, Phaedos and Prakordian had butchered the acolytes who had followed the skinless man. Amakyre walked over to the bloodstained ridge and spotted a corpse with rather more elaborate robes that the rest, its upper body shredded by Vrox's heavy weapons fire. Amakyre picked up the corpse, which flopped like a dead fish in his gauntlet.

'This is what happens, brothers, when your eye wanders from the true pantheon of darkness! This is what we will become if men like Karnulon can rebel with impunity.' Amakyre cast the body aside. 'Never forget why you fight.'

CHAPTER THREE

THE ROLLING, GRASS-SPECKLED foothills rose all around like the swells of a stone ocean. The peaks were pale fangs that jutted in the distance behind the caravan. The way ahead was well-worn by marching feet and rutted with wagon tracks, and wooden frames supported lookout platforms where tall warriors with spears were silhouetted by the orange evening suns. The foothills of the Canis Mountains were every bit as treacherous as the mountains themselves, but it was the tribesmen themselves rather than dizzying heights of bitter cold that took men's lives with such regularity. Grik ruled these parts, and those loyal to him would kill without thought for his favour.

The trail had become more and more well-defined in the two days' journey from Arrowhead Peak to the outer foothills. Deep ruts were worn in the path where wagons had rolled this way and alongside the steeper parts were well-worn steps cut into the stone. Small settlements, no more than handfuls of tents, clung to the slopes around the road, and peddlers would sometimes emerge from the huts and hovels to hawk their wares before seeing that the stern-faced men of the caravan would probably make unappreciative customers. There was no need for fences or fortifications to mark out the borders of Grik's sphere of influence, for the road was one of a very few safe routes towards the current site of his city, and these were well-watched by many eyes loyal to the chieftain.

Golgoth had taken care to make sure his own warriors did not look suspicious. The fine and exotic weapons they had looted from the cargo were hidden under the hide coverings of the wagons, and the iron tokens that Grik's men had carried were hung around their necks on thongs of sinew. Kron was seated alongside Golgoth on the rearward wagon, the cowl of his cloak pulled down low over his face. If they were questioned intensely, Kron would take the place of the sorcerer who had guided the caravan to the Snake's Throat. In a sense this would not be a deception at all, because if Kron wasn't a sorcerer then no one was.

Hath, on the lead wagon, jabbed the flanks of the pack-beasts with a pointed staff and drove them forward. The closest sentry clambered down from his post and jogged down to the lead wagon. He was an old and grizzled warrior, who had so many scars on his face that it was hard to discern his features. He was wrapped in furs and had a brand of the quartered circle, the same symbol as appeared on Grik's tokens, burned into the back of his spear-carrying hand. He was one of Grik's own circle, warriors chosen for their loyalty and usefulness who would follow their chieftain's orders without question. There would be many such men surrounding Grik, strong and utterly loyal. They owed their lives to Grik in often the most literal sense – they had mostly been abandoned by poor or migrating parents, then taken and raised in the chieftain's own tent to act like extensions of his own body. This man, who had reached a great age considering the lifespans of the mountain peoples, must have been inherited by Grik from the previous chieftain. He, and dozens like him, stood between Golgoth and the future of the Emerald Sword.

Hath showed his iron circle token and the sentry looked under the hide of the first wagon, glancing over the weaponry and bundles of tribute tied there. Satisfied, he waved them on.

The caravan moved on, and Golgoth watched as the tented city emerged from between the foothills. A patchwork of muted colours nestled between rolling foothills, and from this distance the tribes people thronging its streets were teeming dark specks. The city was the largest settlement in the mountains, certainly the largest there had ever been since the fall of Arrowhead Peak – to Golgoth, who had grown up in a settlement that was little more than a village, it seemed almost impossibly huge. A man could become lost wandering in the avenues between the tents, and there must be a thousand hidden corners for scheming. Even from this distance Golgoth could just catch the smell of the city – smoke, sweat and cooking.

Huge and mobile, the city migrated with the seasons from the foothills to the edges of the plains within sight of Lady Charybdia's walls, its population carrying their homes of hide and cloth on their backs and loaded onto pack-reptiles, herding their flocks of sheep and goats before them. Every tent was dyed a different colour and bore a different clan or guild symbol on its side. Columns of smoke rose from cooking fires and hearths where the weapons of Grik's soldiers were forged from black mountain iron. Soldiers were staging mock duels in clearings between the tents, and Golgoth knew that other, far more real combats would be in progress in the dark corners of the city.

Golgoth estimated there must be over twenty thousand souls there, as many tribes people as had gathered in any one place since the fall of Arrowhead Peak. Fighting, drinking, rutting, smelting the iron and hunting the food that would be needed to survive the next migration. At the centre of it all, so travellers told, was a vast tent made from hundreds of stitched hides, emblazoned with a huge quartered circle and guarded by burly fur-clad soldiers. There Grik would be waiting on a throne of carved bone, thick bearskins under his feet and a dozen wives watching from the shadows. Grik was the judge and the patron of the city's populace, choosing warriors and settling disputes, ordering deaths when his anger was high and pardoning the weak and treacherous when he made himself lenient with ale.

If they knew what a weak man Grik really was, and the calibre of leader they could have if they wished it, the Emerald Sword could be great again. But they did not know, they were blind, and Golgoth would have to make them see.

'Time to take your leave, Kron,' said Golgoth quietly as the caravan trundled past the first few tents of the city.

'Of course. This will soon be no place for an old man.'

They both knew the truth. This was Golgoth's fight. Kron had taught the warrior as much as he could, but Grik's blood was Golgoth's to shed.

The two men dropped from the wagon to the ground. Kron swept his robes around him and was gone, melting into the unwashed gaggle of tribes people. Golgoth tried to catch sight of him but the old man simply disappeared. More sorcery, perhaps. Or just a life unseen.

The caravan moved into the earthen streets of the city, passing hovels that clustered alongside fine tents of cured hide with banners fluttering from them, pens of animals and gaggles of children. Crippled beggars gave the caravan a wide berth, doubtless knowing that Grik's guards were not generous men. Tribes people watched the caravan from the doorways of their tents, perhaps wondering if this year's tribute would be enough to make Grik a more merciful man for a while. The smells were stronger now, unwashed bodies and a hundred hearths cooking, and the sounds rose to match them – murmurs of conversation punctuated with shouts or distant peals of laughter.

It was a world away from the solitude of the mountains, but Golgoth fancied it was no less dangerous. He could all but feel Grik's eye upon the city, a constant vigilance to weed out enemies and enforce loyalty.

The people's eyes were darkened with the weariness of fear. Watchtowers cast shadows like iron bars across the city. Every street the caravan passed had parties of swordsmen patrolling. Golgoth knew little of cities, but he felt instinctively that this was one held tight by the chains of its ruler's will.

Golgoth jogged towards the head of the caravan. Hath handed him his axe, the iron still rust-coloured with dried blood, as he passed. He could feel his warriors tensing – any moment now one of Grik's men would fail to see a familiar face in the caravan guard, someone would demand to know why they had not brought their sorcerer back. An arrow or a sling bullet or a thrown blade would hit home and they would be surrounded.

Sentries on towers dotted throughout the city glared down. The reptile-beasts growled and a party of hunters, their faces blooded from the kill, stared at Golgoth as the caravan passed.

The road they were following led deeper and deeper into the city, until finally they could see the enormous chieftain's tent, wreathed in a pall of smoke from the guards' fires around it. Golgoth's men were close enough now to make a break for it and hope to reach Grik's compound before they were cut down. Golgoth could see the thick greasy smoke coiling from between the hides of the chieftain's tent and the breath of the fifty-strong guard white in the cold.

Focus had been Kron's last and most important lesson. Control. Colder blood and a stiller heart. Golgoth had never valued such things before but here, stalking through a city that was itself an enemy, he realised it could be all he had. The claws and teeth of the bear were there again, the swiftness of the mountain carrion raptor and the pin-sharp senses of the snake lying in wait. But there was also the steadfastness of the rock itself, the chill of the autumn rains, the cold and solidity of the world around him. Golgoth would need to bring all these things together as he had never tried before. He could already tap into the power that Kron had spoken of, but could he control it?

Yes, he could. Because Golgoth would survive, and Golgoth would win, and even in death he would forge the Emerald Sword again. He could not return across the mountains now, not after he had come this far. Fighting Grik and freeing the city was the only plan he had left. There was nothing else. He would defeat Grik or he would die, and he would not die because Kron had taught him how to win.

A trio of young soldiers, carrying shields and spears, blocked the road ahead.

'Fealty and purpose?' barked the leader, who had one eye missing and a snarling face aged beyond his years.

'Fealty to Grik of the Emerald Sword,' replied Golgoth. He held out the iron token. 'Here to deliver the three-year tithe to our chief.'

The leader beckoned and a dozen more warriors jogged over from the campfires, spears and axes ready. There were some Touched with them, one with an extra set of arms, another with long and powerful legs with knees that bent the wrong way like the legs of a warhorse. Amongst them was a man who was not a warrior, and whose skin was pale shimmering silver, naked to the waist. There were pages of cured and cut skin, covered in arcane scribblings, nailed to his shoulders and ribs. A sorcerer, and one of higher authority than the one Golgoth had killed, judging by the burly four-man guard that surrounded him.

'Give the watchword,' said the leader. Golgoth could see the tendons in his forearms tightening as he got ready to hurl his spear, should the wrong word be spoken.

But there was no word. Golgoth had known that Grik might have some such ruse to identify stealthy attackers. His plan in such a case was simple.

Suddenly, the leader's head snapped back and there was a thin black-fletched arrow jutting from his good eye. Golgoth glanced backwards and saw Tarn, the assassin, nocking another arrow to the bow he had taken during the fight at the Snake's Throat. Before he could fire again arrows began lancing in reply from the two closest watchmen and Grik's warrior guard were charging, some to the side of the convoy to surround it, others straight towards Golgoth.

'Cast the net!' someone yelled, and the sorcerer made a complex gesture that hurt to look at. Spikes of light speared up from the ground, describing a cage of light around the convoy, a cage that trapped Golgoth's men with their attackers.

Golgoth swept his shield off his back and drew his axe. The bear's claws were hot in his fingers. His eyes burned as he threw his senses out and the cage was full of movement, battle-cries and screams, the sigh of metal through the air and the rending as it passed through flesh.

And deep inside his chest he imagined a sliver of ice where his heart should be, pure and uncaring, that would bind all his power to his will. It stabbed down through his soul, pinning it to the only desire that mattered – the death of Grik and the end of the long night of the Emerald Sword.

The first attackers reached him and their shields clashed with Golgoth's own, the shock driving Golgoth back a step. It was one of the Touched, using his powerful altered legs to barge at full thrust into him. Golgoth was supposed to buckle and crumple to the ground, where the Touched's fellow warriors could finish him off.

Golgoth took the impact and let himself slip to the side, spinning and bringing the head of his axe slamming into the Touched's shoulder as he fell past him. The Touched pitched into the ground face-first and Golgoth slammed the edge of his shield down onto the back of his neck.

Something crunched but Golgoth didn't pause to see the Touched spasm and die – already his axe was up, turning aside a spear thrust and twisting in the air, catching the spear shaft and pulling the attacker towards him. Golgoth could smell the meat on the guard's breath as he drove his knee up into the man's groin, punched his shield into his face and let the unconscious body fall.

Golgoth had a split-second to take stock. Lonn, the Touched youth with the all-seeing eyes, was lying broken and bloody by the wheel of the middle wagon. Another of Golgoth's warriors lay beside him, keening with pain as he tried to pull an arrow from his gut. One of the reptilian beasts had been struck and was rearing up, scattering both side's men as it trumpeted in rage. The fight was raging everywhere, Hath and Valin were back-to-back and surrounded on top of the lead wagon, Tarn using a thin golden sword as he duelled with three men at once.

All around was the cage of light, blue-white and burning, ensuring that no matter who won, Golgoth's men would not escape. The sorcerer, hands held high and light bleeding from his eyes, was on the other side of the cage behind the shields of his three remaining guards. There was a score of enemies between Golgoth and the sorcerer, knots of men surrounding and killing Golgoth's men.

Golgoth didn't care about his men. The cold of control told him that he had never really cared, because they were ultimately irrelevant to his goal. If they were of use to him here as they died, then so be it. And if any of them happened to survive, then they would be honoured by the new Emerald Sword for their strength. But for now, there was nothing in the world that mattered but the sorcerer and the malevolence of Grik, hiding beyond the bars of the sorcerer's cage.

Every step was a battle. The many-limbed Touched parried a dozen of Golgoth's strikes, and Golgoth called on the bear to help him swat the deformed warrior aside with his shield and slam him against the side of the wagon, cracking his skull open. One of the guards cut at Golgoth's legs but he stepped out of the way with the raptor's quickness, pivoting on his forward foot and tearing his axe-head through the man's neck without breaking step.

The fire was gone. Instead, the cold was in command, reading every movement and dictating a pattern of strike and counter-strike. The stabbing spear was ducked, the shield cloven open, the warrior behind the shield kicked on the face and hewn through the stomach as he fell to the ground. Golgoth saw the arrow in mid-flight and caught it on his shield, using the motion to bring the edge of the shield into the face of the nearest enemy and shatter his jaw.

The sorcerer must have seen Golgoth carving his way through Grik's warriors, for he was suddenly burning with blue fire and drawing his arm back, as if to throw a spear.

The sorcerer cast a bolt of blue lightning straight at his attacker. Golgoth's reactions were superhumanly fast but the lance of energy still raked down his side, shattering his shield like glass, tearing from his ribcage down to his knee. He hit the ground, blue flame rippling across his fur cloak and seething through his skin. He tore off his cloak and rolled on the earth, trying to smother the flames against the

blood-soaked soil. The magical bolt had hewn through five
or six men before it hit him, boring through torsos and sep-
arating limbs from bodies, and the remains were strewn
across the ground. Golgoth's warriors were few now, surrounded by Grik's soldiers, many reeling from the sudden
discharge of energy, all covered in dozens of minor wounds.

The flames were gone but the pain was not – Golgoth was
still burning, his skin and fat sizzling, threatening to char
down to the muscle and leave him helpless. But he had suffered pain before, and he had known how to master it even
before Kron had taught him to armour his soul with ice.
Pain could be ignored. The threat of failure could not.

Golgoth commanded his body to obey and lurched to his
feet. He cast aside the smoking remains of his shield and
pulled a short sword from a severed hand on the ground.
The sorcerer's guards were the next obstacle, and Golgoth
refused to give up now when he was so close. He caught the
spear of the first man with his axe, stabbed him in the stomach with the sword, withdrew it and hurled it through the
neck of the second. The third was a big man, with a face grizzled by a lifetime hunting in the mountains and countless
kill-braids knotted into his hair. Golgoth saw the sorcerer
about to unleash another spell and grabbed the arm of the
big man, hauling him between himself and the sorcerer just
as a hail of molten silver needles scattered from the sorcerer's hands. They speared through the warrior's body and
many punched through into the muscles of Golgoth's
shoulder, studding the head and haft of his axe, stabbing
through the back of his hand. Hot lances of pain joined the
raging agony of the burns that he was barely able to sup-
press.

Golgoth threw the dead warrior into the last guard, and
turned his attention to the silver-skinned sorcerer. The man
was rangy and wide-eyed, no warrior. He pulled a short
sword from his belt but Golgoth shattered its blade, his
return stroke slicing through the sorcerer's neck.

The head flopped back on a scrap of skin, pale blood like
milk spattering from the wound. The sorcerer's skin shrivelled as the magical power flooded out of his body, beams

of blue light shining through the tears in the skin as it burned away. The body dissolved as Golgoth watched, until there were only charred, fragile bones that crumbled to the ground.

The bars of light flashed and dimmed, and suddenly the cage was gone entirely.

Golgoth saw others rushing to aid Grik's guards, but there were few and they were not prepared for someone like him. He sprinted for Grik's tent, swiping his axe at anyone who got in the way. Women screamed and men yelled curses as Golgoth's surviving warriors rushed to join him, running through tents and hacking their way through the gathering crowd.

Golgoth ignored them. The chieftain's tent loomed large, its arcane symbols burning with the strength of the violence erupting so close by. Golgoth leapt over one of the campfires that ringed the tent, kicking a pot of boiling stew into the face of a warrior pursuing him, and suddenly he was there.

He tore open the side of the tent, the hide coming apart in his hands. It was dark inside and stank of sweat and meat, unwashed bodies and smoke. There was commotion within and Golgoth could make out bodies scurrying away from him: Grik's concubines and catamites fleeing from this apparition of violence.

Golgoth stepped inside, the cloying smoke filling his nostrils. As his eyes adjusted to the gloom he saw the roof was held high by tall poles and trophies of bones and severed heads dangled from the poles on lengths of sinew. The rotting remains of old meals lay scattered around the filthy furs that covered the ground, half-devoured carcasses of spit-roasted animals and empty earthenware ale flagons.

The chieftain's throne stood in the centre of the tent. It was made of pitted, stained bone – legends had it that the bones were those of a sky-whale brought down in distant times by the tribe's forefathers. On that throne was a massive, shaggy-haired figure, deep red eyes glowering in the gloom.

'Chieftain Grik the weak-blooded,' said Golgoth slowly. 'I am Golgoth, come to claim the headship of the Emerald

Sword. For too long the Sword has been blunted. I shall make it sharp again. Yield, and your name will remain though you will not. Resist, and I will make sure not even the memory of you survives.'

The figure smiled, bright white teeth picking out an impossibly wide mouth, gleaming in the dark. 'You have lived too long away from my city, whipling cur. You cannot begin to understand.' The voice was thick, dark and treacly.

Grik stood. He was a clear two heads taller than Golgoth. 'What you call weakness is strength. I could have conquered the tribes a dozen times over, wasting the lives of my tribesmen on some petty feud. The Canis Mountains could have been mine, and I would have paid for a worthless mountain kingdom in the blood of my people.

'The Sword are not mindless barbarians who make war to give their lives meaning. I have seen the way. When my patrons have seen my worth, I will be a god and the Sword will be my church. You cannot imagine my plans. You cannot imagine what I know.'

Grik was Touched. It was no real surprise – those mutated by the winds of magic were often as deformed in mind as they were in body, and Grik was clearly insane. But Golgoth had expected an old, corpulent or weak man, perhaps welltrained but no match for real strength. A Touched was a random factor – there were any number of powers or deformities that Grik might possess. And this was the chieftain's home ground.

Grik walked closer. He shrugged the thick furs off his shoulders and Golgoth saw the chieftain was a hulking, muscular creature. His face was flat-featured as if pushed in; his hair, black and lank, stuck to his face with grease and sweat. There was something wrong with his mouth – it turned down at the corners and carried on down either side of his throat under the layers of hide and leather he wore. Those glowing eyes were pits in Grik's face, no pupil or iris, no lids.

Golgoth weighed his axe, the sorcerer's silver spines now melting from its haft. He had nearly lost control, he knew, in the fight by the wagons. Now this hateful creature was laughing at him, this mockery of a man, boasting that he was using the Emerald Sword as a tool for his own ends. He had to keep his ice heart from melting. He had to keep his power in control, when all his life he had let his rage loose to overcome any obstacle.

In Grik's hand was a glaive, with a long handle and a thick, chopping blade pitted with age and nicked from a thousand butcherings. 'I will show you weakness, Golgoth. You will know what weakness is when you are on your knees begging for death.'

The glaive cut the air as Grik swung it, lumbering closer. Golgoth tensed, feeling the ice within him melting. Surely it was only rage that would take him through? Surely only hatred could win?

Grik roared and slammed the glaive down into the ground, carving through the furs and into the earth. Golgoth swiped at Grik's torso but the big man was suddenly quick, darting back too fast to see, and the butt end of his glaive slammed into Golgoth's chest. Golgoth stumbled back and felt the heavy blade slicing into his burned shoulder as the chieftain hacked down at him. The tip of the glaive cut through the hide of the tent and light flooded in. In daylight Grik's skin was pale and sallow, and the chieftain bellowed as Golgoth rolled away from him.

As he roared, Grik's mouth came fully open. It gaped from his upper lip to his lower chest, a huge wet red maw studded with irregular teeth, a glistening flap of dark flesh pulsing deep inside. Golgoth stumbled to his feet and Grik lunged, the huge mouth snapping wetly shut a hand's span from Golgoth's face.

Golgoth swung heavily and his axe bit deep into Grik's arm, only angering the monstrous warrior more.

Grik struck out and Golgoth had to leap back to avoid disembowelment. He parried Grik's return stroke and felt the chieftain's bestial strength.

Grik was an animal. A monster. He was impossibly strong, as fast and deadly as he was deformed. In a brawl such as this contest was becoming, Grik would win by strength and bloody-mindedness alone. That must not happen. The odds had been heavily against Golgoth even surviving the mountain journey, but he had made it all the way here, to the chieftain's tent and the presence of his enemy. He would not fail now.

Control was the key. Grik was a beast, who had no control. Golgoth could be something more. And that was how Golgoth would kill him.

He wouldn't cleave open Grik's stomach or slice off his head. Grik was too huge and powerful for Golgoth to despatch with one heroic killing blow, such as he had used to sever the heads of lesser men in the days before Kron had taught him there could be more.

The strength and the speed and the accuracy that Kron had given him were bound even tighter by icy bars of control: Golgoth forced every instinct he had into a cage where he could command them like soldiers. He wanted to plunge his axe blade into Grik's stomach – he promised himself he could, if he was only patient. His warrior's spirit demanded that he batter Grik to the ground and stamp down on his mutant face – Golgoth silenced the voice and commanded his body to weave and parry, draw blood and weaken his opponent, frustrate Grik's rage and torment him into making mistakes.

Grik seemed slower already, his glaive ponderous as it swung. Golgoth met it and turned it aside with his axe, gauging the return and dodging it entirely. The edge of his axe grazed Grik's skin and with every cut Grik bellowed, the massive distended jaw jabbering and strands of saliva flying. Golgoth parried and counter-struck, the axe quick in his hands, Grik's blood soaking into the furs on the floor and flaps of slit skin hanging off the chieftain's frame. Grik was enraged and every wound made it worse, anger and pain clouding his reason. He charged and bludgeoned over and over again, missing and exhausting himself while Golgoth kept himself in check and, patiently, slowly, bled his enemy to death.

Golgoth was aware of others gathering, watching through the tears in the tent's hide walls – Grik's warriors and even those of his own men who had survived. They knew better

than to intervene. Grik would never forgive them if they
won his duel for him, and none dared risk helping Golgoth
in case they found themselves on the losing side. This had
become a duel, and only one man was permitted victory.

Grik was all but on his knees. Golgoth stepped round a
clumsy lunge and hacked downwards, cutting through the
back of Grik's thigh, severing the hamstring. The chieftain
crumpled, his breathing heavy like a tired horse, sweat a
glassy sheen on his face, his red eyes dull and bleeding.
The blade of his glaive touched the floor as the energy
bled out of him. He looked up at Golgoth who stood over
him.

What he saw was not hatred; it was not rage. It was control.

Golgoth drove his axe into the back of Grik's head, shattering the spine where it joined the skull.

Control.

Grik kneeled upright for a few moments, as if trying to
shrug off his death and fight on. Then the final drops of
energy seeped from him and his monstrous bulk toppled to
the floor, the breath rattling out of his cavernous mouth.

There was silence. The warriors and tribes people gathered
outside the tent had been holding their breaths as Grik died,
unable to believe it was true. Now their chieftain was dead.

Golgoth knew they could kill him now, if they wanted. It
didn't matter. Grik was dead. The Emerald Sword stood a
chance of survival. It was done.

He had been planning this victory, in one way or another,
for his whole adult life. Perhaps it was the mind-spell of
control that Kron had taught him, but Golgoth still felt cold
inside. The hollow in his soul, which he had dreamed of filling with triumph, was still there. Had he done anything
more than kill a man?

The Emerald Sword could still decay and fall. The mountain peoples could fragment, never to be bound by the
Sword, to be absorbed by the empire of Lady Charybdia or
whatever might come after her. Even the memory of Arrowhead Peak would wilt into nothing, disappearing into the
sea of Torvendis's legend.

Golgoth could die that very moment and still have woven a story worth telling. But how long would it survive? When a man no longer had stories told about his life, then he was truly dead. The greatest legends let their creators live forever. Could Golgoth be something more than another killer?

Golgoth stepped out of the tent, the harsh daylight almost painful. The people of Grik's city were staring at him, this blood-covered warrior with one arm charred and oozing, hair thick with gore, blinking in the light.

No. This was not Grik's city any more.

Golgoth saw Hath in the crowd, one eye swollen shut and crusted with blood.

'Get men back on the watchtowers,' said Golgoth. 'Pull this place down and have them put up somewhere fit for a chieftain. And gather healers, we are all bloody and wounded.'

Hath nodded and turned to bark orders. Golgoth limped over to Tarn, who still had a stained dagger in each hand and the blood of a half-dozen men spattered on his face. There would be elders and adopted foundlings who would still owe loyalty to the memory of Grik. Tarn was the perfect resource for dealing with such obstacles.

Yes, the new chieftain of the Emerald Sword had much to organise.

PRAKORDIAN, PHAEDOS DECIDED, had proven to have uses.

Though his devotion to the pantheon of Chaos was worrisome, Prakordian's skills as a deadspeaker had put the coven firmly on the track of the renegade at last. Between the Word Bearers' guns and Phaedos's own chainsword the coven had left nothing alive at the temple seven days before, but even death could not silence what Prakordian desired to hear.

That the acolyte was already dead hadn't deterred Prakordian – in fact, it made things easier, for a dead man had few defences. Sorcery had forced the lips to open and speak, condemning the tattered lungs to draw breath and the pulped brain to remember. On the stone floor of the temple, the forest of chains sighing above and the torn banners still smouldering, Prakordian had forced out the truth.

The one they had chosen to start with had been lowly, his body was the most intact. Bullets to the gut had blown out his spine – the upper half of his body had been relatively unblemished. Prakordian mumbled spells with words that could not be spoken by weaker men, cast a complex gesture above the body, and wove a spell that dragged the acolyte's tainted soul back from the world of Torvendis's dead.

It was a form of torture almost by proxy – though there were things more terrifying than looking out from a tomb of dead flesh, those things were not very numerous. The acolyte had babbled in his horror, about the dreams he had suffered where pleasure became pain and back again, about the secret war in every Slaaneshi follower's mind between the demands of the god and their own human decency. It told the coven much of the perils of honouring one power of Chaos over another – the whole essence of Chaos was anarchy where any power might wax or wane, and giving fealty to any one alone would lead to decay of the soul and madness. But amongst the babblings, the truth could be filtered out, even as the dead soul disintegrated in the bounds of Prakordian's spell.

The acolyte had known little. The temple was an outpost of faith, an epicentre for the spread of the Slaaneshi worship that Lady Charybdia fed upon. The temple's chief priest, a degenerate named Yrvo, had been of little importance outside the strange silken cage of the temple. The sacrifices, the crude pleasure-sorcery, the divination through blood and agony – it was all typical of blinkered, unenlightened creatures made up the population of Lady Charybdia's empire.

But there had been something else, hidden deep in the dying spirit's insanity.

An order, issued by Lady Charybdia herself and hence of paramount importance, had arrived carried by a bound messenger daemon several days before. A spacecraft had arrived unbidden on the planet, on the unpopulated side of the mountains, evidently small but alien and invasive. It was commanded that all temples offer shelter to any riders travelling to investigate the trespass.

There were many such commands, proscriptions and enforced celebrations, new and sometimes bizarre laws, or just scraps of Lady Charybdia's thoughts disseminated for her subjects' benefit. But this one nugget of information caught in the minds of coven like prey in a snare.

A spacecraft, one that shouldn't be here.

Karnulon.

If anything, it was better than a sighting of the man himself. There was little doubt that the renegade could change his appearance almost at will – a Space Marine could be three metres tall and almost as broad even without armour, but Karnulon's magics would definitely stretch to giving him normal human proportions. A Chaos Marine's wargear could be cast aside, implant scars covered up, all signs of Karnulon's true heritage obliterated. But a spacecraft would be harder to hide.

Captain Amakyre had sent Phaedos, Skarlan and the hulking Vrox to investigate their first lead. Amakyre himself, Makelo, Prakordian and Feorkan had remained in the temple, to divine other anomalies from the magical atmosphere of Torvendis.

SKARLAN WAS A soldier, nothing more. Vrox was a monster, blessed by Chaos with a very special flavour of corruption, but a monster with a monster's intellect. So it was that Phaedos was in command.

One day, Phaedos would carry the accursed crozius of the Word Bearers' Emissary, and fight as a battle-chaplain to the Dark Gods, instilling their majesty into his brothers. He would have to spend centuries honing himself in action and meditating on the mysteries of the Chaotic pantheon, but it was through success on missions such as these that he would win the attention and favour of the Legion.

It was late afternoon when Phaedos clambered over the last ridge and saw what lay east of the Canis Mountains. It was like an open wound in the earth, a boiling, steaming expanse of swampland, a landscape of pure decay. At some point in Torvendis's past the power of Chaos that pulled on the planet had tugged a little harder, and like a spring tide corruption had been forced to the surface and saturated the ground. Stagnant lakes bubbled in the distance. Strangled, twisted trees were black against plumes of marsh gas. The ground was a sodden mire where thin strips of stable ground gave way to sucking marsh, and a gauze of brownish mist and swarms of swamp insects lay over everything.

The information on Torvendis had suggested there were inhabitants in those swamps, and Phaedos could imagine what devolved wretches they must be. There was nothing to eat but the scum of algae and the inevitable marsh lizards, no shelter but the rotting boughs of fallen trees that had yet to be swallowed by the swamp. Phaedos was looking down from the rock slopes above the edge of the swamp and even from here the dark, damp stink of the marshes filtered up to him.

The grey-brown swamps stretched as far as Phaedos's enhanced vision could see, dissolving into the distance. For most of Torvendis's population, this sight marked the edge of the habitable world. That made it a good place to hide.

'Anything?' came Skarlan's voice over the vox. Phaedos glanced across the rocks and saw the red-armoured form of Skarlan stalking down towards where the rocks met the swamp, bolter readied.

'Nothing yet. Stay in contact. All praises.'

'All praises.'

Satisfied there was no immediate threat, Phaedos beckoned and Vrox lumbered over the ridge behind him, eyes bulbous magnalenses. Phaedos headed downwards, scanning the swamps. If there really was a ship down here, it could have been swallowed by the marshes or even towed away by scavengers into the heart of the corruption where even the Word Bearers might never find it. Just because this was the ship's supposed location it didn't mean it was still here.

Beneath Phaedos's feet the rock became crumbly and gave way to the edge of the marsh. The boots of his armour sank up to the ankle, then to the knee. Vrox lumbered into the marsh, tearing through the fibrous ground and releasing gouts of greasy marsh gas. A couple plumed into flame, washing inconsequentially over Vrox's biomechanical skin. Phaedos let his auto-senses sweep over the sickly landscape, trying to pick out a foreign shape amongst the broken forms of trees and bulges of debris-choked ground. The mist exuded by the marshes formed a pale canopy, turning the suns overhead into smears of light. The only sounds were the footsteps of Phaedos and Vrox, the whirring of armour servos, and the ugly sucking of the marsh as it swallowed the spectral shapes of fallen trees.

'Possible contact,' came Skarlan's voice. 'We've got an artefact. Sending coordinates.'

Twin crosshairs blinked on Phaedos's auto-senses, projecting from the inside of his helmet onto his retina. Phaedos peered towards their location and made out a tiny dark glint amongst the rot. He picked out Skarlan a few hundred metres away, keeping his bolter trained on the artefact as Phaedos approached and Vrox stomped along behind him. Phaedos saw the anomaly was a teardrop-shaped bulb of metal, sides ribbed, engines flaring from the rear, long horizontal viewports like reptilian eyes.

It was a pre-Heresy craft, such as roosted in the vast raiding capitol ships of the Word Bearers. It was a single-man vessel but a large one with room for lavish chambers within the bulbous hull. It was Karnulon's craft, without a doubt, for only one who had been with the Legion since the Heresy would have a personal ship like this. It had crash-landed at a shallow angle, leaving a long furrow behind it that had filled up with brackish water, and looked like nothing so much as a huge metallic beached whale.

Phaedos approached the side hatch, bolt pistol drawn, and saw it was open. Karnulon must have abandoned the ship, not caring if the swamp scavengers looted it, a sure indication that whatever his plan, Karnulon was committed to pursue it, and was not planning to return.

Skarlan was backed up by the door, ready to pivot in through the hatch and bring his bolter to bear on whatever waited inside. Phaedos reached his side and looked in through the hatch to the indistinct darkness beyond.

'Go!' he called and ducked in through the hatch, Skarlan entering beside him, each covering all the possible angles of threat.

Phaedos let his augmented vision cut through the darkness. Instantly the fact registered that Karnulon had stripped out all the decks and bulkheads, leaving only the engines partitioned from a cavernous interior lit by suspended glowglobes high above, like the night sky. A ship of this size should have had three or four decks divided into private quarters, a bridge, an armoury, a galley, and as many other rooms that the owner could fit in. But this ship had only one chamber, vast and dark. Into that interior was crammed ten thousand years' worth of a sorcerer's obsessions.

Books lay about in huge piles, some with covers bound in ensorcelled chains to keep their knowledge from leaking out, others burst like seed pods in drifts of loose pages. Towering cabinets, some leaning against each other precariously, held trophies and trinkets from millennia of battles – skulls of aliens from the bestial to the delicate, flayed skins with intricate surgical patterns or lurid tattoos, weapons of astounding design, brutal or artistic or both. There were captured banners woven from threaded gold, chunks of scorched metal torn from Titans, brains of psychics in jars of preservative, age-stained reliquaries looted from Imperial chapels.

Bottles and jars of chemicals were racked around scorched alchemical altars. Narrow catwalks high above linked the heads of gargantuan statues.

Phaedos flicked on his auspex scanner, the screen pulsing but failing to show any bright tell-tale of life. He and Skarlan began to move through the labyrinth of detritus, passing avian skeletons in jewel-studded cages and shrivelled, severed hands that were nailed everywhere. The ceiling high above was like a steel sky lit with electric stars, casting strange fractured shadows over everything.

'Vrox, keep watch outside,' ordered Phaedos over the vox, and an acknowledgement rune flashed. It would not do to have the massive Obliterator blundering through the ship, for he could bring all this junk down on their heads.

'There's a stone pyramid in here,' voxed Skarlan. 'Thirty metres high. Looks like he's built it himself, block by block. I'm checking it out now.'

Skarlan clambered up the pyramid as Phaedos swept a warren of stained wooden torture engines for signs of life. This was surely confirmation that Karnulon was insane. A Word Bearer, especially one who delved into the darkness of sorcery, had to possess iron discipline of mind. Phaedos himself had spent untold hours in meditation, hearing voices in his head and feeling unseen hands pulling at his soul as he strove to understand Chaos. Karnulon had once reached peaks of enlightenment that Phaedos barely dared aspire to, but this ship was evidence that the crucial balance in Karnulon's mind had been disturbed.

Chaos was power, and Chaos was majesty. But it was incalculably dangerous, and madness was the gravest threat. Phaedos had heard those voices and known he could not believe them all – his reward had been a sword-arm faster than lightning and a place with Captain Amakyre's elite coven. Karnulon had fallen into insanity, and when a Word Bearer's knowledge was coupled with madness, that Word Bearer had to die.

'I've found something,' voxed Skarlan. 'He has definitely been here.'

Phaedos jogged through the blackened wooden racks and brass-banded iron maidens to the tumbledown stone pyramid. He saw every stone was carved with strange alien script. Skarlan stood on the upper levels, beckoning Phaedos up.

At the top was a flat stone surface inscribed with a circle, the carvings black with dried blood. Chunks of desiccated flesh were spattered across the stone, pooling in grooves scratched by fingernails. There were scraps of skin and shards of bone. And in the very centre, the armour.

Karnulon's armour lay disassembled in the pool of dried blood. The crimson ceramite was edged with carved jade and covered in eyes, hundreds of them staring blindly from the chest, forearms and shoulder pads. Karnulon's affinity with sorcery had warped his body and his armour to the extent that he had been able to see with those eyes as if they were his own – but now they were dried out and dead. A combat knife, forged from a single jagged monster's tooth, lay beside the massive chestplate alongside a bolt pistol with casings of gold.

'It's his,' said Phaedos. 'I recognise it from the hypno briefing.'

'Agreed, said Skarlan. 'But why take it off?'

'A disguise. He doesn't want to be recognised. Whatever he intends to do, he must do it alone and in secret.'

The armour would have fused with his skin so that Karnulon and his wargear were one. To remove it would have caused immense pain, as skin and muscle encased for millennia were exposed to the air. The blood and flesh were testament to the violence Karnulon had done to himself just to tear off his armour, and even a Chaos Marine would be sorely weakened by such an ordeal. Phaedos knew of older Word Bearers whose armour digested or even breathed for them, and removing it in any case rendered a Marine more vulnerable than was decent for an emissary of Chaos.

Only some terrible imperative could force a Word Bearer to do that to himself. But Karnulon was not a Word Bearer any more – he was a renegade, a wild animal that had to be put down for the good of the Legion.

To Phaedos, Karnulon's existence was an insult, symbolising as it did the rejection of everything Phaedos had striven for so long to achieve. Every Word Bearer would feel the same. When Amakyre had been informed that Karnulon was definitely on Torvendis, and the dog had been hunted down by the coven, Phaedos would be proud to have a hand in his death.

To THE SOUTH of Lady Charybdia's borders, between the Canis Mountains and the southern oceans, was the desert. Like everything on Torvendis it had not always been like this – a scant few centuries ago there had been lush forestland here, populated with ravenous trees that snared travellers and kept them as biological slaves bound in their roots. Flocks of rotting, feathered things had gathered thick enough to turn the sky black. But the jungle, that huge slab of hungry life, had fled south and east, cramming itself onto the precipitous ledges of the broken peninsulas, leaving behind utter desolation.

The ground it left behind was so dry it was petrified and cracked in the heat. The desert was a flat sheet of hot sandy-coloured rock. Sometimes, it rained stone, and huge boulders lay where they had dropped from the sky. Dull glows from cracks in the ground told of the immense heat simmering just beneath the land, which would on occasion bubble up and scour the desert in a flood of fire.

It wasn't just dry or hostile, although it was both those things. The desert was malicious. Even when there was only one sun in the sky, the heat washed off the endless cracked stone underfoot and leached the very life out of anything that walked there. The land was still hungry, inheriting its hunger from the voracious things that had left so suddenly. Aside from the lone skeletal carrion birds circling overhead and scuttling lizards that scampered between patches of shade, there seemed to be no living things here. Certainly a normal human would have a life expectancy of scant hours in the southern desert of Torvendis.

The man who some called Kron, and who was currently satisfied to use that name, was not a normal human and had not been for some time. He felt the desert trying to drag the life out of him through the soles of his feet, but he was made of tougher stuff than that and ignored its hunger.

He gathered his cloak around him, shielding the back of his head and neck from the glare of the three suns burning in the mauve sky. He had been glad to cast off the cold weather gear he had worn in the mountains – he hadn't even kept the walking boots because, though the journey here from Grik's city had been a long one, Kron had not walked it. It rarely did for a sorcerer to walk anywhere.

In the distance was his objective. Where the massive chunks of rock had landed here and there at random, ahead was a formation that might almost have been put there deliberately. It was lopsided and ugly, like the rest of this place, but the great rock spears jutting from the ground were almost like pillars, the boulders scattered around almost

border stones marking out a temple precinct. Perhaps, seen
from the right angle, a long stratified slab of stone was a
fallen lintel and roughly rectangular chunks were the
remains of a fallen wall.

Kron could see how the place could have been missed.
First choked in carnivorous rainforest, then entombed in an
equally deadly land of fire and death, the few who had seen
this place in the last millennia had no doubt paid little
attention to this particular collection of rocks. But Kron was
nothing if not a man who paid attention to the worlds
around him, and as soon as he saw it there was no doubt in
his mind that he had found what he was looking for.

He clambered nimbly over the stones marking the outer
boundaries – he was not a young man, but he was still as
spry as he had ever been – and glanced around the interior
of the collapsed temple. He knew what it once looked like,
and was not surprised that it had weakened and fallen, for
he also had some idea of what it had been built to contain.

Kron spoke a few words that should never issue from a
human throat, felt their power, felt his soul squirming
against the corruption they held. The ground beneath his
feet trembled, not with power but with fear, fragments of
rock tumbling to the ground. Kron took a deep breath,
remembering how he had used this power long ago for very
different ends, and spoke the final syllable.

The ground opened, like clockwork. The mechanisms
were very old and the shriek of metal on stone keened up
from far below as huge sections of the ground pivoted, the
stone columns sunk like the tumblers of a lock, and
immense black metal counterweights swung up from
beneath the ground on long armatures. The circular section
of the ground on which Kron stood shuddered and began to
sink, forming a platform fifty metres across that bore Kron
down into a deep, dark shaft. Arcane machineries whirled
massively around him as the platform continued its descent.
Cogs span in the darkness, and the rhythmic thunder of
titanic clockwork boomed.

After many long minutes, the walls of the shaft vanished
above him as the platform passed through the layer of metal

and machines into a vast open space. Above all was solid black; below hung a landscape of cold metal. As Kron sunk lower into the chill subterranean world he could make out massive curved walls reaching up and down, for this cavern was a hollow sphere, perhaps ten kilometres in diameter. Kron's jaded eyes let him look on it without being dumb-struck, but even he was impressed by the sheer size of the cavity. The circle of stone on which he stood dropped like a mote of light into the darkness, towards the structure the sphere had been built to contain.

A half-glimpsed web of cables suspended a platform in the sphere's centre, larger than a city might be on a saner world, fully five kilometres across. Upon this immense sus-pended plateau was a complex of temples and pyramids, necropoli and sepulchres, built of blue-black metal that glinted strangely in the light filtering down from above. Bridges spanned canyon-like avenues. Pinnacles reached up like blocky metallic fingers towards the open entrance, now a tiny circle of tantalising light in the surface far above. The buildings reached right to the edge of platform, maintaining a rigid design that spoke of how the city had been created for some purpose other than to be lived in. At the metal city's centre was a wide plaza marked out by arti-ficial rivers of quicksilver, with a cluster of buildings in the middle.

The platform on which Kron stood reached the silent metal city and dissolved into droplets of mercury, leaving Kron standing on an avenue of polished iron. The metal glowed a faint shimmering blue-grey as the power evapo-rated off every polished surface. The metal was cold and pale, haloes of condensation formed where his fingers touched it.

Even after all this time, Kron was glad to realise he could still be amazed – for this temple-city was amazing, and a tes-tament to the desperation that had once stalked the planet. That terror had forced whole populations to labour to build this temple, breached terrible secrets to create its designs, and demanded untold sacrifices in the hope that the Dark Gods would leave it inviolate. They had truly been afraid.

Kron knew true fear very well – he could taste it here, in the metallic air, and see it in the dull blue shimmer of the buildings.

Down here it was silent, and Kron's footsteps echoed as he padded through the streets. Tomb-complexes were stacks of steel slabs, with faceless monumental statues looming overhead. Kron could smell the age here, and see the terror in the immense mechanisms swinging through the shadows overhead.

He reached the central plaza, stepping over the geometric channels where runnels of quicksilver ran. The plaza was hundreds of metres across and empty aside from the cluster of buildings in the centre. The rest of the open space was criss-crossed with miniature artificial rivers of mercury and overlooked by five tall towers like the claws of a hand reaching from the plaza's edge.

The buildings in the centre were graven with peculiar straight-lined lettering – a normal man's eyes would bleed from looking at them, for they spelt out the sternest of warning signs as well as complex and powerful spell-boundaries. Kron knew languages that had never been spoken by human tongues, this ancient rune-script amongst them, and he knew how to divert their power around his soul. To actually speak them, of course, was another matter entirely.

The runes glowed as Kron began to speak. His tongue burned and he could feel the skin of his lips splitting in the heat, but he had woven such powerful magic before and could take the pain. His cloak caught fire and he pulled it over his shoulders, casting it to the ground without missing a syllable.

They were dark and dangerous words. They told of power and pain. They had never been written down, because they would come alive and flee from the page.

He felt the fire in his lungs. The runes were almost too bright to look at now, emitting terrible waves of power as they tried to resist Kron's counterspell. The buildings were shuddering, the power within them threatening to break out. Sounds like thunder from deep within the metal of the floor cracked and rumbled, and mercury hissed as it boiled and evaporated.

Kron was forced back but kept on his feet, a bubble of force striving to drive him away from the heart of the tomb-city. He was yelling now, flame licking from his mouth; throat raw and burned with every breath. A voice was answering, bellowing from beneath the precinct, a voice that had not been heard for thousands of years.

With a thunderclap, the metal shattered. Kron flung a mental shield around himself as white-hot shrapnel exploded all around him, surging in gouts of molten steel around his sphere of protection. He felt himself being flung backwards and the buildings flickered by as he hurtled away from the eruption of power. He smashed up against the wall at the edge of the city-platform and grabbed onto it desperately, the skin on his fingers soldered to the hot metal, chunks of wreckage coursing over the edge around him like a waterfall. The din was so vast he didn't hear it at all, his mind blocking it out with a wall of white noise.

When the light died down, Kron hauled himself back onto the platform of smouldering metal. His hands and feet were scorched through to the muscle, but he had suffered such things before. He had felt bullets shear through his body and watched his blood drain away. A few burns were nothing to a man who had lived through as much as Kron.

The billows of smoke gradually dissolved into the gloom, revealing a huge glowing crater where the plaza had been. The city around it had been blasted to molten slag, the towers bubbling stumps, the bridges spindly threads collapsing into the blasted remains. Rivers of black-flecked molten metal oozed towards the crater in the centre where the blast had exposed a chamber hidden within the platform. It like a burst abscess in the metal, where something had been revealed for the first time since fear and desperation had managed to shut it away.

'Rot flesh and splinter bones! Boil gore, snap spine! The light! All pain to the light!'

The voice was a vast cacophony, like a thousand instruments playing at once, all out of tune. It filled the immense spherical cavity, echoing around its distant metal walls. Even from where he stood, Kron's sharp eyes, so much better than a normal man's, cut through the heat haze and could see the creature he had awoken and set free.

'The rage. I remember such rage, like a wall of fire...' The daemon breathed massively with the shock of its release, its chest heaving. It was thirty metres tall, the size of a Titan war engine. Grey flesh throbbing with muscles glistened in the glow of the crater. Its heart was a slab of brass machinery punched through its chest, valves pumping, cogs grinding, driving pistons stabbing from its biceps and thighs, fired by steaming furnaces that gaped from its back. Wings of thick skin stretched between steel frameworks unfolded from its shoulders, and it shook its huge equine head, the fleshy mandibles grinding, the wet red slits of its eyes glowing with anger and joy. 'Such desire it was that caged me, such suffering it took. So much blood! Such a river of hate!'

The monster flexed its taloned hands, breathing in the sulphurous air. It gouged one forearm along the jagged, exposed metal of its prison cell and watched the thick, steaming daemon blood flowing across its skin. It held the arm high and let a few drops spatter onto its face, into its eyes, into its mouth, roaring with its lust for violence.

'Blood!' it keened to itself. 'The blood! The pain!'

Kron stood on the threshold of the crater, and spoke in a sorcerous voice he knew it could not hear.

'Welcome back,' he said.

'Blood for the Blood God!' bellowed Ss'll Sh'Karr.

CHAPTER FOUR

WHILE NO LEGEND gives enough detail to piece together the
face of Arguleon Veq, there is more than enough detail
about the panoply of war that once clad his body and killed
in his hands. Everything Veq touched turned into a legend
of its own.

Slaughtersong, a steed either jet black or deathly white
depending on the tale and the teller, was faster than light
and spat fire from its eyes, and had skin (or scales, or feathers) that could turn aside thunderbolts.

Veq's armour was, rather than just another item of
wargear, a loyal retainer and vengeful bodyguard, more
astute than most mortal commanders. It would give Veq
counsel and, it is said, saved his life many times and had a
gauntlet in many of his victories, always facing destruction
to protect the semi-divine body of its master.

And then there were the weapons. No library could hold
the volumes of tales that are told about the many weapons
that Veq wielded in his long and terrible life and in the
struggle with the Last. If every one was true then Veq would
change his weaponry as often as Torvendis changed its suns,

and yet there must be some truth in every story. They tell of
the bow bent from the spine of a dragon that fired arrows
tipped with its teeth, the whip of spiked chain with links of
gold, the sword of purest emerald that put out one eye of the
Last midway through the battle, and the massive spiked
gauntlets with which Veq tore down mountains and cast
them at his enemies.

Many rulers on Torvendis had claimed ownership of one
or more of these items, and many of them are widely
believed to have been correct. It was surely the spell-staff,
forged by Veq from the molten core of Torvendis, which the
self-styled Pontifex Infernum used to boil the southern
ocean and scour every living thing from the hemisphere. It
is almost certain that the shield worshipped by the Crimson
Knights who ruled a century of insanity was indeed the same
one that fended off the fiery breath of the Last, or a fragment
of the same. And for every such artefact there were a hundred fakes, some of them masterpieces believed sacred by
their discoverers and others deliberately concocted.

Anything believed touched by the hand of Arguleon Veq
became something holy, a fount of power that shone with
the unseen favour of Chaos, such was the power of legends
on Torvendis. And though there are many swords and spears
and even body parts that are described as having belonged
to Veq, there are far more legends than artefacts that mirror
them. It was reasonable, then, to assume that some of
Arguleon Veq's wargear still lies somewhere on Torvendis,
waiting to be found, or kept secret by those who fear what
power they might hold.

THOUGH GOLGOTH HAD seen few before, and then only from
a distance, he knew what the creature was. It looked something like a woman and could probably have disguised itself
as one if it had been given the chance – but bound in sorcerous chains of meteoric iron, mewling on the dirt floor of
Golgoth's new chieftain's tent, it was clear this had never
been mortal.

Its noseless face was dominated by eyes three times the
size of a human's, pupilless and tinted red, with dreadlocks

of flesh instead of hair. Its skin was a pale blue-grey, rows of hermaphrodite breasts ran down the front of its torso, and its feet were like bird's claws rendered in lizard skin. It had no hands, and in their place were long claws of ridged carapace.

They called it a daemonette – mistakenly, Golgoth knew, because the name made them sound like a diminutive version of something deadlier when they were in fact some of the most savage creatures that Torvendis had ever seen. They killed with corruption and lust like men killed with blades. They said daemonettes were the instruments of the Pleasure God, the same decadent force that Lady Charybdia's hordes worshipped. Which rather begged the question – what was it doing here?

'We found it in Grik's harem,' said Tarn, who had brought this unusual prisoner before the Emerald Sword's new chieftain. 'His other wives tried to protect it. Mykkros lost an eye.'

Golgoth knew from the blood crusted under his fingernails that Tarn had made sure none of the women would threaten Golgoth's men again. 'Did they say what its purpose was? Besides the obvious.'

Tarn shrugged. 'They said it was Grik's favourite. He kept it behind his throne in these chains. Like a pet.'

'What kind of man keeps a daemon for a pet?'

'Perhaps there was a daemon in him. Perhaps it controlled him.'

Golgoth thought. It instinctively occurred to him to ask Kron – but the sorcerer had not been seen since before the fight with Grik, and Golgoth would have to learn to live without his counsel.

Then it hit him. The daemon was not a master, or even a pet. What if it was a gift? Could it be the symbol of some pact between Grik and the lust-god, or even Lady Charybdia herself?

Golgoth ran from the tent followed by Tarn, ordering a trio of warriors to butcher the daemon if it so much as uttered a sound. He headed for the wooden lodge at the edge of the tented city, which was rebuilt at the end of every migration to house Grik's cabal of sorcerers. Those sorcerers had been rounded up and were now held, minus their tongues and hands, in cages ringed with guards, but the paraphernalia of their black magic would still be at the lodge. It was commonly believed that grave things would befall whoever entered a sorcerer's home, so it was a good hiding place.

The people of the city stopped their business to catch a glimpse of their new chief. Already most of the warriors had pledged their swords and their lives to Golgoth, and Tarn had organised a highly efficient fate for those who had not. Grik had lasted longer than most and for the majority of the population, Golgoth was the only other leader they had lived under. There was fear in the city as well as hope. That was how it should be, thought Golgoth as he passed through the crowded alleys between the communal warriors' tents heading towards the low log-built lodge.

The place stank. It was not just unpleasant, but a warning, for anyone who had been on a battlefield recognised death when its stench rolled over them. The sparse grasses of the foothills were blackened and dead for fifty paces around the place. No birds sang here. Death bled out, seeping from the corruption the sorcerers had wrought.

Golgoth stepped across the blackened, spongy ground and pulled aside the hide covering that hung over the door. It was not hide, he realised with distaste, but skin, human skin. And inside, it was worse.

The walls were covered with skins and chunks of meat: arms and thighs hung by hooks from the ceiling. Rows of heads lined the floor, marking out the rolls of shorn hair on which Grik's sorcerers had slept. Idols of nailed bones stood in mockeries of the victims used to construct them, and cast strange shadows across the gore-coated walls and ceiling in the light of candles that still guttered in eye sockets.

Pits of ash were sunk into the floor, where the sorcerers had divined the future from the flames. On the hanging skins diagrams were scrawled in languages never spoken, describing complex spells. This was the place where the sorcerer Golgoth had killed, along with all the others Grik had used for counsel, had lived and concocted their magic. They had written down their secrets here.

Golgoth entered the room, willing himself not to vomit at the stench of blood and rot. At the far end of the room was a pile of debris, sheaves of parchment and loops of dried entrails and other detritus he did not want to identify. He scraped through it with his hands until he felt something solid, and pulled it out. It was a casket, wooden and bound with iron. It was locked – Golgoth slammed it against the floor and, when it would not open, hacked the lid off with his axe.

Inside lay the corpse of a bird, a dry skeleton with multi-coloured feathers like jewels. Golgoth took the thing out and looked at it with curiosity, peering into the empty sockets of its skull. Its bones were starting to crumble at his touch.

There was a band around its withered leg, gold studded with jade. Golgoth picked at it and a long strip of parchment that had been wound inside the band fell out. There was writing on the strip, in a thin, spidery hand. It appeared to be written in blood.

Golgoth looked towards Tarn, who stood in the doorway. 'Read this to me,' he said, handing the dead bird and the message to the warrior. Golgoth had never had any need of reading or writing, but Tarn counted such things amongst his other, more manly skills. It had doubtless made him more useful to Grik, when he had served the chieftain many moons ago, and in any case no one had dared mock him for it in a long time.

Tarn began to read, and Golgoth listened. When he was finished, Golgoth thought for a moment.

'Gather the sorcerers and tribal elders,' he said coldly, 'and that she-daemon, too. Shut them in here, make sure nothing can escape. Post a guard of twenty men you can trust around the place. Then gather wood from the people's hearths, pile it around, and set fire to the place. Stand the guard until everything and everyone is burned.'

AMAKYRE NEVER SLEPT. Space Marines rarely did, for a sleeping man was vulnerable. Marines had a complex set of organs implanted during their selection and training, one of

which allowed them to shut down one half of the brain at a
time, entering a half-trance where the mind was rested but
the senses remained alert. The world around sped up but the
slightest sensation of threat or change in environment
would send the Marine's mind snapping to full attention at
the speed of thought.

It was while in such a half-trance that Captain Amakyre of
the Word Bearers first heard the call of Ss'll Sh'Karr.

So HIDEOUS AND guttural was the daemon's cry that it cut
through the purple scents and rainbow screams of the spirits kept chained to the walls of the bedchamber in the heart
of Charybdia Keep. Their lullaby was shattered and Lady
Charybdia was racked with the atonal tremors of the sound,
dragging her senses down from their rarefied heights to keep
her from being blinded and deafened.

The violet drapery of her chambers swam back into view.
Even the faces that writhed in the walls showed more than
their customary terror – the daemon's waking scream was
something more than just a sound, it was something that
echoed in the soul.

Lady Charybdia slid her elegantly elongated body from
under the covers and threw her silks around her. She would
have to consult her sages about this latest invasion of her
sensory worship – she was angered at its incivility, and perhaps a little afraid. There had been grave omens lately,
starting with the elimination of one of her temples and the
curious motions of the Slaughtersong in the heavens, up to
importune mutations and purposeless riots in her city. Torvendis knew that something grave was soon to occur, and
Lady Charybdia knew she had to understand it if she was to
continue in the Pleasure-God's service.

The scream had stunk of the Blood God. If she hadn't
known better, she would have thought that Ss'll Sh'Karr had
returned – but Sh'Karr was dead, she had his skull nailed up
as one of her exhibits, she knew it had to be something else.

IN THE CITY, orgies and complex blood-ceremonies paused as
the scream washed over them. Far below, in the mines, final

tendons of sanity snapped and for a while there was pandemonium as the slaves fought each other at the rock face, trying to anoint themselves with one another's blood to appease a waking god. The legionaries laid into them with nerve whips and painglaives until they had been battered back into obedience.

On the battlements surrounding Charybdia Keep, the Space Marines of the Violators Chapter made new patterns in their devotion-scars, to signify that a new enemy had arisen.

THE CALL ECHOED around the Canis Mountains and barren rocky plains to the north. Flocks of carrion-things took flight all across the foetid swamps. Phaedos, Skarlan and Vrox were making their way back through the mountains when they were shocked into stillness by a cry that bypassed their auto-senses and rifled right into their souls.

AT THE BOTTOM of the ocean, flat-bodied scavengers flopped blindly in fear. In the skies, hollow-boned sky-whales circled, blind with shock. Even the stones and the trees and the rivers of Torvendis shuddered – because they had been there when first a similar cry, but one of triumph, had been heard on the planet. They had been soaked with blood in the mad reign of the daemon prince Ss'll Sh'Karr – one of many but one of the worst.

'BLOOD!' CAME THE call. 'Blood for the Blood God!'

CAPTAIN AMAKYRE SNAPPED out of his trance and saw his bolter was already in his hand, readied in a reflex action. He glanced around the temple, chains swaying with the shock. The portable holomat still stood unfolded on the floor, where a few hours ago it had transmitted the image, sent by Phaedos, of Karnulon's bloodstained armour. Bodies of novices and initiates were still scattered around the temple, body parts dangling from the chains, blood spattered across the charred banners.

Amakyre switched on the vox. 'Word Bearers, report!'

'Standing ready, sir,' came Makelo's voice.

'Ready,' said Feorkan. 'Nothing on the auspex. What was that?'

'It was a sign,' replied Amakyre. 'Prakordian?'

The sorcerer didn't answer. Amakyre peered with enhanced senses around the temple and saw Prakordian stumbling, catching at an iron pillar to keep himself from falling. His nose and ears were bleeding. Prakordian was more sensitive than most to voices not spoken by mortals, and the cry of a powerful waking daemon had taken its toll.

Amakyre hurried up to Prakordian. 'Who was it?' he asked. 'Karnulon?'

'Ss'll Sh'Karr,' gasped Prakordian, gagging on blood from his bitten tongue. 'They said he was dead...'

'You can't kill something like that,' said Amakyre impatiently. When it had become clear Karnulon was heading for Torvendis, Amakyre had made sure he read up on the historical files the *Multus Sanguis* carried. Torvendis had too long and complex a history to ever be written down in full, but there had been mention of Ss'll Sh'Karr, daemon prince of the Blood God who had ruled Torvendis for a number of centuries and who had very nearly killed every living thing on the planet before he was destroyed by the desperate survivors. There were untold numbers of prophecies that told of Ss'll Sh'Karr's return, and it stood to reason that one of them might be true.

'Can you tell where it came from?' asked Amakyre.

Prakordian nodded, blood scattering from his nose. 'South. Three weeks' walk for a man, five days for us.'

'Good. Phaedos and the rest can catch up with us when they can.' Amakyre opened up the vox. 'Word Bearers! If Karnulon has woken this daemon as an ally, we will never have a better chance to hunt him down. Say your prayers and prepare to move out. All praises.'

'All praises,' came the replies.

Amakyre's mission was to find out what Karnulon's plans were, stop them, and kill him. Because of the presence of the deadspeaker Prakordian, these objectives could be accomplished in any order. If the coven had to deal with Ss'll Sh'Karr before they could get to Karnulon, then so be it. Only one of them had to survive to challenge Karnulon – and Amakyre had fought a ten thousand year war against anyone who angered his Legion. No matter what happened, Karnulon would die, because Amakyre had decided it would be so and he was a man who refused to suffer failure.

THE WRENCHING, METALLIC screaming was the temple-gaol of Ss'll Sh'Karr falling apart. The place had been built as a prison and now, as if it knew its prisoner had escaped and its purpose was gone, it was self-destructing.

Sheets of metal and enormous cogs were falling like guillotine blades. The mystical words inscribed on the shattered buildings had broken loose and flailed, chains of glowing syllables flickering white-hot with anger that their enchantments had been broken. The vast spherical abscess beneath the ground was imploding even as Kron watched, plumes of strange-coloured fire lashing from the black metal walls.

A massive girder plunged through the suspended city-sized platform and Kron felt the ground tilting beneath his feet. The whole platform, already gouged by the eruption of Sh'Karr's escape, was fractured, the two halves tilted violently, threatening to pitch the buildings into the darkness. The gulf beneath him yawned blackly, and in spite of the pain that was washing over him, he forced his tongue to pronounce a few more magical words.

Kron began to float as showers of sparks spat from the metal, like rains of razors against his skin. He saw the painful bright glow of Ss'll Sh'Karr's molten prison, and saw the huge winged form of the daemon itself, whose laughter echoed even above the screams of the collapsing palace. Slabs of metal broke as they crashed against Sh'Karr's titanic form. Fire rippled across the daemon's muscles and dripped from his twisted mandibles.

The platform finally gave way and tilted wildly, plummeting from beneath Sh'Karr's feet – but Sh'Karr stayed in mid-air, wings spread, the machinery hammering into his flesh pistoning and sending gouts of steam spurting from the valves and pumps working wildly.

Kron willed himself upwards, rising on a billowing cushion of superheated air. The lower half of the sphere was filling with liquid fire, as the falling metal was melted by the energies unleashed by Sh'Karr's release. Symbols flashed in the air around Kron, the last echo of the spells that had cost so much to cast and taken one man to break.

Kron flew higher, trying to put as much distance between himself and the growing inferno as possible. The machinery that worked the entrance to the sphere was falling like steel rain and whole vast sheets of curved metal were peeling off the inside of the cavity. Finally Kron spotted the entrance shaft, a pinpoint of light far above him, obscured by chunks of broken machinery and growing ever smaller.

Sh'Karr was laughing, insane with the novelty of release. Shards of falling metal were spearing into his skin and melting, flowing into the machinery, forming new clockwork organs to stud his flesh. The great wings were flapping and he was heading upwards, too.

Kron soared up the shaft, dodging falling machinery and sheets of torn metal. The mouth of the shaft was closing and Kron reached up to grab the edge, the metal hot against his hands. With a last mighty effort, he hauled himself up into the open air. Above him, the skies of Torvendis were agitated – stars were flitting across the sky, banks of cloud were billowing and boiling away, and twin suns were circling one another like wary predators.

Kron's last sight, before he had escaped, had been of Ss'll Sh'Karr waist-deep in molten metal, wings beating as he flew upwards to keep himself above the surface of the fire. The sphere was filling with fire as the whole temple complex liquefied in the heat. But it would take far more than mere fire, Kron knew, to hurt the daemon prince who had once wallowed in a literal ocean of blood and had whole armies break against him like a wave.

Kron knew he was no longer strong enough to face something like Sh'Karr. He had made great sacrifices to bring himself to Torvendis, and it was in many ways a miracle that he had made it this far. He was under no illusions that now, when he was nearing the end of his journey, was no time to get himself killed. Banishing the pain from his limbs, Kron ran.

The sky flashed bright and dark. The very atmosphere of Torvendis was reacting with confusion and anger – everything that could feel anything on the planet would be aware that something terrible had been released, such was the resonance that great terror, anger or suffering had in the very fabric of Torvendis. Kron could feel it, thick in the air around him – the fear of those who had managed to imprison Sh'Karr, and the fear of a planet which had endured the daemon prince's rule once before.

But for Kron, it was just one step of the plan. In many ways, it was the first – everything that had gone before was just preparation. If he had laid his plans with enough accuracy, Sh'Karr's release would be the first in a cycle of events that would end in victory.

There were so many variables, so much unseen. The balance was so delicate, and it would take great fortune, diligence and courage for it to unfold as Kron had planned. The result would either be triumph or death – but in many ways Kron didn't mind which it was. Either would be a release, but that didn't mean Kron couldn't give himself the finest send-off.

Kron hauled himself over the rocks that marked the boundary of the surface temple and ran as fast as he could across the parched ground. The earth shook violently beneath his feet and suddenly lurched, pitching Kron unto his face.

A fountain of molten metal gouted from the ground, dissolving the ruins of the temple and casting a sea of fire across the sands. Clouds of black smoke bloomed as the fire condensed into a gnarled hail of glowing metal. Chunks of superheated steel fell like daggers and Kron rolled away from a chunk of smouldering rock that thudded to the ground just a few metres away from him. He risked a look back and saw that in the heart of the fire was Ss'll Sh'Karr, soaring on his bat-like wings and trailing fire like a falling meteor.

Kron knew Sh'Karr's first instinct would be to kill. Once the exultations of his release were done with, the daemon would revert to the purpose for which the Blood God had created it – murder and violence, taking skulls for the throne of its god, spilling blood as an act of worship.

As Kron scrambled to his feet and ran further, he felt the spattering of warm rain against his face. He tasted it, and realised it was horribly familiar. The desert had once been a forest, before that a slab of ocean floor, and a hundred other landscapes before that. But now it would change again and become something terrible – because in the southern desert, it was raining blood.

GOLGOTH HEARD THE scream, too, but it was of little interest to him. Nothing much mattered at all any more – the Emerald Sword had died long ago, perhaps even before Grik had taken the chieftain's throne. But its death had been hidden, and Golgoth's hope that he could save it was a lie only now revealed. The tribe that had once been proud and warlike he now knew to be nothing more than slaves and cattle, betrayed by its elders and headmen until it was just a hollow shell of the majesty that had once ruled from Arrowhead Peak.

Golgoth still stood on the outskirts of Grik's city, within sight of the smoking ruins of the sorcerers' lodge. The crowds had departed now the fire's rage was spent, but it still smouldered, and Golgoth would wait here in the shadow of the mountains until it finally died. The sky above was agitated, unable to decide if it was day or night. The sharp white-edged light of the Slaughtersong clashed with the rosy glow of the Jackal-sun and a handful of hot red stars high in the black and red-streaked sky. The smoke still coiling from the sorcerer's lodge made strange patterns in the mismatched shafts of light. Golgoth could smell the charred meat that filled the lodge, mixed with the smoke and the ugly taint of burned daemon's flesh.

The elders had been herded into the lodge, hands bound, alongside the broken-bodied sorcerers that had survived Tarn's purges. The daemonette had followed them, whimpering and pleading for its life even as it strained to shatter the chains that held it. Then firewood had been heaped over the lodge and all of them had been burned alive. The population of the city had been ordered to watch as the flames grew higher and the feeble screams filtered through the roar of the flames. The daemonette had burst from the side of the lodge, wreathed in fire, to be stuck with a dozen arrows by the guards Golgoth had posted on the watchtowers.

The patch of charred earth where the daemonette had fallen was still there, smouldering even after all these hours. Golgoth had been watching all the time – when the fire finally burned itself out, he would have his men open up the lodge and make sure his tribe's murderers really were dead.

Hath approached from the city. 'They're packing up,' he called. 'The whole city. The people have guessed we can't stay here.'

'How much do they know?'

'That Grik was not to be argued with. That people disappeared, and he had daemons and sorcerers under his command.'

'They must have realised. How long has Grik been selling us? How long was it happening before Grik was even born?'

'No one can answer that, Golgoth. The question is, now you have the Emerald Sword, what are you going to make of it?'

Golgoth spat into the smouldering pit where the daemonette had died. 'The Emerald Sword is dead, Hath. I'm going to make sure it knows it. Have all the warriors armed and the people ready to march to war.'

'Against who?'

'Against Lady Charybdia.'

It was the only way. The message Golgoth had found in the sorcerers' lodge was a simple one – Lady Charybdia guaranteed the Emerald Sword safety, when it would take relatively little effort for her to eradicate it. In return, Grik would send the tribe's healthiest newborns to the temples of the Pleasure God to feed the city's constant hunger for slaves, and the best of the Emerald Sword warriors to be indoctrinated into Lady Charybdia's legions. The daemon-ette and sorcerous tricks were to sweeten the deal.

Grik had conspired with Lady Charybdia to turn the proud Emerald Sword into a farm growing a human crop, feeding the monstrous hordes that Lady Charybdia ruled over. The corruption of the betrayal had turned Grik into a monster and given him the power to speak with the dae-mons, and had robbed the tribe of the fire that once so nearly took it to dominion over the whole Canis Mountains.

'Not one of us will survive, Golgoth,' Hath was saying. 'We won't get past the first wall. We will find ten thousand legionaries against us, maybe even the Violators. They will summon daemons to face us.'

'I don't care. I have always known I will die in battle, Hath. There is nothing left for us to fight for, and this is as good a battle as any. The people must be punished for letting their tribe die. And with the Sword finally gone, it will give Lady Charybdia no more cattle to slaughter. We must hurt her, Hath, it is the only cause left on this planet. This is the only way we can strike back.'

'You have my sword, Golgoth,' said Hath, 'and you always will. But this will be the end. Do you wish to be remem-bered as the chieftain who led his tribe to extinction?'

'Grik already did that,' replied Golgoth bitterly. 'I am putting the Sword out of its misery. Find some messenger birds and get Tarn to write down a proclamation. Every liv-ing thing in these mountains will know the Emerald Sword is going to war one last time.'

LADY CHARYBDIA WAS agitated. When Lady Charybdia was agitated, Slaanesh did not get his due of pleasure from the great altar of the city, and hence Lady Charybdia's unhappi-ness was a heresy in itself.

Ss'll Sh'Karr was, of course, dead. The proof was nailed to the pillar in front of where Lady Charybdia now stood, in the nave of a chapel with soaring fluted walls and a vaulted ceiling so high it sometimes rained inside. The light from a million candles filtered through stained glass windows and filled the nave with shafts of beautiful, sickly colour.

Ss'll Sh'Karr's skull glared down from the pillar with its many empty eye sockets. The skull had been plucked from a seam of Lady Charybdia's mines thick with the bones of daemons and those they had crushed. Sh'Karr's reign had provided plenty of raw material for the city and the keep – the bones from those times lay in battlefields thicker than those from almost any other time in Torvendis's history, redolent with the laughter of the killers and the screams of the killed. The skull could only belong to the daemon prince himself – séances and divinations held over it confirmed the imprint of Sh'Karr's memories. Even now angry madness emanated from the relic, and Lady Charybdia could feel the lunacy all around her, like something boiling beneath the surface, a thousand tiny angry fists beating at her skin. Normally she enjoyed it in here, bathing in the warm malevolence to unwind, safe in the knowledge that no one else could even survive in here without her permission. But now there was much troubling her.

The chapel doors opened, letting the cold air sweep in. A gaggle of sages hobbled in, along with the walking nightmare that was Caduceia, commander of Lady Charybdia's legions. One of the sages was probably Vai'Gar, the chief soothsayer, but Lady Charybdia had long ceased to bother remembering which underling was which.

The sages were men aged prematurely by the proximity to the keep – Lady Charybdia usually remembered to dull the sensory output of the building whenever lesser mortals like these had to enter, but even so the singing of imprisoned souls and the incense of distilled innocents took their toll on those who had to experience them. To Lady Charybdia's jaded eyes people all looked the same unless she forced her senses down to a normal mortal level, so she had them dress in distinctive colours to tell their various functions apart.

'My lady,' said the leader of the sages. He was dressed in white. This man was probably Vai'Gar, but it didn't really matter to Lady Charybdia who he was as long as he did what she asked and gave her answers she wanted to hear. 'We have answered your summons. It ails us deeply that you are so disturbed as to ask for our counsel.'

'Something has awoken in the south that claims to be a descendant of Ss'll Sh'Karr. Strangers have come to my world and killed my priests. Torvendis feels threatened, and I want to know why.'

'The omens have proven complex,' replied another sage vaguely, whose robes were red.

Lady Charybdia glared at him. 'You exist to serve,' she said sternly. 'If you choose not to serve, then you choose not to live. Is there a power on Torvendis that threatens me? Are our uninvited guests conspiring to raise a force against the city?'

The white sage gesticulated grandly. 'Fear not, my lady, we do everything within our power to soothe your concerns. We are merely… very aware of the importance of the task you have blessed us with.'

'Very aware,' said the red sage, smiling forcedly, and all the other coloured sages nodded in agreement.

'The Slaughtersong is particularly active,' continued the white sage. 'As your Ladyship will of course be aware, it is a sign of change and conflict. The Vulture is high, too, and the Jackal has been seen in strange configurations. Everything points towards conflict, with much desperation.'

'Is the city in danger?'

'Nothing on this planet can threaten us, my lady. But… there is perhaps some ill will towards you from some of the satellite peoples.'

'I would be most upset if there was anything but ill feeling,' said Lady Charybdia. 'Caduceia?'

The commander of the legions stepped forwards. Caduceia was half-daemon, and it was the better half – the rest of her was pure malicious human. It was said that when Lady Charybdia had ordered a great summoning of daemons, Caduceia had been one of the sacrificial victims. But Caduceia was anything but a victim and she had refused to let the daemon burst from her flesh, leaving the two melded into something that was quite horrible to look at and hence wielded a natural authority that only a true monster could. Caduceia had been a warrior before and there had never been a time when she didn't have a weapon in each hand –

the daemonic possession had continued the habit to the extent that one arm ended in the flaring barrel of a plasma gun and the other was a vicious claw.

Her body was subtly malformed by the daemon's struggles to escape, but the daemon and the mortal had reached a truce. The body they inhabited together was powerful and lithe, with beautiful, pale, patterned skin and a hideous wide-eyed, sharp-toothed face. Caduceia wore little armour, not to display her disturbingly perfect body, but because for some reason her body warped to refuse any armour made to fit her. In the end it mattered little because it would take much more than a mortal wound to kill her.

'Your wish, my lady?' said Caduceia, a slight hiss in her voice as her snakelike tongue flickered over her lips.

'The western defences. Any news?'

'We anticipated your concerns, my lady. The guard has been doubled on the outer walls. We are pooling sacrifices in case summoning is required. Our tame harpies and spies have reported movement in the mountains. There is a suggestion that there is a new leader amongst the tribes people who may be less accommodating to your offers. Grik of the Emerald Sword is dead and judging from his treatment of the tribe's headmen the new incumbent is unlikely to accept your generosity.'

Lady Charybdia smiled. The sages visibly cringed at the sight. 'Ah, the barbarians. They have tough children, it would be a shame to lose such a resource. It doesn't seem that long since I conquered them and it would be inconvenient to have to do it again.'

'Maybe so, but at your word we can scour the Canis Mountains until nothing larger than a corpse-rat survives.'

Lady Charybdia waved a dismissive, spider-fingered hand. 'Such a campaign would cost us manpower. We might ill afford it if there really is a new daemonic force intending to make its presence felt. Keep up the guard to the west but make sure we can marshal our forces to wherever they might be needed.'

At any one time there might be a quarter of a million legionaries on the outer wall. Caduceia could marshal a full million to the walls if they were needed – if, somehow, the walls were breached, the invaders would only pour into a killing zone packed with Lady Charybdia's legions. And even if something got through, Lady Charybdia had the Violators stationed on the keep's battlements, waiting for the chance to plunge into the din of battle.

But still, she was distracted. Torvendis simply didn't feel right, the echoes of the rocks around her were a semitone out and the fear in which the keep was steeped was more immediate somehow, sharper and keener. Lady Charybdia always relished a new flavour of experience, but was there something the planet knew that she did not?

She looked at the massive, bestial skull. 'Ss'll Sh'Karr is dead, is he not?'

The sages made noises of agreement.

'Good. See that my will is done, and keep me informed of the omens. I would not want our attentions diverted from the majesty of Slaanesh by some inconvenient war.'

The sages bowed and scuttled away, waves of relief flowing off them as they realised that none of them would die this time. Caduceia swept away with inhuman elegance.

Their echoes would stay for many hours, ringing where only Lady Charybdia could hear them. She was always suspicious of those around her – were their voices coloured by lies? She filtered through the remnants of the conversation – she felt they were afraid, and all but obsessed with pleasing her with meaningless counsel. This she knew already. But there was something else there, a bitter tang which she had not felt before.

Pity. They pitied her. Was it born of their horror at her unique appearance? No, there were more spectacular sights on every corner of the city. What, then? Was something going to happen to her that they did not wish to tell her? Something they didn't think she would understand? She made a note to have a couple of them thoroughly interrogated to see if they had divined something they dared keep from her.

Lady Charybdia tutted in annoyance. More distractions. She had half a mind to exterminate the tribes who had the potential to cause such trouble, but it wasn't worth the effort – if the tribes attacked, they would destroy themselves by marching into the teeth of her legions. When she looked at the whole picture, of her stranglehold on Torvendis and the inviolable defences of her city, there really was nothing worth worrying about.

But something had awoken, and it seemed to be calling itself Ss'll Sh'Karr. Sorcerers were stalking her world uninvited. The suns and moons were leading a frantic dance, as if trying to communicate something to those living on the world below. How much of it mattered? Were these the Chaotic nature of the Maelstrom pulling on Torvendis, just to make sure that nothing on the planet was routine? Or omens of something more?

There were millions of legionaries that Lady Charybdia could call upon, howling daemon packs and the shock troops of the Violators. There was nothing she could not cope with, even if doing so broke the city's concentration on the glories of the Pleasure God. A small sacrifice to be made if necessary, and then she could get back to doing the work of Slaanesh.

This is what Lady Charybdia told herself as she walked out of her chapel, trying not to feel the dead eyes of the daemon's skull staring at her as she left.

RUNNERS AND MESSENGER birds went in every direction across the mountains, from the salt-sprayed coastline of the far north to the baking volcanic peaks bordering the southern desert. They each bore the same message, written in blood and charcoal on flayed skin as a sign of the sender's seriousness. They said that the Emerald Sword was marching to war against Lady Charybdia, and all blood-vengeance and honour-debts would be cancelled with regards to those who would join them. The proposal even extended to the Sword's traditional enemies, like the blood-drinking peoples who followed the Bear totem on the edge of the swamps and the pale-skinned, yellow-eyed Serpent tribes whose longboats raided the length of the northern seas.

When the replies began arriving at the site of Golgoth's city, many of them were flat refusals or elaborate insults, reminding the Emerald Sword of long-distant battles or massacres that made any alliance impossible. But others were offers of warriors, or weapons, or the allegiance of whole tribes.

Word was spreading that the Serpent were willing to join with the Sword, for Lady Charybdia had decimated their raiding fleets and had even begun converting their members to the worship of the lust-god through the temples built on the northern shores. Lesser tribes who had not even been contacted began asking if they could have the honour of fighting and dying alongside Golgoth. Other tribes were thrown into rebellion as they discovered their leaders, like Grik, had sold them out to feed Lady Charybdia's slave-mines. Others still were simply spoiling for a fight, and gravitated towards the growing encampments in the western foothills as if drawn by the scent of conflict.

Golden-eyed assassins from the edges of the desert rode northwards on pale horses. Pack-lizards carried howdahs of massively muscled thugs from the valleys in the heart of the mountains where the sun never shone. Over two weeks Golgoth's army swelled until it was not an army any more, but the gathered anger of a new nation, the Canis Mountain tribes at last united not by a ruler's conquest but by rage against Lady Charybdia.

She should have killed us when they had the chance, they said. She should have finished the job she started at Arrowhead Peak. Now, we'll show her how the free tribes repay their debts.

By the time Golgoth had given the order to pack away the tented city and march, the army of the mountains was two hundred thousand souls strong.

CENTURION KOLKIS HAD not slept for twenty-two years. Ever since, as a child, he had first been thrown into the selection pits to prove himself worthy of Lady Charybdia's legions or die in the attempt, he had hungered for sensation. He could not sleep, because every second sleeping could have been spent seeking out new experiences. At his blooding as a soldier, the din of battle had been so imprinted on him that he thirsted for something equal in intensity.

He had seen the thick of the fighting at the Bloodstone Falls, and been enthralled by the screams and the stench. He had led patrols deep into the southern rainforests and been immersed in their lethal strangeness. Now, posted to a command manning the outer walls, there was little save the view to stretch his senses.

It was dull compared to the many flavours of battle he had tasted, and longed to taste again. But he had a job to do. Lady Charybdia commanded, and he had to ensure she was obeyed on his watch.

Kolkis had emerged from a night spent disciplining the more slovenly recruits, to watch the morning break over the mountains. Three suns were competing to be the first over the distant peaks. The sky was orange this morning, studded with stubborn stars, with the hard point of the Slaughtersong staring from one horizon. A fine view.

All along the walls the guard was changing. The legionaries were strapping on their scaled armour wrapped in pastel silks, and taking over from those who had stood lookout throughout the nights. Other legionaries were keeping their muscles and reflexes in trim with spear-duels fought along the broad stretches of ramparts, between the narrow bottlenecks where attackers would be bunched up and killed. Far along the wall some of the defence guns – rare, ancient, monstrous weapons that fired explosive rounds from snarling, daemon-carved muzzles – were being test-fired in the daily drills.

The walls themselves were a masterpiece built, they said, by enslaved monsters and designed by Lady Charybdia herself. The sheer surface presented to the outside world was of orange-pink rock that looked like sandstone but was harder than any granite. The massive buttresses served to shore the wall up from any direct assault, and it was doubtful that even an orbital strike could breach it – not that anyone would be insane enough to pilot a whole warfleet through the Maelstrom to reach Torvendis in the first place.

The wall kinked in many places, forcing attackers into places overlooked by two faces of the wall where missiles could be poured into them from both angles. Ditches and toothed barricades described a maze leading through the approaches to the walls that would break up a massed assault and leave its elements charging the walls in fragments. And if anyone managed to get a foothold on the walls themselves, individual sections could be closed off and barricaded, trapping the attackers inside to be eliminated at leisure.

But it was not the wall itself that was the true defence. Every wall section was commanded by a centurion, like Kolkis, with the experience, steel, and sheer devotion to the cause of maintaining Torvendis as a vessel for the worship of Slaanesh. Under every centurion were upwards of a thousand men, every one of them trained in archery and close-quarters bloodshed. The barracks complexes that filled the ground just behind the wall could disgorge enough men to pack the battlements within half an hour, and there was always a formidable guard posted that could be expected to see off just about any threat that currently existed on Torvendis. Amongst the legions manning the wall were a great many mutants who might vomit acid on attackers or tear them apart with inhuman claws, and the secretive robed figures occasionally sighted were battle-mages who could conjure up a rain of lightning if it was required.

But only centurions like Kolkis knew of the weapon that would be employed when the threat was truly great. There were elaborately decorated towers at regular intervals along the wall – these were not watchtowers or even mere decorations, but temples to the Prince of Pleasure, their interiors stained with blood and their floors marked out with complex symbols of summoning. Lady Charybdia had a pact with the warp, they said, that welded an army of daemons to her will in return for the reverence she gave Slaanesh. Such daemons could be summoned to defend her realm – the ordinary legionaries knew nothing of this, of course, because they would be the ones whose sacrifices would be used to power the summoning rituals, and as less experienced soldiers their devotion had not always been tested unto death.

One of the legionaries – a young man, his skin hardly scarred – hurried up to Kolkis.

'Sir, seventeenth cohort have been observing movement on their watch. They thought you should know.'

The lad was frightened of him, Kolkis realised. At over two metres tall with scarcely a scrap of skin unmarked by the scars of devotion, Kolkis knew he looked something like of a monster. 'Movement? Scavengers?'

'Probably, sir. But with the new orders they thought they should send me to tell you.'

'Let us hope it is something more. We have had too long without bloodshed. Show me.'

The legionary led Kolkis to the watchpoint where the seventeenth cohort had just stood down. This section of the wall overlooked rolling foothills where a forest had found purchase, a dark blue-green blanket lying heavy over the plains. Scavengers, who lived off the detritus and the dead cast down the wall by the legions, used the place for cover – the legionaries, in turn, used them for archery or gunnery practice. Lady Charybdia had often ordered the razing of the forest, but every time it had been scoured with axe and fire it had grown back twice as dense within days, as if Torvendis was trying to remind them how even Lady Charybdia couldn't have everything her own way.

Kolkis held out a hand and one of the legionaries on watch passed him a brass telescope. The centurion scanned the edge of the woods, about two kilometres from the base of the wall, trying to pick out a shape against the darkness. He saw movement but it could just have been the stiff breeze blowing across the foothills.

A flash caught his eye, like the glint of the sun on something reflective. He tried to focus on the spot and saw a tiny, wiry, dark figure darting back into the treeline.

There was a sudden, sharp sound and Kolkis looked away from the eyepiece, to see the young legionary clutching at his throat and the slim shaft of black wood that jutted from his neck, fletched with white feathers. The lad coughed and a gout of blood spurted from his mouth as, eyes rolling, he pitched backwards to land, spasming, on the floor of the battlement.

'To stations!' someone yelled and the legionaries on guard quickly hunkered down between the crenellations. Calls went up for archers and more spotters, and one of the legionaries unhooked a long curled horn from his belt, ready to give the general alarm if Kolkis gave the order. The clatter of armour and weapons rippled down the wall.

Kolkis bent down and pulled the arrow from the dying legionary's throat, yanking hard to dislodge the barbed arrowhead. He put the tip to his tongue and ran it across the surface, breaking the skin and letting his own blood touch the metal. Instantly he felt the tingle of sorcery in his mouth, hot and metallic, dissolving into a dozen aftertastes of spices, sweetness and decay.

'Magical,' he said to himself. And magic meant something more than scavengers.

It was probably nothing, just a gang of barbarian youths claiming nobility from their chieftain fathers, testing their manliness by killing someone on the walls. But it was still an insult that deserved punishment if possible, and the orders for heightened vigilance had been very clear. Any threat was to be considered extreme.

'Sound the alarms!' shouted Kolkis and the horns sounded, braying a long atonal note that carried far down the length of the defences. Already Kolkis could see spear-points bristling up and down the walls as the legionaries on guard took up defensive positions, ready to protect the archers and sorcerers and, if it came to it, form a formidable hedge of spears against anyone scaling the walls.

Then there was a streak of silver above the lip of the battlements, and a stray arrow clattered against the stone. Another, and someone screamed, grabbing at a shoulder. Kolkis glanced between the teeth of the battlements and could see arrows darting up from the edge of the woods, each one enchanted to give them greater range and accuracy than any mundane archer could manage. He had heard that the nomads who lived on the edge of the desert hunted with such weapons, and that only they had them in such numbers – but the deserts were thousands of kilometres further south.

They had said there was something going on in the mountains – Kolkis had heard the rumours gleaned from the legions' spies and infiltrators, telling of a new leader and a rash of rebellions. Had the tribes united, and gathered here? Was this a major assault on the walls, an attempt by the mountain peoples to bring Lady Charybdia's forces to battle for the first time since Arrowhead Peak?

Praises to the Prince, Kolkis hoped so.

The arrows flew thicker, spattering against the ramparts like rain. The spear-armed troops crouched for cover while the parties of swordsmen, who would form a fighting reserve to block off sections of the defences if enemies made it onto the walls, raised their shields overhead for shelter. Legionaries who were too slow were falling as arrows punched near-vertical through their faces and shoulders, others were dragging themselves with speared arms or legs to take cover. Trails of blood were being left across the stone. But they were the exception – the walls had been built with just such an attack in mind, and most of the legionaries on guard were well in cover.

'They think they can take us like this?' said the cohort leader, his back against the wall next to Kolkis.

'No, soldier, they don't. This isn't an attack. This is a signal.' Kolkis looked back over the battlements and saw that the forest seemed to be creeping forward, and knew that the approaching black mass was a seething horde of warriors breaking from the cover of the trees and swarming towards the walls. There were trenches and barricades to tackle first, even before they ran into the teeth of the wall's archers – but there were so many of them...

Some of them might reach the walls themselves, in great enough numbers to make this a decent fight. The dark, shuddering thrill, which Kolkis knew was his bloodlust, had ignited inside him and he prayed to Prince Slaanesh that he would have the chance to let it take over.

'Get the archers to mark their ranges!' he called to the trumpeter. 'And keep lookouts posted, I want to pick off any infiltrators before they reach us. Empty the barracks and man the counter-charge ports. Send up the flares, and give thanks to Slaanesh for this fight!'

ALL ALONG THE wall the signals went up, the multicoloured glow of the signal flares turning the morning sky into a riot of colours. The clashing din of the trumpets called streams of warriors from the barracks just behind the wall, some heading up the complex stairways towards the top of the wall, others into the underground muster halls from where counter-attacks would be led through hidden ports amongst the warrens of defence ditches. Arrows lashed down as archery teams checked their ranges, picking out a line beyond which anything advancing would be met with a hail of arrows dipped in poisons and hallucinogens.

Combat teams, who would take the fight to the attackers if the ranks of spearmen gave way, surrounded their mutated leaders and chanted songs of praise and hatred. Sorcerers, wizened and wasted by decades of service to Slaanesh's dark arts, hurried up winding stairways with their elite body-guards to unlock the chambers hidden within the ornate towers, readying them in case they were needed to summon the Lust God's own servants. And corpse-teams, devolved creatures barely human, gathered around the rearward working of the defences, ready to take the bodies of dead defenders and spirit them away to whatever pits they lived in when battle was not in their air.

And along the wall a new sound arose, growing louder and louder until it could be heard above the blaring trumpets and clatter of arriving soldiers. It was a low, angry growl, and as it swelled it became clearer. It was the combined battle-cry of hundreds of thousands of warriors, who charged as one from the treeline towards the walls, a seething dark mass covered in silver sparks where the morning sun glinted off their weapons, teeth bared and eyes wild.

The spotter teams made out many different manners of weaponry and dress, scores of skin colours, cavalry on white desert horses or swift lizardlike predators, hulking mutants and lightning-fast cave dwellers, sallow-fleshed ocean raiders and stocky barbarian tribesmen. There could be no doubt now – the Canis Mountains had united, and the only force that could bring such people together was the prospect of war against a mutually hated enemy.

Lady Charybdia's legions readied their spears and drew their bows, and prepared to give these animals something they could really hate.

CHAPTER FIVE

IN THE END, it had happened almost by itself – as if it was always meant to be, waiting in the souls of every one of them for a leader to act as a catalyst. This was no longer the Emerald Sword, for the Emerald Sword was dead. There was no Serpent tribe, either, or Bear, or anything else. There were just the people of the Canis Mountains, the inheritors of Arrowhead Peak, a single nation welded together by war.

The Emerald Sword had been destroyed, and with it any hope Golgoth really had of becoming a truly great leader. But even if there was nothing left for him personally, this was a fine way to die.

Around him was a wedge of twenty thousand men and not a few women, pouring screaming from the muster camps in the forest, forming the heart of the attack. The ground was mud under their feet and every one had a weapon drawn as they ran. They had been hand-picked from the Emerald Sword and the first tribes to ally with them, and Golgoth could see Hath leading his own contingent across the foothills. Far to his left was a spearhead of cavalry on pale horses, and to the right was a massive mob of warriors from the northern coasts, led by the Serpent warriors who looked sick and loose-skinned but who were as cruel and murderous as anyone on Torvendis. The wings of the attack, too distant for Golgoth to see, were anchored to the north by strange warriors with great ogrish bodies and huge eyes from living in the darkness of the valleys. The south wing was a mass of warriors mounted on the strangest of creatures, scaled monsters and long-legged avians, along with southern desert nomads on pale horses. The sight was awesome, a line of men pouring forward like a carpet of insects, flowing over the foothills towards the wall that separated the mountains from Lady Charybdia's domain.

The wall stretched as far as Golgoth could see in both directions, sheer and unforgiving, with massive buttresses and a formidable overhang. It must have been a hundred metres high, five hundred metres between buttresses. On the battlements at the top could just be glimpsed tiny figures gathering – legionaries preparing to receive the attack. Many of Golgoth's warriors carried ladders or grappling hooks – others intended to rake the battlements with bowfire. Others just wanted to lure the legionaries into open battle, and lose themselves in a chaotic killing ground beneath the walls. Golgoth, truth be told, was one of them.

The ground ahead of them was broken with ditches and rows of spikes. The mobs flowed over them, heedless of danger. So few of them had ever seen battle of the magnitude that was promised here that they were almost mad with the lust for war, and they cared nothing for the dangers. A mass of unwashed bodies crowded around Golgoth as he clambered over a barricade of sharpened logs, knowing that as he did so he was climbing on the bodies of his own warriors who had stumbled and been impaled. Even as he reached the other side he saw the ditch ahead was filling with bodies, and he joined the horde around him scrambling over the fallen.

They were screaming, some with panic as they were trampled, others with joy as they felt a rush of rage and adrenaline such as they had never felt. The first arrows began to fall, inaccurate ranging shots that still hit because the only place they could land was in the mass of warriors. Golgoth saw a warrior – one of the Sword, he was sure – stumble as an arrow punched through the side of his chest, then disappear beneath the feet of his comrades like a drowning man beneath the waves.

Golgoth pulled the shield from his back as the arrows began raining thicker. Clusters of arrows tore chunks out of the advance, gouging holes quickly filled by others eager to be in the front line. The ground was broken and deadly, with concealed spikes skewering unwary feet and hidden pits swallowing a score of men at once.

Golgoth could hear the trumpets on the walls, a hideous sound calling the Pleasure God's soldiers to battle. He could see the glints of their spearheads and the glare of explosives they used for signalling. There was a distant flash and a plume of dust and broken bodies erupted nearby, a thundercrack washing over the advancing warriors. Golgoth looked up and saw the emplacement on the wall above where a huge war machine had been mounted, lobbing explosive shells into the heart of his army.

They were cowards, these slaves of a degenerate queen. They would rather butcher real men from a distance than face them with sword and axe. Golgoth was filled with hate, at Lady Charybdia who had bled the Emerald Sword of its honour, at her soldiers who he would gladly butcher in their thousands if he could but reach them, at the planet around him that had let such a cancer take power. His hate carried him forward over the smouldering craters and through the falling arrows, over the barricades and ditches.

'Forward!' he screamed at the horde around him, by now covered in blood and stumbling. 'Forward, you dogs! For your honour! Die like men!'

Explosions racked the ground. Blood and earth rained down. Bodies were thick beneath his feet and the defence ditches were like swamps of gore. Spring-loaded spears shot from the ground to transfix men through the stomach.

Golgoth tried to make out what was happening further down the line. The cavalry was a mess, horses tangled in the barricades and contorted masses of men and beasts trampling one another to death. Some elements had avoided the scrum and were spread out as they galloped forward – some were even at the wall itself, horse archers firing arrows straight up and soldiers manhandling ladder segments in the hope of ascending the massive wall. Already sheets of shimmering acid were running down the walls to soak those trying to climb them, and arrows fell in thick waves.

Hath was doing better. The impetus of the Serpent's warriors was dragging his men forward. They were more broken up by the defences, but that meant those strong enough to make it were unimpeded by those who had already fallen. Hath wasn't really in command – no one could truly lead a horde like this, and it was carried forward by its own momentum rather than orders – but Golgoth had wanted to make sure that his old friend was there to represent the Sword.

Bright magical arrows were spearing up from all over the barbarian lines, fired by the mysterious southern assassins, and with every one a tiny figure seemed to topple from the battlements to land broken far below. Bright spears of lightning suddenly arced down in reply, leaping from one of the towers down into the heart of the milling cavalry. There was a white flash and a cloud of vaporised dirt, horse and human flesh rained wetly back down onto the barbarian lines.

They were dying, just as men were dying all along the wall. Golgoth didn't care – he had seen enough men die and had killed enough himself. There was no room to care, not with all the anger that filled him to bursting. He waded through the gore towards the wall, the warriors thinning out beside him, as arrows began to stud the shield he held above his head and his hair and skin became sticky with the thin drizzle of blood.

IT WAS DARK and dry inside the wall. The sounds of battle were beginning to filter through the rock, a dull throb of war-cries and screams, punctuated with sudden roars as the guns were brought to bear and bolts of magic hit the ground.

Tarn drew his dagger and placed it between his teeth. He wedged his body sideways into the crack and began to force himself upwards, the tough leathers he wore protecting his skin from the sharp stone. The dagger was his only weapon, because here within the structure of the wall there was no room to carry a shield or a sword. Tarn didn't mind – he could kill with a dagger better than most men could kill with anything. He was tough enough to never need anything other than his bare hands, truth be told. Grik had chosen him at birth, weeding him from the weaker infants by the simple expedient of exposing them for longer and longer periods until there was only one left, and that one was Tarn.

The gap would have been too narrow for most, but Tarn was slim and lithe, his body all muscle and bone. The massive stones that made up the wall had settled over the centuries and they had moved ever so slightly, leaving gaps between them that were just large enough for a slender man to squeeze into.

As he clambered higher the dim sounds of battle shifted, from the thunderous noise of the horde below to the recoil of guns and crackle of magic from above. He could smell the incense and perfumes with which the Pleasure God's followers anointed themselves and conducted their rites – many would call them effeminate, but Tarn had seen the hideous mess they had left of hunters and scavenger packs that had been caught by their patrols, and knew they were as utterly ruthless as the proudest barbarian. He had heard tell the legions did not feel pain like other men; their magic was as deadly as that of the most powerful tribal sorcerers and they spoke with daemons to lay their plans.

In some ways, Tarn wondered if he wouldn't have made a fine servant of Lady Charybdia. The gods knew he had little enough allegiance to the Emerald Sword or to Golgoth – he had fled Grik's employ when it became clear the old man was mad as well as mutated, and had joined with Golgoth mainly because he could not survive alone in the mountains and Golgoth seemed the best option for his continued survival. Tarn didn't even hate the legions as most of the tribes did – he didn't hate anyone particularly, and considered everyone else to be subordinate to his immediate desires for survival and adventure. But fate had seen fit to deliver Tarn to the Emerald Sword rather than Lady Charybdia, and so Tarn would kill for Golgoth and enjoy it while he could.

Tarn forced his way up through the crack until he emerged through the floor of a tiny chamber, set deep within the wall, where the air was close and hard to breathe. The smell of spices and some strange alchemical substance was strong and stung his eyes. There was a single lit torch guttering on the wall – Tarn guessed it must be some forgotten spell that kept it alight. He took his dagger in one hand and glanced around the room, making sure he was safe. At one side, the floor had collapsed, presumably as a result of the fissure in the wall below, revealing the crack from which he had crawled. The walls were odd, covered in intricate designs with a strange texture – it was only at second glance that Tarn realised they had been covered in skins, stretched and cured, that were scattered with tattoos. The designs twisted and swirled as he watched, spectral eyes seemed to stare – he shook the idea out of his head and moved silently through the room's only door.

He came out under a wooden staircase. It was obviously carrying troops up onto the battlements, judging by the clatter of armour and the pounding of tramping feet. He could smell the troops' sweat and perfumes, hear their voices muttering incoherently in what must be prayers to their god. Tarn peered between the planks of the steps and saw dozens of bare feet, many covered with old, shallow wounds, self-inflicted.

The gaggle of troops passed and Tarn quickly hauled himself up onto the stairway. It was narrow and the air was still close, but this time the smells coiling down from above were mixed with blood and death. Tarn knew those smells well – this place, strange as it was and filled with many things he would not understand, was still just a battlefield like all the rest of them. And the battlefield was the only place Tarn felt at home.

Golden icons hung on the walls, carved into shapes like coiled snakes or twisted branches. There were scratch marks

in the walls, and over the doorway at the top of the stairs
had been nailed a corpse, old and mouldering. It was wearing the tatters of a legion uniform and Tarn guessed it was a
malefactor, killed for some indiscipline and displayed as a
reminder to others. These people were not so much unlike
his own, thought Tarn.

For the moment, he was alone. But Tarn knew that not
only were the walls crammed with legions, there were several other infiltrators like himself making their way into the
heart of the defences. Some were to head for the barracks to
kill the reserves and draw legionaries down from the walls.
Others, like Tarn, were to cause as much bedlam as possible
on the walls themselves. Most wouldn't make it through the
walls or onto the ramparts at all, but those who did had
been picked from the coldest killers in the mountains.

There was a guard on the other side of the door – Tarn
heard his breathing through the wood. He silently opened
the door a crack and stabbed the guard behind the ear without even peering through the doorway. He caught the body
as it fell, wiped his blade on its satin uniform, and dumped
it just behind the doorway, closing it behind him. It was
Tarn's first kill of this enemy – another for the endless cata-
logue of killings that he kept filed away in his head. Few
men like him kept count of their kills for long, but Tarn had,
although he would have needed some time to calculate
before he came up with a final tally.

Tarn saw the staircase had ended and he was now in a
corridor just below the level of the battlements – the corridor's ceiling was the floor of the ramparts above, and the
tramping of dozens of feet filtered down along with
shouted orders and the whistle of arrows let fly. Tarn
darted down the corridor and emerged in the open air, on
a ledge on the rear of the wall leading up towards the ramparts. The ledge was narrow to hamper attackers coming
down – the only other way to reach the vulnerable barracks
and command posts behind the wall consisted of a very
long drop. The defences were well-constructed, designed to
funnel attackers into bottlenecks where they could be confronted and killed by a relatively few trained men, or

bunch them up on the wall where guns and archers could be turned on them.

A short, narrow flight of stairs led to the ramparts and Tarn could see the frenetic activity. Gangs of archers were firing volleys then moving as a smattering of arrows clattered against the ramparts in reply. Spearmen were forming reserves to plug gaps in the walls as men fell. Units of soldiers armed with swords, shields, and more exotic weapons besides, were taking up position at junctions and doorways to face any attackers that might find their way onto the walls.

Tarn watched as a creature appeared that was, presumably, human, but had little of a human's shape – it was twice as tall as a man with dark red scaled skin and tentacle-fingered whips for arms. It had no legs but a thick mantle of skin, like the foot of a slug, showing beneath its kilts of scale and wrappings of silk. It was barking orders from a great wide mouth, and from the elaborate decorations of its misshapen uniform Tarn guessed it was an officer of some kind. Tarn would have called it Touched, others would refer to it as deformed or mutated – Torvendis produced a great many malformities in its offspring and some were strong enough not just to survive but to prove superior in some respects to normal humans. Some tribes killed them at birth regardless of their strength. Lady Charybdia evidently valued those that were useful to her. Tarn certainly saw this particular monstrosity as a formidable soldier that evidently held no little respect amongst the other legionaries.

Tarn had no respect for anyone or anything save himself. He jogged up the flight of steps, crouched low until the mutant was just above him. It was facing the other way and pointing with its snakelike fingers to the battlefield below it, yelling out targets in a strange language for the archers to launch their volleys at.

Tarn silently stalked up the last few steps until he was standing in the mutant's shadow, acutely aware that just one pair of sharp eyes could pick him out and raise the alarm. He stood up and saw the battlefield for the first time. A dark writhing mass seemed to be oozing across the landscape towards the walls, thinning out as it coursed across ditches and walls of spikes. Explosions flashed as guns and magic sent what looked like showers of dark dust into the air – Tarn knew those specks would be bodies and fragments of bodies, torn apart in an instant.

It was no way to die, either beneath the hammer of the guns or beneath the feet of your fellow warriors. Tarn had hoped Golgoth would let him fight his battle up here, where the killing was clean.

It was time to join in.

One of the archers paused to draw a handful of arrows from his quiver and happened to glance backwards. His eyes met Tarn's and for a second they just stared at one another. The legionary was older than most, with sunken eyes and features that were not just lined by age but riven with straight vertical scars, self-inflicted, a measure of devotion to the Pleasure God. The legionary yelled a warning and the mutant commander turned, eyes on stubby stalks fixing on Tarn.

Tarn never made mistakes. Sometimes, he unwittingly created a situation which, although unplanned for, could nevertheless be turned into an unusual advantage. Not mistakes.

He threw the dagger hard and dropped out of sight onto the stairs as the first arrows flew – he heard the thunk of metal through bone and knew that his blade had punched through the mutant's skull. With luck, its brain would be in the normal place and it would be dead before it hit the floor.

Tarn pressed up against the side of the stairway, keeping low so he would see anyone coming onto the head of the stairs before they saw him. He heard footsteps and darted forward on instinct, ramming an elbow into the first face that appeared, shattering his opponent's jaw and driving the bone through the arteries at the top of the throat. In the same motion he grabbed an arrow from the dying man's quiver and stabbed it into the groin of the archer following, seizing the back of the man's neck as he doubled over squealing, and pitching him over his shoulder to tumble brokenly down the stairs.

More would come, and he was trapped on the stairway just as the builders of these fortifications had intended. Tarn reached up, dug his fingers into a crack between two stone blocks of the wall, and jamming the side of his foot against the wall took two long strides straight up it, vaulting over the rear parapet and onto the main ramparts. He landed behind the archers who were gathering to rush down the stairs at him. He wrapped an arm around the neck of the nearest and snapped the spine where it met the skull, a trick he had learned as a child and which was little more than a reflex action to him now. The other hadn't even noticed he was behind him when he grabbed the dead man's bow, took a handful of arrows and loosed off three shots into the archers. He counted quickly as he fired. Six – no, nine left. Two of the arrows hit home. Seven.

He glanced behind him. There was a bizarrely ornate tower a short sprint down the ramparts, a ribbed column topped by jagged ramparts like a crown and a tall, slim steeple. The tower had a solid-looking door covered with runes. It might open, it might not, but the other options were through the archers or over the front of the wall.

Arrows spat towards him from the quicker-witted archers. Voices were yammering in a foreign tongue, but Tarn knew what they would be saying – he's behind us, you morons, kill him quickly.

If Tarn backed away, even if he picked a man off with every shot, they would stick him full of arrows before half of them were dead. He was good with a bow, but better with his bare hands. He charged.

The bow was thin but strong, made of some matt-black substance with a gold handgrip. The ends were tipped with gold, too, which tapered to a sharp point. Tarn sprinted a few steps and plunged that sharp tip into the stomach of one archer and let the momentum of his charge carry him into the other six, bowling them over. An arrow shot wild, arcing high into the air.

Tarn scrabbled and found a short sword scabbarded at the archer's waist. He ripped it free and let his motions slip into the old grooves that had been worn into his movements by countless training duels and battlefield scrums, lashing and parrying, jabbing up underneath the jaw of one man, withdrawing the blade and slicing the arm off another.

Four.

The pommel, formed into a golden orb, shattered a temple and the blade skewered a thigh.

Three.

The fight was over. Three-on-one odds basically meant victory – the legionaries were well-trained and, perhaps more importantly, utterly dedicated to their fight, but Tarn had taken on more men than this a hundred times and won. Back when he had worked for Grik, he had become notorious for taking on tasks that required more than just slitting men's throats while they slept, so eager was he to prove he could fight anyone, on any terms, and win.

Three men? Three dead men, as far as Tarn was concerned. And they were dead, before the thought had even left his mind.

The warm, sticky blood in his hair was almost comfortingly familiar, like the numbness in his palms from the jarring of blade against bone. The burning in his limbs would ache like hell the next morning, but for now it told him of the strength and speed that let him kill men before they could make a sound.

After a lifetime of it, killing should have become a dull routine, but for Tarn, there was nothing else in the world worth doing more.

The noise of the dying archers had attracted attention. He heard voices and the clatter of spears from down the ramparts, and even spotted the muzzle of one of the infernal guns swivelling towards him, ready to blast point-blank into the ramparts in case attackers had made it onto the walls in numbers.

The tower it was, then.

Tarn ran down the battlements and up the steps. The door was made of heavy wood, stained black, and engraved with runes. His eyes refused to focus on them, as if a part of him was afraid to look at them. Blurred shapes snaked around the wood.

Tarn realised he had wasted precious moments standing glaze-eyed at the door.

He tried the door. It swung open. He darted inside sword-first, ready to take on a gaggle of vengeful legionaries.

The room inside was lit by a quartet of braziers that gave out a painful dark red glow. The same weird, eye-burning runes were carved everywhere, on the walls and ceiling, and on the floor where concentric circle designs radiated out from a single squirming symbol of a knotted snake.

The room had too many walls. Tarn couldn't count them.

The door behind him swung shut of its own accord. There were no other obvious exits.

Tarn did not panic. He had been in situations that were technically hopeless before. His warband had been surrounded on some lonely mountain slope by elite houseguards of the Serpent tribe, and he had crawled from the resulting pile of corpses, wounded but alive. He had killed his way through a longhouse of Grik's enemies to find himself ambushed by bowmen who rained flaming arrows down at him, but he had thrown himself insanely at the closest and come out alive. He had even set out to help kill Grik himself, and he had not only made it out alive but seen Grik dead and bagged not a few of his tribesmen besides.

No, it was not panic. Tarn looked at the possibilities – go back out onto the ramparts and die, or stay here and die. This was a horrible place that repulsed him for no obvious reason, but it had a doorway wide enough to admit two men at most and at least he could kill his share of them before they piled through and overwhelmed him. Not such a bad way to go – and plenty of the whoresons would remember Tarn for a long, long time. How many men had made it alive onto the battlements of Lady Charybdia's walls and spilt the blood of its defenders with his bare hands? Not many. Maybe none.

Tarn had never regretted anything. He had killed more men than most people had ever met. He had never wasted his life in loyalty to anyone he would be better off killing than obeying. He had never lost a fair fight. There were no good days to die, but this one was better than most.

He had no way of barring the door. But when he heard the legionaries scrambling up the steps, the door did not fly open. Something heavy bashed against the solid wood and the door buckled – they were trying to batter their way through. Was the door locked? Tarn couldn't see a lock or a bolt on it.

Probably magic. Tarn ignored it, and took up position with his back to the wall beside the door, on the opening edge.

Another hit, and the door bulged and splintered. The runes were agonised squiggles, running like drops of water down the wood.

The door burst inwards and the brass-shod head of a four-man ram ripped into the room. Before it had time to withdraw Tarn's blade lashed through the opening and cut deep into the throat of one of the legionaries – he heard the cry of anger and pain. Two men tried to scramble into the room and Tarn caught one in the side of the head with a vicious side kick, cracking the sword's pommel onto the back of the other's neck. He glanced through the wreckage and bodies and saw there were maybe two dozen legionaries lined up on the battlements, queuing up to kill the infiltrator.

Arrows lashed in and Tarn ducked back. With a roar, the legionaries charged inside, hoping to fill the small room with their bodies and pin Tarn down with the sheer weight of numbers. Tarn stabbed twice, felt more blood spurt onto his gore-covered arms and chest, as three or four legionaries pitched through the door spear-first. Tarn weaved between the stabbing spearheads, swivelled and sliced, taking the head clean off one man. Then he leapt on his attackers, pinning two down onto the floor, kneeling on their backs and slamming the small of his palm into the jaw of the next man through.

Tarn thrust again with the short sword in his right hand, pulling a spear from the mess with his left. More legionaries were charging, yelling words Tarn couldn't understand, cascading through the doorway with no fear.

Tarn grabbed them and hauled them onto his blade, parried with the spear, stepping back into the room as the

tumbling pile of bodies grew. Men clambered up from the
drift of corpses, wounded and spewing blood, to be killed a
second time. Blood spurted from cut throats and severed
limbs to spray across the walls. The hungry runes seemed to
drink the blood, growing larger and beginning to glow.

Arrows were raking in from archers just outside, but by
now the bodies were piled halfway up the doorway and
most of the shafts thunked into dead men's flesh. Tarn was
by now dragging spearbearers and swordsmen over the
rampart of bodies to kill them. Reinforcements had
rushed down the battlements and Tarn had taken them on
too.

How many would they send? How many would they let
him kill before they shattered the tower with a massive shell
from a gun, or sent gouts of lightning crackling through the
door from some magician's hand? How long before they
hurled in flasks of oil and flaming brands?

Tarn didn't care. It would happen sooner or later. But for
now, he was determined to spend what was left of his life
killing, just as he had spent the years that had gone before.

A mutant barrelled through the pile of bodies, with four
massively muscled arms and a huge, horned, equine head. It
carried no weapons, but one great paw slammed Tarn
against the room's back wall. It stamped through the corpses
and stood over him, ready to drive its huge balled fists down
towards Tarn's prone body. Tarn rolled to the side as a fist
splintered the stone beneath him, reached up and dragged
the sword's blade through the meat of the mutant's thigh.
An artery was severed and blue-green blood gouted out. The
mutant stumbled as Tarn ripped the sword through its hamstring, and it fell against the back wall – Tarn squirmed up
behind it and cut through its spine at waist height. The
mutant slumped further and Tarn stabbed it in the back of
the head.

Tarn let the pain register, to gauge his injuries. He was cut
in a hundred places. He had broken a couple of fingers on
the hand that now only held the splintered shaft of a spear.
The monster had broken several of his ribs – his sternum
had separated and moved agonisingly as he breathed.

Shards of bone could have speared his lungs, or cut through some artery or vein. He could be filling up with blood.

He dropped the shaft and braced himself for the next assault. But none came. Through the human wreckage piled up at the doorway he could see the battlements were clear of troops, right up to the next bastion. Beyond that, spear-points glistened between the bastion and the gun emplacement, but none seemed to be rushing to avenge the dozens of fallen. The gun roared – not at the tower, but almost straight down. The explosion echoed from far beneath and Tarn realised the horde must be right at the base of the walls, trading arrows and trying to find some way up.

Had they run out of men? Had Tarn killed every last legionary on this stretch of wall, and had their deaths not been missed yet in the confusion?

No… someone was approaching. Tarn looked in the man-gled bodies for a bow and arrows, so he could pick them off before he got here, but there was none. He realised the room was knee-deep in blood.

The figure approaching was not a legionary. It was dressed in a cloak which hung from its shoulders down to the ground, dark blue with swirling purple embroidery, trimmed in gold. In one hand the figure held a tall staff of brass with the head wrought into a rune like those covering the room's walls – like them it was shifting and painful to see, the eye refusing to focus on it.

The figure had a tall collar that went right round its head save for a slit at the front. For this Tarn was grateful, because as the figure approached he could just see grey, bloodless skin and a ragged hole where a nose should be.

They said sorcery took its toll on the body, ageing a man well beyond his years. But those who mastered it could ignore the body entirely, living in a cadaver and yet staying as lithe and strong as they had been in youth. This had to be such a creature.

The figure waved its free hand and the bodies started to rise. Tarn slashed at them as the oozing torsos and severed limbs began to float. But they drifted out of the room and hung above the rampart floor as the sorcerer walked through them. The blood stayed, though, a pool knee-deep and rising.

The sorcerer was at the door. Tarn held the sword in both hands, rising onto the balls of his feet ready to strike, but knowing instinctively that something as mundane as a blade through the heart wouldn't even discourage a creature like this.

The blood was running up the walls, feeding the runes that were huge and fat, writhing and shuddering. Tarn tried to look at them, but his eyes forced themselves away from the blurred shapes.

Cataracted eyes gleamed through the shadows of the sorcerer's face. Desiccated lips mouthed words in a language that Tarn had never learned, but somehow understood.

'Thank you, my friend,' it said. 'You have saved me a lot of trouble.'

THIS WAS THE worst it had ever been. Hath had been at the last stand at Vengeance Pass and the massacre at the head of the Blackwater River. He had seen it when battle plans went utterly wrong, and seen it from both sides. But this was worse. There was no way on Torvendis that they would take those walls. The ladders and grapples that were carried in the barbarian throng wouldn't be enough, not when the walls were so tall and sheer – there would be more than enough time for the defenders to cut down or shoot anyone who made it that far.

But Hath couldn't stop it now. No one could. He had to do as warriors always did. He had to fight on, do everything with courage and strength, and hope he would be alive when the madness ended.

Hath knew something was wrong even before he hit the wall. Far up the line he could just see the section of the line led by the Serpent tribe – if anything he had expected them to travel faster than his own men. The Serpent were accustomed to lightning raids on the coast, beaching longboats, pillaging and butchering, then melting away again into the darkness of the ocean.

But they had broken like a wave halfway across the defences, well shy of the wall itself. They were being hammered by two guns and countless volleys of arrows, but so were the Emerald Sword and Bear tribesmen swarming around Hath and they were carrying forward on a tide of death and anger.

There had to be something else. The Serpent were oath-breaking, degenerate murderers to a man and never ran from anything. Something was wrong.

But there was plenty wrong around Hath, too. He had never seen madness like this. Ahead of him was an enormous fortification, a solid block of heaped earth bristling with spikes. Most of the barbarians – the clean-shaven, axe-wielding Emerald Sword and the bearded Bear tribesmen who carried maces and brought many of their women to the fight – were going around the mound but some were clambering over it, becoming ensnared in the near-invisible threads of some strong, sharp metal or slipping off the crumbling side to fall beneath the feet of those below.

Arrows were sheeting down and there was some kind of rapid-firing war engine mounted on the rampart directly above, stitching explosions back and forth across the crowds surging across the defences. The din was appalling. The smell, of burning bodies, loosed bowels and blood, was worse.

Hath held his axe high, trying to thrash aside the press around him. 'Make way! Go round! Go round!' He bellowed at the top of his voice, but his command was still lost amongst the din. A swarm of what looked like bright glowing insects poured down off the walls and plunged into the crowds some distance away from Hath, but even then he could hear the yells of confusion as the golden-orange sparks buzzed in and out faster than the eye could follow. Men clambered over one another to get away, their bodies on fire.

Another spell lanced down, and thorned vines writhed from the ground, dragging men down and into the blood-sodden earth, strangling and ensnaring. Many were trampled as Hath watched, the pull of the throng taking him ever closer to the walls.

Another line of explosions raked through the press, blasting broken bodies high, with an earsplitting sound that left Hath's ears full of white noise.

Then, the thunder of magic and crack of the guns stopped. Hath wondered if he had been deafened, but no, he could still hear the battle-cries and the moaning of the dead like a rumble all around him.

The whistle of falling arrows had gone, too.

If Hath could have turned back, he would, but there were still crowds of warriors surging in and carrying him around the fortification, over staked pits and body-choked ditches.

The soil began to lift off the heaped fortification. Bodies were carried up, too, dead and alive – Hath looked up and saw a trio of Lady Charybdia's sorcerers on the battlements, hands held high, white sparks flashing in their eyes and between their fingers. The body of the fortification was dissolving into a rising column of earth, exposing foundations of stone between which yawned a great black pit.

It was the damnedest thing Hath had ever seen. He had a suspicion it would be the last thing, too.

The column disintegrated and rained black, wet earth down over Hath and the warriors crowded around what was now a huge dark tunnel entrance.

From that entrance came hundreds of legionary spearmen, silks billowing as they leapt from the concealed tunnel and charged into the barbarian mob.

FAR TO THE south, white horses were galloping up the wall. The remnants of the desert horsemen were riding vertically up the battlements, swapping arrows with the archers like punches. They had lost perhaps nine out of every ten of their number, but this was still enough to lead the assault on the ramparts. No one really knew anything about the desert raiders, least of all that their steeds were as magical as their arrows and throwing blades. Perhaps it shouldn't have been surprising that the decision to take their horses against the wall, seemingly the maddest of a whole cacophony of insane risks, turned out to be the single best tactical choice in the entire assault.

Ladders rose from Golgoth's horde in the centre, propped precariously against the immense walls. Only the bravest had made it that far, so there was no shortage of madmen to clamber up the tall, narrow ladders one at a time into the storm of arrows. Spearmen pushed ladders away from the wall to fall like felled trees back into the throng. It rained warriors as well as arrows.

Two spell-wrought sally ports opened and legionary shock troops poured out into the Bear and Sword surrounding Hath and the Serpent swarming to Hath's right. They had large round shields as well as spears, and barbed daggers for when their spears broke and they were crammed nose-to-nose with the barbarians. The combat was hellish with the barbarians pushed forwards by the masses to the rear and the legionaries with nowhere to retreat to. These shock troops were pumped up with freakish concoctions that turned their eyes into pupil-less white orbs and shut all pain out of their minds. There was nothing but killing there, no retreat and no skill, sheer butchery in the shadow of the walls.

The Serpent had been halted entirely, facing the legionaries with a solid wall of shields and longswords, taking charge after charge, bending as their front ranks were felled but never breaking. The Serpent were winning, but they wouldn't get within easy bowshot of the walls before darkness fell.

The muscular, pale-skinned valley tribes people died almost to a man, pummelled with the fire of half-a-dozen guns and drenched in hot oil and acid as they scrabbled up the ropes of their grapples. Perhaps a tenth of their number survived to retreat, the rest dead or dying in heaps at the foot of the wall.

The desert horsemen reached the battlements and kept going, charging two abreast in both directions. The defenders had been drilled well, but a cavalry charge along the top of the wall had not been anticipated, and the spearmen couldn't form hedges of spears dense enough to deter the desert men's charge. The battlements were swept from bastion to bastion along nearly two kilometres of wall, three guns were rid of their crews. When the bastions were collapsed with explosive charges to block their passage, the horsemen regrouped, made a silent decision, and charged down the narrow stairways into the columns of legionaries ascending to attack them. They had decided to die there, and many of them did, man and horse tumbling down the back of the wall or charging onto the spears of the legionaries. But a fearsome spearhead made it into the barracks, butchering scores of men as they were still chanting their battle-prayers.

The survivors, their honour satisfied, turned around, swept back up to the wall and back down the front. As purple-grey twilight took over from the blood orange day, a gaggle of proud white horsemen galloped in quiet triumph through the routing masses of the valley tribes people.

Few others made it onto the wall. Through sheer bloody-mindedness many of the Emerald Sword under Golgoth crammed themselves onto the walls, hacking with their axes before they were surrounded and slain, at huge loss, by legionary swordsmen. Golgoth was not among them, though not for want of trying.

A substantial knot of Emerald Sword, along with Bear tribe warriors who had been forced wide from Hath's group, found themselves scaling ladders unopposed and emerged almost intact on a wall completely empty of defenders. Thinking they had the luck of heroes, they prepared to charge down into the vulnerable rear defences of the wall when a torrent of lithe, sinisterly beautiful daemonettes poured from a blood-filled tower. The warriors were transfixed by their sensual movements right up until the moment when sharp claws and needle teeth bit through their armour and into their flesh. As night began that stretch of wall was manned, not by fanatical legionaries, but by the summoned servants of the Pleasure God himself.

The assault had failed everywhere. Nowhere were there warriors still on the walls in any numbers, but nowhere could the barbarians approach and ascend the walls with impunity. The night, which on Torvendis could turn from glimmering moonlight to complete darkness for no reason and without warning, was entirely on the side of the defenders. Some madmen carried on fighting, giving their lives with no hope of success. The barbarian horde fell back, mostly in disarray, some like the Serpent with a good day's battle under their belts, a very few like the horsemen riding with the aspect of victory.

TORVENDIS WAS CRUEL. It sent out a night that would shine down in mockery on the battlefield. The Slaughtersong, ever-present since Golgoth had first met with his mentor high in the Canis Mountains, was low and central in the sky, larger than in living memory with a blue-white corona around a pinprick of light. The blood soaking into the trenches and corpse-heaps glowed white, and the walls looked as if they had been gilded with silver.

No one had even tried to recover any of the bodies. The only movement had been the scuttling corpse-eaters who had melted out of their forest hovels, and the flashes of the arrows sent by the sentries to chase them off.

The cold light filtered down through the thick canopy of the forest, pooling between the trees, illuminating the stragglers still making their way back from the battlefield.

Golgoth watched them as he crouched in the foliage. The forest around him was thick and dark, the gnarled trunks covered with mosses. Though the forest edge was razed regularly by the soldiers on the walls, it grew back almost immediately and each time looked older and denser as if in mockery of their efforts. Thick moss and mulched leaves were heavy underfoot and the dark greenery was like a close green sky. The smell of moss and the forest's quiet exhalation was almost enough to cut out the reek of blood rolling off the battlefield.

The forest was full of survivors, many of them wounded, filtering through the dense trees back towards the grassy foothills where the army had first gathered. The moans of the dying could be heard through the sighing of the leaves,

as could the heated arguments where men tried to appor-
tion blame for the failure to take the walls.

Twining roots snared many of the stragglers on the edge of
the forest as they tried to reach the cover of the canopy. Golgoth could swear he saw some forms moving that were not
survivors but scavengers, drawn from the depths of the forest by the promise of wounded prey struggling through the
undergrowth. Surviving the battle was not necessarily
enough to survive until nightfall.

It had been carnage. Golgoth had seen it raining corpses
as the ladders went up, and walked over a thick swamp of
gore as he fell back with the twilight. He had seen war
before, more than enough to make him utterly certain of his
worth as a warrior. But he had never seen anything like this.
He had never seen, with his own eyes, the sort of bloodshed
that would one day become one of the legends that made
Torvendis the world it was.

The Emerald Sword had lost a quarter of their entire population, easily. The valley folk had lost more like two thirds,
and they were still dying – Golgoth could hear their gurgling
screams as the acid poured from the battlements finally ate
its way into their lungs. Even then, hearing the broken remnants of his army struggling to make it through the night,
Golgoth knew they would never be able to count the dead.
One hundred and fifty thousand dead would probably be
understating the butcher's bill.

The night turned colder, and suddenly Golgoth was aware
of a blade's point on the back of his neck.

'You're too damned ugly to hide, Golgoth,' said a slick,
slimy voice. The point was pulled back to let Golgoth turn
his head, and he saw standing above him a pale, loose-
skinned woman with deep-set black eyes and straggly raven
hair. Golgoth had never met her, but he knew her by
description and reputation: Lutr'Kya, of the Serpent tribe.

Lutr'Kya stepped out of the foliage into the hollow where
Golgoth crouched. The scaled armour she wore like a cloak
was scored and spattered with dried blood. 'I thought I
would find you skulking. Look at you, son of the Sword.
Covered in filth. Cowering.' There was a sneer on her piscene

face. She lowered her long, thin sword, as if daring Golgoth to attack her. 'I hope you can think of a reason why I should not kill you, Golgoth, because I fear I never will.'

Golgoth struggled to his feet. He was covered in cuts, and he had probably cracked a couple of ribs falling from one of the siege ladders. 'Kill me if you will, Lutr'Kya. Lady Charybdia couldn't do it, Grik couldn't. Maybe you will have more luck.'

'Damn you, Golgoth! You joke with me? You have murdered my tribesmen! You led us against the walls to die!'

Golgoth thrust his face close to hers. 'You are already dead! You have been dead for generations! Look at us, Serpent bitch. We're nothing! The Sword sold its children as slaves. The Serpent live on desolate rocks and work their men to death before they grow beards. We only exist because it isn't worth Charybdia's attention to have us exterminated.'

'Then we could have fought back! Damnation, Golgoth, you could have fought her on our terms, not thrown your brothers and sisters against the walls to die!'

'Better death now than slavery forever.'

'Golgoth, our tribes have been at one another's throats for generations. But I have worked without cease to keep the Serpent tribes together, and I thought for the mountain peoples the best chance for survival was to fight as one.' Lutr'Kya's voice was cold. 'Now I see I was betrayed. You have butchered my people as sure as if the Emerald Sword themselves were manning the walls.'

'There is no Emerald Sword. There is no Serpent.' Golgoth held out his arms, indicating the ragged bands of survivors in the forest and the blood-soaked expanse of the battlefield. 'This is all we have! For this one battle, we were something other than slaves. I gave you something to fight for. Your people should be grateful. They would have died as nothing just as they had lived as nothing. I don't care about you or your people, or mine, or Lady Charybdia or anything else. All I want is a decent funeral pyre for a tribe that was dead before I was ever born.'

Lutr'Kya backed off warily. 'You are insane, Golgoth of the Emerald Sword.' She took up a fighter's stance, sword-point

hovering in front of her. Her reputation was of one who preferred to have men killed, but who was willing to kill with
her own hand when circumstance required. Doubtless surviving Serpent warriors would be shadowing her to protect
her, but Golgoth's hide would be hers alone if she wanted it
so. 'You promised hope, and for that I was willing to break
the vows of my fathers and join with you. But your anger
was so deep at the weakness of your own tribe that you
would rather lead us all to destruction than admit the Sword
is the weakest-willed of us all. You have slain my people in
your madness, and I claim your life.'

Golgoth stood, hulking in the darkness, grinning with his
axe limp in his hand. 'Make it slow, bitch,' he said.

Lutr'Kya circled, stepping warily to avoid tripping on the
roots underfoot, sizing up Golgoth and trying to decide if he
really wanted to die so badly. In the end, she never found out.

A shadow passed over them, blotting out the bright stars
for a second. There was a concussion in the air, a beating of
great wings and a whining of machinery. Something huge
and very heavy landed with a wet thump beyond the treeline, where the battleground started, and then the heat hit
them – a wave of blistering hot air that seemed to blow
straight off the parched desert. Leaves were torn from the
trees and swirled blindingly through the air. As the wind
passed Lutr'Kya turned and Golgoth followed her gaze to
where an orange-red flare plumed outside the forest, bright
and hot. People were screaming and running through the
forest, away from the new arrival, yelling for others to follow
who were too dazed or wounded to move.

Golgoth, hunkered down low, hurried forward, to the forest's edge. Lutr'Kya didn't stop him but followed, hanging
back and still wary.

A gaggle of valley tribesmen struggled past, covered in
blood, many missing limbs, supporting each other as they
tripped and swore their way through the undergrowth.
There was fear in their eyes – these were men facing death
for the second time in a day.

Golgoth reached the edge of the forest, and peered out
between the trees. The flare was a muddy glow, wreathed in

steam and smoke. He could make out a shape now, humanoid but deformed with hulking shoulder muscles and strange protuberances. It was very close indeed – no, not close, but huge.

For the moment, Golgoth forgot about the death of the tribes and the funeral pyre he had tried to build for them. Was this some secret weapon of the legions, a daemon of the Lust God sent to scatter the remnants of Golgoth's army?

Somehow, it did not seem that a fire-wreathed monster would be the sort of creature summoned in the name of the lord of pleasures. What was it, then? An omen? An ally?

'Voice of the oceans...' cursed Lutr'Kya behind him, as she realised the true size of the thing. Golgoth moved forward to get a better view. He could see the creature reached a third of the way up the wall. Its flesh was an ugly grey and there were chunks of machinery, like that of the legionaries' guns but glowing hot and dripping gore, stuck into its body. Metal wings spread from its back. Silhouetted in the fire flaring from the joints and pistons of its machinery, it was truly immense, and Golgoth reflected that had he not lost everything he cared about, he would be afraid.

The monster looked up at the walls, and laughed, a sound like a thunderstorm. Hurriedly, legionaries were scuttling across the battlements to meet this new threat and one of the guns fired. An explosion ripped apart the ground at the monster's feet and another hit it square in the chest – it was thrown back a step but when the smoke coiled away it was unharmed.

The monster strode over the carpet of bodies, its feet sinking into the blood-soaked earth. In seconds it crossed ground that had cost tens of thousands of lives to take just hours before. It raised its taloned arms, and roared in anger.

It was raining. It was raining blood.

The ground was squirming. As Golgoth watched, dark forms started to claw their way up out of the ground, slumping half-formed onto the wet soil and thrashing as they threw off birth cauls, unfolding limbs and tails. Tens, then hundreds, their yowling joining the roars of their master as they dragged their malformed bodies from the earth. Fiery red eyes glared and mouths filled with bestial fangs opened to howl. Like smaller versions of the beast that had summoned them, yet still each taller than a man, they unfolded hands tipped with wicked claws and stalked through the wreckage of the battlefield.

Arrows were lashing down and cannon roared. The monster was peppered with bowfire and battered by shells, but it didn't even move. Many of its offspring pulled arrows from their muscular bodies and yelled defiance back at the walls.

'Blood!' the huge beast bellowed. 'Blood for the Blood God!'

Perhaps this creature really was an ally. Perhaps it or its brothers would kill Golgoth on sight if they bothered to notice him. But either way, Golgoth knew he might have achieved something here, after all. The sheer magnitude of carnage had spilt enough blood to attract this creature, surely a daemon of the Blood God. And though Golgoth could not claim to know the ways of daemons, he could guess that those who owed allegiance to one god had little love for the followers of another. The walls had held out so far, but if this daemon chose to take out his rage on them, they might not stand for much longer.

And there was more. There had been tales of daemons summoned on the ramparts during the battle – now it seemed another power was doing some summoning of its own. Daemons were still writhing from the earth and forming bestial packs that roamed towards the walls, loping around the monster's feet.

The daemon stomped towards the wall, the ground shaking with every step. It reached down and dug its talons into the stone of one of the buttresses, tearing deep into the crack between the stones. It pulled, and an immense block of stone was wrenched from the wall, rolling onto the ground and kicking up plumes of blood-soaked earth.

The rampart sagged and cracks ran up the wall. Several legionaries tumbled over the edge and the rest fled as massive cracks ran up the front of the wall with a sound like a glacier's thaw. The daemon reached into the gap it had opened and pushed against the sides, opening up the wound it had made. The battlement above crumbled and more legionaries fell as the top of the whole wall section cracked and bowed, pitching men over the teeth of the rampart.

The daemon put a massive clawed foot into the wound and clambered up the wall, claws tearing chunks from the edifice. It reached up and pulled down a long section of battlement, broken rocks tumbling over its body. It bellowed with joy as it bored its way deep into the wound it had opened and tore out whole blocks of stone, opening up hidden passages and cramped chambers. A bank of pale dust was kicked up by the crumbling stone as it fell and the smaller daemons started swarming up the broken wall, up the ragged edge of the crack and vaulting up onto the battlements. The sound was awesome, like an earthquake, and the rumbling of the falling rock travelled through the ground right to the edge of the forest where Golgoth stood.

Golgoth ran out past the treeline and held his axe high. 'All who can hear me!' he yelled. 'All who call yourselves men! Torvendis has sent us an omen! It has sent us destruction! All who wish to see the city fall, charge!'

He ran out alone towards the daemon and its infant army, suddenly light on his feet and feeling as strong and deadly as a hundred men. Maybe there were some warriors following him, maybe he was completely alone. He didn't care.

Because, as Ss'll Sh'Kar tore at the battlements and his daemon followers gained form at his feet, Lady Charybdia's wall was falling.

CHAPTER SIX

TORVENDIS CAN NEVER be fully mapped. The deserts change to forest, the glaciers to rivers of lava, the mountains to ocean troughs and the cities to plains of dust. Trying to chart it seems to make the landscape change even faster, as if Torvendis takes exception to any attempt to unravel its secrets with compass and map. No one on Torvendis ever wakes up to the same world twice, and in a world where even the colour of the sky mutates from hour to hour nothing ever stays the same.

But even the land never changes as much as the patterns of power that have played across Torvendis for aeons, like wildfires flaring and burning out. The undersea empire of the Pontifex Infernus where columns of lava were formed into mighty fortresses and temples, the blood-soaked reign of Ss'll Sh'Karr, the Coven of a Thousand who ruled a nation of black glass golems, the endless episodes of complete anarchy when banditry and madness were the only laws – each of these seemed an empire that could never fall. But the truth was that every one was just a single face of the endless puzzle box of power on Torvendis, and they lasted no more than the briefest phase of the planet's past. Just as no map can ever be drawn of Torvendis, no history can ever be written.

There are only legends, and when they are compiled they are revealed to be contradictory and vague, but all equally true. Chaos on Torvendis manifested itself as change and inscrutability – many sages and prophets had tried to divide the planet's history into neat slices of time, and all died insane. Chaos does not allow itself to be codified, and Torvendis was a world of pure Chaos, deceptively disguised as rock and ocean.

Everyone on Torvendis ended up a legend, or a part of one. The innocents crushed beneath Ss'll Sh'Karr's daemon legions were more in death, as a part of the daemon lord's legacy of madness, than they had ever been in life. Those who eked out an existence in the mountains, forests and deserts played their part, unknowingly forging the borders that separated warring nations. But no one, no matter how great, ever left more than a ripple in the lake of Torvendis's legends – even monsters like Sh'Karr or the Crimson Knights would become no more than additions to an endless gallery of tyrants, heroes and butchers.

The only legend that mattered was the tale of Torvendis itself, conquered by Arguleon Veq, pulled at by every Chaos power that dared take part in the endless war for domination of the warp. It was a story of how no one man or daemon could ever truly rule, of how Chaos was change and uncertainty and madness, of how every action on Torvendis was a triumph and every change a tragedy. And if anyone on the planet were to be asked, they would agree that this was the one legend that would never end.

THE AIR WAS thick and hot, and caught in Kron's throat. Everywhere he moved, the dense foliage of jungle shuddered and scattered drops of warm condensation down to sting on his burned skin. His burns were red and raw, chalky where they had scorched down to the muscle, and every step ached like hell. And Kron knew very well what hell felt like.

He had been walking for perhaps three days. In that time he had managed to crawl out of the desert and out of the rain of blood that still clotted his straggly hair into congealed knots. He had found the edge of the jungle and dived in. There were few better places on Torvendis to hide, and he knew that he would have to stay hidden until he was healed and ready to implement the last stages of his plan. Kron was not such a fool that he did not anticipate someone following him to Torvendis. The Word Bearers, for a start. Maybe others.

Even so, Kron wished from time to time that he had never chosen the jungle. The humidity was crushing, and every plant seemed to bristle with thorns and crawl with parasites. There were no paths, and every step Kron took forced him to push through branches and vines that clustered round him. Parasites had flocked to him – lice were feasting on the blood in his hair and clothes, wriggling things had burrowed beneath his fingernails and there was something long and slimy rooted in the skin of his back, its circular mouth eating an inflamed crater out of his shoulder blade. He hadn't eaten or drunk anything, save for rainwater, but he knew that something must have got into his guts and was eating him away from the inside. Normally such things would be beneath his notice, but he was exhausted from sorcery and the fiery escape from Sh'Karr's tomb, and he had never been more vulnerable. It would only be a few days before he was back to something approaching full strength, but for those days, he was all but helpless should one of his pursuers find him.

He knew he was being watched. There were a hundred birds of prey and predatory reptiles creeping after him, hoping he would eventually drop dead like every other lone traveller. The night was layered with sounds, claws against bark, the thrum of wings and the hiss of skin against skin. Kron had been in enough hell-holes to know that some of those eyes on him were human.

He reached a tree with a wide bole that had been killed by lightning or disease, and was now a hollow shell of blackened wood. It was a rare piece of shelter and, with the night sky oppressive overhead and heavy with smudges of nebulae, Kron knew he needed some rest or risk letting his immune system wind itself down. The jungle would have killed a normal man by now, with disease and infection. Kron didn't intend to go the same way.

He stepped over the slippery undergrowth and peered into the darkness of the hollow. A spider with an odd number of legs lurked deep inside, on a sparkling web heavy with mummified insects. Eye-stalks flicked up at Kron's approach.

Its leg span was as wide as Kron's arms. He took a knife from his belt. The creature tensed its legs and leapt, its body splitting open into a cross-shaped mouth crammed with teeth.

Kron swiped twice and the creature came apart in mid-air, legs sliced clean off. The parts of the spider scattered into the thick undergrowth.

Kron was old, and hurt. But he was still quick.

There was a rustling and suddenly the ground was alive, crawling with creatures that had sprouted from the severed limbs of the spider. They swarmed into a single ugly mass, surrounding Kron, each one ready to leap and inject poisons that even Kron couldn't shrug off.

Kron whispered words that burned in his throat and traced a shape in the air. A circle of flame flickered around his feet and spread outwards, lighting up the dark green of the jungle with a flare of orange light. There was a cacophony of hooting and screeching as all manner of creatures fled the trees on wings and spindly legs. When the fire had burned away the scorched undergrowth was littered with the charred husks of spider-parasites and countless other creatures.

Kron coughed and slumped to his knees. His strength seemed to drain out of him – he had not slept since he could remember and had not had anything to eat for days. It had been so long since he had last used his powers to anything like their full potential that his body had become weak and rusted around him. Even this minor sorcery had taken its toll.

Kron crawled the last few paces into the hollow tree, the undergrowth thick and warm around his burned hands. He had never felt so old, never felt the centuries weighing down on him so heavily. Doubtless there had been a time, forgotten now, when he had wondered what it would be like to live an impossibly long life. He would have wondered how those Traitor Legion heroes and champions of Chaos felt as they endured and fought well beyond the limits of a normal human body.

The truth was that by the time Kron had begun to worry about such things himself, he had fought the wars of Chaos for hundreds of years already and lived unnatural years without even noticing. That was the kind of life his had been. He had become something other than human without realising, and even now he couldn't put his finger on when Chaos had really got a hold on him, body and soul.

The blanket of stealthy sound draped back over the jungle. The pale light filtering down through the canopy picked out hunched feathered shapes on the branches and nictitating eyes watching from between massive snaking roots. Kron's eyes, still keen after all these centuries, caught the gleam of starlight on flint spearheads and sweating skin. They were quieter than most of the animals, these tribes people, but Kron could still see them.

They would probably be waiting for the same thing as the carrion birds. They were all waiting for him to die, maybe out of curiosity since very few outsiders must have ever survived this long in the jungle. Kron counted a dozen watchers, golden-skinned with heads half-shaved and with bones and feathers thrust through their skin. They were probably a roving patrol, the toughest of the whole tribe, headhunters, cannibals or scalptakers.

Kron smiled. Even now, wounded and tired, he could have fought them to death. It would hurt like hell, but he could take them all. In fact, with them scaring away the larger predators, he was probably safest with them watching him.

As he looked on, one warrior made a near-invisible gesture and a handful of the tribesmen peeled off, slinking through the vegetation to surround the hollow tree, to keep this unusual quarry from escaping. Perhaps they would try to kill him in the night with a poisoned dart or a thrown knife, but there had been a time when Kron could catch bullets. Maybe he still could.

With hungry cannibals creeping towards his hiding place, Kron shut down half his brain and caught some rest at last.

IT WOULD BE impossible for any mortal to properly understand what thoughts went through the mind of Ss'll Sh'Karr, if they could be called thoughts at all. They might resemble, in the most approximate way, a constant scream, or the word 'blood' bellowed over and over again, or an overarching thirst, or pure hatred, or the sensation of being immersed in fire. But nothing would fully describe what made Ss'll Sh'Karr, avatar of the Blood God, do what he did.

But it was still with something resembling nostalgia that Ss'll Sh'Karr watched his army reborn. Hell was oozing up from the ground, the half-formed bodies of his legion dragging themselves from the blood-sodden soil. He had known they would find him – a daemon of Khorne was born of the concept of violence and anger, and Sh'Karr's brothers had always been waiting in the earth of Torvendis, fed by every act of bloodshed. It just took the will of their lord released, and the lake of blood that saturated the earth beneath the walls, to bring them back.

A hundred hulking creatures, each twice the height of a man, yowling as they threw off their birth cauls and let iron claws tear out through their skin. A hundred could become a thousand, a thousand a million, all they needed was more blood. And there was no shortage of blood on Torvendis, or of ways to spill it. Ss'll Sh'Karr could taste millions of packed bodies beyond the wall before him, weak and ripe and waiting to be torn apart for the glory of the God on the Throne of Skulls.

And to get to it all, they just had to get past the wall.

TARN WATCHED AS the wall tumbled down around him. He was in the area immediately behind the wall, between the rear of the fortification and the barracks, grimly aware of the cruelty that his death now would represent when he could have died so many times over already since the previous morning. The wall, he knew, would fall in a great avalanche of stone, sweeping everything away, and that would be no way for a man to die.

Men were running everywhere, funnelling the wounded from the shattered ramparts and charging up the rearward working to relieve those who had fallen. There were terrible sounds from the front of the wall – the rumble of torn stone and the howling of daemons. Men were screaming as they were dragged down, limbs crushed by falling stone. There were shapes moving at the top of the wall, lumpen and shambling but with claws that took a head with every flash.

Tarn had woken beneath a pile of bodies, his head still aching from writhing, reeking dreams. He had crawled from the shattered tower to find the battle was over, the battlements strewn with the remains of Emerald Sword warriors. The stink of magic was still heavy and he could see, in the back of his mind, the rent in the air and the horrible things that had tumbled out of the tower walls at the sorcerer's command, silken-skinned and clawed.

But that was before. Tarn had seen strange and terrible things and learned to shake them out of his head when he had to concentrate on survival. He had scrambled back down the walls, blocking out the pain from his many wounds, and made it into hiding in the shadow of the barracks complexes behind the walls. Right now he was lying in the shelter of a drainage ditch, brackish water up over his shoulders and his nostrils just above the film of clinging scum. Nearby lay a complex of barracks buildings, long, low dormitories with pastel-shaded banners flying along the roofs, along with silos for storing grain to feed the legionaries and paved roads for supplies and marching columns. It was impressive to see the workings of Lady Charybdia's military machine – not for the first time, Tarn wondered how high he could have risen had he been born within the wall instead of outside it.

He had hidden there as the sun sank. The last moans from the battlefield had died down. And now, this.

Tarn risked putting his head above the lip of the drainage ditch. The barracks complex didn't look quite so impressive now, as knots of men ran here and there in confusion. Reinforcements clashed with wounded men trying to get down the wall in the opposite direction.

Tarn looked up and saw movement on the top of the wall, something huge – bigger than anything he had ever seen, bigger than the sea monsters that hunted off the northern coasts and the roc-birds that carried the unwary from the western peaks. Horns and bloodstained metal jutted from the monster's skin, gleaming wetly as it clambered onto the top of the wall, bellowing, sweeping its massive clawed paw through the legionaries trying to hold it at bay with spears and bows. It was a daemon, a huge beast of legend formed from the pure will of Chaos, and around its feet were swarms of smaller daemons enthusiastically mirroring its butchery.

A score of defenders was thrown down the steep stairways, bodies breaking as they tumbled down the steps and walkways. A troop of legionaries ran past Tarn's hiding place, a centurion screaming orders, trying to forge some discipline from the confusion.

A sorcerer staggered past blindly, eyes and ears bleeding, from the massive feedback of sorcery rolling down from the wall – even Tarn could smell blood in his nostrils and taste it on his tongue, and hear the whispers in his head from a thousand thirsty daemons' mouths. Hundreds of legionaries were swarming from the barracks but Tarn knew they couldn't stop it. Arrows were raining against the daemon's skin but it was ignoring them, digging its claws into the stone and pulling. The wall sagged and daemons were scrambling down into the barracks now, butchering their way through the legionaries massed to defend the rear of the wall, a tide of grey-skinned, half-machine monsters.

The wall was coming down like a tidal wave breaking. Palls of dust billowed and massive chunks of masonry rolled down its sides, smashing through barracks buildings and crushing whole centuries of troops.

The daemon strode down through the carnage. The legionaries were in full rout now – the few centurions who tried to stop them were ignored. The smaller daemons were amongst the barracks and supply lines, leaping hither and thither and killing anything they found. Tarn scrabbled through the foul water of the ditch to where a handful of legionaries were wading across – he grabbed the last one and pulled him under the water, holding him down until he stopped kicking. As the screams came closer and the stench of blood overpowered the stink of the ditch, Tarn tore off the dead man's silks and wrapped them around his own leathers, grabbing the spear and hauling himself out of the ditch – at a glance he would pass for a legionary, and no one would pause long enough to get a decent look.

Tarn had never been ashamed of running, for a man who killed for any master could hardly be ashamed of anything. He joined the rout at full sprint, heading away from the walls and further into Lady Charybdia's kingdom. Daemons loped like wolves, tearing men apart. Showers of arrows plunged into battling knots of men and daemon, fired by archers willing to see their own side killed if it meant thinning out the enemy pouring over the ruined wall.

The footsteps of the daemon lord were like war drums. The stench and the noise were awful. Tarn knew this was no longer just Golgoth's desperate attempt to fight one last battle – something new and terrible had awoken, and this wasn't Golgoth's fight any more. That meant it wasn't Tarn's either, and so he ran, the seething blood fighting with the writhing images in his head.

If he lived, he would seek out another master, as he had done a dozen times before. But for now, his only ally was survival.

LADY CHARYBDIA HAD not been so distracted for some time. Everything around her was wrong. The breach in her kingdom was like a wound in her side. Primitives and outsiders were spreading like diseases through Slaanesh's domain. There was a bad taste in her mouth and an ugly screeching sound at the back of her hearing. Sometimes, she wished she could suffer the world with the crude senses of other mortals.

This chamber of the keep had been drained of its extreme sensory input, so the others seated around the wide hardwood table could survive. A chill breeze keened in from the balconies that ringed the tower, bringing the echoes and scents of the city, rippling the war banners brought back by the legions from past campaigns and causing the weeping clusters of candles to flicker. Lady Charybdia did not like this place, high on a pinnacle of the keep, and she hoped that if she had to be uncomfortable then the others would be too. The white sage (whose name she still did not care to remember) was certainly utterly terrified, every muscle tensed, wizened eyes darting. The sweat was rolling off him. Lady Charybdia stifled a smile – at least, there were still the small pleasures.

Caduceia, the one person in her kingdom for whom Lady Charybdia had anything approaching genuine respect, lounged in a massive hardwood throne, one clawed hand lolling, her tentacled head relaxed. She licked her lips with a forked tongue and ruffled the gills ranged down her neck. Nothing frightened Caduceia – whether that was the daemon in her or just her natural state of mind Lady Charybdia was uncertain.

Lady Charybdia's chancellor, Mape, had shrunk back down into the upholstery of his chair and was shivering. He was a tiny, monkey-like man with shrivelled eyes like black beads, who had been drained of his free will by his soul-destroying duties in calculating the total resources of the city. He alone actually had an understanding of just how much was hacked from the earth and then destroyed, poured down the throats of revellers or forged into buildings and weapons. The mathematics of this process were infused with Chaos and hence were fundamentally illogical, and trying to comprehend them had sucked out all the interesting parts of Mape's mind. Lady Charybdia valued her chancellors and their staff as tools to calculate just how great her service to Slaanesh was, but as individuals they meant nothing. She went through chancellors quite quickly – Mape had held his position for three years and was on his last legs.

The door to the chambers swung open, and the last member of Lady Charybdia's council of war entered.

Commander Demetrius of the Violators Space Marine Chapter was about four metres high and the same across, a massive metallic block mounted on hydraulic claw-footed legs. Each articulated shoulder ended in an arm-mounted weapon, a four-barrelled assault cannon on the left and a bouquet of barbed energy-lashes on the right. The flat surfaces of his ceramite-encased body were painted a pale blue-grey, like dead men's lips, with the symbol of the Violators – a lightning bolt crossed by a dagger – wrought in gold over one side of the chest. On the other, dense script had been etched telling of the hundreds of engagements in which Demetrius had fought and the kill-marks of the important foes he had slain. On the centre of the chest, the sarcophagus where Demetrius's physical body was held, was a fleshy knot like an unopened flower, pale and dead but pulsing with the machine's heart.

The dreadnought stomped up to the table, servos growling. The petals of the sarcophagus opened and Demetrius's old body was revealed, a scorched corpse with arms and legs sheared off, the face rotten and drained. Fronds, like the tendrils of some sea creature, waved from the skin – they were exposed and elongated nerve endings, the only way that any sensation could be delivered into Demetrius's sense-dulled mind.

He had been horribly wounded on some distant battleground and recovered – though his body had been wrecked his tactician's mind was intact, and his Chapter had entombed him in a dreadnought's shell so he could continue to lead them in the eternal war that Chaos demanded of them.

'I am glad you could make it, commander,' said Lady Charybdia. 'How is life on the walls?'

'Tolerable, my lady,' replied Demetrius, his voice a low, cracked rattle from his ruined throat. 'The air tastes of war. We shall serve our god soon, I think.'

'That is looking very likely. I can trust you and your men to ensure that the current situation is resolved rapidly and with a minimum of disruption to our sacred work. Is my trust justified?'

'It is, my lady. Every one of my Marines is worth a thousand barbarians and more.'

'Good. I suspect that I shall be calling on you soon.' Lady Charybdia's voice was cold. Compared to her Demetrius was a brute, his own lust for experience limited to the violence of warfare. Lady Charybdia had once been like that, revelling in slaughter, but she knew now that it had just been a phase on the way to the current perfection of her senses. Demetrius was stuck in the pattern of bloodshed which became ever more ordinary for him as he absorbed every experience that battle could give him. One day he would become unable to experience anything at all and his mind would wilt away, leaving just the dreadnought to house some other butcher. The Violators were extremely valuable, undoubtedly the best troops on Torvendis, but their presence reminded Lady Charybdia of the stagnation that was the fate of every unwary servant of Slaanesh.

'Caduceia,' said Lady Charybdia, 'appraise us of the situation, if you will.'

Caduceia stood up. 'Of course, my lady.' She waved her clawed hand and an old, tarnished servitor-creature, which had been fitted out as a holoprojector, shone an image of Torvendis's prime continent into the air above the table. 'The initial attack was on the western walls, here.' The image closed in on a section of the wall bordering the foothills of the Canis Mountains. 'The mountain people mustered a surprisingly large horde and assaulted the walls directly.'

Demetrius snorted a laugh. 'Hah! How many did we kill?'

'About half of them,' continued Caduceia unperturbed. 'For minimal losses. Then, we believe an ally of theirs arrived.'

The image was blurry – compiled from the various seances and remote viewings of Lady Charybdia's pet sages, it was distorted by some sorcery. But it was clear enough to show something huge and monstrous tearing through the walls with its bare claws.

'We believe,' said Caduceia, 'that this is the creature refer-
ring to itself as Ss'll Sh'Karr. Daemons of the Blood God
followed in its wake and brought down the wall. The
remains of the barbarian forces followed. Our legionaries
have fallen back to the outskirts of the inhabited city but they
have been severely mauled. I have despatched several divi-
sions to defend the western outskirts of the city in depth.'

The tension grew higher, if such a thing was possible. The
borders had been penetrated. The sanctity of the city was
violated. It had been a long time since anyone had given
Lady Charybdia news this bad – anyone other than Caduceia could not have expected to survive her disappointment.

'Mobilising the reserves will take time,' said Lady Charybdia, calmly.

'We have deployed a force to slow them down,' continued
Caduceia. 'Slaves mostly, culled from the western mines. The
Blood God's minions are notorious for their love of slaughter for its own sake – they are unlikely to resist the
temptation of such a weak foe.'

'And when the slaves are dead?'

'The legions will mass in the west of the city. If the barbarians attack, we will hold them off. If they do not, we will
launch a counterattack and drive them back against the west
wall.'

'How many invaders are we talking about?'

A scattering of markers appeared on the flickering map,
speckling the breached wall like a disease. Green for barbarians, red for daemons. 'Perhaps a hundred thousand of the
tribes people. We killed a great many but more are flocking
to their cause. We cannot estimate the numbers of the daemons. Ss'll Sh'Karr once commanded millions.'

'But this is not Ss'll Sh'Karr. Sh'Karr is dead.'

'Yes, my lady. But some inheritor of his could rival him in
power.'

'Not if we send him back to his god first. Commander?'

'My lady?' answered Demetrius.

'The daemon lord is yours. The Blood God is the foulest
of all our foes in the heavens, I expect your Marines to execute the full anger of Slaanesh against his creation.'

Demetrius's smile split the skin of his cheeks so a rictus grinned down from the width of his face. 'A pleasure, my lady.' His servos buzzed with excitement.

Lady Charybdia looked towards the white sage. 'What can we expect from the warp?'

The white sage looked startled to have been addressed. Lady Charybdia noted that she often had that effect. 'The city is disturbed, as you are, my lady,' began the sage falteringly. 'Their pleasures are… qualified. Tainted. Fleshly abandon is not quite so abundant. However, the Prince of Pleasure surely sees how important you and the city are to his worship, there is no doubt our ministrations will summon a great many of his servants should the need arise.'

'No doubt? You do not sound so certain.'

The sage was shaking. His old man's eyes were wet. 'Very little is certain any more, my lady. The Slaughtersong has been above the horizon for weeks. Strange things are being born in the city.'

'The city is full of strange things already, sage.'

'My lady, do not misunderstand us, Slaanesh would never desert you, but… but there are many prophecies, and many of them are coming true. A calf with three heads, as the seers of the Crimson Knights foresaw, and a litter of half-devils with tentacles for hands such as was written by the prophets of the undersea kingdoms. They are omens of destruction and mistrust, the oldest there are. They say that something has returned that means the Pleasure God ill.'

'Indeed it has. The Blood God's spawn walk Torvendis again. Prophecies can come true all they like, sage, no number of daemons can hope to breach the city and hold it against us.'

Demetrius laughed, a rasping, throaty sound. 'You have fully one quarter of the Violators Chapter on your walls, lady. They could throw the whole Maelstrom against us and we would hold.'

'Indeed. Mape?'

Mape started, as if he had been woken from a nap.

'What can we pull from the population?'

Mape scrabbled around inside his oversized, filthy dark brown robes, pulling out sheafs of yellowed paper. 'The... the able-bodied population stands at rather more than a million, of whom half are suitable for the press, with the same again in raw slave manpower...'

'Can they be mobilised?'

Mape scrabbled some more, spilling paper onto the flag-stoned floor. 'Three hundred thousand useful troops, at the last census.'

'Good for dying at the barricades,' said Caduceia.

'Then that is what they will do, if necessary. And the slaves?'

Mape continued, speaking faster and faster. 'They will walk into battle like they work on the mine face. Under lashes and dying. An obstacle, nothing more, but there will be hundreds of thousands of them...' Mape's speech degenerated into rapid mumbling.

'Have the slavemasters ready,' said Lady Charybdia. 'They must be able and willing to put up a wall of slave flesh at a moment's notice. But do not let their labours cease, the city must not starve of pleasure while we wait for our enemies to move.'

Lady Charybdia stood up, drawing herself to the full impressive height that her elongated spine would allow. 'You have your orders. Seal my city and butcher this foreign infection.'

As her advisors left the chamber, the sage scuttling, Demetrius stomping heavily, Caduceia loping like an animal of prey, Lady Charybdia left the holomat image shimmering over the table. Her city was beautiful, a glittering jewelled scab over the surface of Torvendis's largest continent, an open wound bleeding grace into a benighted world. Lights glimmered and silver threads of suspended walkways shone against the velvet black of the mine pits. The keep was a diamond on a silver mount, perfect and precious.

How could anyone harm such a masterpiece? No one could understand the ways of the Blood God, but his lust for destruction was to Lady Charybdia the utter opposite of the

most basic logic. He was a god who refused true worship
and embraced only heresy – slaughter and ruination in his
name. His followers were the basest and most bestial. The
times when Torvendis had been in the grasp of the Blood
God's followers had seen tides of warfare wash over the
planet like waves of flame, destroying anything worth ruling,
butchering any population worth subjugating, leaving a
world of ash to be reconquered. Those times had left battlefield strata redolent with hatred and pain, heady pleasures
for Lady Charybdia to refine from the earth but a vivid
reminder of the hell the Blood God called power.

The holomat image flickered and grew dim, letting the
black pillars of the room show through against the milky
night sky. Then it shuddered and shut off, its old circuits
burned out.

The city would not fade out and die. Slaanesh would keep
his most diligent servant drawing worshipful pleasure from
Torvendis in his name. She vowed that no barbarian or daemon would stop her. She was, after everything, a high priest
of Slaanesh, and the city was her church. She would do her
sacred duty, and the final pleasure of death would be an
ironic gift to anyone who stood in her way.

GOLGOTH HAD NEVER truly thought, in all his days, that he
would ever actually set foot on soil like this. Lady Charybdia's realm was holy ground, and he was not invited. He felt
like a trespassing child. He felt like he had done when he
went to kill his first men, creeping onto the battlefield
before his years.

The sacred earth was dry and cracked, drained of life. Here
and there chunks of architecture were slowly oozing from
the ground or being melted back into it, pillared arcades
and flagstoned courtyards. The morning sky was bright yellow, shot through with purple streaks by the horizon, and a
dozen suns burned down, competing with bright patches of
nebula and the hard white spike of the ever-present Slaughtersong. In the distance rose the city, strange bulbous towers
leaning at insane angles – even from this far away Golgoth
would make out the lengths of chain that held some of

them up, and the spindly walkways between them. The deep pits of the mines were dark stains beneath the towers – even now, in the middle of the day, points of light shone in the darkness below.

Between Golgoth and the city was the battle, if it could be called that. The barbarian horde had swarmed through the breach created by Sh'Karr, and advanced into the forbidden heartland of Lady Charybdia's domain. The daemons had chased those who lived in the city's hinterland, scavengers and subsistence farmers who were simply carried away on the tide of the retreating legions. The barbarians toyed with the few legionaries who were left behind, but wasted little time, eager to make headway in what had turned from a catastrophe into an invasion. Golgoth reflected that his grand attempt at suicide had shifted into something different entirely. He had brought the tribes together, but instead of destroying them to punish their weakness, had he taken the first steps in making them strong again?

Lady Charybdia's slaves had been herded into the path of the invading force, lashed into a massive milling crowd, half of them unarmed, some dressed in rags and most little more than naked. Hath had counted tens of thousands of them, but by the time the barbarians caught up with Sh'Karr's daemons, half the slaves were dead.

The battle was in its closing stages. The thin white line of pale, starved slaves was thinning out by the second, crushed against a swarming black mass of barbarians. Knots of grey-skinned daemons leapt about here and there, sating themselves with blood.

An extraordinary thing was happening, quite apart from the merciless removal of an obstacle thrown at them by Lady Charybdia – an alliance was being formed. Golgoth was watching from some distance behind the front line, from where he stood the battle was almost abstract, and he was hard pressed to imagine that the faint pale line of resistance was composed of human beings. But the meaning of the victory was not lost on him. Man and daemon were fighting side by side, and it was hard to tell which was the more determined to punish Lady Charybdia.

The ground shook and a shadow passed in front of the suns behind Golgoth. He turned and saw the form of Ss'll Sh'Karr towering over him, seemingly as big as a mountain, dripping a rain of blood and oil from the machinery that clattered and pumped through his skin. His talons were thick to the elbow with gore and sheets of blood ran from his fleshy mandibles.

'You,' it said in a massive, earth-shaking voice, 'are their king.'

Golgoth craned his head to look up at the daemon. They said it really was Ss'll Sh'Karr – even Golgoth, who could not call himself a learned man, had heard that name whispered with awe by storytellers who spoke of a reign of blood-mad monsters and the tyrannical daemon lord who ruled over it. Now, a creature calling itself by that same name was towering over him.

'I am,' he said.

Ss'll Sh'Karr's mandibles twisted in what Golgoth guessed to be a smile. 'The Blood God is pleased. Much blood! A fine welcome, a fine awakening!' He laughed, and pistons pumped from the blood-spattered skin of his chest.

'Lord Sh'Karr,' said Golgoth, forcing his voice not to falter, 'we have won more than we could ever hope. Do we have a common enemy here?'

Sh'Karr turned his many eyes past the seething battlefield, to the distant city. He spat a massive smouldering gobbet of boiling gore onto the ground. 'Weak-flesh-god! Prince of cold blood! I ruled a true world. The flesh-god rules a shadow. This cancer of feebleness knows nothing of strength! Of rage!' Sh'Karr's fists clenched and his vast metal wings flapped angrily, gears and motors screaming. 'Of power! Of death!'

'We can kill them together, Lord Sh'Karr!' shouted Golgoth over the din. They could, he realised then. The barbarian horde would grow with every victory, victories made possible by Sh'Karr and his daemons.

They said that daemons were kings amongst liars, and that any alliance with them was death. But Golgoth had felt death already when the Emerald Sword was proved to be a breeding ground for slaves – if it cost his soul to fight this war of revenge, then he would gladly give it, because it meant little enough to him now. 'Your daemons and my warriors,' continued Golgoth. 'They fight alongside one another even now! You can have Torvendis if you want it. I just want revenge.'

Sh'Karr glowered at the city. 'Kill the flesh-god. Take back my world,' he rumbled to himself.

'Do we have an alliance, Lord Sh'Karr?'

There was only the sound of the daemon's massive breathing and the clanking of his machinery as he thought. Golgoth knew that Sh'Karr was insane, in a way that all daemonkind was said to be, but he also knew that daemons responded to the basest of desires like anyone else – Sh'Karr was driven by lust for battle and blood, and to see his god's enemies butchered. Sh'Karr could kill Golgoth where he stood, regardless of Kron's sorcery, and Golgoth felt his stomach knotting with apprehension – but if the deal was made, it would be worth the risk. Worth it all.

Ss'll Sh'Karr spread his iron wings, and a rain of blood began to fall. 'Ss'll Sh'Karr decrees! The king of the warriors and the legions of Khorne are one, as long as the flesh-god's whelps draw breath!' Sh'Karr's voice was a bellow as loud as a thunderstorm. Golgoth glanced around and saw the misshapen, loping daemons heading back from the picking of the battle, bestial faces wild-eyed and snarling. 'This world shall be cleansed and bathed in blood for the glory of the Throne of Skulls! From the ocean depths to the heavens, a reign of war to purge the reign of weakness!'

They were oozing from the cracks in the ground, greyskinned monsters, with long slick talons and faces that were tangled messes of skin and bone.

'Death to the flesh god!' bellowed Ss'll Sh'Karr, as the blood-rain lashed down. 'Blood for the Blood God!'

Daemons were all around, baying and screaming. Golgoth could smell their sickly rancid blood and the greasy smoke coiling from their smouldering skin. He was surrounded by daemons, summoned by Sh'Karr's words, and there seemed to be no end to their number.

If Golgoth went to one of the many hells when he died, it might look something like this. But these were his allies, his to follow and command. He felt his heart swell as it had not done for many years – he could taste victory in the stench of congealing blood.

'Blood for the Blood God!' came the chant, raised from more and more daemonic throats. And then, it was sung by Golgoth himself, and the warriors returning from the battle, until the praises of Khorne on the Brazen Throne of Skulls were being sung by the whole invasion force. It was a challenge to the forces of the city of Slaanesh, an insult to Lady Charybdia herself and everyone that followed her.

Ss'll Sh'Karr had returned. The mountain tribes were united. Nothing could stand in their way now.

WAR WAS COMING. War was already here – it was just waking up, thrashing itself awake with bursts of violence. Captain Amakyre's entire life had been one long war, either preparing for it, meditating on it, or engaging in it. He knew war inside out – he had lived for ten thousand years, since the bloody fracture of the Horus Heresy that capped the Accursed Crusade when half the galaxy had been swallowed by the Imperium, and he had followed the banner of Chaos and the Word Bearers in all that time. His memories were galleries of battle, regimented fragments of a thousand combats, a hundred burning cities and shattered planets, all like polished gems in his head. Ten thousand years of distilled battle, and every one of them bitter with the same taste of war that carried on Torvendis's winds.

Prakordian had told him the same. The deadspeaker had thrown fits, thrashing suddenly and foaming at the mouth, as he let the voices of the dead come to him in the sundown ritual when the pantheon of Chaos was appeased. They were being consumed by daemons and ground against massive fortifications. They were being run down by monsters and trampled by their fellows under the lash. But more than anything else, they were dying afraid, convinced that millions more would follow. The slaves in the mines and the serfs in the field could feel it – they had heard the cry of Sh'Karr's rebirth and seen the bands of tribal warriors running amok. War, thick and bloody, was descending on Torvendis yet again.

Amakyre peered through the wind and the rain that had begun to lash down. A wild storm was approaching, one that would probably have tested the ability of a normal man to survive. This was unusual because the place where Amakyre sheltered behind a pile of boulders had until recently been in the middle of a desert.

The dark, rocky landscape was streaked with black, tarry deposits that Amakyre knew from experience were congealed blood. The sky was as grey as the earth, with sporadic bursts of sheet lightning sending stark silhouettes across the ground. In the centre of a massive depression, as if some vast hollow beneath the earth had collapsed, lay a crater. It appeared as if something had erupted from beneath the earth, scattering chunks of rock like shattered mountains all around. Amakyre's augmented senses picked out twisted metal at the edge of the hole, and the chunks of metallic architecture that had rained down with the rock. The whole landscape was an echo of destruction, a memory of the same cataclysmic event that had woken Amakyre from his half-sleep.

Amakyre spotted movement to the north, flitting over the horizon, coming closer. He drew his bolter and slipped into the shadows behind the rocks, scanning the darkness, breath held.

'Prakordian?' he voxed.

'Captain?'

'Take cover. Targets approaching.'

'Understood.'

Amakyre checked Feorkan and Makelo – all four Word Bearers had been approaching the desert in scattered formation, and only Amakyre had made contact.

More movement, about half a kilometre away, something like a man but rather larger, glinting faintly as it moved between cover. Amakyre risked dodging out of his own cover, moving from shadow to shadow, steps light, bolter raised.

'Captain? Got him.' It was Makelo.

Amakyre froze.

'To your left. Seventy degrees.'

Amakyre glanced up and saw Makelo, scarlet armour dull in the darkness, squinting down the barrel of his bolter. Makelo was amongst the Word Bearers' younger Marines, and one of the brightest – they said there would be great things in store for him if he could survive long enough to call himself a veteran. He was a crack shot, too, even for a Space Marine, and he habitually loaded his stripped-down bolter with silenced shells.

'Clean shot, captain.'

'What's the target?'

There was a pause. Then–

'Gods below,' voxed Makelo. 'You never could keep hidden, Vrox.'

A metallic growl sounded over the vox in response. Vrox hadn't been able to speak since the Obliterator virus had overtaken him, but the emotion was clear.

'Phaedos?' voxed Amakyre on the all-squad channel.

'Greetings, captain,' came the reply. 'All praises.'

Phaedos. Good. Amakyre had known it was a risk splitting up the coven – now Phaedos, Skarlan and Vrox had returned they were at full strength again.

'All praises, Marine,' voxed Amakyre. 'Try not to advertise your presence quite so obviously, Phaedos. If Makelo had been an enemy you would have lost half your firepower.'

Phaedos clambered over a nearby knot of rocks, waving Vrox and Skarlan forward. Phaedos said nothing – but Amakyre knew Phaedos would be meditating on his error at every opportunity, as if somehow acknowledging his failure would give him strength. Phaedos had a burning ambition to become one of the Legion's priests, a Dark Apostle leading the Word Bearers with prayers in battle. He might even make it one day. Stranger things had happened in the Maelstrom, although Phaedos wouldn't be taking up the accursed crozius for a long time yet. He had to suffer a great deal more before he could truly begin to understand Chaos.

'We have heard many things,' Phaedos said as he approached, 'from the natives. We interrogated those we came across. There is great movement between the tribes. They are even coming from the southern forests and the oceans. They have a leader now, a man called Golgoth. There is talk of daemons returning. Could this be Karnulon?'

'Possible,' replied Amakyre. 'But unlikely. He must know we are here, and he would not come so far out into the open. This, however,' – Amakyre gestured at the massive rent in the ground – 'is his doing. Something was let out here, and it would take a sorcerer of rare power to do it.'

Phaedos led Vrox and Skarlan over the rock to Amakyre's position. He looked towards the huge crater and murmured a prayer to the Pantheon under his breath, realising the sort of power that must have been unleashed to create such a wound in the earth.

'A sorcerer's stink is all over this place,' said Prakordian, emerging from the gloom. 'He is haemorrhaging power. If he doesn't stop soon, he will bleed himself dry.' He paused, considering. 'He doesn't care if he dies.' Prakordian's pupils were dilated and he swayed as he walked, as if drunk. And he was drunk, on the sorcery that remained from the spell of release and the energy that had bled out of the tomb when it had been shattered.

'What does he want?' said Makelo, who was still on lookout on the pile of rocks. 'It makes no sense, captain. Karnulon has served since before the Heresy, he has learned at the court of Primarch Lorgar himself. He has had more than enough opportunity for sabotage and treachery. If he just wanted to make the Legion suffer, he could have done it without running. There is nothing on Torvendis of any significance to him. What is he trying to do? Why start a war here, when his whole life has been war with the Word Bearers?'

Makelo was right, as was often the case – this was not just a mission to find and eliminate Karnulon, but to find out what could cause such a senior member of the Word Bearers to abandon his Legion. Of all the Traitor Legions, the Word Bearers could claim the greatest discipline and fanaticism to the cause of Chaos – anything that could sunder that discipline was a far greater danger than Karnulon himself.

'If Karnulon is with this Golgoth, then we must hurry, or we could easily lose him,' said Amakyre, addressing the whole coven. 'Prakordian says his army has broken through Lady Charybdia's outer defences and is invading the kingdom itself. When the battle for Lady Charybdia's city begins, there will be half a continent of war for Karnulon to lose himself in. Feorkan?'

'Captain?' voxed the scout.

'You have the point. Makelo, Vrox, take the rear. Prakordian, stay with me. Head for the southern wall, we need to be where the killing is. All praises, Word Bearers. Move out.'

WORD SPREADS, ON Torvendis, faster than the suns travel across the sky. An event momentous enough will be known within scant hours on all corners of the world, as if the rocks and seas and winds carried the news.

It took a cataclysmic event indeed to cut through the chatter of legends and grab the planet's attention. But a threat to Lady Charybdia, who had dominated Torvendis for so long, was something worth talking about. The planet had known there would be war – there always was eventually, if it was only patient enough. It just needed a spark to set the battlefield alight – the stain of Ss'll Sh'Karr was spreading again. Someone had managed to weld the rabble from the mountains into something to be feared, and there was a breach in the western walls through which an army had poured. It could be the start of a new cycle on the daemon world, a new dance of powers to see who had the honour of holding the planet for another century.

The Canis Mountains emptied of the tribes that remained – some inspired by tales of Golgoth's victories, others in fear that Golgoth would return in triumph and exterminate those who had not marched alongside him. The Raptor tribe and the scattered swamp nomads who followed the totem of the Lizard made their way across the mountains and through the breach, mixing with the growing horde blazing its way eastwards.

Nations of headhunters and shamans uprooted themselves from the steaming jungles and headed northwards, some claiming they had been directed by a mysterious wizard to join Golgoth's crusade, others following the howls of daemons. Canoes hacked from sentient trees swarmed up new rivers running through what had once been the deserts, and columns of warriors snaked their way northwards as they followed the dance of the stars.

Longboats from the fractured mountain coast brought a host of raiding tribes, subjugated for so long by the Serpent, who saw in Golgoth a leader who could elevate them above the Serpent if they proved their worth in battle. At the breach they met raiders from the other side of the planet, who had sailed junks from the broken islands to the south of the continent, looking to build a nation of their own in the ruins of Lady Charybdia's city. There were even desert tribesmen, their homelands destroyed, who were just looking for something or someone to fight for and were drawn towards Golgoth's horde as if by gravity.

From every corner of Torvendis they came, peoples too few or powerless to be worth exterminating, who Lady Charybdia's advisors had never heard of but who, when they came together under one banner, numbered too many to count. By the time Ss'll Sh'Karr and Golgoth of the Emerald Sword reached the boundaries of the city proper, they led an army bigger than any seen on Torvendis for hundreds of years.

Torvendis loved wars, for nothing created legends like the sound of steel through flesh. As the taste of slaughter found its way into the air and the rivers of the planet, the soil readied itself for yet another soaking of blood and the air prepared to carry ever more screams to the heavens.

CHAPTER SEVEN

THE FEW SOULS who tried to record Torvendis's history inevitably went insane, but what few cohesive threads they found were usually those that linked the titanic battles of the daemon world's past. And many of the most revered legends of Torvendis concerned those battles – the explosive fractures in history when one power gave way to another, or a ruler emerged from anarchy. Many, many forces had staked a claim to Torvendis – some sponsored by the dark powers of the warp, others acting entirely alone as opportunists or usurpers – such was the symbolic power of the world at the centre of the Maelstrom. And always, when one power wished to wrest control from another, the incumbent was not willing to give up Torvendis without a fight.

The Crimson Knights took hold of their kingdom after a year-long siege of the Pontifex's island fortress, sending huge war-junks bearing terrible daemonic siege engines and galleys crammed with rotting slave-warriors to assault the granite walls. Ss'll Sh'Karr's daemonic legion shattered a massive psychic army of the Change God on the plains of frost. Mutander and his diseased warrior-monks fought a guerrilla war against the iron empire of the Thousand that, in the end, lasted far longer than Mutander's reign itself. Even the skies of Torvendis were repeatedly fought over, such as when clouds of harpies fought for supremacy in the ancient monstrous ages and the silken bird-engines of a hundred nations competed for a newly-risen continent in the southern seas.

It was through cataclysmic battles such as these that the landscape of power on Torvendis changed even more rapidly than its geography. The greatest of them all, of course, was that first contest between Arguleon Veq and the Last, a fight between two individuals which nonetheless saw greater destruction brought to bear than any single clash in the planet's history. Others have claimed that their victories eclipsed those of Veq, and even that the enemy they vanquished was more terrible than the unknown horror of the Last, but their rantings are little more than gossip in the endless web of history that forms all life on the planet. But there are always new prophecies and predictions that one day there will be an even greater battle on the planet, just as there are those who claim that the greatest days of Torvendis are gone and there will never be bloodshed as majestic as that unleashed by Veq and the Last.

Only one fact is never disputed. No one dares predict the future. The wisest sage and the most deluded prophet would dare claim that Torvendis will ever be at peace.

TARN CRAWLED FORWARD on his belly, keeping his profile lower than the rocks and the undulations in the earth. It was a real thieves' curse of a night – the sky was milky with stars that covered the land with a gloomy half-light, while the Slaughtersong was dilated and wan. A decent eye could see a rat moving on a night like this, but Tarn was under no illusions that he could afford to put the foray off for another night – Golgoth's army had swollen to awe-inspiring size and he would have to make his move on the city now or the horde would fall apart.

The landscape could, at a glance, pass for natural, but it was anything but. The rises of land outside the boundaries of Lady

Charybdia's city were not hills, but half-buried buildings, melted organically into the ground like animals wallowing in a swamp. Clumps of trees that nestled between decaying galleries and amphitheatres were not trees at all, but clusters of listing columns. The cruel starlight picked out sculptures on pediments lolling from the sandy earth. The city, they said, was always expanding because it grew of its own accord, seeding itself in its hinterland and sprouting buildings and roadways that would migrate towards their parent.

Tarn waved forward the closest men, most of them Serpent warriors who, it had turned out, excelled at stealth and were almost as hard-bitten killers as Tarn himself. There were a few others, too, desert tribesmen whose innate magic made the shadows gather around them and a couple of reeking swamp nomads who could kill a man so fast he didn't know he was dead.

'Anyone lost?' whispered Tarn to the closest man, a sallow-skinned Serpent with black teeth and a twin-bladed dagger permanently in his hand.

'Kin'rik's mob took a wrong turn an hour back,' replied the Serpent.

'We won't see them again,' said Tarn. He didn't care much for the Serpent – he had killed almost as many of them over the years as he had of his own tribe – but they were admirable butchers and he needed to keep as many of them alive as possible to ensure that someone got back to Golgoth by daybreak. 'Over the next rise and we'll be in bowshot of the outskirts. Give the word, everyone moves as one. Find out what you can and get back without being seen. If anyone's out here when the suns come up, nothing can save them.'

The Serpent nodded and slunk off. Quickly, silently, the order would be spreading. The infiltrating force was in position, and now the mission proper began.

Tarn dragged himself along the ground. The highest pinnacles of the city, topped with pinpoints of light, came into view past the lip of the rise. Even Tarn's mind registered astonishment as the city came into view and he saw it for the first time, huge and terrible, bristling with light and malice.

The city was a hideous masterpiece. Tarn wondered how it could possibly still be standing – immense top-heavy towers were suspended over the endless pits of the mines by walkways and bridges that looked from this distance like lengths of silver gossamer. Every one of those bulbous towers was ringed by galleries and balconies, and on those balconies were untold thousands of legionaries and armed citizens, bows and spears catching the sickly light, lashes and pain-goads deadly in the hands of the civilians who had given up a night's revelries to stand their watch. Tarn knew very little about what went on in those buildings – very few from outside the city would want to – but he had some idea of how serious Golgoth's threat must be for the city to give up a night of its sacred pleasure to stand guard. The whole city seemed alive, and Tarn would have sworn the towers pulsed slowly, almost imperceptibly, as if they were breathing.

The city was Tarn's target. The order of the night was not killing for once, but information. Golgoth was not a leader of much finesse, but even he liked to know what he was up against. He had few seers in his army (not least since he had burned all the Sword's own wizards alive), so that knowledge had to come from the sharp eyes of men like Tarn.

A bright lance of fire leapt from the top of one tower and, in the flash of light that bloomed further along the slope, Tarn knew that infiltrators must have been spotted by lookouts and died for their clumsiness. The hot whistle of bowfire sounded sporadically as archers on the outer towers of the city loosed shots at movement they sighted. Few Serpent or nomads would survive this night, thought Tarn. Not that it really mattered, as long as someone returned – preferably him.

The wind was a low steady keening and Tarn could pick out few sounds from the city. But beneath his hands, vibrating through his prone body, he could feel the drone of thousands upon thousands of voices murmuring prayers and threats, moans of pain and growls of anger. Tarn couldn't see them but he could feel them – slaves, immense herds of them, lashed into crowds ready to be forced forward into an unwilling army. The tactic had already been used once and Ss'll

Sh'Karr had rolled over them just a handful of days before. But Tarn knew that if every slave in the city were to come pouring out of the mines into the path of the attacking horde, Golgoth's warriors and the Blood God's daemons could become mired in carnage while the city remained untouched.

Ah, the daemons. Tarn had fought alongside all manner of savages and butchers, men he would not turn his back on lest he get a dagger through his ribs and men he would have killed on principle had he a scrap of morality in his heart. But even he felt sourness in his mouth at the prospect of daemons calling themselves his allies. He had seen the daemons in the service of Lady Charybdia kill with lust, and still bore the writhing, fleshy scars on his mind's eye. Daemons were monsters, human neither in form nor in thought, fragments of the will of their god and hence with intentions impossible to predict. And the concept of the Blood God filled Tarn with terror. Tarn killed with skill and speed, but those who followed the Blood God – they called him Khorne, the Taker of Skulls, Lord Gore, and all manner of other titles – fought with nothing more than blind savagery and bloodlust. They would throw wave after wave of willing soldiers into any hopeless fight, and they fought not for victory but for the sheer joy of carnage. Victory for the Blood God's worshippers consisted of spilling as much gore as possible and, preferably, but not essentially, surviving to do it again the next day.

But Lady Charybdia called daemons of her own god from the warp to kill for her, so it made sense that Golgoth should find a similar ally. And there was no doubt that Ss'll Sh'Karr – whether he was the daemon prince of legend or not – led the most brutally effective shock troops Tarn had ever seen in a lifetime of slaughter. But still… daemons. Gods above, that it would come to this!

There was no more he would find out this night. The city was brimming with defenders and more slaves than a man could count. They would have to be carved through before any man even set foot in the city itself. It was as he expected. Golgoth would probably be pleased, for Tarn suspected he wanted as hard and cruel a battle as possible.

A couple more Serpent warriors died as flaming arrows lanced down, like fireflies scattering. Tarn turned and writhed back over the rise, to head back to Golgoth's camp and report what he had seen.

If the battle that Golgoth wanted took place, hardly anything would survive. Tarn reasoned that he would be unlikely to be amongst them, having ridden his luck far too much over the last weeks. But he didn't really mind. Most people died eventually, and if there was any battle in which to meet his end, this was it.

NIGHT WAS DAY to auto-senses. It amused Commander Demetrius of the Violators that lesser, unimproved men thought darkness was an advantage. He could see the arrows from his vantage point on the inner walls of Charybdia Keep, as they flitted down from the city's edge towards some enemy infiltrator. A few of the enemy might return with intelligence about the city's defences, but what could they really tell? There were more than enough soldiers garrisoning the many buildings and crossroads to face any invader. And even if the enemy knew about the four hundred Violators Space Marines forming a ring of steel around Lady Charybdia's Keep, by the time any of them reached this far they would be few in number and bled nearly dry. It would be good sport, thought Demetrius, for the men he left behind to defend the keep. Not as good, though, as the quarry for which he would lead the hunt.

Demetrius flexed his massive metal frame, feeling the weight of the assault cannon and the sinuous, living tendrils of the neuro-lash. He racked smoke grenades into the launchers on the upper surface of his carapace, feeling the ovoid canisters filling the breech, spinning the barrels of the cannon and letting the massive-calibre ammunition trickle enticingly through the chambers. Demetrius itched all over for battle, from his wet fleshy core to the sensitive sheets of armaplas protecting his sarcophagus.

Once, he had been terrified of being entombed in a frigid cold ceramite box, unable to feel the sensations that gave him reason to kill. But Demetrius's nervous system, refusing to give up its lifeblood of pleasure-pain, grew like roots into the fabric of the dreadnought body and made him more sensitive to the tide of battle than he had ever been as an able-bodied Space Marine. Yes, it would be a good fight. He longed to feel fire scoring his paintwork and blood spattering his artificer-honed armour plates.

'Commander?' voxed a voice in Demetrius's ear. Demetrius turned to see Techmarine Klaes, a tendriled servo-arm reaching blindly over his shoulder pad.

'Techmarine. We are ready?'

'The fleet is prepared. They were hungry after so long, it took some effort to wake them up and get them fed. But they can fly at an hour's notice.'

'Good. I want you with us, Klaes. Nothing can succeed without the fleet, and they listen to you above all other.'

'I am proud to serve.'

'You will be proud when the Blood God's whelp is dead, Klaes. For now, revel in the battle and remember for whose praises you fight.'

Klaes nodded his helmeted head. Like many Violators he never removed any part of his armour – Slaanesh looked favourably on the Chapter and often altered their bodies so their sensations and pleasures were more immediate. No one knew for sure what Klaes really looked like any more – and that was part of what made the Violators beloved of Slaanesh. Every Marine was a temple to the Pleasure God, his flesh sacred and inviolate, and displaying those holy mutations was like throwing open the doors of a temple to any passer-by. Demetrius himself rarely revealed what he looked like beneath the massive armoured hull of the dreadnought body. When he did, it was in the presence of only those who truly represented the ideals of Slaanesh, like Lady Charybdia herself, or that of a great enemy before the kill.

'The force is selected then, commander?' said Klaes.

'Our best,' replied Demetrius, voice grating from the dreadnought's vox-casters. 'Koivas. Haggin. Most of the Assault units. Plenty of steel, plenty of battle-lust.' Demetrius turned back to look out over the city, with its millions of lights and glittering seas of spearpoints. 'Lead the battle-brothers in their wargear rites. They must feel every bullet they fire. There will not be another fight like this on Torvendis for a good long time.'

Klaes headed off below the battlements, to bless the bolt-guns and armour of the Violators, that Slaanesh might send every sensation they felt straight into the soul of the wielder. Haggin would be murmuring prayers devotedly, while Koivas would be filling his system with the cocktails of combat drugs he had become all but immune to. Devriad's squad would be carving devotions onto one another's armour. Every Violator would be shuddering with anticipation for the battle – Slaanesh had ordained that every one of them would see bloodshed when the sun next went down, both those who stayed to defend the keep and those who accompanied Demetrius on Lady Charybdia's own sacred mission.

It would be a good day, thought Demetrius. One of the best.

LADY CHARYBDIA LOOKED down from the balcony over the assembled seers and sorcerers. Plucked from all over the city and brought into the gatehouse of the keep, they were young and old, deformed and pristine, male and female and everything in between. There were hundreds of them in the crowd below, and only a very few knew why they had been called here. The tall stone walls of the gatehouse cast a shadow over the crowd and they shivered in the lightless cold. Most of them had been dragged from their beds and herded through the streets to the keep – some were still naked and painted from the pleasure-domes.

Lady Charybdia had her spies keep a record of all those born with sorcerous talents. She knew she would need them in a situation like this, because she liked to know who she was fighting, and the best way to know was to ask her enemy. For that, she needed a plentiful supply of those born with sorcery in their blood.

The few below who saw her and recognised her through their fear flinched and went pale.

A gaggle of sages, swamped in voluminous robes, trailed in Lady Charybdia's wake, keeping a respectful distance.

Lady Charybdia waved an impatient hand and they scuttled
forward, murmuring sacred words, making complex gestures with their hands. A filmy white light, like a pale gauze,
fell over the crowd below – some of them whimpered in
fear, others said their own prayers for salvation.

'Have you found him?' asked Lady Charybdia of her sages.

One of the sages was thrust forward to speak. 'Yes, my
lady. He is not a difficult target, we can smell him from here.'

'Good. You are ready?'

'A last few syllables and it will be complete, my lady.'

'Then proceed.'

A few moments more, and the spell was cast. Shapes
and lights flickered in the air in front of Lady Charybdia,
powered by the energy of her unwilling sorcerers and
focused by the lore of her sages. The image hardened
until it was something shaped like a man, then like a
deformed man, then like something else entirely with
strange growths sprouting from its back and its forehead.
Nauseating energy rolled off it, pure malevolence. Low
moans rose from the crowd as the older and more infirm
dropped dead, drained of their lifeforce by the hunger of
the spell.

'Ha!' cried the image. 'She watches! She sees! She sees her
death!'

'You are the one who calls itself Ss'll Sh'Karr,' said Lady
Charybdia coldly.

The image coalesced into the form of the daemon prince.
Life-sized, it towered over the balcony, massive bestial head
thrust forwards out of the nimbus of power that formed the
scrying window. It could see her, too.

It grimaced at her. Lady Charybdia could not remember
seeing an uglier creature. 'The flesh-god rots you, lady. He
drains your strength. This land will be bathed in blood to
wash away his stink.'

'The Blood God abandoned this world long ago, daemon,'
replied Lady Charybdia coldly. 'Ss'll Sh'Karr was trapped and
slain by those he tried to subjugate.'

'I am free!' bellowed the image, and with the exclamation
more of the crowd died, blood pouring from their noses and

ears. Lady Charybdia shut out the annoying buzz of their death cries.

'The Blood God saw his world made weak and set me upon it!' continued the daemon. 'I am his hound of war! My hand is his hand!' The daemon's voice was a bellow so loud it shook the stones of the gatehouse and knocked the frailer sages off their feet.

'You are not Ss'll Sh'Karr,' said Lady Charybdia calmly. 'Ss'll Sh'Karr is dead.' She clapped her hands briskly and a quartet of well-muscled legionaries marched out onto the balcony, holding between them the massive skull that had been nailed up in the chapel of the keep. The monstrous skull of Ss'll Sh'Karr. 'They took his head,' she continued. 'The same as I shall take yours.'

The daemon peered out from the image at the immense skull, the empty eye sockets returning his gaze. The daemon's face twisted, its mandibles parting, and Lady Charybdia realised it was smiling.

Then it began to laugh. It was a hideous, hacking, roaring sound, and with every bark of laughter members of the sorcerous crowd died as their bodies ruptured wetly. The daemon lifted a steel-taloned hand to its face and dug the claws into its ugly grey flesh, tearing at the rubbery skin and into the dark wet muscle underneath. The monster that called itself Ss'll Sh'Karr dug its palm into its face, grabbing a massive handful of flesh, and pulling.

Like scraps of a wet, gory mask, the daemon's face was torn out, stringy sinews snapping, hot gobbets of ichor raining off the image. The illusory blood mingled with the real blood welling up from the crowd, now a heaving, moaning mass of the dying.

The burning eyes smiled hideously. The fanged mandibles leered in a broken rictus, slick with the daemon's own blood. As the gore ran off the ruined face, Lady Charybdia saw what the daemon had found so amusing.

Its skull was forged of brass. Its mandibles were hinged sheets of metal, with steaming pistons powering the throat. Alchemical fires burned deep within its jaws and flickered in its eyes. Exposed to the air, the brass was beginning to smoulder with the heat.

'They thought they had killed me, the vermin and slaves who tried to face me! They thought I had been banished, just because they took my head! It takes more than one wound to bring down the Blood God's will incarnate. I forged a new skull, and showed them how the soldiers of Khorne avenge themselves!'

It occurred to Lady Charybdia that what the daemon said might actually be true. Her sages certainly believed it – many were voiding themselves in fear, quaking even more than they did when Lady Charybdia herself was displeased. She had, herself, bowed in awe before daemons in her distant past, and if truth be told she felt no little apprehension at the fact that Ss'll Sh'Karr himself might really be camped outside her city with untold legions of daemons and barbarian followers.

The titanic image of the daemon shuddered and faded. Lady Charybdia glanced down from the gatehouse balcony to where the heaped bodies of the sacrifices lay, their life-forces drained by the effort of powering the sages' spell. Only a few still lived, and they were thrashing as their lungs collapsed and blood seeped from their noses and ears. Even once the survivors had crawled off, thought Lady Charybdia, it would leave a terrible mess.

A shame. They might have one day served her as sorcerers and seers – but their sacrifice was a small price to pay if it gave some clue as to the nature of her enemy. The image was gone now, leaving only the fading pinpoints of fire that had burned in the eyes of the brass skull. A few more divinations would give a better idea of whether this really was the daemon prince who had forged a reign of blood that still left scars on Torvendis, but for now the ceremony was over.

One thing was certain. The invading horde would have to make their attack before the night was over – the barbarian army would fall apart without food or water, and only by attacking and seizing the city would they hope to keep up the momentum of their invasion. All the signs spoke of another well-lit night, with the stars and moons gathering to watch the battle – it would happen tonight, when the barbarians would think the city's archers were at a disadvantage. If Ss'll Sh'Karr was at their head, he would carry with him the weight of legend, but Lady Charybdia had not been idle as queen. Her city brimmed over with traps and killing grounds, where even unarmed slaves and slovenly hedonist-priests would have their uses in blocking up the narrow arteries of walkways.

Ss'll Sh'Karr could attack if he wished. His army would be repulsed, and the Violators would see to it that even forging a new skull wouldn't be enough to save the daemon. Lady Charybdia swept back into the keep, leaving her sages to deal with the cleanup. There were new legends to write before the sun came up again.

GOLGOTH CROUCHED BEHIND the tangle of rocks, painfully aware of how exposed he was, almost within bowshot of the city. He knew that it would take little more than a sharp-eyed archer and a quick-witted sorcerer to put an arrow in his eye. But Ss'll Sh'Karr had insisted that Golgoth be present to see this, and he imagined that it would be unwise to snub his ally. So Tarn had led him to this spot and told him to keep his head down as he watched what Sh'Karr had planned. There were others here, too, infiltrators culled from the Serpent and the desert peoples, who would raise the signal to the rest of the horde when the time was right.

Golgoth knew Sh'Karr's plan. The key tribal leaders knew – Lutr'Kya of the Serpent was even now leading the warchants of her warriors and the south island headhunters had picked their deadliest butchers to fight alongside the Serpent in the spearhead. It would be better killing than either had seen for decades. It was, quite frankly, an insane way to begin a battle, but then Golgoth had rarely placed much faith in a balanced mind. And whatever happened, it would be as good a way to die as any.

Ss'll Sh'Karr stomped over the nearest rise, massive strides taking him towards the city. Sighting shots whistled down from the city, and one or two even hit and bounced off his thick daemonic skin. Ss'll Sh'Karr had torn off his face to reveal a dimly glowing brazen skull. Golgoth found it hard to imagine that anything the monstrous daemon prince did could surprise him any more.

Silver flashes marked spell-wrought arrows that stuck into Sh'Karr's flesh and dissolved in the heat rolling off him. He ignored them and began to chant.

These were old words and the language was painful to hear, rolling and guttural from Sh'Karr's inhuman throat. The wind rose to echo the daemon's words and Golgoth recognised the intricate patterns of sound and the reverberations of power that had haunted Kron's spells. But this was on a different scale – this was massive, setting the rocks shuddering and the very fires on the city's watchtowers flickering.

Sh'Karr was yelling now, bellowing prayers to the Blood God that were old when Torvendis was young. Golgoth's view of the city blurred as the air itself shook with power, and strange lights were flashing in the skies. The stars began to fade from view, recoiling from the magnitude of sorcery that Sh'Karr was calling up.

Then, there was another sound, rolling beneath the wind and the chanting. It was a sound Golgoth had heard many times before – too many times, in the thick of battle and dead of night alike.

Screaming.

In the endless pits beneath the city, millions of slaves were screaming.

THE CITY HAD been built on the site of a great plain across which had been fought battles without number. Some of the greatest conflicts the Maelstrom had ever seen had ebbed and flowed across that land, one of the few stable places on Torvendis, and lain down the endless layers of war dead that Lady Charybdia's slave hordes had mined for the pure experience of conflict. There were near-limitless mounds of corpses compressed and ossified into fossil strata, massive daemonic war engines and gargantuan beasts of battle. Bullet shells were sown in the ground like crop seeds. The ground yielded an unending crop of corroded blades and arrowheads.

But the most potent of all the layers was the furthest down, beneath the bones of prehistoric monsters and the skeletons of daemons, bound to their mangled remains but far from dead. It was the place where the heat of Torvendis's core met the corrupted outer crust.

It was where the blood from all those battles had flowed down and settled, an ocean of gore filtering through layers of the dead. It was a vast, invisible underground sea lying under immense pressure in the pores of fossilised bones and between strata of stone.

The blood had been there ever since the first drop had been shed on Torvendis, from the days when the Last ruled the planet and Arguleon Veq had the strength to challenge it. Every creature killed on the plains was represented by a drop in that ocean of death.

A lake of blood lay beneath Lady Charybdia's city. It was to this that Ss'll Sh'Karr spoke, for there was nothing more sacred to unholy Khorne than an ocean of the blood that was shed in his holy tribute.

The slaves knew it first. The walls of the mines were bleeding, and blood was pooling up around their feet. Many tried to run, whole gangs breaking from their chains and charging in huge scrums up the slopes of spoil, guards lashing at them. Many others gave thanks to whatever god had taken pity on them for letting them die at last.

The blood burst in torrents from fractures in the mine faces. It fountained from the ground in hot red geysers, it crashed against the foundations of the city's mightiest towers. The level rose and closed over the heads of the slaves who had given up on any hope of freedom, and swirled around the ankles of those who tried to flee up the sharp rock faces. It even carried some of the most resourceful, those who had managed to find something that would float, upwards towards the lowest walkways of the city itself.

The magnitude of the death dealt in the first few minutes of Ss'll Sh'Karr's attack sent hideous dark waves of death throes pulsing through the sensitive streets of the city. They rippled up the walls of the keep, fouled the wine and wilted the plants in the pleasure-gardens. Not even Mape and all

Lady Charybdia's counsellors and sages had ever been able to calculate the true numbers of the slaves that toiled in the mine-pits – anything up to two hundred and fifty thousand drowned in the half-hour it took the mines to fill with blood.

The defenders of the city looked on in horror as the corruption of the Blood God befouled their city, waves of it crashing against the lower levels of the towers, huge swells swallowing the guard outposts suspended above the pits and sweeping away the lowest walkways. When elaborate stained-glass windows gave way, gouts of blood pumped into the towers and exploded upwards to fountain spectacularly over balconies and through the mouths of doorways.

The centurions bellowed to the defenders to hold fast. The assault had come from an unusual quarter, but then what was to be expected when the Butcher God sent its minions against the fair city? They had all heard the legends where nations were drowned in rivers of blood during the days of Ss'll Sh'Karr, but they had also heard of how that daemon was defeated and killed. Nothing could destroy the city that Lady Charybdia had built, much less unclean barbarians and the remnants of a foul empire that had already outstayed its welcome on Torvendis.

This was just the prelude. When the real attack came, it would hurtle into the teeth of a city now brimming with the rage of Slaanesh.

THE HORROR UNFOLDING beneath the city was the cue for the attackers to advance. When the first waves of blood lapped at the edge of the mine pits, the desert folk sent up bright alchemical flares and the Serpent sent signal arrows shrieking. The spearheads, assembled in narrow columns behind ripples of high ground, picked up their heavy loads and began the charge towards the city.

Ten thousand Serpent under Lutr'Kya, and a contingent of near-naked headhunters under Skorkan the Gouger of the Southern Ocean, formed the first wave. The Serpent hauled longboats edged with shields, and every warrior had an oar alongside their axe or sword. The headhunters carried eight-man canoes hacked from thick-boled jungle trees with the withered heads of their enemies nailed to the prows, and were armed with stone-headed picks blessed by the thousand snake gods of the islands. Skorkan himself was at the place of honour at their head, the skulls of his most notable enemies forced under his skin so they bulged from his torso like cancerous growths.

They charged towards the city under the cover of a swirling sandstorm conjured up by the desert nomads. The headhunters, with their lighter craft, leapt into the blood ocean first, pushing off in their canoes and paddling furiously towards the closest towers. The Serpent launched their longboats in the headhunters' wake, arrows plunging into the blood ocean around them. Just as they had done down the corpse-choked rivers of the southern islands and along the broken northern coasts, the first raiders attacked by boat, and there was little the massed defenders of the city could do to stop them in the first minutes of the horde's attack.

The defenders had imagined almost any method of invasion, but an amphibious assault had not been anticipated. There were precious few legionaries defending the lower levels and the ranks of archers had to redeploy hastily before they could send accurate volleys of arrows into the sea of blood directly below them. Thousands of warriors on hundreds of boats were launching from the western shore of the blood ocean, chanting battle-songs to the sound of tribal drums and shrill war-skirls. They seemed without number, and they very nearly were.

Skorkan the Gouger reserved for himself the honour of being the first invader to set foot in the city, as his royal war-canoe burst through the scenic window of a low-level pleasure dome, carried on a cascade of blood into the worship-pit where a few drained revellers still lay. The stone-headed weapons of Skorkan and his retainers tasted their first kills of many as they cut through the degenerate pleasure-priests and charged up the winding stairways.

The battle had begun. The horde of Golgoth and Ss'll Sh'Karr had done the unthinkable and violated the city itself. As the word went round the defenders that there were outsiders within the bounds of the city, the message became clear.

Slaanesh was angry with this unprecedented offence. Slaanesh would be avenged.

COMMANDER DEMETRIUS FLICKED through the vox-channels, relishing the taste of the confusion. He revelled in the potential of his allies' terror – the graver the threat, the more profound the thrill of battle. It was clever, he thought, how the horde had attacked, raising the ocean and sending in those who had survived raiding the rivers and seas. Worthy, almost, of a Space Marine's planning. But not quite.

Below Demetrius, the waves of the new blood ocean crashed against the walls that ringed Charybdia Keep. Floating bodies were gathering against the buttresses of the defences, and as more rose to the surface there would be a formidable, stinking flotsam at the base of the walls. But it made no difference how many slaves and conscripts died this day. No matter what the attacking hordes could dream up, they would never be able to get past these walls and into the keep. Not when the Violators were here to meet them.

Demetrius would not be among them. He had other matters to attend to.

There was a sudden roar behind him. He pivoted his massive dreadnought body to see the beast rising from its moorings behind the wall, as did all the hundred Marines Demetrius had assembled on the walls. They were mostly Assault Marines, trained for close-quarter bloodshed, armed with chainswords and other, more exotic weapons they had fashioned or found. Haggin, who led one of the largest warbands, wore a huge scissoring crab-like power claw on each hand. Koivas fought with the barbed tendrils that grew from the lower half of his face as mandibles, keeping his hands for the twin bolt pistols he always carried. Their armour was pale blue, often stained with the juices of their bodies that ran from the joints or riven with battle-scars worn proudly. Every head was turned towards the beast that rose level with the battlements amidst the bellowing of its engines.

The Thunderhawk gunship was monstrous. Its wings were covered in thick, gnarled skin, between which was suspended the huge underslung fuselage painted in the Violators' colours. Muscular tentacles had grown through the metal and clung all over the hull like roots. The front viewports were deformed into warped metal slits, pale glows leering out. Nothing living had been into the cockpit of the Thunderhawk gunship for centuries, ever since a daemon had first been enticed into the craft's machine-spirit. Now the whole fleet was a menacing flock of huge winged beasts, able to strike from the air with greater speed and precision than even a Marine pilot could manage.

A further pair of Thunderhawks, similarly mutated, rose above the battlements. They turned and their bellies opened, revealing payload compartments ringed with grav-cushioned benches. Demetrius waved his whip-arm and Koivas yelled an order to his men, who clambered up into the belly of the first Thunderhawk. The other warbands followed suit, a hundred Marines in total, enough Violators to grace any battlefield. Demetrius himself stood under the last Thunderhawk as tentacles draped down from the payload compartment and wrapped around him. They hauled his huge metal body up into the heart of the craft and the fuselage closed beneath him.

There were thirty Marines in here with him, seventy more in the other craft, bathed in the dim biological glow of the Thunderhawks' innards. The air was thick and close, and smelled of the potent warrior-hormones that coursed through the veins of the Violators.

'Klaes?' voxed Demetrius.

'Commander?' replied the Techmarine.

'Take us out.'

'Yes, sir.'

The grav-couches engaged as the Thunderhawk shot forward, carrying with it the intention to slay the Blood God's spawn for a second time.

GOLGOTH FELT THE arrow thunking into the wood of his shield as he held it over his head and pushed hard against the hull of the longboat. The stink and shouting of the Serpent and Emerald Sword warriors was all around him, as a hundred-strong wave of boats was launched along the edge of the blood ocean. Above him loomed the bulbous-headed towers ringed with balconies and strung with walkways, on which Golgoth caught glimpses of tiny, distant figures launching a rain of arrows against the attackers. Before him stretched the choppy sea of blood, criss-crossed with the waves of a thousand boats storming across it. Already they were saying that Skorkan had spilt blood. Golgoth felt a sharp pang of jealousy – he wanted to kill. Rarely had he felt it this strong. Maybe it was Ss'll Sh'Karr bringing the influence of the Blood God, or maybe it was just that he was so close to the tyrant who had corrupted the Emerald Sword. Either way, soon there would be more blood on his hands, and he thanked all the gods for it.

A final heave, and the longboat slid into the pink-foaming surf. Golgoth leapt on as the boat was launched, and twenty other warriors did the same. Every man grabbed an oar and began paddling to the beat of the helmsman's drum, the dragon-headed prow cutting through the waves of gore.

Golgoth clambered past the warriors and leaned out over the prow, the blood waves speeding by beneath him, the boat knocking aside floating bodies. He could see the southern islanders speeding their canoes towards the lowest towers, and one tower was even now teeming with warriors trading blowpipe darts with arrows.

'Where are you?' he yelled above the chanting and the drums. 'Where are you? I'll tear your guts out, you bitch! I'll eat your heart!'

He could feel her, somewhere up there in the heart of the city – a cancer, an arrogance that dared corrupt the souls of his brothers. Lady Charybdia had given Golgoth a reason to fight, and she would regret it for the rest of her short, painful life.

He pointed towards the nearest tower, a huge-bellied construction of black stone lapped by the waves of blood from which projected a long, slender spire topped with a glass sphere. 'There!' he cried to the helmsman.

The men cheered as the longboat swung round towards the tower, and they saw the archers scrambling over its upper surface to take up firing positions.

Arrows were falling more thickly now. Golgoth spotted warriors flailing and tumbling over the side of their boats, or falling back into the hull and being pitched over the side by their comrades as dead weight. A sorcerous blast, like a lightning bolt, shattered the prow of one ship, sending broken bodies flailing into the blood. Somewhere in the distance, through the forest of towers, a pleasure-barge with pastel silken sails had been launched and was fending off swarms of headhunter canoes.

Arrows thudded into the woodwork of the longboat from the fat-bellied tower. One man screamed, his arm pinned to his oar by a white-fletched shaft. Golgoth wrenched it free, kicked the wailing man over the edge, and took up the oar himself.

The helmsmen steered them towards a yawning hole in the tower wall, where a huge window had shattered under the pressure. The drumbeat hammered faster as the longboat hurtled through the gauntlet of the archers, volleys of arrows splintering against the shield they held overhead. Another man's death-scream was a strangled gurgle as an arrowhead tore open his throat. The helmsman was pitched backwards over the stern, two arrows in his chest, and another warrior took up the tiller to hold them on course.

The side of the hull scraped angrily against stone as the longboat coursed through the window and into the body of the tower. Golgoth's eyes adjusted to the darkness and he could see writhing, humanoid sculptures encrusting the walls, silks and bodies bobbing, shafts of weak light filtering in through skylights stained with incense. Spices and burnt offerings formed a scum on the surface of the blood. The inside of the tower was a single spherical cavity covered in sculpture. The lantern-spheres had been snuffed out by the cascade of blood when the window had first shattered and now the place was lit only by faint shafts of light filtering down from where the hollow spire joined the top of the sphere, and a few round skylights in the upper surface.

'Up the walls!' someone yelled, and warriors reached out to grab the gold-leafed sculpture and drag the longboat to the wall. Clambering out, they began to climb the sculpture just as the first arrows came whistling down through the sky-lights. The warriors slung their shields over their backs to protect them as they climbed.

Golgoth could smell the enemy, perfumed and effemi-nate. He could taste their cowardice and degeneracy. He dipped into the well of power inside him that Kron had taught of, sent it coursing through his arms and into the hands that dragged him upwards. An arrow spanged against the perverse sculpture by the side of his head, but he ignored it. One of the Serpent soldiers was hit in the thigh and fell spiralling into the filthy gore below.

Golgoth's hand reached a sill and suddenly he was in the open air again, out on the upper surface of the tower's base. The dark stone beneath him was smooth and mottled. The shadow of the spire fell on a unit of archers, maybe twenty-strong, who had been using the surface of the tower's belly as a platform to fire on the attacking boats. Golgoth pulled him-self onto the stone and saw other warriors doing the same, clambering out around him and through the other skylights.

Golgoth left his shield on his back, unhooked his axe and swung it two-handed at the nearest thing that moved – a legionary archer, whose nocked arrow sped upwards as his shoulder and arm came away from his body and Golgoth felt the hot spatter of blood against his face.

Golgoth didn't care about control any more. These men were vermin – not men at all, but the tools of a sick and cor-rupting god, manipulated by their queen who was no more than a puppet herself.

Arrows sped towards him. He knocked them aside with the haft of his axe, letting Kron's sorcery give him the reflexes of a striking snake and a madman's disdain for harm. He ran towards the closest knot of archers, hacking two apart before they had a chance to draw another arrow from their quivers, kicking the other so hard in the jaw that his head snapped backwards and he rolled down the side of the tower.

Emerald Sword warriors would, only scant weeks ago, have killed Serpent soldiers on sight, and would die a terrible death rather than fight alongside them. But now Lady Charybdia had dared make herself a common enemy of all the tribes, and so it was together that the Sword and the Serpent fought, butchering anything that opposed them on the tower surface with sword and axe.

A lance of light spat down and scored deep into the black stone of the tower. Golgoth dived as two warriors came apart in a blinding flash and earsplitting noise. He looked upwards through the glare and saw a spindly figure composed of flame sending bright bolts of power down at them from a walkway high above.

'Upwards!' cried Golgoth. 'With me!' He ran towards the slim main body of the tower, spotted a closed doorway of black wood, and charged through it like a bull through a fence. A stairway ran in a spiral around the inside of the tower and Golgoth led the way upwards. Legionaries were heading down towards them, hoping to block the attackers' path on the narrow stairs, but Golgoth was almost ablaze with power and smashed into them, hardly bothering to swing his axe, simply swatting the men aside. Blades found his flesh, but the pain just made him stronger. Bones shattered as his shoulder hit shield, but he called out to the sorcerous potential within him and they were knitted back together before he reached the next man.

All the hatred was flowing out of him through the violence he did to the enemy. It was the same lust for battle he had always had, but a hundred times stronger and a thousand times better. He had seen his tribe brought low, seen his army thrown back from the walls, felt the contempt of Lady Charybdia and the uncaring cruelty of the gods. Now, he forced all that hate into a tiny white-hot spark and let it power the tricks that Kron had taught him back in the Canis Mountains. He hurled legionaries from the stairway with one hand, split them clean in two with the axe in his other, and left the survivors to be trampled by the warriors who followed him, bellowing their own war-cries.

They were like him. They wanted to write their own legends, too.

Golgoth burst out into the open air again, this time dizzyingly high, on a balcony that ran round the tower. A slender walkway spanned the gulf to the next tower, blocked by the fire-skinned sorcerer and his twenty-strong legionary bodyguard who made a formidable ring of spearheads around him.

The sorcerer spoke a few syllables of command and the legionaries, unquestioning, charged, spears held low.

Golgoth tore the shield off his back and threw it, so its iron-banded edge caught the closest legionary square in the face and pitched him off his feet. There was only room on the walkway for three men to fight side-by-side, and soon a Serpent warrior with a shock of white hair and a pair of livid scars through one eye was at Golgoth's shoulder. The Serpent had a sword with a blade at each end and a two-handed grip in the centre. Looking at Golgoth, there was a smile in his one good eye as he cast his own shield idly over the edge of the walkway. There would be no need for it here – Golgoth clearly cared nothing for his own safety, so neither would those who fought by his side.

Fire washed through the air, swirling around the legionaries and flowing over Golgoth and the warriors emerging from the doorway behind him. Golgoth hit the polished stone floor as the white magical flame carved through a half-dozen warriors like a knife, searing off limbs and heads. The stench of burning skin and the alchemical stink of sorcery almost overwhelmed him.

The Serpent warrior died as a spear punched through his gut, thrust by a legionary charging through the flame. Golgoth kicked the legionary's feet out from under him and knocked him off the walkway. An axe thrown from behind him split open the face of the next legionary and by then Golgoth was on his feet, axe cleaving through anything that stood in his way – warriors clambering over themselves to get closer to the sorcerer who dared threaten their leader.

One of the Emerald Sword had grabbed the dead Serpent's strange double-bladed sword and leapt past Golgoth's swinging axe blade, slicing through the stomach of one legionary before being pitched off the walkway to fall, flailing wildly, towards the crashing crimson waves.

A legionary archer fired. Golgoth caught the arrow and jabbed it through the eye of the nearest enemy. He batted aside the weapon of the next and simply trampled him beneath his feet, using the added height to swing his axe down at the heads of those guarding the sorcerer.

White fire rained down on him. Hot lightning crackled, conducted through the legionaries and up into Golgoth's body. Sounds and lights flashed in Golgoth's mind. But he was no longer afraid of sorcerers – he was a sorcerer himself, who turned his power inside himself and used it to kill up close, rather than from afar like a coward.

The palm of his hand blistered as he closed it around the neck of the sorcerer, whose long, thin, lizardlike face was blurred with the heat and flame rolling off it. His eyes were flinty black, like gemstones, skin puckered and pale with flame rippling over it like liquid. The sorcerer's mouth opened to scream, but its forked tongue just rattled as Golgoth squeezed the life out of it.

His enemy's spine snapped and Golgoth shook the body violently to make sure it was dead, swinging it left and right and sending enemies flying. Warriors ran past him, dragged the sorcerer's body to the ground, and hacked it to bits with their own swords. They threw the mangled limbs down towards the blood surf and cheered.

THE DESERT NOMADS galloped across the surface of the blood sea, the hooves of their horses throwing up crimson plumes of spray. Alchemical charges, made of powdered dragon bone with fuses of harpies' hair, were thrown through the windows of the nearest tower as they galloped past – the explosion tore out the root of the tower and sent it toppling, shedding legionaries like lizard scales, to crash onto the shore.

The next wave of warriors went on foot, using the fallen tower as a bridge, clambering up the spindly roadways that still connected it to the rest of the city. They were funnelled into bottlenecks and the kill from the watching archers was huge, but there were too many of them to be stopped. Like blood from a severed artery, they bled into the city, Emerald Sword and Serpent, reeking swamp-dwellers and lithe, white-haired raiders from the eastern seas. The first of the city's major temples to be overwhelmed fell as the flood of warriors coursed over its razor-studded battlements and into the sacred precinct, overwhelming even the daemons summoned there by its priests and befouling Slaanesh's sacred icons with their presence.

The dead of the battle were falling like snow, their bodies adding to the scum of corpses choking the dismal corners where the blood tide met stone. A thousand men died when retreating legionaries destroyed the tower that the few remaining Bear tribe warriors were using to enter the city. The same number of legionaries were blown to bits when the desert horsemen galloped up the side of a tower and captured one of the few guns that besmirched the skyline of the city – they blasted great holes in the closest defences before detonating the weapon's ammunition stockpile.

No one had ever got this far before. Lady Charybdia's soldiers had never died by enemy hands within the city itself.

THE PLEASURE-BARGE raked the approaching canoes with shots from the bolt throwers mounted in its prow and stern. Archers high up in its rigging added their arrows to the fire that was peppering the red waves and picking the crews off the attacking boats. The waters around it were thick with bodies, both of the headhunters and of the barge's crewmen, who had been killed when blowpipe darts hit them or daring boarding parties had made it onto the deck.

The barge was protecting the immense, glass-domed palace of pleasure that formed one of the city's most sacred sites. Silver struts like the legs of a spider supported a crystal canopy above a network of pleasure-pits. The most elaborate and intense rites of Slaaneshi worship were conducted in the sunken pits and across the upholstered surfaces, fuelled by the censers that breathed hallucinogens and the labyrinth of tunnels that would bring in slaves and

revellers from all over the city. Priceless works of sensual
arts stood alongside perfume-soaked altars to the Lord of
Pleasures. No bare-chested savage could be allowed to set
foot on that holy ground, where the praises of Slaanesh had
been acted out by revellers for centuries. The crew of the
barge were bound by the worship of their god to protect the
waters around the dome, and they were doing a very good
job of it.

The headhunters were dying. They were fighting with
bravery far beyond that which might be expected of such
primitives, but with every volley of silver-tipped bolts more
of them were toppled into the waves. The pleasure-barge's
crew – press-ganged revellers and hardened legionaries –
were fighting back, fuelled by the righteous anger of
Slaanesh. When the Prince of Pleasure was angry, he was
angry indeed.

The blood-ocean swelled beneath the barge and the canoes
were scattered. Something huge welled up underneath–

–and then the air was filled with splintering wood and
broken, flying bodies, the screech of tearing metal and the
bestial roar of something singing the praises of the Blood
God. Ss'll Sh'Karr burst up through the hull of the ship like
a sea monster of legend, metallic jaw ripping through the
rigging, smouldering claws tearing the keel in two. The daemon prince erupted clean out of the blood and landed on
the side of the pleasure-dome, shattering its crystal walls.

The headhunters joined him as Ss'll Sh'Karr ripped
through the dome, toppling the monumental statues of living flesh and smashing the works of sensual arts that
radiated Slaanesh's power.

As the waves of warriors charged into the city on foot, they
were joined by a huge shoal of daemons, following Ss'll
Sh'Karr against the defences of the city. They clambered onto
the wide avenues suspended between the towers and tore
through the pleasure-caverns. Legionaries were moved in
their thousands to form massive barriers of bodies at the key
intersections, so the tide of warriors and daemons crashed
against them and a hundred bloody, savage, face-to-face battles erupted.

A million legends were written in the first few hours of
the battle, about towering daemons who scattered dozens
of men aside with a single swipe, and soldiers who per-
formed acts of insane bravery on both sides. There was
cowardice, too, and madness, and flashes of brilliance
that turned defeat into victory, incompetence that saw
legions of men killed like cattle, savagery and the beauty
of killing.

There was, however, no mercy.

GOLGOTH RAN THROUGH the broken ruin of men's bodies and
ducked down beside the entrance to the next tower. Behind
him stretched a wide thoroughfare suspended on silver
chains hundreds of metres above the waves, now piled with
broken corpses. There were half-a-dozen such miniature battlefields behind them now, for Golgoth had led a growing
spearhead of warriors deep into the city, heading straight for
the imposing slab of the keep. The losses they had suffered
were made up by warriors from other waves they picked up
as they charged from tower to tower, carving their way
through the defenders.

This last knot of legionaries had been tough, determined
veterans formed around a formidable commander an
armspan taller than the rest. Golgoth had taken the giant
himself and his brother warriors had pitched the legionaries
off the edge. The warriors in the rear were finishing off the
wounded as Golgoth peered into the gloom beyond the
doorway at the end of the thoroughfare.

The place was deserted. The chamber within the next
tower was divided by standing screens painted with sinister
designs that seemed to writhe. Embroidered cushions were
piled high on the floor and elaborate hookahs lay smashed.
The sounds of battle filtered through the banners hung
around the walls, silver threads glinting in the light oozing
in shafts from holes in the high ceiling.

Golgoth waved forward Kyarados, a thin brittle-looking
woman whose speed and cruelty made her one of the most
dangerous of the Serpent warriors. She had joined Golgoth's
spearhead shortly after they broken through the defences of

the first tower and afterwards had killed at a rate almost equal to that of Golgoth himself.

'Kyarados, take six men and hold this entrance.'

Kyarados nodded and began barking names at the crowd of warriors who had made their way across the gore-slicked thoroughfare.

'The rest of you,' said Golgoth, 'follow me.'

He led them into the chamber, many of them choking on the heavy, thick scents that hung in the air like smoke. He yelled at them to spread out and find a way forward – one of the Emerald Sword called back that there was a spiral staircase leading down to a larger chamber below, from which sounds of vicious combat could be heard.

'Good man,' said Golgoth. 'Is there anything alive in here?'

Swords were shoved through upholstery and banners were torn down. The revellers, wisely, had fled.

'Follow me!'

There was a sudden warning cry from Kyarados. Golgoth just had time to see her diving in through the doorway when a deafening peal of explosions tore through the curved wall of the chamber, blasting shards of masonry everywhere. Sharp flashes of flame erupted all across the upholstered floor, throwing men aside, kicking up clouds of shredded fabric. Great holes were blasted clean through the walls and the mid-morning light streamed in, shining off the wet remains of those who had been blown apart.

Golgoth jumped to his feet and sprinted to see what had attacked them. He spotted a dark shape wheeling outside, then another, just as lances of fire burst into the chamber through the opposite wall.

'Take cover!' someone yelled unnecessarily as another volley of explosions were stitched across the inside of the chamber. Golgoth grabbed the edge of one of the holes in the wall, leaning out to see their attackers.

They were massive flying monsters, not quite giant birds or huge bats, not dragons or winged daemons. They were covered in patchy yellowing skin that was peeling from ichor-splattered pale blue bodies, and their eyes were slitted triangles of malice.

Guns on the tips of their wings and mounted beneath their chins chattered, and bright flashes of explosions rattled along the towers and walkways. The thoroughfare Golgoth had just crossed splintered and fractured, the silver tendons snapping as half of it rolled to one side and the rest gave way completely.

Suddenly, as if they had spotted something, the three flying beasts banked sharply with a roar and dropped down towards the blood ocean below.

Golgoth didn't know that the monsters were Thunderhawks of the Violators Chapter of Chaos Space Marines. But leaning out over the dizzying drop beneath him, he could guess what they had seen. Far below, kicking up a foaming pink fountain of blood, was Ss'll Sh'Karr.

CHAPTER EIGHT

THE STENCH OF blood was overpowering. Lady Charybdia had to drag her senses far, far down to the level of mere men, otherwise she would have passed out. The keep was dull around her – the songs of imprisoned spirits were no more than echoes and she couldn't tell that the blood-warm walls of the tower chamber were any more than stone.

It was a small place, perched high on one of the keep's many towers, a cylinder of stone where an array of crystal prisons hung like a massive chandelier. Each polished, fist-sized crystal contained some heretic or rebel, captured and sentenced to imprisonment here where their emotions were magnified for Lady Charybdia's pleasure. When the city was at peace she would climb the spiral stairs to the chamber so she could feel their betrayal and hear their remorse, tinged with loneliness and despair. But now, with such discord drowning the city, even those simple pleasures were denied her.

She looked down from the arched window. Concentric circles of defences stood proud around the keep, and Lady Charybdia could see the hulking forms of the Violators on the

203

walls, in full battle-array. Beyond them the city was ravaged –
a foul red-black stain where there should be emptiness, knots
of distant fighters struggling at every intersection, banners
being torn from the temples and whole towers collapsing
slowly into the ocean of blood. She could hear steel against
steel and the ragings of daemons. The electric tang in the air
told her that daemonettes, and worse besides, had been summoned to every altar to aid in the defence. But there were
other daemons, too – the grotesque, gibbering thug-daemons
that sang the praises of the Blood God.

Ss'll Sh'Karr was out there, rampaging at will, befouling
the sacred city. Unwashed barbarians were doing the same –
she had heard tell of fur-clad mountain men and bronzed
jungle hunters fighting side by side, of primitive hedge-wiz-
ards casting crude spells of destruction and nomad
horsemen galloping up the walls. It was as if someone had
skimmed off all the scum of Torvendis and poured it into
her city.

Lady Charybdia spat. Disgust filled her. How dare they
destroy such beauty? Nothing sentient could do such a
thing. The attacking army was composed of little more than
animals, with matted hair and stinking sweat, mindless
beasts who knew nothing of beauty and grace. None of
them had known Slaanesh's sacred pleasures. None of them
knew what it meant to worship truly, to give their whole
selves over to a worthy god. This whole city was a temple to
Slaanesh – they knew nothing of the sacredness of the
ground they befouled.

There was a crackling and spitting behind her as a tiny ball
of blackness winked into existence, hanging in the air. A
message-spell, such as she entrusted only to her most valuable servants.

'My lady?' came a deep, metallic voice, distorted as though
from a distance.

'Commander Demetrius?'

'We have him, my lady.'

'Good. Then kill him.'

The message-spell ended and the point of blackness vanished. At least something good will come of this, Lady

Charybdia told herself. *At least I will know it was on my word that Ss'll Sh'Karr was killed for the last time.*

'OPEN!' YELLED COMMANDER Demetrius, and the belly of the Thunderhawk gunship split open like a seed pod. The city whirled beneath, dizzying towers and clouded sky alternating with the swirling blood, as the noisome air was sucked out of the passenger hold and replaced by a howling wind.

The noise was vast, air rushing through the hold mixed with stuttering explosions from the gunship's cannon. Commander Demetrius's eyes peered through the dreadnought's ocular sensors and picked out a sudden ripple of grey flesh shot through with greasy, smoking machinery.

Not that he needed to see. His mutated nervous system could feel the Blood God's taint all around. Sh'Karr was in the blood ocean right below them.

'On my mark!' yelled Demetrius over the vox. 'The landing zone is the Temple Precinct of Opulence Inflamed!' He jabbed his whip-taloned arm towards a circle of purple-streaked stone sweeping by beneath them, supported on a column above the blood surface like a huge stone mushroom. 'Mobile fire pattern and keep your wits about you, we'll lure him up!'

His vision strobed as acknowledgement runes flashed on the back of his eye. His sergeants were ready.

'Drop!' ordered Demetrius and suddenly the grav-couch restrains were disengaged, dropping the thirty Space Marines packed into the Thunderhawk straight down. Their jump packs ignited as one, slowing their descent and giving them control over where they fell. Demetrius himself didn't bother – his sarcophagus split open and he angled the thick metal plates like fins, guiding his massive metal body as it fell.

His skin was open to the rushing air. It pulled at his exposed nerve endings, sending a thrill of pain through his broken body. It was like plunging into an ocean of razor blades. It was for experiences like this that Demetrius held Slaanesh above all other gods – but it would be just a taste of true sensation before the killing began.

Demetrius slammed into the sacred precinct, smashing a crater in the stone around him. The shock absorbers of the dreadnought's legs deadened the impact and in an instant Demetrius was battle-ready, assault cannon scanning for targets, sarcophagus closing around him like the carapace of a beetle.

The precinct was circular, and complex diagrams were etched in white on the black, purple-shot surface. A cluster of sacred buildings stood in the centre – several temples to minor aspects of Slaanesh, a life-torch like a huge brazier where sacrifices were immolated, a statue of Arguleon Veq and attendant shrine. There were no worshippers here now, though. A few legionaries were taking shelter amongst the buildings, firing paltry volleys of arrows at the tribesmen clambering over the far side of the stone disc.

Demetrius fired a salvo from his assault cannon, rejoicing inwardly at the feel of hot shrapnel bursting from the many barrels. Explosions stitched along the platform edge and several southern barbarians were burst apart by the cannon fire. Violators were already landing all around Demetrius, chainblades drawn, snapping off bolt pistol shots at the invaders.

Demetrius left the warriors for his men to deal with. He stomped towards the nearest edge of the precinct platform, looking down at the blood ocean that churned beneath it.

Where was he? Where was the daemon?

There! Looping in and out of the blood, swimming at supernatural speed, leading a shoal of his lesser daemons. One of the Thunderhawks swooped low and kicked up fountains of blood with cannon fire – and with a sudden roar Ss'll Sh'Karr leapt from the water like a sea monster, massive mechanical wings thrusting him from the blood.

His head was a fanged bronze gargoyle's mask, and those huge jaws slammed shut on one of the Thunderhawk's wings. Demetrius could hear the shriek from where he stood as the wing came away in a fountain of fuel and ichor. The Thunderhawk banked insanely, flipped, and spiralled towards the platform.

It overshot Demetrius and ploughed into the precinct in a shower of gore, skidding on its torn belly and careering into the cluster of temples. The monumental statue of Veq was toppled like a great tree. A fuel tank ignited and a blossom of flame erupted.

Violators sprinted from the wreckage, ignoring the flames that wreathed their armour. Many survived. Many died. Ss'll Sh'Karr, Demetrius vowed, would pay for every death with a hundred deaths of his own.

Demetrius swivelled his chassis and blasted a volley of assault cannon shells at Ss'll Sh'Karr, who was clambering up the side of a nearby tower. Shots stitched around the daemon prince, bursting against its flesh and the pulsing machinery. The arriving Violators were at Demetrius's side, and Demetrius heard Haggin yelling for disciplined fire – those Violators armed with bolt guns or other longer-ranged weapons opened fire at Sh'Karr, spattering his hide with small weapons fire. A missile launcher barked and a trail of smoke led to an explosion just above Sh'Karr. The daemon prince's metal head turned towards the precinct, and the baleful fiery eyes focused on the Violators forming ranks around Demetrius.

Ss'll Sh'Karr leapt off the tower and plunged back into the blood. Ripples carved through the water towards the precinct, scattering bobbing corpses.

'We have him!' voxed Demetrius. Above him, the third Thunderhawk was swooping low, belly open, to deliver the last payload of Violators. 'Marines, prepare for counter-charge!'

Assault Marines were forming up behind their commander. Demetrius's own neuro-lashes were charged and buzzing.

Demetrius's ocular sensors scanned the surface of the blood just beneath the lip of the stone platform. The ripples were gone – Sh'Karr had dived deep. He calculated the daemon prince would leap when he emerged, one kick bringing him up over the edge and onto the platform, right into the middle of the Violators…

There was a thunderous sound of breaking stone. The platform cracked and a huge section of it was raised up, spilling Traitor Marines off their feet. Another, and it was split apart entirely, Sh'Karr's metal head breaking through and his talons hauling him up.

The whole platform tilted. Demetrius kept his footing, as did most of the Marines, but Sh'Karr's huge metallic beak snapped and Demetrius saw armoured limbs severed. Every bolt pistol let fly at the daemon prince as he hauled himself up through the broken platform, the bolts blowing chunks from his flesh and raining down boiling daemon blood and spatters of oil as he lunged at Koivas's warband.

They had him at bay. Now it was time for the kill.

Demetrius stomped forward, assault cannon barrel red hot as he sprayed shells at Sh'Karr. He lashed out with his other arm and the barbed whips tore deep into the daemon's thigh, carving right through the muscles, exposing glinting brass bones through rents that rained gore.

Sh'Karr bellowed in pain and swiped down with a taloned paw. Demetrius met it with his own whip-fingered hand, deflecting the force of the blow and ducking beneath Sh'Karr's reach. He was blasting away into the daemon's torso at point-blank range, lashing out at his leg again.

The whips twined around Sh'Karr's ankle and tightened, biting through the muscle. Demetrius dug a foot into the stone and the servos of his legs screamed as he pulled as hard as his dreadnought's body would allow. The power plant mounted on the body's back glowed red-hot as its reactors pumped every last scrap of energy. The whips bit against the bone – but it was not bone, Demetrius realised now, for Sh'Karr's entire skeleton seemed to be made of hot brass and steel.

The weight of gunfire battered Sh'Karr like a gale. His skin was puckered with bullet wounds and the membranes of his wings were in tatters. Chunks of daemonic flesh flew everywhere. The beast howled and, as Demetrius pulled its monstrous body toppled, crashing slowly to the floor of the platform.

Violators gunned their jump packs and leapt onto the huge heaving form, hacking with their chainswords like woodsmen chopping up a fallen tree.

Demetrius wrenched his whips free from Sh'Karr's leg and dodged past the daemon's lashing arms. Raising his assault cannon, Demetrius emptied his ammunition hoppers directly into Sh'Karr's face.

The brazen skull bent and fractured. Writhing metal mandibles splintered. Flame glared from the sockets and Sh'Karr bellowed in pain. Blood and meat was still raining down, kicked up by the chainblades of the Violators and the bolters still pumped shells into the heaving body.

Demetrius wanted to feel the death of the daemon prince who had waged war on Torvendis twice. There might never be a death like this again. He split open his sarcophagus and exposed his desiccated body to the outside air, so Sh'Karr's death-throes would flood directly into his nervous system.

Sh'Karr thrashed wildly but most of the Violators held on or avoided his claws, tearing at his skin with guns and blades. Demetrius felt the pain flooding off the daemon prince like a heat haze, pure and monstrous, the anger of the Blood God mixed with the anguish of a cornered beast.

It was raining blood. Blood spattered against Demetrius's bare skin and set his nerve endings afire. Hot pain flooded through him, igniting old pleasure-centres he thought were long dead. Slaanesh would be well praised by the intensity of experience Demetrius was absorbing in the Pleasure God's name.

Sh'Karr was keening a high, terrible howl. There was a sudden commotion amongst the Violators at the edge of the platform and Demetrius tuned into the vox channel to see what was happening, angry that he might be disturbed during such a holy act of experience.

'...hundreds of them, fall back by fire teams, fall back...!'

It was Haggin's voice. His warband were already turning and retreating, forming up around their flamers and plasma guns. And suddenly, like a dark tide washing against sore, a wall of grey daemon-flesh erupted over the edge of the platform in a shower of blood.

A hundred daemons of the Blood God poured onto the platform, summoned by the howling of their prince. The first ranks were toppled by Haggin's bolter fire but there were too many of them. Demetrius watched as half of Haggin's warband disappeared beneath bronze talons and snapping jaws.

Ss'll Sh'Karr bucked like a wild animal and was up on his knees as the Violators began to fall back from the daemons.

'Kill the prince!' bellowed Demetrius. 'Kill it first! Hold! Hold!' But it was to no avail. Individual warbands were being swept aside by the hundreds of attacking daemons. Ss'll Sh'Karr brushed off the Violators who still clung to his back – some escaped on the jets of their jump packs, others were cast brokenly to the ground and crushed by Sh'Karr's massive feet.

This could not be. Sh'Karr could not live, not when Demetrius had vowed his death to Slaanesh. Daemons leapt at Demetrius but he knocked them aside, battering them with his whips and stuttering assault cannon fire into them. The vox was alive with calls to fall back – Demetrius tried to halt the retreat but those who obeyed his orders were dying as they were surrounded and overwhelmed. Koivas was still alive, his Assault Marines completely cut off in the shadow of Sh'Karr, fending off ranks of daemons.

Demetrius would have to finish this himself. He was angry beyond belief that he had been robbed of Sh'Karr's death. His Violators, the greatest warriors on Torvendis, were in disarray. The enemy they had been charged with destroying was still alive, standing over them and bellowing in triumph as more Marines were snatched between his claws and crushed.

But Demetrius had vowed to kill Sh'Karr. If he had to do it alone, then so it would be. He threw aside the daemons lunging at him and strode towards the towering daemon prince, daemons' blood sizzling against his exposed skin. He knocked daemons aside with the barrel of his assault cannon as he ran, clearing a path in front of him with the barbs of his whips.

The assault cannon chewed through the last daemons that stood between Demetrius and his quarry. He felt the ammunition hoppers were almost empty, and his power plant almost rupturing with the effort. He didn't care. Even if he had to spend a year inert while the Chapter artificers mended his dreadnought body, it would be more than worth it.

Sh'Karr saw Demetrius, and lashed down at him. The Violator ducked past the gore-slicked talons and charged into Sh'Karr's leg, barging him back down onto his knees, as he emptied the assault cannon into the daemon's torso.

Demetrius's whips wrapped themselves around Sh'Karr's neck and dragged his huge equine skull down, the last few assault cannon shells rattling into the daemon's face.

Huge taloned fingers wrapped around Demetrius's sarcophagus and he was hauled off the ground. Sh'Karr pulled and Demetrius felt a flash of pain as the whips were torn from the arm of the dreadnought body. Sh'Karr reached up with his other hand and tore the assault cannon arm off at the shoulder.

The world span around Demetrius. The shock of such massive injury sent the overcast sky swirling over his head, the towers of the city dancing. A thousand daemons gibbered up at him, their din mixed with the gunfire from the last resisting Violators. The vox was a wild cacophony of death, and Demetrius realised that he was screaming, too.

There was one chance. The power plant of his dreadnought body was white-hot with exertion. If he overloaded the plasma conduits he could rupture the casing and disappear in a ball of plasma fire, taking Sh'Karr's head and upper body with him. He would die, but then he had often contemplated the ultimate sensation of death and that, mingled with Sh'Karr's demise, would be a greater sensation than could be imagined.

Demetrius was still thinking this as Sh'Karr ripped free the power plant and hurled it off the platform into the sea of blood below. Then, forcing the side of Demetrius's sarcophagus further open, he reached in with a claw and hooked out the morsel of living meat.

Ss'll Sh'Karr dropped the scrap of wriggling muscle into his maw, and felt it slide, still moving, down his throat. Then he turned to the daemons milling around his feet, and beckoned to them to follow him. They had seen off a

troublesome enemy, but there were many more battles here
for them to slake their thirst.

LADY CHARYBDIA LOOKED out across the ruins of the outer
walls, trying not to gag on the stench of congealing blood.
She had retreated into her private chambers where surely
nothing could get to her – but as she watched through the
scrying orb that hovered in the centre of her bedchamber
she began to wonder if anything in her city was safe any
more. The dim noises of battle penetrated the walls of her
keep, drowning out the droning of the souls imprisoned in
the stones, echoing the carnage on and around the walls.

The Violators were holding out as best they could. She
had chosen well when she had brought them to her walls,
for every one of them was the equal of a hundred of the barbarian animals. But there were far more than a hundred
invaders for each Violator Marine, and Demetrius had not
yet returned as promised. In fact, Lady Charybdia had not
heard back from Commander Demetrius at all. Caduceia
and her elite shock companies of legionaries were surrounded and pinned down in the west of the city, trying to
stem the flow of invaders still pouring in from the western
coast of the blood ocean. Everywhere Lady Charybdia's
forces were cut off, for very few of them were able to use the
blood as the invaders were to move from place to place
quickly. The city was supposed to be impossible to traverse
for an attacking force, but Sh'Karr and his accursed sorcery
had completely reversed the situation. Now it was Lady
Charybdia's legions who were trapped, trying to face a foe
who could disengage and sail across to the next point of
attack.

And now, that foe had reached the defences of Charybdia
Keep itself.

A tide of men and daemons was crashing against the
walls. Towers nearby had been felled to form causeways
across which horsemen could gallop and footsoldiers could
scramble. The Violators were forming fire teams that faced
every point of entry with a wall of bolter fire, but more sections were coming under attack with each passing minute.

Explosions tore chunks out of the battlements and men clambered up from boats beached on the growing reef of corpses beneath the wall. Walkways and towers were brought down, forming bridges onto the walls. For every breach swept clear by the Violators, another one opened up and vomited a torrent of enemy warriors onto the walls.

There was the sound of tramping feet nearby. Lady Charybdia looked away from the gruesome scenes on the walls and strode out to see a troop of legionaries hurrying down the corridor. Their faces were drawn and many bled from their ears and noses – even in its present state the keep, Lady Charybdia realised, radiated experience rather too pure for most mortals to endure without ill effects.

'Centurion, does the keep hold?' demanded Lady Charybdia.

The leader of the legionaries stopped and bowed. 'They are coming in through the north-west, my lady. They came up the sacrificial causeway. We have sealed the area, but there will be more to follow them.'

'This is the holiest of ground, centurion. Every enemy foot that steps here is a blasphemy. It will not be permitted.'

'There are so many of them, my lady. They say the Violators are all but lost.'

'I am sure they say many things. But if you are still alive, then the enemy has not won yet. Where are you headed?'

'The waste conduits, my lady. With the causeway blocked, that is where they will attack next. Headhunters, I saw them. Half-naked, daubed with paint. They must have come from all over the planet...'

'You will see to it that their journey ends here. The keep will remain inviolate or you will die trying to keep it so. Understood?'

'Of course, my lady.' The centurion yelled an order and his men followed him down the corridor and down the grand staircase.

Even the very heart of the keep was disturbed by the cacophony of war. When the enemy was seen off, there would be unending sacrifices to cleanse the city of the presence before Slaanesh received his due of pleasure again.

There was a sudden dull crump from beneath Lady Charybdia's feet, and the rumble of falling rock. Something had exploded and taken a sizeable chunk of the keep down with it.

Almost immediately there came the dim sound of men's voices, hundreds of them, raised as they charged into the keep. Somewhere, floors below, the invaders had got in through some subterfuge or stealth. The sounds of steel on steel marked the point where they met her legionaries – but almost as soon as one influx was halted, there was another crash, closer this time, and Lady Charybdia heard more barbarians charging into the keep.

Lady Charybdia ran back into her chambers, but the warmth and solitude of her haven was fragile compared to the anger of the war outside. She willed the violated floors of the keep to exude their sensations at the level she normally preferred, pure and intense. This was the keep's last line of defence – the labyrinth of pleasures built into its stones, that allowed her to worship Slaanesh purely, could overwhelm and destroy the minds of lesser men. It was the last chance. She would have to kill the invaders with pleasure.

The souls would be singing more sweetly and the tapestries shining with impossible beauty, enough to bewitch or destroy any mortal. There were censers that would be burning musk so potent it would utterly paralyse anyone who breathed it and carpets that sent bright stabs of pain through anyone who walked on them. Lady Charybdia felt the heightened, pure pleasures faintly as they echoed up to her chambers – rather more clearly, she heard the screams of barbarian and legionary alike as they died.

But it would not last forever. As the fabric of the keep was damaged, its power to produce such heady sensations was diminished. The hardier of the attackers might run the gauntlet of pleasure and survive.

Lady Charybdia glanced one more time into the scrying window. The Violators were now little more than a pocket of blue-armoured figures, surrounded by a baying horde of enemies. There was still no sign of Demetrius or his

Thunderhawks, but Demetrius was her last hope. If just one of his flying craft remained, she could call for it to land on the roof of the keep and pluck her to safety.

With a sudden shock, Lady Charybdia realised that she was genuinely contemplating the possibility that the keep would fall.

Blood was rushing through the lower levels, and there were barbarian feet trampling the works of art Lady Charybdia had spent a lifetime accumulating. Shaking the horror out of her head, Lady Charybdia ran for the stairway that led to the keep's upper levels.

FAR, FAR BELOW, in the channels carved out of the keep's foundation blocks, all was blood. The tunnels and the chambers were immersed, with the bodies of faithful servants and legionaries floating slowly through the darkness. The drowned corpses of prisoners bobbed in their flooded dungeon cells. Long-forgotten storerooms and oubliettes were saturated, and their contents stained the gore strange colours. Priceless tapestries hung ruined. Captured spirits turned angry and violent as they were infused with the Blood God's rage, destroying themselves in their anger.

And along one deep corridor, a row of eldar skulls stared blankly.

CADUCEIA'S COMMAND WAS all but cut to ribbons. Trapped behind makeshift barricades in a wide crossroads high above the western edge of the city, they had been utterly surrounded as invaders poured up the closest towers. Caduceia had begun this battle with a mobile force of seven thousand veterans. She had barely three thousand left now, hardened fighters who had fought through a dozen campaigns but who were now facing their end at the hands of unwashed hordes of thugs who were not fit to speak the name of Slaanesh.

The enemy had attacked a dozen times, each time being thrown back with massive losses. But there were so many of them. Caduceia looked through the broken planks of the makeshift barricade, watching enemy warriors scurrying

along the balconies of nearby towers and behind the
defences that had been erected on the three roads that led
from the junction. Sporadic bowfire and volleys of hurled
javelins arced into Caduceia's position, thudding into the
barricades and clattering against the stone of the road's surface, sometimes whistling into the flesh of a legionary with
a lucky shot.

One of her centurions hurried up to her, head bent low in
case some sharp-eyed nomad speared him with an arrow.
Caduceia recognised him but could not recall his name – he
had served the armies of the city for well over a decade, as
had Caduceia herself. 'There's movement to the south,
below us,' he said. 'Some of the men think it's Charrian's
reinforcements...'

'There will be no reinforcements,' replied Caduceia
shortly, her forked tongue flicking over her lips. 'We are all
that is left. Our purpose is to hold up as many of these hea-
thens as we can and make sure none of them bleed further
into the city. Stop such talk amongst the men, their hope
will make them weak.'

If the centurion objected, he did not say so. With a nod,
he headed back towards where his command was manning
a south-facing barricade.

Caduceia had told the truth. A force surrounded and isolated would not be rescued. They were more use as
obstacles, and the men who might rescue them were more
valuable elsewhere.

The daemon half of her reminded her that she had been
sacrificed to Slaanesh once before, and would be honoured
to do it again.

'Attack from the east!' came a yell from the barricade at
the other side of the position, just before a hail of arrows
and throwing spears heralded another barbarian assault.
Muscle memory kicked in and powered Caduceia across the
open ground, ignoring the raining steel as she loped on
long, strangely-jointed legs that carried her faster than her
legionaries.

An arrow thudded into her shoulder and a spear cut a
long gash down one thigh as she ran. She reached the

shelter of the eastern barricades and tore out the arrow – brackish, daemonic blood spurted corrosively before the wound closed itself.

She pushed in amongst the legionaries and glanced through the planks of the barricades. The enemy were stationed within the bulbous midsection of a tower a short distance down the road – Caduceia could smell them from here, the heat of their breath, the sweat on their skin.

The clatter of arrows abated. The enemy charged – hundreds of them, a thousand, streaming from the windows and doors of the tower towards her eastern barricade.

The legionaries were still. None would kill without Caduceia's word.

The first of the barbarians were casting spears and throwing axes, which skidded onto the roadway, well short.

Caduceia withdrew the fingers of her right hand into the fleshy orifice that sprouted from her wrist. White-hot fire flickered inside as her limb shifted into the grotesque biological weapon her invasive daemon had gifted her. Her right hand, a chitinous crab-like claw, snapped impatiently. The daemon wanted blood, but the woman commanded it to wait.

A hurled javelin thudded into the barricade.

'Ready!' called Caduceia. Those legionaries with spears to spare drew them back, one hand on their back-up weapons.

The stench of the barbarians was unbearable. Caduceia knew that only the smell of blood would mask it.

'Throw!' she ordered, and a wall of spears hurled over the wall like a wave that broke against the charging warriors in a spray of blood. The front rank was broken up just before it hit.

The enemy was bloodied but they were swarming all over the barricade, many climbing onto its top and stabbing down with swords and axes. Caduceia reached over and fired a blast of superheated plasma down the barricade, the stench of burned meat washing over her as three men disappeared in a crimson cloud of vapourised blood.

The legionaries were all around her, jabbing with their spears, those with only swords clambering onto the

barricade and matching sword-strokes with the attackers.
Barbarian corpses were falling on both sides and the clam-
our was appalling, a terrible song of wounding and death. At
the flanks, details of legionaries charged over the barricades,
driving a wedge of men into the barbarian line and pitching
scores of attackers over the edge of the roadway before
falling back behind the barricade.

Hundreds of attackers were dead already, and scores of
legionaries. How many were there? How many would they
have to slay?

Not enough, said the daemon, and Caduceia let it take
her over, claw severing limbs and heads, gun blasting
chunks from the seething mass of barbarians. She revelled
in the stench of cooked flesh and flowing blood, in the
heat of gore against her skin and the pain of a hundred
tiny wounds from arrows and lucky sword-blows. A flicker
of the daemon's insanity drove her onward – it was a pure
delight in destruction, as if she wanted to tear apart the
real world and see only the undiluted Chaos of the warp
in its place.

When the red mist in Caduceia's mind died down and the
daemon retreated from the forefront of her mind, she was
standing in the middle of the road with the barricade far
behind her, a mound of broken bodies beneath her feet. The
last few barbarians were fleeing into the tower, and the enemies in the windows were preparing to launch another
volley at the legionary position.

Caduceia hurried back to the barricades, as something
caught her eye.

It was the keep, far across the city, dimmed by the distance
and the palls of smoke billowing from those towers that had
been blown up or set ablaze. Blood was fountaining from
the windows of the lower levels, and the walls around it
were teeming with combatants. The invaders had reached
the keep, and Lady Charybdia herself.

The daemon in her said that it didn't matter, her fight
was here and there were more foes to slay. The woman in
her agreed, and she ran back into the barricaded enclo-
sure as the arrows began to fall. There would be many

more battles here before night fell and the fate of the city was decided.

LADY CHARYBDIA SAW her city in agony. From the observation dome at the pinnacle of the keep, she could see across to the far borders of her masterpiece. Flames glowed bright on the tops of a hundred towers. Others had been toppled like trees, or were cut off entirely from the rest of the city, their connecting roadways brought down. Seething swarms of barbarians were everywhere, and in the few places that the bright silks of her legionaries were still visible, they were outnumbered ten to one by the enemy.

The walls were lost. The Violators had withdrawn into the keep itself, leaving a trail of heaped bodies – Lady Charybdia could hear the ugly barking of their bolters from the dome, and feel the bloating as the keep's doors and staircases were choked with the dead. Imprisoned spirits were being set free by the destruction, flitting away into the night like wisps of smoke. The sky above was bleeding like the city, nebulae weeping sores that oozed torn stars, comets falling as if fainting in horror. Only the Slaughtersong was unmoved, its cold light a hard jewelled pin stuck into the sky.

There was commotion directly below the observation dome. Something was scrabbling angrily at the hatch in the floor.

Lady Charybdia looked around the lavish decorations of the dome. She caught sight of a jewelled dagger, maybe a gift or a tribute, or something her armies had captured – there were untold thousands of such things all over the keep. She picked it up and drew its blade from the scabbard. It was sharp, at least.

Lady Charybdia had been, at one point or another, almost every type of sensualist that a devotee of the Pleasure God could name – including a warrior. She had fought in battles that had raged across the whole world and taken her place in the armies of Chaos. But that had all been long ago. How much would she remember? Was her elegant, perfect body any use for fighting now?

The noise was louder now – something had got a purchase on the hatch and was trying to wrench it free. Lady Charybdia backed against the crystal wall of the dome, and for the first time in a very long time, she felt fear. Her city was in ruins. Her armies were reduced to tiny pockets of doomed resistance. And though she glanced in hope at the sky outside, there was no sign of Demetrius or his Thunderhawks.

The floor collapsed and something reached through the hole. Its stench came before it – fire and blood, anger and revenge. A hand followed the reek, grey and gnarled with talons of brass.

The misshapen, hulking thing that clambered up into the dome had once been a daemon of the Blood God, but it was now something less. The machinery torn from its body had left hideous puckered scars in its unnatural flesh and its twisted limbs had been broken many times and not set – but it was healthier now than it had been, for it had been immersed in blood and had gorged itself. Its muscles bulged wetly, even as hot gore ran from the many scars re-opened. Slits of red anger marked its eyes, and they were fixed on Lady Charybdia.

A chain hung from one wrist. A chain with links of human tongues. There was a recent, weeping spear-wound in its side.

'You,' said Lady Charybdia.

The beast did not answer. It took a step forward, the razor-sharp claws on its feet slicing through the cushioned floor of the dome. Lady Charybdia held the dagger out in front of her, gripped tight in her delicate, spiderlike hand.

It was faster than her. It was faster than anything mortal. She slashed at it as it charged and cut a deep slash in its chest, ducking its snapping jaws. But its hand clamped onto the back of her neck and picked her up, slamming her against the wall of the dome.

Her sculptured skull cracked, and hollow bones shattered. Lady Charybdia glanced crazily through a gauze of blood as the daemon lifted her again and hurled her against the far wall. The crystal cracked. So did her spine.

She couldn't move. She couldn't breathe. Her body was a mass of pain, porcelain-delicate bones reduced to sharp splinters. The dagger dropped from her broken fingers. The daemon reared up and punched a fistful of claws through her stomach, sending a hot tide of agony washing over her.

She could hear the gunfire of the Violators, and the war-cries of the enemy as they charged. She could hear the tide of blood washing against the foundations of the keep, and the splintering of stone as another tower fell. In those last few moments, her heightened senses brought her the sound of a city dying, of a mighty temple falling. And the smells hit her, too – the burning wreckage and the overwhelming stench of congealing blood. A hot wind of suffering blew over her and she could see the pale light of death dawning over her city.

It was the final sensation, the ultimate blessing promised by Slaanesh. Even in death, his followers were to worship him with the experience of their death. But this was no act of piety – this was pain, and sudden cold, and utter futility. Lady Charybdia had failed Slaanesh, and as her punishment her death was no ultimate thrill but a wretched flash of pain followed by emptiness.

Lady Charybdia was still suffering the betrayal of her god when the daemon began to eat her.

THE DEATH OF Lady Charybdia, for those who were attuned to such things, was every bit as loud as the awakening of Ss'll Sh'Karr. It was a pathetic thing, a distant, despairing whimper. The wave that rippled across Torvendis at the shock of her death carried a cry of abandonment and pain, and then silence.

Kron heard it, far south in the depths of the jungle. He marked the passing of Lady Charybdia with some satisfaction that she did not have a heroic death. Then, he ignored it for the time being, because he had matters of his own to worry about.

The jungle was thick around him. Moving was like pushing through a solid wall – every plant had spines and every creature had a stinger. Kron's body was covered in scratches and puncture marks – he could heal them quickly enough, but pain was pain and it seemed the whole jungle was determined to inflict as much of it on him as possible.

He risked a flash of sorcery, and held out a palm wreathed in black flame that caused the malevolent plants to wither and die in front of him, opening the way into a clearing. The wan starlight filtered down through the canopy and mottled a circular patch of rocky ground.

It was familiar, this clearing. Of course, when Kron had last seen it the jungle had yet to encroach, but there was no doubt about it. The rocky ground sloped down into a depression that Kron recognised as an impact crater. He picked his way across the broken stones and headed downwards, lizardlike creatures slithering out from under his bare feet.

At the bottom of the depression was a patch of earth. Kron dug at it with his hands, until finally he touched cold metal. A word of sorcery carried the soil away and revealed a curved metal surface with blistered paintwork and a small round hatch.

Kron passed his hands over the hatch. Gene-sensors beneath the surface bleeped and the locking mechanism clicked into place. The hatch swung inwards and old air, carrying a smell of machinery and fuel, rolled out. A light flickered inside, revealing a single grav-cushioned seat with a life-support hood bolted in front of a bank of controls and readouts, crammed into a tiny space barely large enough for one man.

Kron smiled. It was good to see that the saviour pod was still where he had left it – as if Torvendis, sensing that the pod was a foreign object, refused to swallow it and left it near the surface.

Kron eased his old body through the hatch and into the seat. The hood lowered itself over his head with a hiss of hydraulics and the hatch closed above him. The readout began to flicker on – temperature, air mix, hull integrity. A topographic map of the area appeared on one screen and the view of the night sky, straight up, on another. Kron checked the fuel counter and saw there was still plenty. Back when this pod had been built, they made things to last. The pod was still spaceworthy, and while intended as a one-man lifeboat, it still had enough thrust to carry its small payload back into orbit.

There wasn't enough to bring it back down. But Kron had already reached a point where he couldn't go back – the events he had kicked into motion were approaching their climax and he couldn't have stopped them if he had wanted to.

The control stick unfolded from the central console and Kron grasped it, gunning the single large thrust engine and feeling the pod lurch up out of the earth. Another firing and the pod was airborne, slashing up through the jungle carapace, and hurtling up towards the night sky.

AMAKYRE WATCHED THE city aflame. It had been clear for some time that Lady Charybdia's forces were doomed. The surprise assault over the ocean of blood had cut the defending army into pieces, isolated and crushed by mobile barbarian forces that attacked from everywhere at once. The barbarian leaders were evidently rather more astute than Lady Charybdia had suspected – even the Violators had been overwhelmed. There were no better troops in the Maelstrom (save, of course, the Word Bearers) and it took a stroke of tactical brilliance to force them into fighting a losing battle. SS'll Sh'Karr had broken down what obstacles were beyond the barbarians, and the resistance in the city had been squeezed until the keep was in the invaders' hands. The last of the fighting might take weeks to conclude, but it was clear that, as night descended, the city of Slaanesh had fallen.

From the ridge overlooking the north of the city, the Word Bearers' coven had seen the battle unfold in all its beauty. But their immediate purpose was unfulfilled – there had been plenty of explosions of sorcery, but nothing that might lead the coven directly to Karnulon. They weren't even sure he was in the city at all, and even if he was it would be all but impossible to find him in such a place.

Vrox, perched on an outcrop a short distance away, kept up a constant perimeter sweep with his many guns. Skarlan,

Feorkan and Prakordian were in half-sleep, while Phaedos and Makelo took the watch. Amakyre was sitting on the rock, watching the fires of the city when the communication came.

The vox was suddenly alive with noise. Not voices – a horrible, guttural, bubbling sound, like the death-rattle of something huge.

'Makelo?' voxed Amakyre.

'Captain?'

'Wake Prakordian.'

There was a pause as Makelo scrabbled down from his vantage point and shook Prakordian from half-sleep. When his acknowledgement rune flashed, Amakyre played the sequence of noises back from his communicator.

'It's the *Multus*,' voxed Prakordian as the noise finished. The sorcerer was the only one of the coven who could translate the machine-spirit's communications without using the ship's bridge controls. 'It's seen something.'

Amakyre had left instructions with the insane machine-spirit of the *Multus Sanguis* to watch the skies, in case Karnulon tried to leave Torvendis by spacecraft. It mildly surprised him that the ship had actually kept its watch and had the presence of tech-mind to inform the coven.

'Tell it to get us target details. And a trajectory.'

Prakordian transmitted, not by vox but by linking his own mind with the festering psychic lump that was the *Multus's* spirit.

'It's a spacecraft, probably a single-seater,' voxed Prakordian after a few moments. 'Unknown design. It took off a few minutes ago from the southern jungles.'

'Can the *Multus* track it?'

'The craft isn't shielded. It can be followed.'

'Good. Tell the *Multus* to pick us up at this location and take us in pursuit. If it's Karnulon, we can't afford to lose him.' Amakyre switched to the squad frequency. 'Word Bearers?' Five acknowledgement runes flickered. 'Break half-sleep and get ready to move out. Karnulon may have fled and we're following him into orbit.'

'Can we hide the *Multus*?' asked Feorkan. 'If we're not supposed to be here…'

'Karnulon probably knows we're here. Speed is more important than secrecy.' Amakyre knew the wily Feorkan would rather keep a low profile than announce to everyone on Torvendis that the Word Bearers were on the planet by launching the *Multus* again. But catching Karnulon overrode all other priorities and, in any case, with Lady Charybdia dead there were few forces on the planet that would be able to do anything about the Word Bearers if they wanted to.

Amakyre jogged down the ridge to where the other members of the coven were already checking their equipment ready for pick-up. Makelo was still keeping watch – Vrox had stomped down and, with Skarlan and Feorkan, was beginning to double-check the landing zone. Prakordian sat cross-legged, eyes closed as he communicated psychically with the *Multus Sanguis*.

'It will be here within two hours,' said the deadspeaker, eyes suddenly open.

'Good. Can it be relied upon?'

'The *Multus* is lucid when it wants to be,' said Prakordian. 'Once it's got something to hunt it can be very cooperative.'

'Has it found the target's trajectory?'

Prakordian smiled. 'Oh yes, captain. He's heading for the Slaughtersong.'

SOME WERE STILL fighting. But most had already begun to celebrate.

Lady Charybdia's keep was a dull shell of the place it had been. The trapped spirits were gone and the living stained-glass windows were shattered, so their writhing images could no longer hypnotise intruders. Some areas were still impossible to enter due to the soporific musks and hallucinogenic incense that hung in the air, but those would be ventilated soon enough, and there was plenty of space for the revellers.

Golgoth had headed straight for the keep when he had learned it was taken. But it seemed Lady Charybdia had either fled or been killed and her body lost. Golgoth had longed to tear her apart with his bare hands, but at least he could console himself by tearing down her priceless tapestries and joining his brother warriors in celebrations.

The sound of raucous song echoed throughout the keep as Golgoth stumbled up a grand staircase, flagon of some captured wine still in his hand, a fog of drunkenness descending over him in the wake of the day's slaughter. The keep was huge and there was plenty to explore and loot – most of it had yet to be ransacked, and Golgoth still hoped to find Lady Charybdia cowering in some alcove, or at least her remains that he could nail to a pole and parade as his personal standard.

He emerged into a ballroom, a vast room with a ceiling so high clouds were gathering in the corners. The floor was polished black hardwood and the walls of plaster sculpted into sinuous, suggestive designs. Hundreds of clocks were set into the walls, each with a different set of numbers on the face, every one powered by the beating of a human heart built into the casing. Every one stopped.

Golgoth wandered across the ballroom floor, down the steps into the orchestra pit where strange instruments lay discarded, and into another room. This was a wine cellar, freezing cold, with barrels of liquid misery and distilled pain. He walked on through an art gallery whose pictures had turned black and dull with only the faint, wriggling traces of the living images they had displayed. Clouds of glowing insects, bound in magical cages hanging from the ceiling, shone onto the pictures with a dim, pale light.

There was a little menagerie with cages and enclosures no bigger than a man's fist, where tiny jewelled insects and perfectly miniaturised beasts were kept. Golgoth recognised a few diminutive versions of mountain predators, shrunk by magic until they were like toys displayed for children too cowardly to seek out the real thing. Very few of the creatures were still alive. Golgoth ignored them and headed onward, aware that the singing of his drunken warriors was growing dim. The occasional report of a stolen bolt gun was distant – Golgoth had taken a bolt pistol himself, but he had discarded it soon after when foul-smelling pus had begun to leak from the workings. Everything in the city seemed tainted. There was little question of his warriors taking over the place. It would be razed, and the mines beneath filled in.

A corridor lined with statues that turned out to be petrified prisoners was next. How many of them had come from the mountain peoples, given as tribute by corrupted chieftains? They said there were dungeons beneath the upper floors where lowing beasts, once human, were imprisoned. How many good, strong men had met a worse end than death here, men who might have helped keep the Emerald Sword powerful and warlike?

Something caught Golgoth's eye. It was a creature – a bird – flitting silently along the corridor towards him. Golgoth at first thought it had escaped from the menagerie, but it alighted on the shoulder of the nearest statue and tilted its head to one side, eying him quizzically. It had iridescent blue-green feathers and tiny, bright eyes.

Around one of its legs was tied a message ring. Golgoth reached out and the bird allowed him to remove it. He pulled a strip of parchment from the ring, and wondered idly if Tarn was still alive somewhere, so he could read it for him.

The words on the parchment swirled and suddenly, Golgoth could read them, as if the message was being spoken directly into his mind. He had never liked his mind being interfered with and scrunched the parchment into a ball, but the message remained, hanging in front of his eyes and reciting itself over and over in his head: *Arrowhead Peak. Hall of the Elders.*

Suddenly there was an image to go along with the message – a huge, dark, dusty hall, quiet as a tomb, with snarls of spiders' webs hanging from the ceiling and… *something…* in the middle, distant and blurred to he couldn't focus on it.

Then, it was gone, and the corridor swam back into view.

A final scrap of the message surfaced in his mind – a signature.

Kron.

CHAPTER NINE

THE *Multus Sanguis* was troubled. Strange groaning sounds filtered from below decks competing with the distant roar of the engines, and the bridge lights kept dimming, casting strange shadows like mottled bloodstains across the floor and walls. There were fewer deck-slaves now cowering at the edge of the bridge. Prakordian had divined that the *Multus Sanguis* had been calling them to its machine-spirit chamber and consuming them while the Word Bearers were away. The old ship was getting worse, as if infected by the same malice that gripped the whole of Torvendis.

From orbit, Captain Amakyre could see the city burning. The holoprojector array sent a bright image of the planet's surface into the air in the centre of the bridge and the plumes of smoke were clearly visible, wreathing the jewelled wound in the earth. Soon, the city would be a torn, burned-out shell.

Feorkan was at the navigational helm, overseeing the machine-spirit's calculations. Prakordian was somewhere overhead in an observational dome, watching the distant destruction with glee, opening his mind to the echoes of the dead. All the Word Bearers were at rest in their own way, because they knew that if they had to face Karnulon, it could be the hardest fight of their long lives.

'We've got something here, sir,' said Feorkan. 'The machine-spirit just put it up on the scopes.'

'Visual,' said Amakyre, and the image of Torvendis shimmered and disappeared, to be replaced by a view of the starscape outside. A cursor blinked over a particular star, an especially bright one.

'Close-up?'

Feorkan worked for a few moments, trying to coax the *Multus's* sensors into closing on the object. Then, the image shifted again.

This time it showed a spaceship. It was wreathed in light reflected from Torvendis's many suns and moons, but it was definitely a ship. From the measurements streaming along the lower edge of the holographic image, Amakyre could tell it was huge, bigger by far than the *Multus*. A massive, curved hull was underslung with powerful engines – gaping particle scoops projected past the prow and led to flared engine exhausts. Clusters of sensor arrays stabbed forward. Sleek windows covered the segmented hull, covering the ship in pinpoints of light.

'Is there a signal?'

Feorkan shook his head. 'As far as the *Multus* can tell, the ship's dead.'

It had made no sense when Prakordian had said Karnulon was headed for the Slaughtersong. The star would have been far too distant for a one-man craft to reach. But this, of course, made perfect sense, for they had found Karnulon's destination and it was not a star at all. Reflected in the light of Torvendis's suns, it had burned bright and cold in the sky.

There was a name stencilled in enormous letters along the spaceship's hull. The name was *Slaughtersong*.

Amakyre strode over to the comms helm and switched on the ship's vox-caster system. His voice boomed throughout the *Multus*.

'Word Bearers, prepare yourselves. We've found him. Make ready for boarding.'

* * *

Ss'll Sh'Karr, if he had possessed a mind approximating that of a mortal, might have been sated. He might have had his fill of blood and killing, even as the ocean of blood drained back into the earth beneath the city. The stench of the bloated corpses left behind as it receded, and the oppressive pall of smoke that hung between the towers, might have satisfied his lust for destruction.

But Ss'll Sh'Karr was not mortal. And nor was he just a daemon – he was a prince among daemons with a soul forged from the will of the Blood God himself. For Ss'll Sh'Karr, there was never enough blood. If there was killing to be done, he would do it. And in the pale early morning light, as Golgoth's barbarian horde slept off a day of laughter and a night of revelry, he did.

Golgoth woke to the sound of screams. He was alone in the keep, in some high-ceilinged, colonnaded gallery where statues of frozen tears had once stood until the keep's fall had caused them to melt. His head was thick with the wine he had drunk by the flagonful and his movements were uncertain as he clambered to his feet. He could smell burnt-out fires and the after-stink of a thousand sleeping men.

They were the screams of men in pain or fear. Golgoth ran to the nearest doorway and peered around into the corridor beyond. Shadows danced round the corner, and he saw a warrior run into view carrying a burning torch.

The man was spattered with blood, his eyes wild. He was from one of the mountain tribes, which one Golgoth wasn't sure. He saw Golgoth, and began to yell a warning, the words of which never reached his throat.

Hulking shapes scrambled round the corner and cut the man down from behind. His midriff came apart in a welter of blood, his legs and lower half trampled beneath clawed feet, the rest of him flipped into the air by the fury of his attackers' charge. The torch fell to the ground and flickered, its dying flames reflected in glinting, asymmetrical eyes.

Daemons.

Golgoth reached behind his back and a silent prayer was answered as he found his axe still strapped there. He had no shield. His head was too thick for sorcery. He fell back on the oldest of instincts – to fight, and to buy himself time to think only after the enemy was dead.

The first daemon charged into Golgoth and just missed as he dodged backwards, into the gallery of tears – the marble doorway splintered as the daemon impacted against it. Golgoth brought the axe down and cut a fearsome slice out of the creature's back, sending bolts of hot daemon blood spattering across his skin. Golgoth ignored the scalding pain as the second daemon clambered over its fellow to attack.

Golgoth hacked wildly at the daemon's flailing claws, hoping to defend himself by wrecking the daemon's hands. But Golgoth knew enough to guess that it couldn't feel pain as mortals did, and even losing its limbs wouldn't be enough to break its spirit.

The first daemon was back on its feet, loping twistedly with its spine shattered. It stepped behind Golgoth and slashed at him wildly – Golgoth ducked and heard a satisfying wet crunch as one daemon caught the full force of the other's blow. Golgoth hacked at the first daemon's leg, carving a meaty chunk out of its thigh, and ran.

He couldn't fight creatures like these, not now. Not when there might be a dozen more at any moment.

They had to be rogues, breaking away from Sh'Karr's authority to feed on their own initiative. Even Sh'Karr would recognise the sanctity of this victory, where man and daemon had joined forces to exorcise a rotten regime of debauchery.

Golgoth was still telling himself this when he blundered out onto a balcony that projected from the side of the keep. Lush plants had once grown here but were now withering and dead. Golgoth could see out into the city around the keep and below him, the walls where so many men had died rushing the ranks of the Violators.

Daemons were feasting on piles of corpses. Men were corralled into frightened knots surrounded by daemons who took it in turns to dart in and carry them off to eat. Blood flowed like water along the battlements, licked from the stones by daemons' tongues or drunk like wine where it pooled. The noise was terrible – the gibbering of the daemons as they slaked their thirst, the screams of the dying men and the defiant taunts of the warriors still on their feet.

The same sounds were filtering up from the lower levels of the keep, and the same scenes were being replayed on the distant towers and walkways where victorious warriors had celebrated and slumbered. It was appalling – Golgoth could hear thousands of men dying at once.

The immense shape of Ss'll Sh'Karr clambered up onto the walls around the keep. His metallic skull was spattered with gore and chunks of flesh. The daemons gathered around him, shrieking excitedly, as he lifted a handful of bodies and crammed them into his mass of bronze mandibles.

The magnitude of the betrayal threatened to overwhelm Golgoth. Sh'Karr had used the warriors to win a victory over the hated Lady Charybdia, and then relegated them to the status of mere sustenance. The hate could destroy him if he let it take him over, as it had nearly done when he had learned of the Grik's betrayal.

It was an awesome effort to force his anger down. But the logical part of his mind, which had barely been there at all before Kron's teachings, took control. There will be time for your hatred later, it said. For now, you must survive.

Golgoth turned and ran again, the scrabblings of the pursuing daemons insistent behind him. There must be a way out of the keep, through some waste chute or sewer, or even just through the main gates past daemons too intent on feasting to notice him. The pits of the city were vast enough to hide in and, when he made it out of the city, he knew exactly where he would go.

Arrowhead Peak. Hall of the Elders.

A HANDFUL OF days had passed since the *Multus Sanguis* had picked the Word Bearers up from the surface of Torvendis. The old ship had made best speed out into orbit but the *Slaughtersong's* exact position had been hard to pin down and it was further out than the sensor readings had suggested. Strange interference made navigation all but impossible – the visual reading of the *Slaughtersong's* white glow had been the most accurate indication of where it was and it had taken frustrating days to reach it, as if the ship had known they were coming and had tried to hide from them. But slowly, the *Multus* had closed in, and now the Word Bearers had reached their target.

The green indicator on the auspex scanner meant the air within the *Slaughtersong* was breathable. Captain Amakyre removed his helmet and let the smell of the place come to him – mechanical, metallic, clean and old. Very, very old.

The *Slaughtersong* was not old in the way that the *Multus* was old. It was bright and clean, with lumostrips picking out the polished chrome surfaces, every curved wall smooth and unblemished. The floor was of bright silver mesh and the walls of mirror-bright metal. Every spacecraft Amakyre had ever set foot on had been rebuilt a hundred times, with massive imposing architecture and a patina of grime. The *Slaughtersong* was so old, it looked new.

Amakyre waved the coven forward. A brief hand signal told them to fall into search pattern – Feorkan on point with Makelo just behind him, followed by Amakyre, Prakordian, Phaedos and Vrox, with Skarlan behind. Feorkan jogged lightly ahead down the hullspace, helmet still on to gain the benefit of its auto-senses.

The *Multus Sanguis's* boarding shuttle had delivered them into the space between the inner and outer hulls of the *Slaughtersong*. The gap was crammed with maintenance tunnels and accessways leading to the external sensor arrays and weapons emplacements, and could take them to any point on the ship if the coven kept their sense of direction.

Amakyre was well aware that there could be anything on this ship. How long had it been up here, orbiting the daemon world? The Slaughtersong had shone down on Torvendis for as long as the legends could remember, so long it had become a part of the immensely complex star-divinations of the planet's sages. And where had it come from? How had it come to Torvendis at all?

'Nothing on the auspex, captain,' came Feorkan's voice on the vox. 'This area's dead. Where do we go?'

'There's no point in scouring this place. The ship will have saviour pods and shuttlecraft Karnulon could use to escape, we must find him as soon as possible above all other priorities. We head for the bridge.'

Feorkan acknowledged and the coven moved swiftly through the hull-space. The corridors and doorways were circular with blank readout screens everywhere, evenly and harshly lit by the lumostrips running along the ceiling. His augmented hearing picked up the faint purring of machinery deep within the craft, even and smooth.

Amakyre had heard tell that before the beginning of history, before the accursed Imperium of man had seeded the stars with weakness and ignorance, before the terrible Age of Strife from which the Imperium had emerged, there was a time when technology had come to rule humankind. Many of the secrets from the Dark Age of Technology had been lost, leaving only the barest scraps of information surviving. Could this craft itself be a relic of that dark age? Was it really that old?

It was impossible, of course. The Maelstrom swallowed up everything, eventually. Nothing could have survived in it for that long. But the idea was tempting – think of the power this craft could have if Amakyre could capture it, and the respect that would be due him from the Word Bearers.

A tempting thought indeed, he concluded, as the corridor passed a huge transparent wall section that looked out on a massive weapons array larger in itself than many spacecraft. But the coven had its mission. Karnulon came first.

'This is his plan,' voxed Makelo from ahead, 'isn't it? This ship. Karnulon must have found it and realised how powerful a weapon it is. Now he just has to start it up.'

Amakyre could just see Makelo's scarlet-armoured form ahead of him, stalking past the bulkheads and machinery. 'Perhaps. We will know for sure once he is dead.' Amakyre switched to Feorkan's frequency. 'Any bearing on the bridge?'

'The auspex scanner shows power conduits radiating out from a central point,' came the reply. 'Somewhere in the heart of the ship. There's lots of interference but it's all coming from one point. There's a lot of power in here.'

'Take us in the next entrance you find,' said Amakyre.

The lights flickered slightly and the purring of the ship's power source went up a notch. Faint vibrations shuddered through the floor.

After untold years, the *Slaughtersong* was waking up.

GOLGOTH DIDN'T NOTICE if the hard, cold star overhead was any brighter. The whole night sky seemed to leer down at him cruelly – nebulae spat stars at him and the clouds of stellar gas were sucked towards black holes as if turning their faces from him. The jagged line of the Canis Mountains, haloed in the starlight, was a grinning maw eager to swallow him.

Golgoth dragged himself over an incline and slumped down in the lee of the rock, where the chill wind sweeping across from the plains wouldn't cut into him. The foothills of the mountains seemed colder and harsher than ever, barren and devoid of life, as if everywhere Golgoth went was destined to be touched with death. He slumped his aching, exhausted body against the earth and willed himself to sleep, but his mind stayed alert, still full of the terrible things he had seen.

It had been a nightmare. The keep swarmed with thirsting daemons, who ran unchecked by the few bands of warriors awake and sober enough to defend themselves. Golgoth had found his way down to the dungeon levels, where acres of cells led into abattoirs where captives were dissected and processed, and then into the waste pits where a slurry of rancid gore hid his scent from Sh'Karr's daemons. He had writhed blindly through the filth, sometimes diving deep and wondering if he would ever find anywhere to come up for air, sometimes struggling wildly against slithering, clawed things that snapped at his feet as he waded.

The pits below the city had been worse. It rained body parts from above. Blind packs of surviving slaves roamed, more predators than bandits, and Golgoth had fought for his life more than once. He had tried to forget how he had eaten those he had killed, and even those he had found, to keep his strength up as the hours turned into days. But he couldn't forget any of it.

He had swum a river of blood. He had climbed a cliff of corpses. Carrion insects had laid eggs in his hands and feet and left them bleeding and raw where ravenous grubs had chewed their way out. His tears had been full of wriggling white worms and things had squirmed under his fingernails. Some of them were still there.

He barely remembered what he had done after clambering up the slope of bodies and out of the pits. He must have run most of the way, knowing only that he had to go east, towards the mountains and Arrowhead Peak. Now he was within sight of the mountains, Golgoth realised he had no idea what he would do once he got there. Would Kron meet him there, at the Hall of the Elders? Where even was the hall? Golgoth had never heard of it, though admittedly all anyone knew of Arrowhead Peak were scraps of legend from before its fall.

But Kron's message was all Golgoth had to go on. It was all he had – his army was gone, his tribe butchered, his honour betrayed by a foe he couldn't face. Only exhaustion kept his anger from boiling up and taking control of him again.

Why? Why couldn't the gods just look favourably on him once? Why was his every triumph followed by despair and treachery? Just when he thought he had achieved a great victory, his greatest ally slaughtered his men as they slept. Golgoth had never been driven this low, not even when he had found out of Grik's wanton abuse of the Emerald Sword, nor below the eastern walls as his attack broke on the impenetrable defences.

If Golgoth could take this whole world and crush it, he would, if it would only mean revenge. If he could face Sh'Karr now, broken and fatigued as he was, he would do it, if only to die in the name of vengeance. But he could do nothing. There was nothing left on Torvendis for him now.

A shadow passed beneath the starlight. Someone was moving behind him, over the ridge. Golgoth turned, but too late, the figure was upon him, standing right behind him, silhouetted against the weeping sky.

'Golgoth,' it said in a familiar, cold-blooded voice. 'If any one of us could have survived, I knew it would be you.'

'Tarn,' said Golgoth. 'I had thought I was the only one.'

Tarn loped over the ridge and settled down next to Golgoth. His thin killer's fingers were bloody and scabbed. There were bite marks in his palms – he must have fought his way out of the city with his bare hands. His face was pale and drawn, but his eyes, rimmed with sleepless red, were wide and alert. 'Have some faith, Golgoth. It takes more than that to kill me.'

'Are there any others?'

'Maybe. I didn't see them. If there are, they haven't come this way. You were the only one I could track eastwards. Which leads me to wonder just why you are heading in this direction, when it would be the obvious route for Sh'Karr to hunt down survivors.'

'Kron gave me a message. I think he will meet me in Arrowhead Peak, if I can reach it.'

'Although it is unwise to speak ill of my chieftain,' said Tarn, 'I will wager you need some rest before attempting the journey. I will find us food and water. You sleep.'

With that, Tarn disappeared into the darkness. And Golgoth, knowing that at least there was one man left who would kill for him, gradually fell asleep.

ON ONE SCREEN, the suns were coming up over the Canis Mountains, framing the jagged peaks in a haze of gold, painting the valleys with a milky grey. On another, the oceans were still wrapped in darkness, starlight playing across the churning surface as sea monsters rose from the deeps to graze on the smaller creatures above. There were a dozen scenes being played out, picked up by the *Slaughter-song's* sensor arrays and transmitted onto flat screens that hovered in the centre of the bridge.

Kron watched a new day dawn and another one end. He watched the city, glimpsing the daemons running wild through the corpse-choked streets. He saw straggling bands of refugees, civilians from the battle preyed on by escaped slaves and vagrant warriors fleeing from Sh'Karr's daemons. Torvendis itself seemed lazy and sated with blood. But the daemon world would become thirsty enough soon, Kron knew. One battle was never enough.

The bridge of the *Slaughtersong* was a shining armoured sphere several hundred metres across, in which hovered circular platforms lit brightly from within. Instrumentation appeared as ghostly lines of light in the air, traced out by hidden holoprojectors, and scanners fed through to broad flat screens that hung everywhere and followed at a command.

The *Slaughtersong* seemed composed of silver and light. It was a world away from the ugliness of the Maelstrom outside, where there was only madness and bloodshed.

Kron stood on the central platform, watching the Canis Mountains as two tiny figures trekked along the upper foothills and into the rugged valleys of the mountains themselves. Soon, he told himself. Soon.

There was a bleeping from one of the scanner screens. The image it showed was filled with static, and Kron knew from experience that the internal scanners must be warped by psychics or sorcery. The screen was tuned in to one of the scanners in the maintenance ducts, and was picking up movement – shadowy forms, shaped like men but far bigger, that were stalking carefully towards the bridge sphere.

A military unit. He caught a dull hint of scarlet – Word Bearers, then. It was to be expected that they would manage to follow him here. A shame that this beautiful ship would have to see violence before this was all done with. But if that was the way it had to be, then Kron would see it through to the end.

Kron waved a hand and a dozen screens clustered around him, each showing one of the approaches to the bridge. There were many – every passage on the ship led here eventually. Gradually the interference was spreading, meaning the Word Bearers had probably brought a sorcerer with them. It seemed the Word Bearers were organised into a coven, composed of specialists who could deal with any eventuality. They would have a commander, a scout or two, someone with heavy firepower. Highly-trained and motivated better than any other troops in the Maelstrom, they would be utterly determined to see their mission through. It was not lost on Kron that this mission probably involved killing him.

'Ready?' Kron said quietly.

The lights of the *Slaughtersong* flickered in reply.

'Good. Open the armoury and prepare.'

'HOLD,' ORDERED AMAKYRE. 'We'll go in guns first.'

Feorkan sent an acknowledgement over the vox and, together with Makelo and Phaedos, flanked the closed circular portal that lay ahead of them, waiting for the others. Amakyre and Prakordian moved as silently as possible up behind him as Vrox lumbered into position. Massive-bore guns extruded themselves from Vrox's forearms, mouth and eyes, heavy chains of ammunition writhing beneath his skin like thick, dark veins.

The Obliterator stood in front of the door into the bridge, armoured legs planted wide for stability. Amakyre gave a hand signal and Makelo and Feorkan took high-explosive krak grenades from the belts of their armour, planting the dull metal discs around the edge of the door. Phaedos unhooked two bulky cylindrical melta-bombs and mag-clamped them to the door, where their ultra-high temperature detonations would cook off the krak grenades.

Silently, Amakyre counted down the seconds on his fingers. Three. Two. One.

The grenades went off in unison, blasting the door into a storm of metal shards. Instantly Vrox opened up, every gun blazing massive calibre shells, red-hot casings fountaining. Chains of gunfire ripped through the air, sending bright points of light streaming into the brightly-lit, spherical room beyond, and the noise was truly terrible.

Vrox took a step into the room, muscles straining between the plates of his armour as he forced himself forward against the recoil of his guns. Phaedos ducked the streams of bullets and sidestepped into the room, chainblade held low, bolt pistol held out in front to shoot anything that still moved. Feorkan followed, Makelo crouched in the doorway scanning with his sniper-stripped bolter. Then, Amakyre charged through.

The room was flooded with light. It shone from the circular platforms that floated in the air like leaves on water, and seemed composed entirely of light that was reflected and re-reflected from the polished interior of the spherical room. Amakyre's enhanced senses instantly picked out the one potential foe – high above, standing on the central platform, was a man.

From here the man looked almost harmless, for he was old and slim, with a beard and straggly hair. His clothes were many layers of dull brown robes, clean but frayed with wear. Yet his face had a look to it that Amakyre was very familiar with, the look of man who, like Amakyre himself, had lived for so long and seen so much that he could hardly be called a man at all.

Karnulon had shed his armour, and a sorcerer of his power would be able to assume any form he wanted. This unassuming shape was the sort of body he would have to wear if he was to hope to act on Torvendis unnoticed.

Bright bolts were already spattering up towards the platform from Makelo's bolter and Phaedos's pistol. Amakyre added his own bolter fire as the old man gestured and the platform sped upwards and to the side. Phaedos was leaping onto the nearest platform, intent on making his way up the chamber to take on the enemy face to face.

The old man was unarmed. Amakyre switched to the squad vox.

'Cease fire!' he yelled. The din of Vrox's gunfire halted, replaced by the tinny patter of shell casings still hitting the floor.

'I have a shot, captain,' voxed Makelo quietly.

'Hold your fire, Word Bearer,' ordered Amakyre. Then, out loud, he called up to the distant figure.

'A brother Word Bearer deserves a proper execution!' he shouted. 'Not this animal's death. We have come to kill you, Karnulon, but you will have some choice over how it happens.'

The old man held up a hand and one of the lower platforms drifted down to Amakyre's feet. Amakyre stepped on to it and was carried slowly upward.

Darkness began to overcome the light. Gradually, the silver walls were turning black, and Amakyre realised they were projecting the image of the Maelstrom around them onto the chamber's walls. It was as if the whole ship was turning translucent, or disappearing and leaving the occupants of the bridge suspended in space.

'We know you abandoned your Legion, Karnulon,' continued Amakyre. 'We know you took your ship and fled from the authority of Lorgar and the commanders of the Word Bearers. You ignored all the orders transmitted to you. You eluded our pursuit ships and forced us to follow you to Torvendis and confront you here.

'What we do not know is why. If you will tell us what business you had on Torvendis, it will not be painless and it will not be quick, but it will end. But if you do not, we will be forced to extract what we can from your soul, and then hand what remains over to blessed Lorgar himself and the arch-sorcerers of the Legion.'

Amakyre was level with the old man now. The man was clearly unarmed, and his posture seemed slightly stooped and weary. He knew he was defeated, and that his lifespan was measured now in seconds. It was a pathetic end for a Space Marine who had done the work of the Chaotic pantheon for so long, but it was no more than he deserved for plotting against his Legion.

'I have been alive for ten thousand years,' continued Amakyre, determined to break Karnulon before he killed him. 'I have seen untold variations in the terrible things that can befall the unworthy. But even I am unable to comprehend the sheer torment they will keep you in. I have glimpsed the court of Lorgar and heard the screams of those who have wronged him, but I cannot know what they suffer. But you will know, Karnulon, if you force us to show you. I can take your head and Prakordian will interrogate your soul, but the Legion will have its due.

'You can stop it, if you wish. Tell us what you were planning against your Legion, and what force compelled you to deviate from the command of Lorgar, and we can end it here. You will suffer, but that suffering will end with your final death. Tell us, and you can die with at least the honour of knowing your fellow Marines can understand your penance. Choose, Karnulon.'

The man straightened, and his face hardened. Standing against the background of the swirling maelstrom and silhouetted by its pale starlight, he didn't look as frail as he had done a moment before. He looked Amakyre right in the eye, and it had been a long, long time since anyone had been able to do that.

'Karnulon is dead,' said the old man. 'My name is Arguleon Veq.'

GOLGOTH AND TARN made it into the shadow of Arrowhead Peak just as the sun was setting. The journey had been cold and often agonisingly slow, but they had never been in any doubt as to their direction. All they had to do was follow the harpies.

A great stream of them poured across the sky in a mass migration, heading towards the city where doubtless mounds of stinking carrion had attracted them. The thick, dark ribbon of flying bodies led Tarn and Golgoth through the dark valleys and frozen ridges to where the many mountains of Arrowhead Peak rose, the mountainsides riddled with gaping doors and abandoned hovel-caves.

Tarn strode on ahead, pausing every now and then for Golgoth to catch up. His leader was still badly fatigued, and it was only his determination to find what Kron had left for him that kept him going.

Tarn had stopped at the edge of the next ridge, beyond which was the rushing sound of a river. Golgoth clambered up to him and looked down.

It was a river of blood, foaming pink where rocks broke the surface. It flowed down the valley from a jagged-mouthed cavern some way upstream, carrying with it wispy strands of flesh that clogged around the rocks. The stench of blood welled up from it, and had Golgoth not been immersed in that same smell for so long beforehand, he would have gagged at it.

'It must have flowed here from the city,' said Tarn, as if to himself. 'There was too much to drain into the earth and it formed underground rivers that spread all over the continent. Half of Torvendis must be bleeding.'

'Can we cross?'

Tarn pointed downstream to where several large boulders had resisted the river's flow. 'Probably. I know I can.'

Golgoth looked up at the pinnacles of Arrowhead Peak, where Kron might be waiting even now. To go around the river would add days. 'We'll cross.'

The two men picked their way along the bank towards the boulders, where the blood was forming fierce rapids. Tarn went first, hopping from rock to rock with agility not dulled by his recent ordeal. Golgoth tried to follow but he felt heavy and clumsy, for the exhaustion of the flight from the city had still not left him. It troubled him that Tarn, who had been subservient to him when the Emerald Sword had existed, was now leading him along like a parent might a child.

Golgoth reached the far bank but as he pulled himself over the last rock his grip slipped and he rolled off into the vile liquid. His footing failed him on the river bed and he fell face-first into the gore, thick freezing blood forcing its way into his mouth and nose. He pushed himself up to his knees and shook his head free, scooping blood from his eyes and hair.

Tarn stood on the bank, looking down at him, and said nothing.

Golgoth waded to the shore. As he clambered up the bank he saw that two whitish stones by his hand were not stones at all, but skulls. Had they been washed down here all the way from the city? It was possible. Maybe Torvendis had swallowed them and regurgitated them here.

He picked one up. It was not human. The cranium was subtly tapered, as were the large eye sockets. The jaw was thin, with a slim point to the chin, and the cheekbones stood out. It would have made for a delicate, graceful, elfin face, with large searching eyes and a tiny thin nose.

Perhaps it was from one of the strange creatures that had languished in Lady Charybdia's dungeons? Golgoth cast the skull into the river and followed Tarn up the slope, forgetting the skull and trying to shake the congealing blood from his ears.

The first scarps were appearing in the side of the valley, where bundles of rags still lay amid the filth of the harpies. Fragmented skeletons that had fallen from above during the battle for the peaks were lying in drifts. Crude stone steps were cut into the slope leading to grander avenues on the towering mountains above. Soon they would pass under the arches that signified the jurisdiction of the various tribes, and the wayside shrines to tribal heroes from the days when the mountain peoples truly ruled their own harsh world.

For the first time in a great many centuries, men of the tribes set foot in Arrowhead Peak.

FROM DEEP WITHIN the ship, a bolt of silvery light shot from the armoury doors straight into Veq's hand. The Word Bearer in front of him had barely begun to raise his bolt gun but already Veq's mind had snapped into the cold, heightened cast of battle. The man who had been called Kron by some, and Karnulon by others, was now content to think of himself by his first and greatest name – Arguleon Veq.

The silver sword, sent by the *Slaughtersong* at Veq's unspoken order, was warm and buzzing in his fingers. It was as if the intervening millennia had never happened. Veq and the *Slaughtersong*, so attuned to one another that Veq had hardly to think before his commands were answered, had one more fight to win. The blade was heavy and familiar – with a flick of his wrist he cut the Word Bearer's gun clean in two.

He had seen the corrupted sparks of their souls as they had entered the bridge. He knew that this one was Amakyre, the captain, whose devotion to his Legion had brought him all the way across the Maelstrom on Veq's tail.

The waking of Sh'Karr had weakened him, but now, back on home ground, Arguleon Veq felt as strong as ever. Amakyre dodged backwards and let himself fall from the platform rather than face Veq's blade, honed from the heart of a star and white-hot to all but Veq himself.

Gunfire erupted again from below. Veq swatted away a score of bullets from the Obliterator and caught three more with his free hand, throwing them back down to the floor of the bridge with a curse. The young one, the most dangerous, fired a well-aimed shot at his temple, but Veq flicked his head to the side and the silenced bolt flittered past him.

Veq took two steps and leapt, dropping through the lattice of bullet trails to land directly in front of the Obliterator whose every weapon was blazing at him from point-blank range. The star-sword cut through the air as Veq met every bullet, sending a sparkling fan of deflected fire in every direction.

The hulking Obliterator reeled as several of its own bullets punched through its biomechanical body. The flesh of one arm became fluid, extruded, and solidified into a blade of bone with gnawing teeth at the cutting edge. Veq ducked the first blow and parried the second, shearing the first blade in two as a barbed whip, tipped with a lamprey-like mouth, lashed from the Obliterator's other arm. Veq grabbed the lash, wrapped it round his fist, and used it to swing the Obliterator hard into the wall by the doorway. Armour split and cracked. Corrupted blood spilled. Veq paused to dodge more bolter fire from the other Word Bearers who were falling back through the doorway.

The Obliterator tried to rise to its feet but Veq was faster by far. One swipe hacked its arm off. Another opened it up from throat to belly, spilling half-machine guts out onto the floor. Silvery, snaking entrails spattered across the swirling Maelstrom visible through the transparent floor.

Veq knew better than to assume the Obliterator would die. A bright line sparked in the air and a twisted, half-machine head rolled onto the floor.

One was dead. The slowest and stupidest. Now, for the rest.

ARROWHEAD PEAK WAS chill and empty. Its interior had been carved out by generations of proud tribes people, each tribe and clan and family striving to outdo one another with the imposing vastness of the architecture. Vaulted naves soared overhead. Hand-hewn chasms joined amphitheatres with throne rooms. Artificial harbours loomed on the shores of lakes gathered in the heart of the mountain. The harpies' filth ran down the walls and lay like a blanket beneath their roosts, but nothing could dull the cold grandeur of the place. Strength and honour were written into the architecture. This had been a proud place, and that pride had not died with the tribes who had built it.

The stink of the harpies' foulness was like a hand in Golgoth's face, but he ignored it. The vast stone tunnel they had entered echoed to their footsteps, and the rock beneath their feet was worn smooth by generations of marching tribesmen that had lived there before the city's fall. The remnants of Lady Charybdia's attack still lay scattered here and there – arrow-stuck skeletons, discarded spears and shields, makeshift barricades that had been overrun and pulled apart.

This time, Golgoth was leading Tarn. Neither man had heard of the Hall of the Elders – they didn't know if it existed, let alone where it was. They had walked for an hour, deeper into the first mountain of Arrowhead Peak, their way lit by faint shafts of milky daylight that filtered in through channels cut for light and ventilation. The wind outside was the only sound, save their own footsteps. It seemed they were the only two things alive.

They had come to a crossroads, where a dozen paths met in a large round chamber, age-worn tribal symbols carved into the floor. This had been a place of trade and parley once, and tarnished gold thrones stood in a circle in the centre of the chamber where tribal chiefs had once sat and glowered as they debated the business of Arrowhead Peak. Now, thick cobwebs hung like banners from the high ceiling and a single skeleton was the only thing sitting on the high thrones.

'Where now?' asked Tarn.

Golgoth didn't answer. How could he know? Determination to find Kron and maybe begin the path of vengeance against Sh'Karr had taken him this far, but how could he possibly find a place he had never heard of in a city his people had not set foot in for hundreds of years? He was livid with himself. A man could die down here. All he had gone through and it would end here, entombed in Arrowhead Peak or wandering lost around the mountains.

He kicked against the wall. He tore the axe from his back and hurled it across the chamber. Tarn watched, impassive.

A movement caught his eye, something small and flittering. Golgoth hoped it was a rat, so he could stamp it to death and let some of his anger bleed out. Or even better, a harpy, so he could hold its wings and tear them off. But it was neither. It was a bird, tiny and quick, with feathers of a brilliant iridescent green. It was the same bird that Golgoth had seen in the keep, and that had delivered Kron's message.

The bird shimmered across the chamber and into one of the side tunnels. Golgoth ran after it and Tarn followed wordlessly, sprinting as Golgoth plunged into the darkness of the tunnel.

It led downwards. Golgoth sometimes thought he had lost the bird, but each time he heard the flutter of its wings or saw a flash of green in the faint light. The light was coming from the walls and floor now, a dim glow let off by some strange phosphorescent matter that clung in blue-white patches to the stone. The tunnel wound further down and Golgoth imagined it was describing a spiral that drilled far down into the mountain.

The tunnel emerged into an enormous underground cavern where the air was close and hot. Stalactites hung, huge and dripping like fangs, and trickles of water spattered down into an unseen pool far below. The walls and floor were too far away to be seen, as if there was a whole world beneath the mountain and the ceiling above was the sky. Golgoth's footsteps seemed to take an age to echo back to him.

The floor formed a bridge that curved down across the cavern towards an immense irregular sphere of stone, like a heart of rock suspended in the centre of the cavern. The bridge led to an archway carved into the stone, with darkness beyond.

A tiny flashing green dot that was the bird flitted through the archway ahead. Golgoth followed it, taking care to keep his footing on the wet stone as the bridge became thinner and thinner. There was a very faint rumbling in the air, as if they were so far down they could hear Torvendis's heart beating.

'Do you know of this place?' asked Golgoth.

'No. And neither did the tribes when they lived here,' replied Tarn. 'Or else they would have held this place against Lady Charybdia.'

'Unless they would rather have faced her up there than be trapped down here.'

The stone heart loomed in front of them. Golgoth could just see that same faint phosphorescence beyond as he approached the threshold.

Carefully, he stepped through the arch, aware that Tarn was hanging back some way behind. The bird was hopping impatiently on the floor just inside, its tiny dark eyes glancing here and there. Golgoth stooped down to see if it was carrying another message, but it took flight, fluttering away across the expanse of the cavern and out of sight. Golgoth stood up, took a breath, and walked into the Hall of the Elders.

The glowing lichen was thick on the ceiling, making the whole room a ghostly pale blue-grey. It was a circular room as large as the grandest feasting halls, with a huge rectangular slab like an oversized sarcophagus in the centre.

The pale light seemed to congeal around the sarcophagus. Gradually it coalesced into human forms, a crowd of them, standing several deep around the slab. More detail emerged from the glow until Golgoth was looking at the faces and clothes of glowing, ghostly men and women. They turned to look at Golgoth as he entered. They were tall and broad-shouldered, wearing the same furs and skins that the mountain peoples had worn for as long as the Canis Mountains had existed. Their ages were impossible to guess, for they had smooth-skinned faces but lined, weary eyes, pure black with no pupils.

'Another one,' said one man.

'Do not sound so jaded,' said a different voice, a woman's. 'How long has it been since the last?'

'It will be the same,' came a different reply, and Golgoth realised that every statement came in a different voice. 'They are always the same. Why don't we ask him? See his face turn pale.' A male ghost walked towards Golgoth – Golgoth could see right through him. 'You. Do you know what this place is?'

'The Hall of the Elders.'

The man seemed young and strong, with hair down to his shoulders and a bow slung at his back. Was this one of the Emerald Sword's dead, a young warrior slain on some ancient battlefield? The ghost smiled. 'And are you worthy to stand within it? If you are not, Torvendis will swallow you and spit you out as a rock or a tree. It has never failed to do so, not once. When this world was founded, we were placed here as guardians. We are the first of the Emerald Sword, our purpose is to ensure that only the one whose soul was pure hate should see this place and survive.'

Golgoth smiled. 'Hate? I know nothing about this place. But I know everything about hate. If I could crush this world, I would, just to give my hatred somewhere to go. If I could drain the Maelstrom dry, I would do it. I would fight the gods of Chaos if it meant I could find an outlet for my hate.'

The ghostly man turned to the watching ghostly crowd. 'Well?'

A woman walked up to Golgoth. She was a warrior-woman such as the Sword had bred before it became weak. Her hair was hacked short and even though it was composed of the same swirling fog as her, Golgoth could see the sword at her side was notched and pitted with use. She laid a hand on Golgoth's chest. It was cold.

Then, pain. Golgoth felt as if he were immersed in ice, the sheer agonising cold flowing right through to his bones. Suddenly, the chamber was gone and he was high in the air, hurtling over the Canis Mountains. The viewpoint shifted and zoomed in to one of the valleys where a brutal battle raged, a half-dozen tribes mingled in bloodshed. A giant warrior swung a halberd and took a head with every stroke. Golgoth could see the red raw hatred in his soul, this man who had given up on his humanity and embraced a life of slaughter.

No, a voice spoke somewhere in the back of Golgoth's head. *This one has far deeper loathing than this.*

Another change. The cold gripped again and dragged Golgoth across the skies of Torvendis and the disease-ridden southern islands shimmered into view. Golgoth's view shot down and into a dark cabin of warped tropical wood. A woman rolled the body of a murdered man under the cabin's single bed. Golgoth knew, somehow, that this woman had killed many like this before in revenge for some wrong done to her, and would kill a great many more, in a fruitless attempt to exorcise the howl of rage in her head. Her hatred consumed her entire soul and drove her every action.

No. Not enough, said the distant voice. *This one has hatred deep indeed.*

Another change. The Crimson Knights of legend, in red robes with their faces cowled, stood in a circle and debated how best they might commit yet more atrocities before the people of Torvendis found the will to rise up against them.

Something huge and sentient beneath the seas built a mighty black reef to wreck passing ships, so it could drag the crews down and feel their lives ebbing away beneath the world. It did this because it wanted the world to suffer.

A mighty sorcerer plunged a staff of awesome power into the ocean and let it boil. His rage was so great that only the eradication of life would sate it.

No, came the voice. *He has more hate than any of them. It is deeper and deadlier. It would drive him to more terrible things than any of these have committed, if he only had the power.*

Ss'll Sh'Karr, in Torvendis's distant past when he first ruled, sat on a throne of bones, thousands of bodies heaped at his feet, drinking in the blood of a tortured world and feeling the Blood God's loathing pumping through his veins.

The cold was terrible. It seemed to chill Golgoth's body and freeze his very soul. He was laid utterly bare, his whole mind open for scrutiny. Everything about him was stripped away, his memories, the layers of his personality, even Kron's sorcery that had kept him alive through so much.

There was only one part of him left. The thing that beat at his core and kept him living when everything around him told him he should die.

His hate.

The cold let him go. He was whole again, lying gasping on the surface of the chamber, the ghostly figures of the Emerald Sword standing around him. The warrior-woman was kneeling beside him, removing her cold hand from his chest.

Her black eyes were wide with shock. 'The… the loathing… the violence… this is betrayal, this is purest hate. It is deeper than that of any other living thing on Torvendis. You have lost everything. Your hatred is pure, born of betrayal. Arguleon Veq told us that one like you would come to the Hall of the Elders. It has been so long, we never thought you would…'

'It is him?' asked a man.

'It can be no other.'

Suddenly, the figures were fading away, coiling up into wisps of smoke that filtered up towards the ceiling and then were gone. Golgoth was alone in the chamber. If, of course, the ghosts had ever been there in the first place. His breath came in gasps – the memory of that terrible coldness, and the after-images of the terrible things the elders had shown him, left him dizzy and shaken.

Had this chamber really been here since the birth of the Emerald Sword tribe? Had Golgoth been the first to survive the test? Perhaps, he thought, here he would be able to find a way to exact his revenge and begin to rebuild his tribe. That strange feeling in his heart was hope, turned savage by the depth of his hatred and rage. Sh'Karr would be bled dry. Torvendis would be his, no matter what it took. The totems of the Emerald Sword would cast their shadows across the whole world.

The huge sarcophagus shuddered and with a grinding of stone the lid moved aside. Golgoth got to his feet and peered inside – his eyes caught a flash of green.

It was a blade, long and thin, with a two-handed grip. It was made entirely of crystal that shone in the milky light, a vivid green crystal.

It was the same weapon that had once found a home in the hands of Arguleon Veq. It had been the subject of legends that Golgoth had heard as a child, told around tribal campfires to remember the days of warlike glory past. It was the Emerald Sword.

It wasn't real. It couldn't be. The Emerald Sword was a legend, gone with the age of Arguleon Veq and the Last. But it was here, right in front of him, and in that moment Golgoth was absolutely certain that this really was the sword itself. His tribe, so abused and corrupted, had been founded to guard the sword on the orders of Veq himself. Golgoth was the last of the tribe, and so it fell to him to take up the weapon and exact vengeance against those who had opposed the word of Veq by destroying the tribe.

Golgoth reached into the sarcophagus. It smelled of dust and age inside, and the air was so dry it seemed to suck the moisture from his skin. His hand closed around the cold, crystal haft of the sword, feeling it tingle against his fingers.

It was light, and so perfectly balanced it seemed to want to swing itself. Golgoth swept the shimmering blade through the air, watching the shining green trail it left behind it like a shooting star.

The rock beneath his feet was rumbling. The wan light flickered like a dying fire above him. Suddenly the walls of the chamber were moving inwards and billowing out like something alive, with a deep, throaty heaving sound. Golgoth ran for the archway and came out onto the bridge where Tarn was backing away, ready to run. Tarn glanced at the sword in Golgoth's hand, then up at the huge bulb of stone, before turning and sprinting towards the other side of the cavern.

Golgoth looked up before he followed.

The stone heart of Torvendis was beating.

PHAEDOS PUT UP a better fight than Vrox had. He was fast and he had learned a thousand different feints in his years as a

Word Bearer. In the endless galleries of the neoplasma generators, where the gigantic cylindrical turbines hung suspended between a web of gantries, Phaedos turned to face Arguleon Veq.

It was brave, in so much as anything a Word Bearer did could be called brave. It showed his devotion to the Legion, which was typical. Arguleon Veq had come to loathe those such as the Word Bearers above all others – mindless preachers who covered up their self-serving conniving with the veneer of a debased religion. They spouted hatred from the pulpit as if it was something sacred, and butchered anything in their way just to prove they were superior to the wretches they ground beneath their feet. That was what Chaos could do – rot away a man's humanity and have the cruelty to let him believe he was still worth something.

Phaedos, backed against the railing around a corner, jumped out as Veq approached in the hope of ambushing his foe. Veq caught Phaedos's chainsword on his own sword and locked the blade between the teeth of the chainblade, twisting it out of Phaedos's grasp. Phaedos let go and rolled beneath Veq's guard, blasting a volley of bolt pistol shells up into Veq's body. Veq twisted and felt the air turn searing hot as the bolts shot past his torso, close enough to singe his robes.

'Armour,' said Veq, and plates of armour shot through the air from the depths of the *Slaughtersong* to slam around his body. Much of Veq's old panoply had fallen into the hands of prophets and tyrants down on Torvendis, but the *Slaughtersong* had kept the starheart sword and the armour of the deep safe in its armoury.

The armour had been carved from the bony exoskeletal plates of the giant sea creatures that scoured Torvendis's ocean bed. Ribbed, roughened plates of bone and cartilage thudded into his upper body and arms, as mail of meteoric iron, like silk carried on a wind, flowed through the air and wrapped itself around his abdomen and throat. Hardened spines sprouted down his back and gauntlets of ensorcelled sharkskin slid onto his fingers.

Phaedos caught his falling chainsword, but his next stab was turned aside by a greave of solid, iron-hard bone that had not been there a second ago. Veq grabbed the collar of Phaedos's armour with his free hand and hurled the Word Bearer into the side of the nearest turbine. Blue-white sparks fountained as electricity coursed through Phaedos and he fell hard onto the walkway.

He fought until the last. But by then his muscles were burning inside his power armour and his arm was slowed. Veq turned the chainsword aside with his boot, kicked it into the air, caught it and drove it through the small of Phaedos's back, chainblade chewing through plasteel and bone. Phaedos writhed like a pinned insect, gasped, and died.

Veq could not deny it felt good. It felt almost as good as it had done all those years ago, when he had tamed the Maelstrom in the name of Chaos, stormed cities and slain armies for the voices in his head he called gods. He had wished to drown in an ocean of blood, revel in a torrent of flesh, delight in decay and wield the powers of change like a weapon. He had done everything they had asked of him, and he had asked only that they honour him as their greatest champion in return. He had given himself over to Chaos, and it had taken ten thousand years to get himself back.

He left Phaedos's body smouldering on the walkway, and moved on to hunt down the others.

THE CURIOUS THING was, almost all of the legends were true. Arguleon Veq really had been tall as a mountain when he wanted to be (which was rare – he had learned early on that a small target survives longer). He had walked the bottom of the oceans to hunt the things that lived there. He had torn down the gates of the Obsidian City and broken the back of the Overdaemon that ruled there. He had taken on an army of alien savages and killed them all with his bare hands. He had done all the things that the legends said he had before he had come to Torvendis, and many of the things he had done afterwards. And, above all, he had fought the Last.

Of course, no one on Torvendis actually knew what the Last was. If any of them had guessed correctly, they had been drowned out by the other theories that survived. The ones that said the Last was a huge and powerful daemon, or a god who fell foul of a conspiracy amongst the innumerable other deities of the warp, or some ancient and arcane war machine left behind by aliens. Veq would have found the lies they told amusing, had they not covered up a more terrible truth.

The truth was that the Maelstrom had not always occupied this tract of space. That the Maelstrom was there at all was, in part, down to Veq, a fact for which he would never forgive himself. Soon, he told himself, soon the truth would be known, and he would have perhaps gained himself some measure of redemption. It would not be enough, not anything close to what he would have to do to atone for all the evil he had wrought. But even if it was just a gesture, it would be more than he had ever truly accomplished before.

Arguleon Veq had fought the Overslayer of the green-skinned barbarians and burned the Immortal Library of the Ninety-Seven Sorcerers. He had waited at the courts of the gods when the Imperium of Man was still throwing off its birth caul and he had seen the universe with eyes so jaded by experience that he could look upon the warp itself and not go mad. But he realised now that he had never done anything of which he was proud. He had seen what Chaos was, what it had done to him and demanded in return, and now nothing he had done seemed to justify a fraction of esteem in which his memory was held.

It was not that he was a good person at heart. Veq could find little place in his soul for those innumerable unfortunates who made up the armies he had slaughtered, and on Torvendis millions of men had died to satisfy the requirements of his plan. No, it was not goodness that gnawed in the pit of his tainted soul. It was anger.

FOR ONCE, GOLGOTH was quicker than Tarn. He called on every thread of sorcery that Kron had left him, leaping down the slope with the legs of an antelope, the tireless energy of a sea kraken driving his limbs, a hawk's eyes looking for the quickest path away from Arrowhead Peak. The Emerald

Sword in his hand covered the mountainside around him with a vibrant green glow, and rocks fell like hail all around him as he ran. A sound like a hundred thunderstorms raged from below, like the bellow of a subterranean god.

Tarn lagged behind, though he was sprinting, too. The two men had made it out of the tunnels of Arrowhead Peak more by luck than forethought, for there was no way they could retrace a route with the tunnels spasming like pumped arteries and the walls of the chambers pulsing in and out. Now, they were separated by the rain of stone and the terrible heaving of the mountainside beneath them.

Golgoth risked a glance backwards. He caught a glimpse of Tarn, stumbling and clutching an arm where it had been broken by falling rock. The mountain slope above him was shuddering violently and huge slabs of rock were detaching to slide down and reveal the bone-white ancient strata beneath. The mountain peaks all around were shaking as they slid out of their stone sheaths, gleaming points punching out and stabbing towards the sky. The Canis Mountains had never looked more like the teeth of the Last, teeth set into a jaw that ran the length of the continent.

The sky above was caught between night and day, the speckled black velvet of the Maelstrom punctured by the violent flares of a dozen suns, gathered sombrely to watch the destruction.

Golgoth reached the bottom of the slope and sprinted down the length of the valley. It was the same one that had held the rushing blood river scant hours before, but now the walls were cracked and the torrent was a churning knee-high mass darkened to purple by detritus thrown up by the quaking underfoot. The whole mountain range seemed to quiver and with a noise like nothing Golgoth had ever heard the ground rose like an ocean wave, carrying Golgoth higher and higher until he was sure he could see clear across the mountains, to the coast in the north and the foothills westwards.

The whole range seemed to be breaking apart, smooth white peaks rising from the grey stone. Here and there deeper fissures had opened and plumes of magma spattered into the air. Avalanches swept down mountainsides. Ice-filled valleys shattered like broken glass. Many-coloured lightning lanced down from where violent air currents had been driven into massive black thunderheads.

The swell died and the ground plummeted again. Golgoth had no idea where Tarn was, or where he was – he felt the shifting land was taking him closer to the plains of the west where he might be safer, but huge chunks of rock were collapsing into chasms and boulders were tumbling down towards him all around.

The Canis Mountain range shattered down its spine, giving way to something far older and more terrible. Beneath the greatest peaks, the heart beat ever stronger as the Last broke ground on Torvendis once again.

CHAPTER TEN

MANY LEGENDS CLAIM to tell of the birth of Torvendis. Creation legends are amongst the oldest of the tales told in the courts of prophets and around the campfires of barbarians, and every people that has ever graced Torvendis has a different tale of how the planet came to be.

There are those that say the planet is an egg laid in the time before the gods, which will one day hatch into a new god that will subjugate the warp and bring about the final war between all forces, from which only Chaos will emerge. Others maintain the world is the heart of the Maelstrom, turned to stone when Chaos infected the warp storm and took it over like maggots infest a corpse. Still others have died to protect the notion that Torvendis was given to the real universe by the gods of the warp, to act as a bridge across which the ignorance of reality might be enlightened by the madness of Chaos.

Arguleon Veq had heard most of these legends and perhaps he alone, aside from the Chaos gods themselves, knew the truth. Because there had not always been a Maelstrom. Once, countless thousands of years before, there was just a tract of realspace, scattered with stars and a handful of inhabitable worlds. Intelligent species, as species would, found amongst these worlds a home for themselves or a colony for their offspring. When the fabric of reality became too thinly stretched and the warp bled through, untold numbers died or were driven mad over the course of a generation as the rules of reality were rescinded. Stars imploded or exploded or mutated into something new. Planets were swallowed and melded and tortuously deformed into daemon worlds. Populations died as one, or fled, or welcomed the daemonic powers as saviours or gods. It was a time of terrible madness and conquest.

Some worlds survived. There were species that were simply too tough to roll over without a fight, like the green-skinned hordes or the nocturnal reptilians that infested asteroid belts. Others were too clever.

Arguleon Veq was not the only one who knew there had once been eldar on Torvendis. He was, however, the only one outside the gods who knew just how long ago they had been there. Torvendis had been a jewel in the now-fallen empire of the alien eldar, a species which prized knowledge and self-mastery over all other things and who at their height commanded technology that bordered on the most powerful magic. Torvendis had been a beautiful world, with verdant forests, shimmering seas, and towering cities of glass and ivory. It had been a world of learning and culture, a place jealously guarded by the eldar as a crucial link of the webway that held their empire together.

Torvendis had been caught in the heart of the eruption of warp space. The systems around it were torn apart and their populations enslaved. Torvendis endured, protected first by a fleet of warships, then a shield of sorcerous energies, and then just the faith and invention of the eldar themselves. The eldar, though long-lived, were still mortal, and they were cut off from their fellows elsewhere. Gradually, one by one, they died. Torvendis, however, did not.

THE HOLD OF the *Slaughtersong* held a flight of fighter craft, huge chromed raptors with delta-swept wings and bundles of particle projectors jutting from the fuselage. There were seventy of these craft lined up neatly in the hold, lit by the stark floodlights high up on the ceiling, waiting to be launched at the will of the ship's master just as they had waited since they had flown against the Last.

It was a good place to hide, a vast space covered with fighters, each one providing formidable cover with its underslung bomb casings and landing gear. And it was here that two of the Word Bearers had fled.

Arguleon Veq could smell them, the oil and age of their equipment, their sweat, their bodies corrupted with the stink of the warp. Veq couldn't hear their vox-communications but he knew from the way they had scattered that it was every Marine for himself now. Their leader and the psyker had gone one way, these two the other, and the dangerous one a third.

Veq moved slowly and quietly, the starheart sword held low to prevent its glow from giving him away, the armour of the deeps dripping with brine to keep its plates from grinding audibly. It felt so good to be back in the chitinous armour, with a blade in his hand and an enemy to fight. Veq knew how that feeling could be so seductive, how it had dragged him into the fold of Chaos and kept him a slave for so long.

He could catch no glimpse of scarlet armour between the forest of landing gear. There had been a time when he could see and hear anything that dared move within a league of him, but he was an old man and his glory days, he admitted to himself, were over. He would have to hunt down his enemy the old-fashioned way.

Veq saw the bolt before he heard its report, like a tiny steel insect buzzing towards his head. His reactions were almost as sharp as they had ever been, he was pleased to note as he ducked the shot and let it thud into the hull of the fighter behind him. The shooter, though, had slipped back into cover.

He was a damn good shot, this one. Probably the scout.

Veq broke into a run and allowed himself a small sensation of satisfaction as his sprint lured the other Marine into spraying a storm of bolter fire, explosive shots rattling around him on full-auto. Miniature explosions studded the hull of the closest fighter as Veq leapt, kicked off the side of the ship and vaulted onto the wing of the ship opposite.

The Word Bearer was almost directly below him, trying to track Veq while firing off the rest of his clip. Veq slashed downwards and the wing of the fighter sheared off in a crescent of sparks, crashing to the floor and forcing the Marine to dive out of the way.

A reflex action forced Veq's blade hand to deflect a shot from the scout, taken in the instant Veq had left himself open. In the split-second the other Marine dived under a fighter.

'*Slaughtersong*! Give me fighter command!' yelled Veq as he dropped off the ship he was standing on, bolter rounds shattering the cockpit behind him.

Of course, my lord, replied the ancient ship in a metallic voice directly into Veq's inner ear, and suddenly the cockpit instrumentation lit up on seventy ships.

They had nearly got him. A split-second either way and they could have got him in the head, or knocked him off his feet with a shot to the body. He was old, and slow, and these were a pair of Traitor Marines who had fought for so long that they acted as one. The scout was a better shot but the Tactical Marine was more reckless, and together they could have killed him.

Arguleon Veq was the greatest champion the Maelstrom had ever known, and he had not got there without knowing not to underestimate the enemy. He raised a hand and a fighter craft suddenly juddered into motion, blue-flamed thrusters flaring as it rose into the air revealing the Tactical Marine sheltering beneath. Veq brought his hand down and the craft fell, smashing into the floor of the hangar and scattering metal fragments as the Marine rolled frantically out of the way. Veq swept a hand sideways and another fighter slammed into the first, rupturing its fuel tank and sending a plume of flame washing through the air.

The Tactical Marine was running into the nearest cover, on fire. Veq knew that power armour meant the Marine could ignore the flames. But he was lit up like a beacon, and Veq didn't pass up opportunities like that.

He charged, kicking off against the hulls of ships nearby, flipping through the air to avoid the bolts the scout sent speeding towards him. He reached the fighter under which the burning Marine was trying to hide, vaulted on top of it, rolled across the top of the hull and swung down behind it, starheart sword slashing downwards as he fell.

The starheart blade had no respect for even the most ancient of power armour. The Marine never even had time to register Veq's presence before the sword had passed down the centre of his helmet and through the armour's collar, splitting the chestplate and abdomen and carving through the groin. Cleanly bisected, the awful stink of the Marine's entrails rolled out as his body fell in two in a welter of blood.

A flash of pain burst against Veq's free arm. His reactions had got his body out of the way but the scout's shot had still winged him, burying itself in the chitin on his armour and bursting deep inside. The muscle was bruised and Veq felt the bone crack.

Stupid, slow old man.

His anger welled up inside him and he willed a dozen fighter craft into the air, wheeled them around the hangar, and dropped them in a rain of falling metal, smashing craft all around and triggering a spectacular chain of explosions. He slammed more fighters into the burning wreckage, sending flaming craft scudding along the metal floor. Floodlights were shattered by flying shrapnel. A wave of hot air filled Veq's nostrils with the overpowering smell of fuel and flame.

A bolt lanced out, shot wild. The scout was panicked. For a Space Marine to panic meant a great deal – he must be trapped somewhere in the mass of burning wreckage, hoping to kill Veq with a lucky shot so he could get clear and put out the flames.

No one had got a lucky shot against Veq for many thousands of years. Another wave of fighter craft piled into the wreckage, bringing with them a slew of ammunition crates that detonated in the flames like huge stacks of firecrackers.

The wreckage filled one corner of the hangar and was piled halfway up the wall, surrounded by a blue-flamed moat of burning fuel.

Amazingly, the scout wasn't dead. One arm hanging limp, wreathed in flames, he was dragging himself from beneath the edge of the wreckage. His bolter was wrecked but he was pulling a bolt pistol from his belt with his good arm.

Veq strode across the burning floor, the fire crackling against the armour of the deeps. The scout emptied the magazine of the bolt pistol but Veq could see every shot coming and swatted them away. The scout's helmet was off and Veq could look into his bare, blistered face. His eyes were defiant and what was left of his lips were drawn into a snarl. He dropped his pistol and pulled a combat knife from his waist.

'Defiant to the end,' said Veq, almost with pity. 'What must they do to your soul to make you so blind?'

The scout didn't answer. Perhaps his lips were burned shut or his throat scorched open. Perhaps he just refused to answer someone who stood so sternly against everything the Word Bearers stood for.

Veq raised the starheart blade, and cut off the Word Bearer's head.

THE SURFACE OF Torvendis was shimmering as if in a heat haze. The sands and rocks were squirming, suddenly free of their bonds. The Emerald Sword had been drawn. The Last was free. Torvendis knew it was the end of all things and, because Torvendis and the Last were one, it was glad.

The gleaming teeth sunk into the earth, leaving the wreckage of their stony scabbards where once the mighty Canis Mountains had risen. The earth groaned as they were pushed further through the ground, spearing through the planet's mantle until they surrounded the city where Lady Charybdia had ruled and where now a howling horde of daemons still feasted.

A new mountain range rose as the jaws of the Last reformed themselves in a ring around the city, forming a huge circular maw a thousand kilometres across. Ss'll Sh'Karr looked up from the corpses mounded at his feet and watched as the bone-white spires rose and began to close in on the city.

No mortal could ever understand what thoughts run through the mind of a daemon. But if Ss'll Sh'Karr could ever be capable of feeling fear, perhaps it was then, when the Blood God's chosen was confronted with a foe that even he could not best.

The oceans were churning as if in ecstasy or pain, thrashing the northern coasts with towering waves and wrestling the southern island chains beneath the surface. Titanic kraken which had not left the ocean bed for aeons reared up, immense living islands themselves, as if to glimpse the sky of Torvendis just once before they died.

And it was a dying sky. Blood-red weals, like infected wounds, burst from the horizon. Thick black banks of cloud were split in two by terrible sudden storms, which opened up the sky to the pure weeping majesty of the Maelstrom. Rifts in the ground spat geysers of lava high into the air to fall as black stone rain.

In what were once the foothills of the Canis Mountains, Golgoth and the few remaining tribesmen cowered as a thick rain of acid fell. Golgoth was no longer too proud to throw himself beneath a slender overhang, bury his head beneath his arms and pray to any god that would listen that all this death around him not take him too. He still held the Emerald Sword – though it was surely the drawing of the sword that had brought such destruction to Torvendis, it was all he had left in the world. Not even his rage could keep him going. He could see huge slabs of land rearing up from where the swamplands had been, and a spider's web of molten rock bubbling up through the wreckage of the mountains.

He had never seen such death. The magnitude of it all was enough to make even Golgoth forget the depths of his hatred.

He could not know that his very hatred had made all this possible, or that the Emerald Sword tribe he had so nearly destroyed was the key to the devastation. He wondered in his desperation if this was the Last, come to reclaim its world as more than a few prophets had predicted throughout Torvendis's history. It would have been little comfort to him to discover he was right.

The jungles were writhing, the dense trees rioting in delight at the terror even as lightning slashed into them and set fires that breathed immense towers of smoke into the sky. Distant places that had taken their leave of Torvendis's history for the past few centuries – the ice caps, the snaking coral sandbars that took up half an ocean, titanic skeletons with ruined cities built into the skulls – suffered too. Some came alive where no life should be. Others sank beneath the waves, or were blown high into the sky.

Torvendis spasmed and screamed. Its very mantle and core in torment, sending pulses of lava gouting from the surface. From orbit, it looked like Torvendis was bleeding to death.

THE YOUNGEST OF the Word Bearers, and the most dangerous, was the last to face Veq. Veq knew the leader was still out there, but as he headed from the burning hangar into the machine-spirit core the *Slaughtersong* told him the Word Bearers' captain was in the maintenance layer. That meant he was trying to escape with the psyker, to go back through the boarding lock of the attack shuttle that had brought the coven here, and return to his own ship.

He would not succeed. In fleeing, he had chosen to end his own life running instead of fighting. He had condemned the psyker to the same fate. The young Word Bearer was cleverer than his captain in one truly important area – he knew how to die, a rare and valuable commodity that Veq had seen very little of, though he had experienced plenty of death.

The machine-spirit of the *Slaughtersong* was, perhaps, even older than the rest of the ship. Veq had found the ship towards the beginning of his career in the Maelstrom and even then he knew it was something special. That is was a relic of the Dark Age of Technology there was little doubt, and the machine-spirit was the strongest evidence. The core was like an arena ringed by towering grey-black memory stacks as tall as buildings, each with a faint ripple of light playing across the surface. The wide circular arena of dark glassy stone was full of wispy lights, forming complex shapes and swirling patterns that broke up and reformed at the speed of the *Slaughtersong's* thoughts. The ship was all but sentient, a companion as much as a vessel, a counsellor and sounding board as well as a weapon.

The Word Bearer had chosen this place because he thought he could hold the *Slaughtersong* hostage, threatening Veq with a battle in the heart of the vessel's mind. It was clever. It was the only thing that would give him a chance. The memory stacks contained more information on Veq's life than Veq could remember himself. There would be no pyrotechnics here.

Veq stalked out into the arena, bathed in the light. There had been a time when he had held a gun that fired salvoes of sentient flesh-grubs which would seek out anything living, or release daemonic riphounds that would hunt down the Word Bearer by scent alone. But his wargear had mostly been lost in the battle with the Last or ended up sacred relics on Torvendis, so his sword and wits would have to do.

'You know you can't just shoot me,' said Veq aloud. 'I saw you on the bridge. You carry a stripped-down old-pattern boltgun with silenced shells and an ocular scope. No autofire, just one shot at a time. You are smart enough to know what little that will do to me. So what trick do you have?'

There was no answer. But Veq could smell the Word Bearer, the spices used in the armour rites and the chemicals of the backpack exhausts. He could feel the unwanted presence in the sanctum of the machine-spirit.

'I know what you have been through,' said Veq, almost conversationally. 'I was like you once. Exactly like you. I was born with a strong body and a stronger mind. I wanted to be somebody, but the universe is so vast and there is always someone stronger.

'Was it a stranger, who told you there was something more? Some old book or a half-remembered rumour?

Perhaps you sought it out yourself because you were convinced it had to be there.

'The Word Bearers found you willing, I would imagine.
Maybe you found them. They told you about the power you
could gain and they showed you, and you believed them.
You're stronger, you're braver, you can face anything. The
gods just asked that you forget a few of the things you never
believed in anyway. Chaos is an unlimited source of power
that you can tap into and they ask next to nothing.'

A suppressed shot coughed out from the shadows. Veq
saw the rippling wake of the shell as it cut through the pattern of light and sidestepped it, letting it gouge an ugly scar
into the floor.

'Nervous, Word Bearer? You can't listen any more, can
you? Not now there's someone who might actually know
the truth about what you are becoming.' Veq followed the
path of the bolter shell but the shadows swallowed what little movement he could see. The Word Bearer was up on the
power conduits that connected the memory stack towers,
moving quickly and quietly, and would take a new position
after every shot. It could go on until the Marine ran out of
bolter shells, or decided to cash in his threat and shatter the
Slaughtersong's soul with a frag grenade.

Veq circled slowly. He had no gun, and the most truly
powerful of his weapons were scattered and out of his reach.
He would have to use the most powerful weapon he had.

The truth.

MAKELO EASED INTO position behind the grey-black tower,
his well-oiled armour making no sound. He glanced around
the side of the tower and saw Arguleon Veq scanning the
chamber for him, sword held ready.

Was it true? Had they been pursuing Veq the legend rather
than Karnulon the Word Bearer? It was insane. But then
again, Makelo had listened to many of the legends of Torvendis in the preparation and execution of the mission to
the daemon world, and never come across one telling of the
death of Arguleon Veq. A champion of Chaos could live a
life of unlimited years – Captain Amakyre had fought in the

Heresy ten thousand years before. Maybe this really was Veq facing Makelo in the *Slaughtersong's* spirit core.

Half of Makelo's mind went through this conundrum. The rest of it, however, concentrated on the task at hand – it didn't matter whether this was Veq or not. It was the enemy, and the enemy was to be defeated no matter who or what it was. That was the way in which the Word Bearers worshipped.

Makelo squinted down the sights of his bolter, its light-weight frame following his eyes as he followed Veq's movements. Veq had been right – Makelo couldn't take him with one shot as he would any other target. Not if he went for an obvious shot – head, throat, torso.

He could take him in the foot. The split-second of pain and confusion would let Makelo follow up with a more dangerous shot, perhaps to the artery in the wrist, or the kidneys. Then another, and another, each one more damaging until the cascade of shells ended in a fatal shot.

If he thought about it like that, Makelo had every advantage. Veq, he knew from the confused vox-traffic that marked the deaths of Phaedos, Skarlan and Feorkan, was without peer up close. But he had no ranged weapon and could not make use of destructive sorcery here when the masterpiece of the *Slaughtersong* was at risk. Makelo could keep Veq at arm's length, and rattle shots into him until he was dead.

Makelo knew he was good. He knew he was one of the best the Chapter had, pure raw talent ready to be moulded into a great leader of the future. This was not a conflict with a terrible and deadly foe – this was conundrum to be solved, and Makelo knew the answer.

Veq was trying to put him off with heretical preachings about Chaos. It was desperation. Ever since he had first been found by the Dark Apostles of the Word Bearers and shown himself to be an avid student of the warp, Makelo had examined the Chaos within himself and never doubted it. Chaos was power, but it was an intelligent power, and did not give itself away lightly. It had to be studied, honoured, and sometimes obeyed, in order to exploit it and become greater than you were. It was as simple as that.

Makelo lined up another shot. Ankle, then knee, then shoulder, throat, head, and heart. Simple.

'If you were lucky, you would have died ignorant, never realising you had been used from the first day you looked up at the sky.' Veq's voice sounded subtly amused and scornful. It was bluster, thought Makelo. The big talk of a man used to winning, who finds himself trapped. 'But maybe you would have survived. You won great victories and thought you had won them for yourself. But everything you do is at the whim of the gods, filtered down through your commanders and up through your soul. They know how you will react in every situation. Nothing you do is your own.'

Makelo had never feared anyone, man, daemon or god. A legend held no fear for him either. The silenced shell slid into the breech, and Makelo let his finger squeeze down on the trigger.

ARGULEON VEQ STEPPED into the brightest part of the arena, lighting himself up in the *Slaughtersong's* thoughts, making him the most inviting of targets.

'Then, one day,' he continued, 'you realise that you fight because you have to. You've done it your whole life. It's all you know how to enjoy. You decide it doesn't matter if Chaos is just using you. As long as you can keep on killing and drinking that power, you can tell yourself you have everything you want.'

Veq felt the bullet before he saw or heard it, sensing the subtle shift atmosphere as the shot disturbed the ship's thoughts. He stabbed down with the tip of his sword and deflected the bolter shell before it thudded into his foot. An old trick amongst those who could pick any shot – distract with pain and shock with a shot to the foot or hand or knee, before going for the killing shot. It had been tried on him before. It had almost worked. Veq had determined a long time ago to learn as much as possible whenever anyone tried to kill him, which meant he had learned all the tricks.

'Eventually, you begin to understand. The power you have isn't power at all. You could run a million kilometres and the gods would still own you. You could fight until everything in the galaxy was dead, and they would still find a war to chew you up.' Veq knew his voice sounded bitter. His bile rose every time he thought about it. 'Is that power? No. That is addiction. Power is something you can use to win your own victories. But nothing you have ever done is your own.

'It is too late. The gods are laughing at you. They own your body and your soul, and what can you do? You can never live a normal life. You are filled with hate. The galaxy is barred to you. You are just a shell of a creature that kills on command. I am the greatest champion of the Maelstrom, Word Bearer, and it took me thousands of years to break free. Even now, I am nothing, just a rogue, neither free nor enslaved. I am reduced to this, wanton slaughter in the name of revenge, because there is nothing else left. My life could have been worth something, but all I achieved was a lifetime of death. The victory I have ever won is to find out the truth.

'Think about it, Word Bearer. What is Chaos? Chaos is a lie.'

The shot was swatted away easily. Too easily. Veq ducked instinctively as the combat knife carved through the air above his head and the dark scarlet form of the Word Bearer leapt down from the towers. The Marine hit the floor heavily, rolling and firing at close range.

Veq glanced at his attacker as he dived backwards from the suppressed blast. Younger than the rest, helmetless like the scout but with a youth's face, sharp-nosed and cold-eyed. His skin was intensely pale, the hair white-blond and cut short. A snarling daemon's head, the symbol of the Word Bearers Legion, was tattooed on each temple. His eyes seemed older than the rest of his face owing to the faint surgical scars that radiated out from them like an old man's crow's feet.

The Word Bearer dropped his bolter and drew two more knives from his belt. They were longer and heavier than the one he had thrown – brutal heavy-bladed weapons designed to be used in pairs and hack through armour.

The Marine slashed low and Veq parried quick as lightning, sweeping his blade over the Marine's guard and slicing one of the exhaust vanes from his power armour's backpack. Veq thrust but the Marine caught the blade between his knives, turning it aside and forcing Veq's guard open to drive a knee up into the side of Veq's abdomen.

The armour of the deep took the blow. But that wasn't the point. The Word Bearer was fighting with the strength of a fanatic – Veq had drawn him into close combat by denouncing the Marine's Chaotic masters, but it had also given him something more than just survival to fight for. The Word Bearers were insane in their devotion to the Chaotic pantheon, and they would push back the boundaries of their bodies to avenge any heresy against the warp.

Veq dropped low and swept out a leg, knocking one of the Marine's feet aside, swivelling and slashing upwards. The starheart sword tore a white-hot gouge up the middle of the Marine's abdomen.

The tip went deep enough to inflict an agonising, fatal wound on a mortal man. The Word Bearer, however, had the training of a Space Marine and the determination of a man fighting for everything he believed in. It would take more than that to bring him down.

The Word Bearer hacked again and punched a blade through Veq's shoulder guard, pain flaring alongside the angry bolter wound from the hangar. Veq ducked forward and charged a shoulder into the massive barrel-chested breastplate of the Marine. The Word Bearer, still off-balance, stumbled backwards a step and Veq stabbed hard.

The starheart sword sheared through the Marine's chest, through the internal breastplate of fused ribs, his lungs, and one of his two hearts, to tear out through the armour's backpack. Veq twisted the blade, felt it lock in the thick bone, and used it as a lever to drag the Word Bearer towards him and headbutt him hard in the face.

The Word Bearer, nose burst in a bloody smear across his face, let his body slump and locked a leg round Veq's knee, trying to drop him on his back. Veq rolled with the motion, pulled the Word Bearer beneath him, and fell on top of him as the Marine crashed onto the floor. Veq's weight drove the starheart sword deeper, its broadening blade slicing further into his organs. The Marine was thrashing like a stuck animal, trying to throw Veq off the blade, but Veq held on grimly, face to face with his enemy.

Veq felt the ribcage splintering and the organs torn apart. The Word Bearer was dribbling blood.

'I don't believe you,' he gasped, spraying red spittle. 'I die not because you tell the truth, but because I will die fighting. Nothing I do will save me now. Chaos demands I fight.'

The Marine's limbs were still. The starheart blade had passed through his spine. Veq stood up and slowly withdrew the sword, the blood crackling on its hot blade.

'How do you know you would die?' asked Veq. 'You might have escaped. You might have shattered the machine-spirit and fled.'

The Word Bearer at his feet smiled, bitterly, blood running free from the corner of his mouth. 'Nothing will survive,' he said. 'You're going to wake the Last.'

Veq stabbed down again, puncturing the Marine's other heart. The Word Bearer spasmed as the life flowed out of him along with the blood spreading across the floor.

'Clever lad,' said Veq, cleaning his blade.

THE SHUTTLE WAS small and cramped, and it stank of slave-sweat and age. It was crammed with too much equipment, as if a larger ship had been crushed. Black wrought iron clashed with stained chrome, flickering holo-readouts with clouded flat screens. The bridge was a wedge-shaped cavity towards the nose of the shuttle, with thick black tubing dangling from the ceiling and painful runes carved into the pitted floor.

Captain Amakyre stomped across the bridge, head bowed as the ceiling lowered towards the front of the bridge where a slave was frantically working the complex navigation controls.

He threw the slave aside and took the navigation helm himself. The shuttle was still attached to the side of the *Slaughtersong* by an umbilical of ribbed steel through which the coven had entered the ship – it would take barely a flicker from the *Slaughtersong's* weapons to turn Amakyre,

Prakordian, and the shuttle into an expanding ball of plasma. It was time to leave.

'I can feel it,' Prakordian was saying from the back of the bridge. 'I can feel it waking up.'

Amakyre glanced round from the navigation helm, into which he was hammering the co-ordinates that would take them back to the *Multus Sanguis*. 'The *Slaughtersong*?'

'The planet.'

Amakyre rounded on the nearest slave, who was cowering in the corner of the shuttle's cramped bridge trying to disappear. 'Get the scope up! Now!' A kick propelled the slave into the sensor station, a sunken pit lined with ornately-wrought readout terminals.

The sloping ceiling lit up with an image of the deep Maelstrom, the hull of the *Slaughtersong* stretching out along one side. The view panned to take in the disc of Torvendis, and Amakyre could see what Prakordian meant.

The seas were boiling. Welters of scalding water were swelling up and pounding the coastlines with tidal waves. The Canis Mountains were gone, fractured webs of lava-filled fissures in their place. The southern islands were gone, too, replaced by fountaining geysers of steam.

The open wound of the city was ringed with teeth, like a morsel in a huge mouth. Strangely-coloured clouds scudded across Torvendis's surface, leaving seething trails of acid-burned earth in their wake. The many moons of the planet were orbiting so fast they slid across the image as Amakyre watched, as if they were so excited by the unfolding destruction they couldn't sit still.

Amakyre looked back towards the navigation readouts. The shuttle still had a lock on the *Multus Sanguis*, but it was dangerously weak. A tiny inset screen showed a composite image of the *Multus*, lit eerily from beneath by the light reflecting the Torvendis's suns. Interference from the planet would soon overwhelm the ageing shuttle's connection.

'Prakordian! Disengage us!' yelled Amakyre. The sorcerer, eyes glazed and moving as if in a dream, pressed the square panel in the console beside him. A shudder went through the shuttle as the docking charges detonated and the umbilical was blasted off the side of the shuttle, spinning off into space.

Amakyre reached up to the throttle slider above his head and gunned the shuttle's engines violently. The grav-dampeners didn't quite compensate for all the sudden thrust and the bridge heaved as the shuttle shot forwards.

'What has he done, Prakordian?' demanded Amakyre. 'How is he making this happen?'

'I don't think Veq did it himself, commander.' Prakordian seemed to be all but in a trance. His eyes were sunken, his skin sucked into his cheeks. The pressure of the psychic shockwave from the planet must be telling on him. 'I think he's having it done for him. Someone on the surface is doing his will. They probably don't realise it. He must have been planning this since he defeated the Last, he must have planted things on the planet that took thousands of years to pay off.'

'You sound like you admire the heretic.'

Prakordian smiled. 'He would have made a fine Word Bearer.'

Amakyre ignored such blasphemy for now. Prakordian could be punished at the Legion's leisure, if either of them survived to see it happen.

Amakyre switched the viewscreen to show the shuttle's destination. The *Multus Sanguis* was a cruelly small bright glint, almost drowned by the nebulae and red giants of the Maelstrom. Amakyre was under no illusions as to what would happen if Torvendis suffered a massive catastrophe, losing a section of its crust or being violently wrenched out of its orbit by whatever Veq was doing to it. At the very least, close orbit would be filled with debris too thick for any craft to survive. An escape via warp drive was the only possible option, and that meant getting to the *Multus*.

This mission was not a failure. The coven had been charged with finding out what had happened to Karnulon. Amakyre had satisfied this objective – Karnulon had been killed by Arguleon Veq, probably for his spaceship so that Veq could get to Torvendis in the first place. There was no defection from the Legion, and the honour of the Word

Bearers was intact. This was what Amakyre would report to the Legion command, and he would be honoured for his duty to the Word Bearers.

There was a piercing shriek from the sensor station as the shuttle's scanners picked up a massive power spike. Amakyre could see the cause right away. It was a searing bright streak tearing across the viewscreen.

A weapon had emerged from the side of the *Slaughtersong's* hull, immense and shining, from which was leaping a solid beam of blue-white light.

'Status on the *Multus!*' yelled Amakyre at the slave in the sensor pit but the slave was already dead, brain fried by the massive feedback from the sensors.

If the *Slaughtersong* had been firing on them, they would already be dead. As far as Amakyre knew there was only one other target in orbit around Torvendis. The *Multus Sanguis*.

The searing beam cut off. In its place, a silent explosion of multicoloured flame bloomed against the darkness. Ruptured plasma generators sent blue tongues of flame out into space. The ancient, insane machine-spirit detonated in an orange flare of dying madness. Torpedoes exploded in cherry-red bursts.

'Veq! Heretic! Traitor!' yelled Amakyre.

By the time the shuttle's sensors had recovered, there was nothing at the *Multus's* location save a cloud of cooling debris.

Amakyre valued iron discipline above all things. This did not stop him from punching his fist through the navigation helm. Prakordian just stared up at the viewscreen like a man mesmerised, a childlike smile on his face as the view panned back across the tortured surface of Torvendis.

Amakyre knew he was trapped. The best he could do was activate the shuttle's distress beacon and wait for the Word Bearers to pick them up. That is, if whatever Veq had planned for Torvendis didn't get them first.

Amakyre had an all-encompassing hatred of weakness. His own weakness was the worst. It was a blasphemy in itself, to be trapped and powerless, totally at the mercy of his enemy.

'All those dead...' said Prakordian vaguely, spittle glinting at the corner of his mouth. He reached out a hand to touch the shimmering image of Torvendis above him.

Amakyre drew his bolt pistol and shot Prakordian between the eyes. Prakordian stumbled and looked at Amakyre, watery blood flowing out of the wound and down his face. 'But... it's wonderful. They're telling me, the dead. He planned it all so long ago, he used so many of them to make it happen. It never died, they're saying... it never died, it was there all along, captive, insane...'

Amakyre wished for once that Space Marines were easier to kill. He emptied his bolt pistol into Prakordian until there was nothing but shattered bone and gristle above the neck. Prakordian's body swayed slowly, as if it hadn't realised it was dead. Then it fell and crashed to the floor of the bridge.

There were no slaves left to clean up the mess. It would have to stay there for the time being. Amakyre looked up at the screen, at the deformed, dying globe of Torvendis, and waited with gritted teeth for the blasphemy to end.

QUITE WHY HE had done it, Veq wasn't sure. Not leaving the Last alive – there was no choice in that. You couldn't kill something like the Last. You couldn't kill a whole planet, not if you wanted to offer it up as a prize to your masters. The question Arguleon Veq often asked himself was why he had left himself some means of waking it up again.

Perhaps it was the feeling of power it had given him. It would certainly have been just like him. To simply cripple the Last forever would have given him less pleasure than knowing he could release it, and yet choosing not to. That might well have been why he had founded the Emerald Sword tribe to guard the weapon that, if removed from the heart of the Last, would let it awaken again.

Of course, he had been very careful to guard against anyone accidentally removing the Sword. The tribe had been bound by his sorcery and will to ensure that they would allow only one of their own member into the heart, and that both the guardians and the Sword would destroy anyone whose hate was not as deep as the Last's own rage against Chaos.

It had taken some effort to find someone whose inherent violence and pride was as strong as Golgoth's, and then to break down that pride so utterly through destruction and betrayal that there was nothing left in the man's heart but hate. To tell the truth, while Arguleon Veq had always been able to read the behaviour of Lady Charybdia and Ss'll Sh'Karr, he didn't know quite how Golgoth would react to the betrayal of first Grik, then Sh'Karr. It had been enough of a risk to assume he would survive at all – Veq had taught Golgoth a few of his simpler tricks, but it had never been certain that he wouldn't get himself killed.

It had all been an immense risk. It could have been just another cycle of war and bloodshed on Torvendis, and Veq could have risked showing his true hand to the gods of the warp without accomplishing anything. But incredibly, it had worked. Though he was immeasurably old and well past his prime, Arguleon Veq still had the power to make legends.

Veq allowed himself some satisfaction at this thought as he walked back onto the bridge of the *Slaughtersong*. It was still transparent, affording an awesome view of the torment that racked Torvendis.

'It has been a long time, my friend,' he said.

A very long time, replied the ship. *I was beginning to think that the probability of your ever returning was negligibly low.*

Veq could understand. It was when he first began to doubt the authority of his Chaos masters that he had left the *Slaughtersong* in Torvendis's orbit, and had wandered off across the Maelstrom to look on it with new, doubting eyes. For years beyond number he had watched the carnage and torture and slavery, and had come to the conclusion that he wanted revenge against the powers that had made him a part of it. 'I hope you haven't been lonely,' said Veq.

I have been able to amuse myself. The planet provides much of interest.

'Not as much as it will do shortly. Torvendis has been everything a planet could be, except for dead. Are you ready?'

I have been ready for some time, my lord.

'Good. Take us to atmospheric depth. I wish to talk with another old friend.'

GOLGOTH'S DEATH, WHEN it came, was not as he had imagined it. He had never doubted that he would die in the teeth of some battle, axes and swords in a storm around him, his shield stove in and a thousand wounds on his body. That was how death happened – it was supposed to be the final step on the warrior's road.

Instead, it was a pitiful fall into darkness. An earthquake ripped apart the ground beneath him and a crevasse opened up. Kron's sorcery had made him superhuman, but it couldn't beat gravity. The ground fell away in chunks beneath his hands and his feet kicked out at nothing. He let go of the Emerald Sword and it tumbled, glittering, into the crevasse to land in the bubbling, glowing red lava pulsing below.

Then there was nothing left to hold onto. Golgoth was falling, tumbling towards the terrible heat below.

What if he had never left the Bladestone settlement? What if he had been content to fight and not to lead? He could have lived. He could have ended his days like a man, not like a pitiful wretch who had died after unwittingly destroying all that he had once dreamed of ruling.

The searing heat enveloped him, chewing up through his legs and dissolving his bones. What if he had stopped at the foothills and been content to rebuild his tribe? What if he had headed back towards the mountains as soon as Sh'Karr had appeared? Why had he wanted a part in such an insane alliance, man and daemon, when only carnage could be the result?

Golgoth died in the fires beneath Torvendis, never knowing why he had died, and never guessing that it was the same reason for which he had been born.

* * *

ARGULEON VEQ LOOKED down on the city directly beneath him as the Last's maw closed. Towers splintered beneath the crushing teeth. Daemons died as the city fell down, a mighty roar rising up in a cloud of debris. Veq could see Sh'Karr clinging to the top of Charybdia Keep, raging insanely and showering blood, lashing out with steel claws at the fangs that bore down on him. The whole city was gone now, crushed and hidden beneath a canopy of mountainous teeth, with only Sh'Karr visible. His huge body was transfixed by a dozen points that sunk into his flesh and came out the other side, holding him fast. Still he bellowed, brass skull shaking with anger, as the maw sunk into the ground.

Sh'Karr was still alive, if any daemon could be alive, when the earth closed over him.

The *Slaughtersong* hovered low over the surface. The maw resurfaced, teeth now picked clean of daemon's flesh. The earthquakes and storms paused as the Last recognised the *Slaughtersong* and the mind of its inhabitant.

The Last didn't speak, as such, but it had been given intelligence by the eldar, who at their height had mastered psychic engineering, and it could talk directly with a man's soul.

It was in agony. It had been that way since the day Veq had defeated it, a hundred lifetimes ago. It had been violated as the powers of Chaos took the planet as a symbol of their power, infected with its war dead and soaked in corrupted blood. Its stones had been ground up and incorporated into terrible temples and bastions that rang with the screams of the tormented, into the very city it had just reabsorbed into its body. It had been suffering most terribly, and it had been driven insane.

Torvendis, last of the eldar maiden worlds, wanted revenge just as much as Arguleon Veq. Revenge against Chaos, which was such a vast and all-consuming power that only the grandest of gestures could hurt its gods. Only the loss of a symbol like Torvendis would be enough for them to notice.

Veq and the Last had fought the most terrible battle of the Maelstrom's long history, but now, when they had both had so much time to contemplate what had happened, they understood. The Last did not hate Veq, though Veq had imprisoned it and introduced it to this torment. It hated Chaos. Veq, for his part, knew the Last was still a maiden world, imbued by the eldar who had lived there with a consciousness of its own so it could be as beautiful and productive as possible. It still valued beauty and justice, and understood the value of sacrifice in the face of evil. It was mad, but those beliefs had not left it.

The only way it could hurt Chaos was to be destroyed. Arguleon Veq, a different man from the one who had defeated it, had let it free to accomplish this. For this, at least, it found space in its rage to be grateful.

It also understood that Arguleon Veq did not expect, or particularly want to survive. So it was with little ceremony that, with a final roar of rage from it very core, Torvendis tore itself apart.

THE VIEWSCREEN ON the bridge of the shuttle blew out as the continents began to detach themselves. Amakyre just had time to see the seas boiling into a cloud of superheated vapour and the main continent tearing itself from the crust like a scab. He saw plumes of lava ejected into space, he saw ice caps flashing into white towers of steam, he saw impossibly bright slashes of red where the rock of the mantle, suddenly relieved of the pressure of the crust, liquified and exploded outwards.

The death of the Last sent waves of unleashed anger lashing across the Maelstrom. The shattering of Torvendis was perhaps the single greatest event the ancient warp storm had ever witnessed – the symbol of the power of Chaos, the lynchpin of power, erupted into a boiling sphere of nuclear fire that expanded as the planet's massive energies were all released at once.

Long-buried palaces were torn from the ground and hurled out into space. The evaporated oceans carried immense kraken and undersea kingdoms with them as they billowed across the vacuum. Sections of crust thousands of kilometres across and hundreds deep fragmented into seething clouds of superheated dust.

The howl of the Last rocked the very stars, screeching into every living mind in the Maelstrom so man and daemon alike would know of its death. Even the gods, in those final few moments of destruction, turned to see their prize disappearing in a cloud of roiling flame.

The shockwaves slammed into the side of Amakyre's shuttle, spinning it wildly and throwing Amakyre against the walls and ceiling as the gravity systems cut out. He heard the scream of a dying world.

Then the storm of shattered rock and unleashed power split the shuttle clean open, and he glimpsed the blinding light of the exploding planet before the massive wave of heat and rage vapourised him.

OF ALL THE legends of Torvendis, the one that is recounted most throughout the Maelstrom is the best one, the last one. It is the story of how a once-beautiful eldar maiden world was defeated by a Champion of Chaos, who then turned against the dark powers. It tells of how he woke the maiden world's spirit, now insane, and let it destroy itself so the daemon world would be lost to Chaos forever.

As is inevitable when tellers of tales gather and try to outdo each other, there are embellishments that go beyond what all the tales agree. Most notably, they question whether Arguleon Veq, the great betrayer of the Maelstrom, is indeed dead. Perhaps, some say, the Last let him live as a final act of vengeance against its imprisonment. Perhaps the gods kept him alive just to torment him with the memories of the atrocities he had committed in their name, as gods are wont to do. Or perhaps Arguleon Veq was simply too powerful a warrior to die like that.

And perhaps they are right. Arguleon Veq could be wandering the Maelstrom, livid that he was robbed of his death, ever searching for new ways to hurt the pantheon of Chaos and ensure they would regret the day they had corrupted his soul until it was no longer his.

But that, of course, would be a different story altogether.

ABOUT THE AUTHOR

Ben Counter has made several contributions to the Black Library's *Inferno!* magazine, and has been published in 2000 AD and the UK small press. *Daemon World* is his second novel.

More Warhammer 40,000 from the Black Library

SOUL DRINKER
by Ben Counter

SARPEDON STEPPED OUT into the battle. Givrillian's squad had torn the first rank of mutants apart, and they were now crouched in firepoints as return fire sheeted over their heads. Tellos had the beast-mutant on its knees, one horn gone, huge blade chipped and scarred by the assault sergeant's lightning-quick chainsword parries. Sarpedon strode through it all, ignoring the autoshells and las-blasts spattering across the shadowy interior of the hub.

He spread his arms, and felt the coil of the aegis circuits light up and flow around his armoured body. He forced the images in his head to screaming intensity – and let them go.

The Hell began.

GENETICALLY ENGINEERED superhumans, the Space Marines stand foremost among the warriors who protect the human Imperium. The Soul Drinkers have served the Emperor loyally for thousands of years, but their obsessive desire to retrieve an ancient relic throws them into conflict with those they are honour-bound to obey. Faced with an impossible choice, will this proud and noble chapter back down, or rebel to forge a new destiny for themselves among the stars?

More Warhammer 40,000 from the Black Library

STORM OF IRON
by Graham McNeill

STUTTERING VOLLEYS OF las-fire blasted from the trench, but it was too little, too late as Honsou dropped into the prepared position. The Traitor Marine worked his way down the trench, hacking a bloody path through the defenders who fell back in horror from his deadly blade. As Honsou killed the Guardsmen, he revelled in his superiority, and could well understand the attraction of Khorne's path. The Iron Warriors swept over the trench killing everything in it with the fury of those who had fought their way through hell and lived to tell the tale.

IN A DARK *and gothic future, humanity fights a constant battle for survival in a hostile universe. Now hell has come to Hydra Cordatus, for a massive force of terrifying Iron Warriors, brutal assault troops of Chaos, have invaded the planet and lain siege to its mighty Imperial citadel. But what prize could possibly be worth so much savage bloodshed and destruction?*

More Warhammer 40,000 from the Black Library

THE GAUNT'S GHOSTS SERIES
by Dan Abnett

IN THE NIGHTMARE *future of Warhammer 40,000, mankind is beset by relentless foes. Commissar Ibram Gaunt and his regiment the Tanith First-and-Only must fight as much against the inhuman enemies of mankind as survive the bitter internal rivalries of the Imperial Guard.*

FIRST AND ONLY

GAUNT AND HIS men find themselves at the forefront of a fight to win back control of a vital Imperial forge world from the forces of Chaos, but find far more than they expected in the heart of the Chaos-infested manufactuaries.

GHOSTMAKER

NICKNAMED THE GHOSTS, Commissar Gaunt's regiment of stealth troops move from world from world, playing a vital part in the crusade to liberate the Sabbat Worlds from Chaos.

NECROPOLIS

ON THE SHATTERED world of Verghast, Gaunt and his Ghosts find themselves embroiled within a deadly civil war as a mighty hive-city is besieged by an unrelenting foe. When treachery from within brings the city's defences crashing down, rivalry and corruption threaten to bring the Ghosts to the brink of defeat.

HONOUR GUARD

Commissar Gaunt and the Ghosts are back in action on Hagia, a vital shrine-world of the deepest tactical and spiritual importance. As a mighty Chaos fleet approaches the planet, Gaunt and his men are sent on a desperate mission to safeguard some of the Imperium's most holy relics: the remains of the ancient saint who first led humanity to these stars.

THE GUNS OF TANITH

Colonel-Commissar Gaunt and the Tanith First-and-Only must recapture Phantine, a world rich in promethium but so ruined by pollution that the only way to attack is via a dangerous – and untried – aerial assault. Pitted against deadly opposition and a lethal environment, how can Gaunt and his men possibly survive?

STRAIGHT SILVER

On the battlefields of Aexe Cardinal, the struggling forces of the Imperial Guard are locked in a deadly stalemate with the dark armies of Chaos. Commissar Ibram Gaunt and his regiment, the Tanith First-and-Only, are thrown headlong into this living hell of trench warfare, where death from lethal artillery is always just a moment away.